She had to do something to distract him.

From the height of the castle parapets one could see much farther than Rosalind had imagined. The cold starlight could show up the smugglers' boat as a dark shadow in the regular march of white breakers to the shore.

"Shall we stroll down below?" she asked, not daring to face Nick.

"I thought you liked it here," he replied. He stepped closer and the heat of his body radiated through her. Prickles of sensation shivered along her skin.

"I cannot tell you how pleased I am that we trust each other now," he continued, his mouth close to her ear.

She stood still in his embrace. This closeness both fascinated and frightened her. But at least with his lips in her hair, he could not be peering down the beach!

Dear Reader,

December is a busy time for most of you, and we at Harlequin Historicals would like to thank you for taking a moment to find out what we have to offer this month.

From author Marianne Willman, we bring you *Thomasina,* the continuing story of a character from *Vixen,* Ms. Willman's first book for Harlequin Historicals. Set in the Mexican countryside, the heroine lives out her dream of becoming a doctor and discovers love along the way.

In *A Corner of Heaven,* newcomer Theresa Michaels has written the touching story of a woman reunited with the father of her child amidst the danger and hardships of the Civil War.

Isabel Whitfield's *Silver Fury* takes place in a California silver town where a stubborn washerwoman and a rebellious blue blood manage to overcome their differences and find happiness. Caryn Cameron's *King's Man* takes the reader to Tudor England where a lady smuggler and a loyal soldier outwit their common enemies.

We hope that you will enjoy our December titles. From all of us at Harlequin Historicals, our best wishes for the holidays and the year ahead.

Sincerely,

The Editors

King's Man

Caryn Cameron

Harlequin Books

TORONTO • NEW YORK • LONDON
AMSTERDAM • PARIS • SYDNEY • HAMBURG
STOCKHOLM • ATHENS • TOKYO • MILAN

Harlequin Historicals first edition December 1991

ISBN 0-373-28706-2

KING'S MAN

Books by Caryn Cameron

Harlequin Historicals

Dawn's Early Light #11
Silver Swords #27
Liberty's Lady #39
Freedom Flame #49
Braden's Brides #61
Wild Lily #70
King's Man #106

Harlequin Books

Historical Christmas Stories 1991
"A Season of Joy"

CARYN CAMERON

is a former high school and college English teacher who now writes full-time and is the author of bestselling historical romances under her own name, Karen Harper. She is a lifelong Ohioan, who, with her husband, enjoys traveling and family genealogy. She also plays the piano and keeps in shape with Scottish Highland dancing.

Prologue

September 22, 1539
The coastal town of Deal, England

"Quiet now, all of you!" the small figure whispered. "Percy's in town tonight, and I won't have him snaring us with this fine haul! Into the tunnel with you now."

Seven burly men, shoulders bent under their loads, hastened to obey. For a quarter hour, they shuffled boxes, rolled barrels and shouldered bolts of fabric up from the beach, through the dark valley and into the even darker, hidden tunnel. Even in daylight, its entrance was obscured by a brushy thicket in the vale behind the gardens of the town's only inn. Inside the tunnel, their leader fumbled to light a lantern and told them where to stash the goods. Soon, the thin man bringing up the rear shoved his way through the others.

"*Sacre bleu,* but you are the only woman I know with a mettle forged from steel, Rosalind!" He shifted to French then, aware that only she among the band spoke his native tongue. "However petite and charming, you make a magnificent general for our bold enterprise! Who else would dare to hide such a cache of French goods under the very nose of the local revenue man, eh? Ah, I adore you!"

"Now, *friend* Pierre," she answered, speaking in French as well. "I told you we are to be just that and no more." Rosalind gave a warning shake of her head, hooded to help conceal her identity.

"What's he jabbering about, Ros?" a big, slope-shouldered man demanded and came closer. "Not wanting more wool or coin for his goods, is he?"

"No, Wat, naught's amiss. He was just complimenting us on daring this under Master Putnam's nose."

Wat snorted. "Got no choice, Pierre. 'Sides, we're not scared o' him and never have been, the bumbler. It's only that big castle down the beach King Henry's building 'gainst you Frenchies case you invade that's got us nettled. Rumor says his high and mighty majesty could send a lord lieutenant here to oversee it. He's the one we don't need the likes o' nosin' 'round."

"We'll handle that just fine when we come to it, won't we, my Rosies?" Rosalind declared. As she turned her head to smile at them, her hood fell off to reveal blond hair that gleamed gold in the lantern light.

Vowing to outfox the king and any of his men, all said their farewells and began to file out. But as Rosalind moved to follow her men, the Frenchman seized her wrist.

"Heed this, Rosalind." His eyes narrowed, his words came in a whispered hiss. "Though things have gone splendidly for us these past three years, a wily king's man here could bring us to destruction!"

"I promise you, Pierre, I can care for such. No lofty lord lieutenant King Horrid Harry sends our way will ever get the best of me!"

Besides, she knew they could not quit. This free trading meant life or death for Deal. Some called it smuggling, but the rewards of it neither filled their coffers nor swelled their purses. Fat coffers and purses were unheard of here. Without a market and with harsh times and seasons, free trading was a necessity for the struggling little town's very survival. But for very painful and personal reasons, smuggling was also Rosalind's protest against their greedy, detested Tudor monarch. She, Rosalind Barlow, mistress of the Rose and Anchor Inn, was now the brains behind all the Rosies' secret doings.

Since her father's and husband's deaths, things had been so difficult. She struggled to keep everything afloat, the inn by day, this covert trade by night. The visits of Percy Putnam, the royal revenue and exciseman from nearby Sandwich, had forced more caution, however friendly he was. So, no longer did they "import" goods from distant Bordeaux but from the nearer town of Boulogne-sur-Mer, just thirty miles across the Narrow Seas. That way, booty could be obtained from a voyage to France and secreted during the same span of time fishermen might be out to sea. But when Pierre, her contact both here and there, delivered things, it was even easier. Still, that did not mean she agreed to become more than a friend to him—nor to any man, not after losing her beloved Murray.

"I will be going then," Pierre told her. He bowed to kiss her hand, evidently realizing that an attempt at more, even in this privy, dim setting, would be bootless. "I will be—in touch, dear Rosalind," he said with a sad smile. He started away, then threw their password back over his shoulder in farewell.

"Ring-a-ring of rosies."

"Pocket full of posies," she responded.

His low chuckle floated back to her as he melted out the far end of the tunnel into the moonless night.

Rosalind edgéd closer to the entrance to make certain her men had closed the brush barricade over it again. She knew Wat and Alf would use a tree limb for a scuffler to cover all tracks in the vale and on the beach after Pierre and his men shoved off. She walked back deeper into the tunnel, holding the small, shuttered lantern. She realized she was exhausted, but she preferred it that way at the end of a day. It helped her to forget the loss of her desire and her hunger for revenge so she could sleep.

She saw the canvas cover had come loose from a bolt of scarlet satin with a broad band of lace sewn to its edge. She bent to cover it. No use things getting soiled before a pack train of black ponies with muffled hooves came through some other midnight to take these goods away to be sold.

She knelt and stroked the sleek cloth and fingered the delicate lace. How thrilling to have a gown made of such luxurious goods. Mayhap she'd wear it to a dance, to a fine dinner with food lining the table. Maybe to court to tell King Horrid Harry what she really thought of him for the tragedy he had wreaked upon them all.

She shook her head to clear it of the foolish fantasy. Mistress Rosalind Barlow would wage her wars from Deal and not at court. But she stood abruptly and kicked the canvas-covered roll as if it were the king himself. Curse King Henry VIII of England for what he'd done to her and Deal! And curse any low, vile, ugly king's man he dared ever send their way!

Tears in her eyes, she strode to the ladder that led up to the hatch hidden in the floor of her bedchamber at the inn. She blew out the lantern and began to climb.

Chapter One

Nicholas Spencer like his women shy, sweet, submissive and shapely. He noticed three comely court ladies looking his way. They might not be acting shy at the moment, but he was certain they were amply endowed with his other requirements.

"Lord Spencer! Nick! O-oh, Ni-iiick!" they called to him from a ways down the bank of the Thames. He shot them a smile as he stepped from the shaded royal barge into the warm noontide sun.

"We've missed you sorely! Wherever have you been hiding, you naughty knave?" one cried, and giggled behind her hand. They waved and beckoned to him, the bright scarves from their gabled headdresses lifting in the gentle river breeze.

He could not recall the names of any of them, but he recognized them as women newly come to court. The blonde had briefly been the restless king's mistress. Once, Nick admitted, their invitation to join them would have been irresistible. But today his future hung in the balance, so he only waved in return as he strode up the gravel walk toward vast, ruddy-bricked Whitehall Palace.

When His Majesty King Henry VIII commanded, Nick gave everything. Since he was nine and the young monarch took him under his wing, Nick had been dedicated solely to the business of the crown and the dynamic Tudor monarch who wore it.

It was not often Nick spent time in his own house upriver in Greenwich; now his majesty had summoned him back to London after two days away. He had returned to court only a month ago from a lengthy military assignment in Calais, France, England's only remaining foothold on the Continent. These were times of terrible threat from France and Spain, so Nick had known it would not be long before his king had need of him again.

He lengthened his strides as he crossed the Great Privy Gardens and passed the yeomen guards at the river gate entry to the massive palace. He hurried along dim corridors to the large Presence Chamber where courtiers awaited audiences, though no doubt most would see not the king but the powerful lord chamberlain, Thomas Cromwell.

He walked into the wood-paneled Privy Chamber with a nod to the next matched set of guards, who looked like colorful chess pieces. Here came Cromwell himself, whom Nick always thought of as a dark raven with his talons in the king's concerns. Cromwell's sharp black eyes swooped over Nick and he nodded. A flock of aides and lackeys swept after the lord chamberlain, but Nick still caught Cromwell's words. "Spencer. His bad leg pains him. He's busy and burdened, railing at everyone. Tread with care."

Nick wanted to ask a question, but Cromwell was gone. As for the warning, he always trod with care around the king. These past few years as the royal age and girth had increased, Nick was even heedful never to beat his majesty at the manly pursuits of bowls, tennis or archery, even when it would have been easy to do so.

The last set of guards recognized Nick, separated their ceremonial poleaxes, and opened the doors to the king's elegantly furnished withdrawing room. Nick swept off his flat velvet cap and stepped into the presence of the man whom he admired not only as his king but also as his mentor and foster father.

"Nick, my man!" the sumptuously attired Henry Tudor called out, and nodded his thick-jowled head in greeting.

It had not been so many years, Nick recalled, since his grace used to bellow out "Nick, my lad!" or "Nick, my boy!" but he had newly turned thirty now.

Still, it was always for Nick as it had been that first glorious day. Here at Whitehall, the robust, red-haired monarch had singled out the tall, gangly, black-haired boy because he had acquitted himself admirably at the jousting quintain. In those days, Nick had felt so alone at court after his widowed mother had married and moved to York. He had been just another face in the crowd of pages and squires until he caught the king's favor and was made his ward.

But that memory faded. This king had faded, too: now gray hairs mingled with the red ones, and the infamous Tudor temper was even more volatile. Yet Nick still cherished the man and the great nation he symbolized.

Nick approached before he bowed. The king sat with his bad leg propped on a pillowed stool under a table where he had been signing documents. He shoved them and the two secretaries hovering over him aside. As ever, Nick and the king spoke familiarly as if no one else were present.

"I cannot apologize for pulling you away from your little place in Greenwich," the king began with a sweep of his beringed hand. "I have need of you again."

"And I stand ready, your grace."

"To be exact, the line of castles I am building on the shores of Kent to guard against French invasion has need of you, the one at Deal in particular. I have my master mason, Franklin Stanway, there with nigh on five hundred laborers, but they are not making headway fast enough to suit me."

Nick's mind raced. He had never been to Deal. He had heard it was some scrubby town. Courtiers had been surprised the king bestowed one of his modern, fortified castles upon it when he evidently did not see fit even to give it a royal license for a market. But Nick knew Deal had a long sweep of unsheltered, stony beach that needed protecting from the French enemy just across the Narrow Seas.

"So you would like me to ride down to hurry the work along, your grace?"

"'S blood, much more than that. On the morrow, I shall send you there by royal galley to spur things on. You have earned your own command. Nick, my man, I am appointing you lord lieutenant of Deal Castle with ultimate power in the region to protect our sovereign shores from this vile foreign threat!"

Nick tensed with pride. He almost went down on one knee in gratitude, but instead stretched erect to his six feet. The king grunted as he lifted his bandaged leg down from the stool. He shooed the others back as if they were pesky flies when they tried to help him stand. He grasped the edge of the table to rise. The royal weight scooted the heavy oaken piece toward Nick, but the king lumbered up and clomped around to lean both hands on Nick's broad shoulders. His grace stood a mere two inches taller than Nick, though he towered over most of his liege men.

"You have always acquitted yourself to make me proud, Nick," the king intoned. "I need a strong hand there, a man who commands discipline and order, as you do. But I have another charge as well for you."

"Anything, your grace!"

"Cromwell tells me there is a band of slippery smugglers in the area who are trafficking with the French. He insists he has ways to ferret them out, but as long as you will be there, see to it. I frown on smuggling in my kingdom in peacetime, but with hostilities looming, these smugglers' ties to the French could breed treason. The French might pay to have some greedy smuggler tell him about our fortifications, you know. Discover the culprits and smash them."

The king shrugged his massive shoulders. "Compared to your other tasks, that will be naught. Simply find who is the most ruthless, brawny lout and make him your prime suspect. It takes a lot of heavy rowing and lifting to be a smuggler, you know."

"Yes, your grace. Consider it done," Nick said crisply. He gave an assured nod, although inside he still felt stunned by the honor the king had bestowed on him.

Lord lieutenant of Deal Castle! The king had helped design that very edifice he had sent his favorite master mason from Hampton Court to build. And now he was sending Nicholas Spencer to command it! He was being given ultimate power to protect his beloved country and his king! And, in his spare time, he was to squash some petty rural smuggling band—an assignment he would fulfill immediately. Then the king would know he had sent the right man and there could be no question of Deal citizens in collusion with the French.

The royal secretaries scurried to hand Nick a pouch with all the necessary legal writs, warrants and orders. He assured his grace he could leave by royal galley from Gravesend on the morrow. They discussed special powers and problems, and shared a toast with the king's favorite French malmsey wine.

"To your immediate success and fair England's eternal glory!" the king declared.

"To your ultimate victory, your grace! Down with the French foe and the smuggling rogues who dare trade with them!"

The king wiped his mouth with the back of his big hand. His narrow blue eyes bored into Nick's steady stare. "But to tell true, Nick, I would favor trading with those blasted French froggies again. This wine and the other Gallic imports I favor are in damned short supply. But I will not have some ragtag band of jackanape smugglers defying the king's taxes to haul in the stuff sub rosa. Especially when little enough of it gets to me out of what my revenue agents capture!''

The king bellowed with laughter and clapped Nick hard on the back of his leather jerkin. At least, Nick thought, Henry of England's flashes of good humor had not gone the way of his bodily health nor the women he had wed. Nick bade the king farewell, bowed again and walked to the door. But he turned back there.

"I shall not fail you, your grace."

"You never have, and that is rare in these tenuous times, eh? Oh, and I regret you will have to put off your wedding to Lady Penelope. A tough little town with five hundred laborers and filthy smugglers running about after dark is no place for a woman."

Nick bowed again and backed out the door. He strode through the clusters of whispering—no doubt plotting—courtiers as quickly as he had come. He was not one to comprehend or thrive on secret doings nor to tolerate the smell—sometimes the stench—of covert alliances at court. Nick liked everything to be done aboveboard. Damned sneaky Deal smugglers!

But what bothered him now was that he had not given one thought to his fiancée Penelope in all this until the king mentioned her. He did not know her well, but, as with his first marriage, the king had arranged it. Neither he nor Penelope had romantic illusions about their match. A practical woman, Penelope was greatly interested in the marriage, for it would elevate her in the realm with a king's favorite on the rise. They both knew full well what they were getting into.

He wished Penelope meant more to him, but then he might long for her while he was away. He wanted no feminine complications in the enactment of his royal duties in Deal. Lady Penelope Wentworth was visiting kin in Suffolk, so he would not even be able to see her before he left. He would simply leave her a letter. He had liked her well enough the few times they had kept company after he returned from Calais. She was well connected, elegant and, thank God, docile.

Ever since he had seen his majesty taken in by clever, deceitful Anne Boleyn, he had preferred tame game in the amorous hunting of wenches. Since Nick kept his life orderly and controlled, he had never been able to fathom how the Boleyn shrew had lured the king and then ensnared him all those years. During the king's courtship, Anne Boleyn had gainsaid his grace at every turn, Nick recalled as he made for the barge landing. And when she finally capitulated, even wilder chaos had ensued. Hell's gates, Nick vowed to himself, he'd turn traitor ere he'd allow such to happen to him!

At least, after Anne's fall, King Henry had wed pliant Jane Seymour, who had finally given him his legal male heir, Prince Edward. Now that Queen Jane had died in childbed, his grace was searching for a fourth wife under the guidance of Lord Chamberlain Cromwell. The alliance would no doubt be with the German Protestants since things were so hostile with Catholic France and Spain right now. It would be, thank goodness, a marriage of politics rather than of passion.

Amorous passion, Nick was convinced, was a great danger. He had no time for any passion in his life other than for his duty to the king, which was the same as loyalty to his country. His brief interludes with court ladies who took his eye had hardly sent him into the throes of permanent passion.

His square jaw was set hard as he leaped onto the waiting barge. He felt relieved the court ladies were gone. Ignoring the bustling city of London that sprawled up and down the broad river, he gazed instead over the glassy surface of the water.

Nick Spencer breathed in deeply. The gentle breeze brushed his brow; the water looked like glass. So calm today, so calm his life. No one would ever command it but his king. And he intended to keep it that way.

"'The queen was in her countinghouse, counting all her money....'" Aunt Bess chanted the old nursery rhyme as she brought in a flagon of Deal-brewed ale and a plate of buttered bread for Rosalind.

Amid a pile of clutter, she scarcely looked up from her counting of coins and jotting of accounts with her quill pen. "I think it says the king is counting his money, and the queen is eating bread and honey, Aunt Bess," she said. "Knowing the vile king who rules us all, *he* is counting the money from his unjustly high taxes and planning either to behead his next queen or let her die in childbirth."

"My, my, poor sweet Queen Jane, wed to a man like King Henry!" Aunt Bess commiserated with a shake of her linen-hooded head. "But Franklin Stanway is only the king's master mason and a nice enough sort. Besides, dear Rosalind, Meg fancies him."

That got Rosalind's attention. Ever since her mother had died bearing her younger sister, Margaret, called Meg, Rosalind had felt she was her sister's keeper. This time, she looked up at her aunt, her heavily fringed, gray-green eyes snapping, lighting the cream-and-roses complexion of her delicate, oval face. Her high knot of honey-blond hair bounced as she jerked up her firm chin and wrinkled her pert nose.

"Indeed, Aunt, I am well aware Meg fancies the king's master builder. Am I to assume she sent you in here to plead for my permission to Stanway's courting of her? By the saints, she knows better by now! I told her no, however many bouquets and pretty poems the wretch sends her. And you, too, know this family's stand on being so much as civil to anyone the king favors!"

Aunt Bess wrung her plump hands. "Your temper is just like your father's when his blood was up. Too much like him for a woman, however hard a yoke you've had to bear since we lost him and Murray."

Despite the fact Rosalind bristled at the subtle scolding, she stood and gathered Aunt Bess in her arms. "I do not mean to snap, dear aunt. It is just that things are getting even more prickly now with this monstrous Deal Castle King Horrid Harry is building here—"

"Which we shall need if the French you think you can blithely trade with attack our shores!"

"Yes, well," Rosalind admitted as she stepped back, "but, *sacre bleu,* we do not need king's men camped on our beach, however welcome their coins in our coffers!"

Aunt Bess squeezed Rosalind's shoulders and held her at arm's length to study her. "Then best guard against such name-calling as that, my girl. King Horrid Harry, indeed! And I meant to tell you, I mislike your picking up those sailors' oaths you've used of late, even if they are in French. You may have a knack for bringing profit to this family inn and tavern and the Rosies, too, but you must guard your temper and your tongue. The king's lord lieutenant will not abide someone cursing our royal master in any language!"

"This king will never be my master—neither the king nor his lord lieutenant, nor any of his men!"

"Nor *any* man, more like. And you've been pushing yourself too hard," Rosalind heard her aunt mutter, though the old woman turned away and went back out into the inn, shaking her head.

The buzz of male voices from the busy taproom floated in louder before the door closed. Rosalind heaved a huge sigh. From her disarray of coins and records on the table she dug out the account book she kept in code. Bound with black morocco leather, it bore an embossed gold rose on the cover. In it she kept "import and export" records for the band of eleven Deal men covertly dubbed the Rosies.

She had chosen the name *Rosies* on a whim, partly because of the cover of this book, partly because this inn with the rose on its sign was one of their major drops for goods. Maybe it made her proud to echo her own name just a bit, too. The name *Rosies* amused her for being so sweet, fragile and, therefore, misleading. After all, most of the band were brawny bruisers with massive muscles from years of sailing or other labors. Also, the name reminded her of her rebellion against the Tudor king who claimed a rose as the symbol of his dynasty. Since she and Murray had had no children, the Rosies were her claim on the future, her heritage to the town, and she loved their families as her own.

During the reign of this king's father, her father and his friends had begun the band under a different name. They imported such things as wines, lace, silk, leather and steel in exchange for wool and coin. Henry Tudor, both father and son, had always taxed imported goods heavily to fill the greedy royal privy purse for pleasure of court and king.

All the years the Tudors lived in splendor, Rosalind fumed, the little folk who filled the realm scrambled for every bite and scrap. Tiny Deal had always struggled for subsistence. Its fields were meager, and its fishing often hazardous since tempests kicked up so suddenly in the Narrow Seas. A bit of extra coin came in when Deal seamen risked their lives to rescue ships that foundered in storms on the treacherous Goodwin Sands just off the coast in the Downs. There, in shallow water in calm weather, ships of many nations could find safe anchorage until a south or southwest wind blew up to take them west.

But in an east wind, the Downs could be a nasty place. Anchors dragged, cables parted, ships collided or ran aground on the Goodwin Sands. Then Deal seamen would launch their sturdy boats called luggers to take out an extra anchor or rescue survivors if ships had snagged or broken up. But risky fishing and an even riskier rescue trade still meant pinched lives in a town to which the king did not even grant a market license. For most supplies, citizens of Deal had to travel five miles both ways to Sandwich, the nearest "royally recognized" town.

And so, all these years, Deal's necessary free trading grew and flourished. If the king had just tried to halt it, which fortunately, with the Rosies' watchfulness, his current revenue agent here would never do, she could have understood and dealt with that. But worse than that had happened.

Three years ago three luggers of Deal men had put out into a wild storm to save a vessel in distress. Proud to be English as they were, despite their free trading, they had cheered when they saw that the flags whipping in the gale were the king's green-and-white banners, and that the Tudor rose was emblazoned boldly on the stern. It had been their honor to rescue men from a royal ship. The town of Deal had lost a boat in the rescue of king's sailors, but that was a risk of life boldly accepted by Deal men when they put out to help others. The lost boat meant both Rosalind's father and her husband, Murray Barlow, were drowned with five others, but if that had been the only loss she could have mourned and then gone on without a bitter heart. The despicable actions of the king had been something else entirely to her.

It was not only that King Henry never sent the standard reward or recognized that some citizens of Deal had given the ultimate sacrifice to save his sailors. It was not only that townsfolk had housed the king's men in their own homes and paid to send them back to London, yet had never been recompensed by the crown. It *was* that a fortnight later the means of any livelihood for Deal—every last lugger on the beach—was staved in and ruined by king's soldiers from London.

When folk tried to stop them and demanded why, the soldiers accused Deal of being a hotbed of smugglers, depriving the crown of its just and proper revenues.

"Just and proper!" Rosalind growled the words through clenched teeth at the memory. "Nothing is just or proper about this king! I swear anew the Rosies shall do all we can to deprive the crown of its 'just and proper' revenues! Even though Horrid Harry smacks that bloated castle in our midst and drops his damned, poxy lord lieutenant there to watch us all! By the saints, I swear it!''

She saw she was shaking and gripped her metal flagon so hard her fingers were white. Noticing she had slopped ale on her records, she swore a French sailor's oath and jumped up to blot things off with her muslin apron. She took the leather book and small sack of shillings and strode to her bed. Careful not to kick off several piles of clothing on her high mattress, she stepped up on it and balanced there. Over the carved head of her bed, covered by an arras, was a tiny recessed cupboard behind the hidden panel. Within, she placed and locked her record books and coins.

This small chamber in the inn was her privy domain for business and retreat. No one entered but her, Aunt Bess and Meg. She let no one tamper with or tidy it but her, which meant it was ever in slight disarray. But it was for a good purpose, she assured herself as she jumped down on the floor and stepped over a pile of fresh, folded linens and a basket of beach shells she fancied. A bit of blatant jumble hither and yon would distract any unwelcome stranger from what was hidden.

So, over the hatch to the tunnel she had laid a thick rug covered with crates of wine. Anyway, she never used that escape but in emergencies, even though it would get her closer to the seaside she loved. From her windows, she could often hear the distant crash of waves. But today it was too noisy here for such enticing sounds to carry: workers on leave from their castle labors caroused in the taproom and the wind howled. With her sense of the sea, she could tell a big storm was coming from what had been a calm beginning to this day.

Rosalind locked her chamber door behind her and went out into the noisy inn. It was bursting with laborers clamoring for drink and the better-paid tradesmen demanding a soft bed for sleep. Sometimes she had a good notion to toss out all these royal workers in defiance of the king. But it perversely pleased her to get the money King Horrid Harry was paying them as well as by circumventing his royal import taxes. By free trading, she proudly brought in fine French goods the common folk of Deal could afford— goods the king himself probably could not get with the French embargo. And if he got them now, let him pay a steep price for them!

But Rosalind knew her family also had paid a steep price for this booming business at the Rose and Anchor. The barracks on the beach left much to be desired for living quarters. So the first months until some chambers were completed in the castle, the king's master mason, Franklin Stanway, had leased a room here, despite the outrageous price. And, residing here in the very bosom of her family, he had seen and desired nineteen-year-old Meg. As a twenty-seven-year-old widow and head of the family now, Rosalind vowed she would die before she would allow any of Horrid Harry's lackeys to worm his way into her family! Surely all any king's man from London wanted from a rural Deal lass was to bed her for sport. Because of Aunt Bess's pleading for Franklin Stanway just now, Rosalind decided she must find Meg and warn her, as she had so many times before.

When she turned the corner to climb the stairs, she ran right into Percival Putnam, the revenue man from Sandwich. Though he was wobbly on his feet, his hand not gripping the banister shot to her waist. Quickly she stepped back against the whitewashed wall.

Despite the fact that he was a king's man with a sworn mission to wipe out smuggling, Percy Putnam had worked his way into folks' affections around here. As ever, when he turned those twinkling blue eyes on her, he flaunted his bright teeth in a wide smile. His cheeks bunched up like pears framed by flyaway, baby-blond hair. His face was cherubic, though his occupation was not.

When Percy visited Deal, she saw no alternative but to harbor him and his companion, Roger Shanks, in their midst at the inn. Here, unknowing, Putnam and Shanks rubbed shoulders with most of the Rosies it was their duty to seek and stop. But Percy never rode down on the beach where he might get in their way. Besides, he brought them the news from Sandwich, where Rosalind's elder sister, Nan, lived with her family, and news of the world beyond.

Still it annoyed Rosalind that Percy's eyes followed her sometimes. At least he did not seem desirous of her, she thought. Besides having one leg shorter than the other from some childhood accident, the man was a bit strange. But instead of disliking Percy, Rosalind and folks pitied him. Unlike Meg's would-be swain, Franklin Stanway, Rosalind thought Percy Putnam harmless, both as a revenue agent and a man.

"Sorry, Percy. I was searching for my sister."

"Upstairs fussing with the linens she dried outside," he told her in an intimate tone, as if dispensing his usual gossip. "Said she had to rescue them from the bushes. Quite a storm coming up."

"Yes. I warrant Alf or Ned have gone to scan the Downs for ships with problems. But favorable winds have emptied it out this week, so we are not expecting anything."

Suddenly the drowning intensity of Putnam's watery gaze bothered her. No, perhaps it was just the increased rattle of shingles in the wind that caused her alarm. The last storm had ripped off several, and rainwater had formed puddles on the floors upstairs. She had to get that repaired along with a hundred other things to keep her busy.

"Excuse me then," she said and hurried past him up the stairs.

* * *

"But Franklin and I care deeply for each other," the dewy-eyed Meg insisted when Rosalind confronted her upstairs. "He is kindness personified, and he writes me the most tender poems."

Rosalind sniffed. "A king's man whose task is breaking stones writes tender poems!" she muttered. "By the saints, now you've got me rhyming! Meg, I just don't trust any man that—"

"Any man at all, you mean," the usually sweet, shy Meg muttered. She clutched a bolster to her breasts and dared to meet Rosalind's intense glare.

Meg was brown haired where Rosalind was blond. She was also bigger boned and taller than the petite, willowy Rosalind. But, despite her edge in size and apparent strength, Meg knew well who ruled the roost here.

"We are speaking about you, Meg, not me," Rosalind insisted. "I will not have you and Aunt Bess gainsay and scold me!"

"We only speak up because we care for you. It is only that you—"

"Ros! Ros, you up here?"

Both women jumped at their cousin Alf's loud shout as he clambered up the stairs. Besides being the local blacksmith, Alf Deland was a fisherman, as were most village men; he and his brother, Hal, a cooper, were Aunt Bess's twenty-eight-year-old twins. Each had his own house in the village, though Hal had been ailing lately and Aunt Bess had been nursing him upstairs at the inn so his wife and children would not be smitten, too. Both Alf and Hal were barrel-chested, brawny men who could row to France without so much as a sore muscle, so it had shocked everyone when Hal fell ill.

"What it is, Alf?" Rosalind cried.

"Just one ship caught in the blow, a small galley. But it's gone aground, an' its men are out scramblin' on the sandbar already. They could lose all hands, so we'll have to launch three luggers, but how's Hal's fever?''

"It broke but he's weak as a babe," Rosalind told him as she made for the stairs. Already she could hear the ding-ding of the warning bell sounding through the village. "I shall take Hal's place at the oars," she clipped out and tore downstairs with Alf and Meg behind her, both protesting she had been working herself too hard to do this, too. Percy Putnam still stood at the bottom of the steps, and he joined the chorus of dissent when he heard she was going.

"Just because your father and husband went out—" he began, but Rosalind dashed past him into her chamber.

Percy was wrong about that, she told herself. She did not just go out because Father and Murray had, though sometimes she thought she did it in remembrance of them. She also wanted to help others and keep family and town pride alive. And also she thrilled at the challenge.

Meg followed her in and began to chatter. "Meg, please just help me into this gear!" Rosalind interrupted as she unlaced and yanked off the sleeves and bodice of her gown and wriggled out of her skirts and petticoats. Meg gathered debris and scurried to help her pull out things stuffed under the bed. They tugged up the oilskin trousers, tied under her armpits the cork belt that smashed her firm breasts flat and lashed the sheepskin jacket on her. She grabbed her rowing gloves. In her boots and sealskin cap with her hair tied up under it, Rosalind looked quite the short, bulky boy.

"I always worry when you go to sea for this—or the other," Meg told her and hugged her sister's rotund figure. "And I am saddened when we disagree."

Rosalind gave Meg's cheek a quick peck. "I, too. But I am thinking of your own good, really! I have done this before, and I shall be careful! Take care of things here."

Hampered by all she wore, Rosalind waddled out to the waiting ox cart, which was filling with seamen in like gear. If their boats tipped, such garb could help keep them afloat and warm until they could be rescued. If, that is, the tempest was not so cruel to drown them first the way it had Father and Murray. But she would not think of that now.

There was little talking as the cart rattled through the rainswept vale and out over the beach to their boats. Several of the men with her were Rosies; all admired and trusted her as she did them. No one here—unlike her own family—ever questioned or denied her right to face danger with them.

Others waited on the beach to help launch the boats. The townsfolk knew each other well; most were involved with free trading at least in a minor way. If they did not put out to sea or unload the goods themselves, they helped to hide them or transport them inland. Everyone in Deal pulled together in times of trial.

But Rosalind had used every last penny of her family's savings to replace one of the luggers ruined by the king's men. And then she had scrimped and saved to help finance a second boat to pull the town from its economic stupor. Once folks got back on their feet to fish and revisit the teeming wharves of France for imported brandy, wine, spices, leather and other bounty, they had been able to buy a third boat. She had inherited the inn, but she had earned her place as town leader for herself.

"Come on, Ros, an' I'll watch you closer'n I would Hal!" Alf shouted in her ear over the pounding crash of the waves. She squinted offshore, looking for the battered vessel on the Goodwin Sands, but wind and rain slashed her face. Already, blowing saltwater made her eyes sting.

Alf and Wat Milford helped her out of the cart and into the right-hand seat in the second lugger. Sitting on the same board seat as Alf, she gripped her propped-up oar tightly through her leather gloves.

"Hold tight!" Wat yelled.

She braced her legs on the deep, slanted floor of the twenty-foot boat manned by seven of them—six on oars, one on rudder. Every muscle in her body tensed as she awaited the cry to launch. Each craft had to catch "a smooth," a wave big enough to take the boat but not too high to swamp it. The strapping Wat Milford, Deal's brewer and another fisherman and fellow Rosie, served as steersman on this lugger. Wat had been her husband's boon companion, and he was her friend now. He stood, holding the rudder up to clear the beach, staring out to judge the waves.

"Go!" he shouted.

With a shove from the launchers, the boat rumbled, bow first, down the steep beach on greased logs. The ride always exhilarated Rosalind; it was hardly the way the Rosies launched some of these same boats for free trading. Then it would be in calmer seas, sometimes at night, sometimes from another beach when the men had supposedly gone fishing. It was quiet with no howling, shrieking wind and rain and voices like this.

The boat rode the first wave and smacked the second. Cold spray doused them. She blinked and licked salt from her lips. A good launch! The stocky Wat steered, and the crew rowed. Energy flowed into the strong limbs of her body. Though she was only five feet two inches and looked delicate, her mode of life had given her a wiry strength and resiliency. She bent, pulled, bent, pulled with the rest of them. The lugger bore two masts for sails, but it would have been suicide to put them up in a gale like this. Their oars would let them maneuver to save whom and what they could in this black toss of steep, sliding waves.

"Holy hell!" Wat shouted out as the ship, askew on the deadly Goodwin Sands, came in view.

Rosalind craned her neck to look. A big, oblong gray shadow, the galley listed at a deadly slant right over the area the local seamen called the Ship Swallower. The sands would suck it down soon; water crashed against its wooden ribs, and the wind tore its flapping shrouds. Grasping tipped railings, its few crew members still on deck gestured and shouted. The other two luggers were already loading men from the sandbar itself; some stood waist-deep in swirling water. Rosalind heard Alf curse before she saw what Wat was pointing at. The other rowers stopped and sat as if carved from wood. Both Rosalind's hands flew to her mouth until a wave yanked her oar away and she had to scramble to grab it back.

For there, emblazoned on the stern of the doomed ship, as if it were a ghost galley from the past, was the gilded Tudor rose. This ship was the first king's vessel that the Sands had snagged since the ship that had begun Rosalind's tragedy and fed her quest for revenge. She had not been at sea that fateful day, but she had heard about the Tudor rose on the ship. And she had suffered for it ever since!

"You there!" a deep voice trumpeted from the deck of the ship. "You men just sitting in that boat, get in closer here! King Henry's men require your help! Row on in here. I am Nicholas Spencer, the new lord lieutenant of Deal Castle. Do as I say! I shall drop men over in order before this thing goes in the tide."

Rosalind gaped up through the brutal slash of rain and wind. Rivulets of water coursed down her face and neck, soaking her breasts and belly. The stern tenor of that voice shook her. The man who shouted looked so big and—yes, even in danger of drowning as he was—threatening, as he leaned over the rail and shouted orders at them. He clung to the rail with one hand, but gestured wildly to them with the other. Black rain polished his leather doublet and high boots, and his ebony hair was slicked flat to his big head. In that moment he was everything she hated, everything she feared.

"We vowed never again. What we gonna do?" Wat's voice pierced her panic.

She jerked her eyes away from the man above them on the ship. He had dared to shake his fist at them! Beside her, Alf looked frozen. She realized the crew was looking to her for orders.

"Get the king's lackeys down here," she shouted. "And then we shall see!"

Chapter Two

⚜

They rowed the lugger closer to the tilted royal galley. Wind shrieked, and the sea threw shattered pieces of the ship at them as they fought to position their boat below the seven men left on deck. The king's lieutenant yet dared give them orders! Rosalind almost shouted back at him. Did the man think seasoned seamen deftly maneuvering boats knew naught of how to rescue them?

The lugger bumped and scraped the hull of the bigger vessel, riding up and down with each roll of water. Before they could throw guy lines or grappling hooks, the lord lieutenant dangled a man over the side by a rope tied under his armpits. Sooner than they were ready, that man thumped into the shifting lugger, almost on top of Wat.

"Hold tight with hooks!" Wat yelled, still trying to do things their way. "No extra lashings! Be ready to cut if the galley goes down!"

It dared not go down, Rosalind thought, as she took another brutal slosh of water. That arrogant king's man would not let it go down until he had everything his way!

This deadly contest with time and tempest made her tremble, but violent emotions shook her harder. Her need for revenge wrestled with her need to rescue. Her fear for those endangered warred with her fearful hatred for their cruel king. If justice held any sway in this world, she thought, these king's men should go down in righteous payment for Deal lives lost three years ago!

Amid the road and whirl, she thought of Murray. Her husband had been a childhood companion, their marriage a union of friends as much as one of lovers. From their youngest days, there had been a slow, steady blossoming of feelings and commitments. Things were always calm and contented between them; they seldom disagreed or argued. The only sadness in their lives had been that they had made no child for her to keep when he was gone. She loved her family deeply, but it was not like having Murray or his child. His image tumbled through her thoughts: sandy haired, blue eyed, smiling. Strong but tender. Then the memories drowned in the turbulence around her.

That other man's demanding voice jolted her again like a trumpet call. "Next man coming! Hold steady!" came his order from above.

Another man thudded into the boat and huddled there, shaking and sodden. The king's lord lieutenant yanked the freed rope back up. Now, they had no choice but to let him do things his way; the threatened position of the ship made it too late for anyone else to clamber off onto the sands for rescue. There was no ladder or netting on this side, and it would be insanity to jump this far into the bobbing, shifting target of the lugger. Another man descended, then another and another until only two were left, clinging to the listing rails of the vessel above.

Rosalind's mind churned with chaotic thoughts. She sat stiff-limbed, frozen with dread as this man dared to take over their lives while he could yet lose his. Ashore later, would he stave in the very luggers that rescued his men? Even if he didn't, she knew her worst fears had materialized in the flesh: his mere presence here could mean the Rosies' ruin, even if he presently knew naught of them. Keeping Percy Putnam and his man Roger Shanks in the dark was one thing, but now they would have to be so much more careful, so very clever!

Shading her eyes from the slash of wind and rain, she looked up again. The man was tall and powerfully built; she could tell even from here. Clinging desperately to the creaking, shaking ship, he tied and lowered his last man. Like all the king's men, she thought, the lord lieutenant was doubtless a selfish glory seeker. Yet however much she detested him and his ilk, she had to admire his steely calm in sending his men down first.

A crack like cannon sounded; a mast went crashing to the tilted galley deck overhead, just missing the lord lieutenant. At a sharp slant, the ship settled lower. He grabbed for a railing, which broke under him, then managed to stop his fall with the next rail. The lifeline he had secured snapped; the sea swallowed the man he dangled.

"Alf, fish him out!" Wat roared. "The rest of you, let go the hooks! Now!"

Rosalind's hook was yanked from her grasp as the others let loose. Had Wat decided for her what she had been too cowardly to do? Had he cut them adrift now to let the lord lieutenant go down with the galley? As they stared aghast, the sands swallowed its stern and licked at midships. Gray waves seethed and boiled.

"No-o-o!" she heard herself scream. The soldier sitting in the hull near her feet stared up slack-jawed at a woman's voice. But her cry was otherwise drowned as the galley gave another groan and upended to slowly, steadily sink to its grave beneath the waves.

The soldier nearest her shouted, "My Lord Spencer!" He got to his knees as if in prayer to see his commander go.

Several Deal men, moved by the commander's bravery, cried out to him, "Jump! Jump!" Alf and Wat, meanwhile, hauled in the other man from the sea and dropped him in the lugger.

"Row away, row, or the whirlpool will suck us under!"
Wat shouted. Rosalind bent to her oars, then stared in awe
as, at the last moment before the ship went under, the king's
lord lieutenant jumped free. Arms and legs outspread, he
seemed to fly toward them like a demon in a nightmare. He
had something big and bulky belted to his middle. He
vaulted into the churning, inky sea with a white splash that
outdid the sinking ship.

Rosalind held to her oar and half stood with the others to
scan the rows of waves. Suddenly she felt desperate to find
him. What if this vindictive king blamed them for his loss
when they had tried their best? Yet she did not want the man
in Deal! She would almost rather have had the French army
than that dark, demanding devil on their doorstep! Still, she
had to find him!

She squinted into wind-whipped waves. Few folks knew
how to swim. Surely he was gone. Then she glimpsed a black
form where the ship had disappeared.

"There, Wat!" she shouted and pointed. "A man? *The*
man?"

It was, but floating facedown and limp. Another slick,
sliding wave pulled him away. They rowed after him, right
over the now shallow whirlpool that marked the sunken
ship. Alf hooked his belt with an oar. Half the crew leaned
the other way to balance the rotating lugger while three men
plucked him out. Two of his own men who could reach him
bent over him.

"Dear God, dead! Hit his head and drowned," Rosalind
heard one of them mutter.

She felt hollow, not victorious or vindicated as she had
thought she would. She tried to tell herself it was for the
best, for Deal and for her. Still, she felt crushed. They
hauled him in and laid him, shiny wet, down the center of
the boat, while others tried to give the corpse room. Even
though he was limp and dead, the size and aura of the man
evoked respect. His left shoulder leaned heavily against

Rosalind's boots, but she had no space to shift away. She saw his head was bleeding. She bent, rowed, bent, rowed as Wat called out, but she did not take her eyes from the man. And what stung her eyes now was not only seawater, but tears.

At least, even in the continued upheaval of the storm, he looked peaceful now. However arrogant, he had been brave and self-sacrificing, she grudgingly admitted to herself.

Still insatiably curious about a man she would never know, she continued to study him while she rowed. His skin was dark as if he had been much outside and not just in the halls of Horrid Harry's plush palaces. Even soaking wet and bloodstained, he looked imposing. A square jaw, thick ebony hair slicked straight back, raven-dark eyebrows. His narrow, firm mouth hung open to reveal white, straight teeth. His nose looked crooked, as if it was broken, but since it was not discolored, she was not certain that had happened today. Strangely, she wanted to know if his eyes were dark brown as she imagined. His shoulders were wide, his wrists sturdy enough to swing a sword well. He was very tall; there was—had been—so much of him. She knew for certain this rugged-looking man was no whey-faced courtier but a fighter indeed. She shuddered to think of having to take him on, and yet, in some strange way, she would have welcomed such an exhilarating challenge. Now she felt only sad that a vital man in the very midst of life was gone.

But as they rowed hell-bent for shore, she was sure he moved. No, of course not; it was just the rocking boat jostling his limbs. But he had such good color, she thought. She had seen drowned men before, and somehow this one did not fit.

"Feel the pulse at the base of his throat," she told the man huddled at his head.

The man gaped at her, evidently amazed anew to find she was a woman. When her words sank in, he hurried to obey. "Yes!" he cried. "Yes, faint. I think so. Captain Delancey," he shouted to the man slumped in despair at the lord lieutenant's feet, "I think Lord Spencer yet lives!"

Delancey scrambled between her and Alf and felt his pulse, then nodded and bent to listen at his chest. He nodded again, then turned the man facedown to get the water out of him.

Rosalind did not know whether to cheer or cry. If King Henry's Lord Lieutenant Nicholas Spencer lived, it changed everything! How could she have thought that rude lout was bold? How could she have grieved?

But there was no more time for tumbled thoughts. Ashore, she herself tumbled from the lugger with the others, while townsfolk hauled it up and emptied it. The wounded or half drowned were lifted into the waiting wagons. Two men carted the lord lieutenant to a wagon. And Wat, as exhausted as he was, insisted Rosalind ride his horse back to town while he walked along beside her.

After she was dry and changed, Rosalind wolfed down the hot stew and biscuits being given to anyone who had the strength or stomach to eat. She left the settling of the wounded to the able care of Aunt Bess and Meg until her head stopped spinning. Fatigue racked her, but the memories of the terrible time when Deal folk had rescued the other king's men and lost so much troubled her even more. She glared into the fire Meg had built in the hearth for her; flame and shadow danced in her brain, too. At last, her strength restored a bit, she rose to help. Also, she had to make certain no retribution was taken against the beached luggers this night. She went out and snagged Alf as he hurried by.

"See to it that someone guards the boats all night," she whispered. He frowned, then nodded and hurried off.

Men from town and castle still bustled everywhere in the inn, speaking about the wreck, buzzing about the ignominious arrival of the commander and his men. "As strong and tight as we are building that fortress at his grace's command,'' Rosalind overheard Franklin Stanway boast to Captain Delancey, ''it is no wonder as small a garrison as you brought can hold it.''

Rosalind went up to them, keeping a good rein on her temper. ''I am going to close the inn early today, sirs,'' she said and leveled a you-know-you're-not-welcome glare at Stanway. ''Many are still sick from saltwater or banged up or swept by chills.''

''I will stay with the commander,'' Captain Delancey, a wiry blond man, insisted. He looked gray with fatigue and what folks called the sea wobbles. He clasped to him a large leather packet that she recognized as having been belted around his commander's waist. ''Your aunt said he would need tending,'' he continued, ''and I shall stay near in case he calls. She wants to put me in a room upstairs, but I'll sleep on the floor of his chamber down here, and—''

''Where *have* they put your commander?'' Rosalind interrupted. She shuddered when she saw the direction in which Captain Delancey pointed. Lord Lieutenant Nicholas Spencer was in Aunt Bess's room, directly across the hall from her own privy chamber. Had her family taken leave of their senses? It was bad enough to bring them into the very heart of the place the Rosies congregated, but to put him right across from her accounting room and the secrets she hid there?

Somehow, she managed to keep control. ''Captain, my aunt is right. You must go up to the room they gave you and sleep so you will be of aid to your commander on the morrow. We shall watch him for you now, I assure you.''

''I could stay with him,'' Franklin offered. ''I've only known him briefly at court, but I would be honored to help you and Meg nurse him.''

''Absolutely not!'' Rosalind snapped at thoughts of Meg and Franklin keeping a bedside vigil together into the night. ''I am closing the inn, I said, so we can help those in need.

And the kind of need from which you suffer, Master Mason Stanway, does *not* have surcease available to you here!"

She thrust the protesting man out the door and shooed Captain Delancey upstairs. Fortunately, he looked so shaky he obeyed. Despite weak legs herself, Rosalind bolted to her aunt's chamber. She opened the door. Both Aunt Bess and Meg bent over their enemy, who was laid diagonally on the bed so he would fit.

"Are you two demented to put him here?" Rosalind whispered as she hurried in and closed the door. But when they both merely shot her a look and then turned back to him, she tiptoed to the bed. His clothes and boots lay in a sodden heap on the floor. Though they had covered him to his flat belly with the sheet, they had obviously just sponged and dried him. Rosalind had never seen such a stretch of brown skin or such a mat of curly, onyx chest hair. It grew in intriguing little whorls and narrowed as it descended from his chest and midriff muscles to point downward in a narrow line toward—

"That blow to his head still has him unconscious," Aunt Bess said, as if Rosalind could not tell. "We fear he's in for a fever, too, but there are others who need our help upstairs, and I must look in on Hal again."

"While we make our rounds," Meg put in, gathering up her nursing herbs and cloths, "you keep an eye on this one, since he is worst off and directly across from your room."

"And *why* is he directly across from my room?" Rosalind hissed.

"You try to cart him upstairs then," her sister countered. "I know all this reminds you of the other time, but it is different. This time these men are to stay here to protect Deal, so—"

"Protect Deal! At what cost, beginning with this man!"

"Just sit with him till I come back down," Aunt Bess put in to head off a confrontation as both women bustled from the room.

Hugging herself for warmth and calm, Rosalind stared down at the king's lord lieutenant. He breathed heavily through his mouth since his nostrils were swollen closed. Yes, he had broken his nose just today. She could tell by the discoloration and the telltale darkening circles under his eyes. It ought to be set and packed while he was unconscious. She had seen it done, but she'd be damned if she'd do it for this man. Let him have a crooked nose to match the crooked morals of one who was in league with and lackey to the king!

She pulled up a heavy chair and plopped in it, her elbows on the wooden arms, her hands in tight fists. As soon as this one and his men recovered a bit, she would like to dump them all in the dry, uncompleted moat of Deal Castle!

But she could not stop staring at this man. How well did he know the king? she wondered. She had never before felt she was just one person away from the hated Henry Tudor, as it were. That is, she had never been with someone who must know the king directly. "Cruel bastards, all of you!" she whispered. Then she stood again to peruse him more closely.

He fluttered his eyelids sometimes as if he were dreaming, but otherwise he did not move. "Nicholas." She tried his name aloud upon her tongue and lips. Did anyone dare call him Nick? His mother, wife or lover? She could see each separate, shadowed, dark eyelash, so long and curved for a man. She could see the pattern of his dark beard stubble, the slant of taut skin under his high cheekbones. Still damp, his raven hair lay straight back on the pillow. It looked thick and crisp, though part of it was covered with dried blood and the bandage over his head bump.

Looking lower on his big form, she could see Aunt Bess had wrapped him snugly; the angular shape of his solid contours made intriguingly shadowed hills and valleys. She blushed when she found she was wondering if they had washed him all over when they had disrobed him. Quickly, she averted her eyes.

He snorted a bit and muttered. She jumped. Someone really should fix his nose before he awoke—if he ever did. Head blows were strange things. Once they had rescued a Dutch woman who had never recovered from such and was now buried in the graveyard of St. Leonard's Church just down the way in town. The dead woman's cousin Frieda had stayed with them for months before her family sent her money to come home. Frieda had taught Rosalind to speak bits and pieces of High Dutch and had told wonderful stories. Such a fine, strong woman that the whole family had been sad to see her go.

But they would not be sad when this one left! Rosalind told herself. A strange sense of power seeped into her at the realization of how helpless this man—this powerful king's man—was now. He lay here completely in her control. She reached out to touch his broad brow: he felt hot. Indeed, there probably was a fever coming. And if he got delirious and tossed and turned, he could hurt that poor, swollen, bluish, bruised nose even more.

Not knowing exactly what possessed her, she decided to set it. She tore a piece of linen in narrow, short strips. Her hand bracing his forehead, she pushed the bone and cartilage into position and carefully stuffed tiny rolls of linen up each nostril. He frowned and growled, but did not wake. She stood back to observe her handiwork.

"Somehow, some way," she whispered to him, "you will pay for this favor—and so much more."

Exhaustion claimed Rosalind after midnight, but her sleep was light and fitful. Her door was open a crack and Aunt Bess's door across the narrow hall also left ajar so she could hear the man if he stirred during the night. She had promised Aunt Bess, who was sleeping upstairs with Meg, she would keep an ear cocked. Aunt Bess and Meg, both dead on their feet from caring for the wounded, had finally gone upstairs to bed only after helping Rosalind tie the lord lieutenant in bed with strips of cloth. How Rosalind enjoyed that, though they only did it in case he tried to thrash in his increasing fever. But even with him bound and the inn lying silent, she did not like having both doors open, almost as if she were sharing her well-guarded privacy with him. She and Meg had learned to be careful at night because they kept so many strangers upstairs with no male family member on the premises, and, of course, her room was always off limits for the Rosies' reasons.

Awake again. It must be nervous tension from all these new strangers packed in the inn tonight that kept her from a sound sleep. As soon as Lord Lieutenant Nicholas Spencer recovered, he could move down to the castle barracks straightaway! Perhaps if he dedicated himself only to protecting their shores from French attack—and left her in peace to protect her French friends who visited here covertly to deliver goods—she could abide his presence. After all, overseeing that big fortress and watching the sea should keep him busy at his own tasks.

She jumped when she heard a low moan and garbled words. Had that been what awakened her? By feel, she slipped into her worn velvet mules and pulled her quilted wrapper over her night rail. She sat in the dark on the edge of her high bed, straining to hear.

"Yes, yes, your grace! At your service! The castle—safe. Tell Penelope. The castle, safe..."

Hearing that, Rosalind stood and wended her way through the familiar piles of things on her bedroom floor and into the hall. She took a low-burning cresset lamp from the table and edged Aunt Bess's door farther open, half-expecting to find Captain Delancey had come down to sit with his commander. But there was only the man muttering from the bed. Holding the lamp aloft, she shuffled silently closer.

"I shall not let you down, your grace," he said. The words were quite distinct despite the packing in his nose. "The castle, crush the French foe, the smugglers, too. . ."

Rosalind gasped. Her lamp wavered. He was dripping wet with sweat, but he turned his head and opened his velvet-brown eyes as if he saw the monarch whom he addressed instead of her. The monarch who must have sent him here not only to crush the French foe—but the smugglers, too! She trembled, and the shadows from the lamp jumped and wavered on his face.

"You've been like a father—a father to me, your grace. I shall not let you down. Soon, soon, down with the French foe and Deal smugglers, too. . ."

He closed his eyes and seemed to doze instantly. She slumped into the bedside chair. Worse than she had feared! This man was like—a foster son, a ward of the king! And he was here to smash them all, all those she had loved and known and sworn to protect.

She jolted stiffly upright. She had this man tied and weak. Why, he could even die during the night, and Deal would be the better for it. His head injuries, his fever—no one would know if he simply stopped breathing somehow. He represented the king here; he stood for everything she hated. The king had not cared one whit that she lost Murray and her father, but the king would suffer if he lost his foster son! To have Murray drowned and this man saved—it was not fair!

She stood and placed the candle on the bedside stand. Trembling like a leaf in an autumn gale, she pressed her clasped hands together in the valley between her breasts as she leaned over him. But whatever this man stood for, he looked so helpless, so battered. He had survived the sinking ship and surging sea. Surely, having such an experience would change a man, make him more humble. It would make him realize that he owed a huge debt of gratitude to his saviors, even to the one who set his nose and nursed him. . . .

As if some other woman controlled her body, Rosalind reached out to touch his hand. He clasped her fingers hard, and muttered something about his mother, whose name was evidently Penelope. He had a family he loved, just as she did, she thought. By the saints, of course, even monsters like King Henry did. But even as innocent and appealing as he looked right now, she did not want to think of him in terms of someone who had people dependent on him. Parents, friends, mayhap a wife he loved as dearly as she had loved Murray. Perhaps he even had children, as she and her husband never had.

Still, standing there, tempest-tossed as she had been at sea, she kept a long vigil, blotting sweat from his face, listening to his ravings. She told herself she was just here to ferret out more of his plans, but she knew that was not all of it. While he was ill and weak like this, she would help him. Though he was her enemy, she felt a strange, shared intimacy with him. Now, he needed her. And if he recovered to be the railing man he was before, *then* she would fight him to the death to protect all she had.

Two days later, Rosalind came in to sit with the lord lieutenant. She had volunteered to take over tending him while Meg and Aunt Bess cared for the others and went about their other tasks at the inn. She had thought at first of bringing her accounts in here to work on, but even though he had not wakened, his fever had broken and she would not even trust so much as her Rosies' records near a man like this. Nor could she trust some of the fantasies she had spun about him these past days.

She had imagined he might awaken with his memory gone. That had happened to a man in Sandwich who was kicked by a horse. Then she would be able to convince Nicholas Spencer to be on their side, and together they would plot against the king. Or she pretended he would become so contrite from being plucked from certain death that he would donate his fortune—surely he had one—to helping the poor folk of the town. And, of course, he would insist on hiring Deal men to help him defend their own shores instead of just sending for more soldiers from London. And he would apologize publicly for how vile the king had been. He would convince Horrid Harry to raise a vast monument to the men of Deal who had died three years ago, and he would go down on one knee before her to beg for her forgiveness and then gaze up at her with such warm brown eyes that—

"Mmm!" he murmured and flopped over on his side facing her. He cuddled his cheek in one hand as if he were all toasty and enjoying some sweet dream. But evidently he was too warm. With his other hand, he shoved at the sheets and blankets she had cocooned around him. He uncovered himself halfway down his chest, then stopped.

She breathed a sigh of relief. He was, after all, still naked under there, though she was going to ask his man Delancey to come by later and dress him in the garments he had been rescued in. Delancey was often in and out to help care for and keep an eye on the commander he greatly admired, but today he had gone after the noon meal to see how the castle was progressing.

Rosalind settled back in her chair. Amazing how she could be content to sit and study this man, her enemy, while he slept. She had memorized each slant and stretch of muscle through the covers; she had wondered endlessly whether his four-day stubble would be sharp or soft until she had dared to stroke it and found it soft. When he was lying here like this, so human in shared intimacy as if she had just awakened from his side while he still slept, he was so hard to hate, and quite the opposite sometimes.

"Mmm!" her patient said again, and to her surprise, he slitted his eyes open to stare at her. She jumped to her feet.

"Are you awake? Do you know who you are?"

"Mmm. Where—am I?" His voice was rough. It vibrated up and down her backbone, making her insides shiver and the hair on the nape of her neck stand on end. She tried to harden her heart, now that he was back among the living.

"If we had not fished you out after you jumped, my lord, for certain you would be in heaven—or the other place." She bent closer. His eyes focused and darkened. He perused her face, then the rest of her, thoroughly.

"You are in the Rose and Anchor Inn at Deal," she told him hastily when he frowned, "and you have been ill for nearly four days. You hit your head, so we have bandaged it. You swallowed a great amount of seawater, but—" she took a deep breath and almost said *unfortunately* "—you will survive."

He rolled on his back with a groan and lifted a hand to his head. "My men?"

"All safe. Someone named Clarence has a broken leg, and they all downed enough salt to never feel its want again."

His hand groped at his flat waist. "Where are the things I had strapped here?" he asked, his voice accusing. "King's official business and—"

"Oh, indeed, if it is king's official business," she interrupted, "I am certain it just walked on water, even though *you* could not quite manage to do so."

His head jerked around. His gaze widened, then narrowed, though she could tell his head still pained him and he felt weak as a babe.

"Actually, your man Delancey has it," she added and saw his big body relax.

"I am Nicholas Spencer, the king's lord lieutenant of Deal Castle," he informed her. "And you are the chambermaid? I want you to fetch Captain Delancey."

Her unwilling pleasure to see him recovered faded with each thing he said. She set her jaw and sat down straight-

backed in the chair. "I am the one who foolishly noted you
were still alive after we saved you from the sea. Of course,
if we had been allowed to try to rescue you our way instead
of having your men dropped into our boat like ballast, we
might have got to you, too, before the ship went down. I am
Rosalind Barlow, owner and innkeeper of this establish-
ment, Lord Spencer. And I am not here to take your orders
or fetch this and that for you."

He still had to breathe through his mouth; it opened wider
and wider during that speech. Had the man never had a
woman say him nay before? she wondered. She reveled in
defying him, yet prayed he was indeed as weak as he looked.

"I packed your broken nose for you," she admitted, "so
you had best not get it farther out of joint!"

"And who disrobed me? I am naked under here."

"That is correct," she threw at him, intentionally ignoring his question. Let him wonder what she had seen, what
she knew! "How disagreeable and disgusting. Then I shall
send for your Captain Delancey, but not because you ordered me to."

She marched to the door and spun back to the confused,
surprised man. "I shall fetch him," she added, "because *he*
is used to scurrying to your orders and will hasten to obey."

He said something else, but she went out and banged the
door. In the hall, she leaned against the wall a moment. She
was relieved he was better, but helpless as he was yet, his
imperious arrogance and disdain were back. He was a formidable foe and she'd not forget that, however fascinated
she had been while she watched him sleep and tenderly
spooned ale and broth into him these past few days. She
only hoped he would not wonder why she had been so short
with him. She supposed a wretch who looked ruggedly
handsome like that—when he was not all black and blue in
the face—had women falling all over him to obey his orders, from court ladies to chambermaids. And now that he
was himself again, she would stay as far from his path as

she—and her Rosies—could possibly manage. This was no "petty Percival Putnam" and she knew it.

Percival Putnam stayed the next night at the inn as was his usual practice, but he watched Rosalind more than ever now. He was curious how she would react to both boarding and bedding—he sniggered at the humor of that—a king's man. Drinking in the taproom, he watched her when she bustled through or greeted friends. Of all he coveted—and would, he vowed, possess!—here in Deal someday, Rosalind Deland Barlow was a great part.

It was not that he loved her, no, just the opposite. She deserved none of the things that should by right be his. With all his heart, he hated Rosalind and her dear Deal.

She, a mere woman, held the place as popular leader of the community that should by all rights be his. She owned this big, sprawling building, the only one of any size in the pitiful little town. He would make this inn his second home once Thomas Cromwell awarded him command of the entire area as a reward for exposing the covert smuggling band hereabouts. When he did expose the smugglers and his reputation rose with Cromwell's, the lord chamberlain had promised him that his cut in the covert market monopoly at Sandwich would even increase! And when together they ruined the smuggling band, glory would redound to both of them, for the king would never suspect their secret dealings!

Folks all believed him to be merely "Petty Percy," just a lonely, friendly hail-fellow-well-met gossip with one leg shorter than the other, whose mind must surely limp along, too. But he would stomp them into the ground! Imagine, a town that hid a group of smugglers befriending the revenue agent whom everyone knew must be dedicated to collecting import taxes and smashing smuggling! It had helped that he was from neighboring Sandwich and not from distrusted London, he supposed.

Percy knew he had managed to work his way into Deal's grudging trust with little acts of charity for the poor. Most in this ragtag town were impoverished, though not the family that ran this inn. But he was convinced that even the Delands' and Barlows' funds had to be low, since they helped everyone else keep going most of the time. He had kissed the dirty children of the townsfolk to win their foolish hearts. He had related time after time to them his heart-rending, embellished version of his letters to the king deploring the fact that Deal had no market town and no recognition or respect. If some Deal folk had not been so set against this castle in their midst, he'd have claimed credit for it, too, as it did bring in some shillings.

As soon as he discovered the identities of specific smugglers, he would complete the job of ruination he had begun three years before when, as officer of the King's Customs and Excises, he had informed Cromwell that there was a secret, slippery band of smugglers here. He had insisted Cromwell send soldiers to stave in all the boats in the area to punish and flush out the lawbreakers. Cromwell had been only too willing to do it, without telling the king, in order to protect the flourishing of his pet town of Sandwich. But the ruin of Deal and its smugglers had not lasted long. Percy could tell from the flow of goods inland and the slight elevation in the level of living here that smuggling must be going full tilt again, so he must try to uncover it anew. He hoped he could even use the king's new lord lieutenant to flush them out, then grab the glory for himself.

He chuckled. He had told the people of Deal that he took their side, but none of the dolts had ever asked to see his so-called missives to King Henry. That was good, for not a one of them existed, including the protest he had pretended to send to the king about their boats being ruined. And how they had all commiserated with him that the king gave him no heed, too, the fools! They would stand in awe of his uncloaked power someday! He would control these wretched dolts as surely as his idol, Thomas Cromwell, would control the king!

Two days passed before Rosalind went to see the lord lieutenant again. It was at his request, relayed by Captain Delancey. Lord Spencer was still weak and slept a great deal, though he was eating like a horse. Meg had said he looked disappointed each time she delivered his tray, as though he were expecting someone else. Rosalind ignored that hint. If her clever sister thought she would get sweet on a king's man and give Meg an excuse to see Franklin Stanway, she was sorely mistaken. The only thing Rosalind intended to deliver to Lord Spencer, once he was back on his feet, was the reckoning for his debts. If Horrid Harry were paying, prices would be steep, she vowed, and that would knock "His Majesty" Nicholas Spencer right off his feet again! No king's man from the lowest castle laborer to the lofty lord lieutenant himself was going to live on her bounty or that of the folks of Deal!

And she had every intention, she thought as she rapped on the door to his room, of turning him out of this chamber so Aunt Bess could have it back. The dear old woman had not complained, but using the tiny room upstairs that Hal had now vacated meant she had to climb stairs all day long. She had refused Rosalind's offer to sleep in her downstairs room with her, and was planning to use the opportunity to visit her sons' families for a few nights.

"Enter!" came the deep voice through the door.

Rosalind went in. To her dismay, the ubiquitous Captain Delancey was not with Lord Spencer, but she refused to show fear or hesitancy. She was convinced this man would devour and spit out anyone who showed him the slightest trepidation. He sat on the bed now, garbed in his only outfit of black hose and padded leather doublet over a white ruffled shirt. Perfectly neat piles of papers covered his lap and were spread around him. Objects on the bedside table were aligned in tidy rows. She came as far as the chair he indicated, but chose to stand behind it, with her hands on its carved back.

"Good afternoon, Mistress Rosalind. I shan't keep you long," he said. But she thought he took a lengthy time just looking over what he could see of her. "I wish to thank you for several things, including the way my nose is healing properly. I shall see you are rewarded."

That surprised her. "I expect no reward, though fair settlement for room and board for you and your men is expected, my lord. And, I must tell you, since some seem to be ignorant of this, that it is customary for a small fee to be paid to the fishermen who rescue folks from the Downs."

She bit her lower lips before she said more. She fought to keep at bay a tirade at the previous cruel treatment of Deal men by Spencer's king. It would not do to let this man know what she really thought of him or his monarch—his foster father!—especially if it was true that he was here to search out smugglers.

"Of course, I intend to settle that with you," he replied brusquely. His eyes still went over her as she held her ground behind the chair. "Were you really there among our rescuers in that little boat tossed by the sea?" he asked, his voice softer now. "You seem so—so petite and delicate."

"What one appears to be is not necessarily the way of it, my lord," she declared, then could have bitten her tongue. "I have rowed luggers and hauled up fishing lines off and on for years. It is not so uncommon for wives or sisters to take a turn at the oars if the men are indisposed."

He lifted his thick dark eyebrows. "But I understand you are widowed and have no brothers."

Her chin jerked up. So he had been asking others about her already. She cursed herself for any sympathy or tenderness she had ever felt for him. "Yes," was all she said and tried her best to return his rude stare, though she did not let her eyes wander as his did. Still, she felt her skin blush and prickle at the thought that she had studied him so intimately for hours while he slept.

"To business, then. I require this chamber for a few weeks until my rooms in the castle are complete."

"I am sorry, but this is my aunt's chamber, and we are full here otherwise. She is too old to be climbing up and down the stairs all day, you see." Her pulse began to pound even harder. It had been trying enough to have him about when he was unconscious, but she would never abide him or trust him awake! She had never been with a man before whose very gaze bored deep inside her or caused such arresting vibrations to her senses!

"If not this chamber, the one across the hall will do, but Captain Delancey mentioned that was yours. Evidently you have enough strength to climb the stairs. I need a place to work and have meetings, too, so a small room will not do. Of course, I shall recompense you handsomely."

"It is not a question of money, Lord Spencer. I use my chamber to work, too—accounts of the inn's business and such," she added hastily.

"Then, have your aunt bed with you. You do realize, mistress, I am here on the king's business and could take over this entire inn or town if I thought it served to protect the realm."

She clamped her teeth together until they hurt. Her toes curled in her shoes. He had her there. If she dared more defiance, he was just the type to do as he threatened.

"I should value your cooperation," he went on, "but I will have your assistance, voluntary or not. Here," he said, and took something from a leather satchel beside him on the bed. "I should be grateful if you would distribute these coins with my heartfelt gratitude to the seamen—and women—who rescued me and my men. Before I knew it was the custom, I had planned such. At least," he added low as if to himself, "I can write his majesty his men are safe, though his galley went down in that damned tempest when ships are in such short supply in this crisis!"

He extended to her a leather pouch, heavy with coins. Her first impulse was to snatch it and dump the contents over his head. But her goal had ever been to take what she could from the royal coffers, one way or the other. She came around the chair. She approached and stiffly held out her hand. With rougher seas in the coming colder season, any extra cache of coins was important to village folk. But what annoyed her was that this offering made it just a whit harder to detest this man.

"I shall see the coins are properly distributed," she said, but her agreement to anything he wanted tasted like bitter gall on her tongue.

When she came no closer, he swung his long legs off the bed and stood. She gaped at his height next to hers; the top of her head came only to his shoulder. She had never felt anything but comfortable with any other men she knew, even if they were as broadly built as Hal or Alf or Wat. But this man made her feel what he had called her—petite and delicate. It was the strangest, headiest feeling. But she felt anger, too, and that confused her. She wanted to fight him, yes, but she wanted something quite the opposite as well.

To her amazement, as soon as he stood, he put his hand to his head and wavered on his feet. His eyes squeezed closed. His knees buckled and he began to topple.

Without thinking, she jumped to help him, pushing him back. But she was not prepared for how much he weighed. He pulled her against him as he fell, and together they tumbled back on the bed, with him half on top of her, pressing her down.

"Oh!" she cried and tried to squirm out from under him. He did not budge, but at least he had not hurt her. The bed was soft beneath her, and though he touched her several places to pin her there, it was not pain that shot through her.

"Dizzy," he muttered. "Tried to stand too fast."

"I see," she managed. "Let me up now."

But he only slowly opened his eyes, as if they had all the time and amorous intent in the world. He propped himself slightly on one elbow, so that his weight was no longer fully on her. They lay amid wrinkled parchment and his leather folders that crinkled or creaked each time she tried to shift away. One heavy thigh across her knees weighed down both her legs; his left arm was draped across her waist, and he made no effort to draw it back. He was so close she could feel his chest and stomach move when he breathed, a bit faster now. She lifted her free hand to her square-cut, laced linen bodice to be certain it was not gaping away and exposing more than the tops of her breasts. He seemed to be looking there as if to ascertain that, too. She could smell his breath—a scent of brandy and cloves—and feel it on her cheek and throat. His nose still looked swollen with her stuffings in it, but his eyes were so intense she felt he branded her. All this had taken only one instant, yet she tingled as if he had caressed her leisurely everywhere he looked as well as touched.

"Yes," he said, when she had forgotten they had said anything. "Mayhap, Mistress Rosalind, it was you made me dizzy."

His eyes lowered to her lips, and like a fool, she pursed them. Panicked at the idea that he would think she offered them for a kiss when she only meant to show disdain, she shoved at him. He let her scramble to the far side of the bed. She stood and fluffed out her russet, embroidered skirt. She retrieved a piece of parchment she had shoved off and, desperate to appear nonchalant, started to place it back on the bed beside him. Then she gasped. In large, bold handwriting at the top, the letter began, "My dear sovereign and liege lord King Henry..."

She strode around the foot of the bed and was past the chair when he called to her. "Mistress, the money!" She turned just in time to catch the pouch of coins he tossed her.

His pitch was so adept, she wondered if his dizzy spell had been pretense. He still leaned on one elbow, staring at her.

"And something else," he said. "I hear my master mason, Franklin Stanway, wishes to court your sister, and you are opposed. I can vouch for his fine character and reputation. He is a most skilled craftsman and valued by the king. You should be honored."

"Should I? Just the way I should be honored that you wish to be housed here? That the king's castle is growing on our beach like a big, gray stone fungus? That all you king's men were rescued without loss of one life when the men of Deal—"

Panicked, she halted in midsentence. She fought to calm herself. From across the space between them, she still felt his eyes as if they pulled her back toward him on the bed. She felt where he had touched her as if yet he pressed her down.

"Besides," she added, trying to speak slowly and deliberately, "the more time skilled craftsmen like Franklin Stanway spend working and not dawdling about this inn for whatever purpose, the sooner you can hie yourself to the castle. We all certainly want that. Good day, my Lord Spencer."

She refused to curtsy, though it was due him, and Meg and Aunt Bess had been fussing about such for days. Let him think she was a green, rural dolt of a lass who did not know her manners. Let him think that she was petite and delicate and a flutterbrained woman too weak to row a boat or tote up sums in a column—or organize the Rosies!

But the last thing she needed was him hanging about like Franklin Stanway—like a clever spider. And now she was stuck in a web with him for a while! He was sleeping in the room right across from her and from her secrets, too! She had to avoid him and that was that. For reasons she did not like to admit or contemplate, when near him she acted like a foolish virgin with her first man! And what scared her senseless was not so much that he would ever discover that she or her Rosies were free trading. What annoyed her no end was that she had never for one instant felt all weak and wonderful like this, even with her beloved Murray.

Chapter Three

"Now that Lord Spencer is up and about," Meg said to Rosalind as they shared a mug of hot cider in Rosalind's chamber a few days later, "shouldn't you be more civil to him? Not let bygones be bygones, of course, but he is not the one who staved in the boats. He has thanked folks for the rescue of his men, and paid for it, too. Besides, Deal needs that castle if we have a visit from the French, and I do not mean your free-trading friends."

"Shh!" Rosalind whispered. "With him about, I feel my own walls might have ears. And I *am* civil to him when business or necessity dictates we speak."

Meg heaved a huge sigh and shot her elder sister a slanted look. "I think he is intrigued by you, but you avoid his path at all costs. He is hardly the sort of man women usually avoid, Ros, and he is the most important person in the entire region now. If you avoid him, whatever will he think?"

"That I am busy at my own affairs, just as he is at his."

"But if you do not want him in your—" here Meg lowered her voice to avoid another shushing "—free-trading affairs, you had best not make yourself so scarce, hence so interesting, to him. He has inquired where you are more than once. Of course, if you actually wish to arouse his interest even more..."

Rosalind ignored the implication the man was one bit interested in or aroused by her. "Don't fret so, Meg. If he thinks I avoid him, I have made it clear why. In the few dealings the lord lieutenant and I have had over arrangements here, I have simply stated that not all of the king's subjects appreciate having their quiet town invaded by five hundred laborers and a demanding commander.

"Yes, the inn has profited, though the king does not deign to bestow on Deal a license for a market. But his 'gracious' majesty gives us all these mouths to feed, and it is Sandwich that profits the most, since they have the market. Besides, Lord Spencer knows I believe his so-called impenetrable castle might draw the French here for battle just as readily as the fine landing beaches will. Of course, as I told him, the further ruination of poor, pitiful Deal would be naught, as the Tudors have ever thought it entirely expendable—"

"You dared to say *all that* to him!" Meg muttered, wide-eyed. "No wonder Lord Spencer glares darts at you. And I thought it was Cupid's arrows! Remember what Mother used to tell Father when his temper steamed—'You can catch more flies with honey than with vinegar.'"

"Lord Spencer is more like a spider than a fly, and I hardly want to catch him," Rosalind protested. "I just need," she added under her breath, "to be certain he does not catch me and our friends!" She downed the rest of her cider and smacked the mug on the cluttered table.

"Do not hurry off yet, sister," Meg said and caught at her arm. "I want to share something with you. If you would but change your mind...about how you treat someone else. About Master Stanway. He may be the king's favored master mason from one of his royal palaces, but— Here, I pray you, read this."

From the tight sleeve at her wrist, Meg shakily pulled a folded piece of paper. Rosalind took it, touched by how nervous Meg seemed to be at showing it to her. A lover's note? she wondered. She opened the paper and, to her amazement, read a poem in rhymed couplets signed by Lord Spencer's frequent visitor, the king's master mason:

My hands and heart do work with stone,
Materials both hard and strong.
So never did I think to seek
Aught that made me frail or weak.

Yet when I breathe the air you do,
My hands and heart doth tremble too.
But when your smile says I belong,
Then my weakness makes me strong.

"Oh," Rosalind whispered, suddenly a bit regretful she had more than once told Master Stanway he did not belong near Meg.

The feelings flowing from the poem surprised her, and its impact seemed to sap her strength. Still, Meg and Franklin Stanway together would be disaster. She refused to have her sister hurt. The man would leave as soon as the castle was completed. Meg simply must fall in love with someone safe in town. And, even if Stanway did want to wed her—which Rosalind did not believe—that would mean Meg would have to live near King Horrid Harry to honor him for her husband's sake.

But what moved Rosalind most was that the poem addressed her own dilemma. She partly avoided and feared Nicholas Spencer because her feelings toward him confused her. It was a paradox. What sane person would ever 'seek aught that made one frail or weak'? Even the strength of her hatred and vengeance weakened in Lord Spencer's presence, and yet that weakness made her feel vital, thrilled and strong. Curse them, but what a tangled web these Deal Castle men spun!

"Ros, do you see what I mean about him?" Meg prompted and touched her arm. "He is not just some king's man merely trifling with a maid's affections. He cares deeply."

"He is very clever," Rosalind admitted as she handed back the poem and watched Meg replace it in her sleeve. "But perhaps overly clever and far too adept in courtly ways. He needs watching. And not the sort of watching you do of him the moment he brings his ale into the common room or comes by to visit Lord Spencer. But I will not throw him out again if you vow not to go traipsing off privily with him somewhere."

Rosalind did not exactly feel she was capitulating. There was no way she could stop Stanway from visiting the lord lieutenant, and she could hardly lock Meg in her chamber. But Meg's face lit like a Yuletide candle at her budging just a bit.

"Then you'll not make a fuss if we are together here on the grounds?"

"Just guard your heart with a king's man, dear Meg. With our heritage—and our present situation—it would create an impossibility!"

The next day, Rosalind began to wonder if there were not a conspiracy afoot to persuade her to be friendly to the king's lord lieutenant. Meg was not the only one to mention it. While Rosalind was standing outside, holding the ladder for fellow Rosie Clint Marlow while he repaired shingles on the inn's roof, Rosie after Rosie stopped by to offer such advice on their way in or out of the taproom for a drink. Will Worthington, a shepherd and fisherman; Charles Seabrook, town carpenter and fisherman; and two of the four Thorpe brothers, Jack and Boyd. Alf and Hal had already made similar comments.

At least Lord Spencer had ridden off on an inspection of the castle, so he would not notice all this chatting, she thought. She was just wondering when Clint Marlow would stop his pounding on the roof to shout down the same advice. When he clambered back to earth and did indeed suggest she be a bit "softer on the new man," she decided to talk to Wat. Her Rosies were acting in just the opposite way to what she wanted and would have expected.

Wat Milford's small brewery was just down the road. With increased demands on it as well as on the inn lately, he seldom got away to visit as he used to. Wat was in charge of one of the Deal luggers, and was, after Rosalind, the unspoken leader of the Rosies. She would just ask him about this little conspiracy.

She started toward town with an admiring glance back at the new patches on the brown shingled roof of the inn. The Rose and Anchor was the only edifice of any size in Deal—before the king had started building his huge castle, that was. Built two generations ago in wattle and daub, the inn's outer walls had been occasionally replastered between its exposed oak-beam ribs. Tall, muted-rose brick chimneys, one for each of the four broad hearths, poked up toward the sky. The building lay in an L-shape around a cobbled courtyard with a big anchor in the middle to which visitors often tied their horses. Roses sprawled up the walls along the facade with its tiny patches of mullioned windows. The gardens and grass lay behind with the small stable on the brow of the vale, which was thick with trees now changing to the October reds and golds. Pride and possessiveness swelled in her as she gazed back at the inn, then turned her face toward town.

The inn stood on the edge of Deal along the road to the bigger town of Sandwich. Next on the road came Milford's combined house and brewery. The town's other plaster or stone buildings with tiled or thatched roofs clustered around the little gray stone Norman Church of St. Leonard. There were only four streets in town, High, Common, South and Valley, but small alleyways and closes laced it all together.

She walked across the cobbled yard at Milford's. Stacked barrels and kegs seemed to guard the door. Inside, holding wooden paddles, Wat and his two workers stirred steaming vats of malted brew; the smell of sweet apples hung heavy in the air. Wat left his task immediately to walk with her out back amid more barrels. As he listened to her question, his rounded face, framed by flyaway brown hair, was intent. He sighed and nodded.

"Not a conspiracy 'zactly," he assured her, "but most of the lads feel your hatred of the man will tip him off to something. For a certain, I admire your honesty and dedication, though," he added hastily.

"But do you agree with the others?" she asked. After she lost Murray, she had relied on Wat a great deal for advice about stocking and running the taproom. She had known Wat almost as long as she had Murray, and she felt sorry he had never wed, though numerous girls had been more than willing. "Wat?" she prompted him again when he crossed his arms over his stocky chest, gazed sadly at her and did not answer.

"I s'pose you'll have to make some effort," he admitted with a shrug. "The king's man is hardly one to be strung along like that bumbler Putnam. With that big French shipment coming in 'bout a week, we don't need him perturbed. Even though our Boulogne friends will land it after dark a ways down the beach, Spencer's strong enough to ride a horse now. We'll have to keep him otherwise occupied that night. We need him to think everyone likes and accepts him, 'specially after your news that he's here to look for smugglers, too. That's what everyone's wanting you to do, I guess."

He looked as if he could have bitten off his tongue after that speech, one of the longest she'd ever heard him make. "Everyone's wanting me to do what?" she demanded. "Let him think I like him? Occupy him while our cache is unloaded? Has it come to that, to sacrifice me to that?"

Wat shook his head. He looked as if he were in pain. She noted his sloping shoulder slumped even more. "No, no, but some of the lads thought maybe you could get a look at the castle or something that night—you and Meg, even Aunt Bess, I thought. But meanwhile, folks are thinking that your standing up to him might—you know—backfire like a bad cannon. Now, I don't like all this no more'n you do, but I s'pose it's best you let sleeping dogs lie."

"He's no longer sleeping, Wat. *Sacre bleu,* I detest that arrogant bastard and what he stands for!"

Wat felt his eyes water in mingled gratitude and grief. He was so glad to hear she hated that tall, handsome man she had to keep under her roof. And so sorry to have to urge her to be kinder to him. Through his tears there were suddenly two blurred Rosalinds standing defiantly before him. He'd always wished there had been two of her! One for Murray and one for him! He'd adored her for so long, but she'd been Murray's. Even these years Murray was gone, she was still somehow Murray's, always so busy, so dedicated, so fiery for the cause. And now there were rumors from the inn that the king's commander had fire in his eyes when he looked at her! 'S bones, it was enough to make a brewer take to his own drink!

He blinked and managed to say, "Just think it over, lass. Too late to warn our French friends to use another beach, and then it would be too blasted far to haul the stuff to hide it."

She nodded. Wat drank her in with his eyes, but she was looking away, evidently pondering other things as usual. "Until Spencer moves into the castle," she said, "we can hardly store our imports in the inn's hidden cellars. It will all have to go in the cave in the vale or maybe even in the empty tombs at St. Leonard's. I just knew this was going to get so complicated...." Her words drifted off.

"I'm so glad you don't agree with the others, Wat," she added.

She patted his arm as if he were a good little boy or a faithful dog as she turned away. Wiping his nose on his sleeve, Wat watched her—as always—leave him standing here while she hurried back to other things.

Rosalind jumped when Nicholas Spencer's voice followed a knock on the door to her chamber. "Mistress Rosalind, if you are in there, I would have a word with you!"

She hurried to the door, patting at her hair, fluffing her dark green velvet skirt. Not, of course, that she cared a whit how she looked for him, but she had been moving wine crates after doing her records, and she did not want him to see her in disarray. She opened the door just far enough to step out into the hall, and closed it quietly after her.

"Yes, my lord?"

"I shan't keep you long, as I am certain we both have things to see to."

She nodded, but offered no information. Standing this close to him in the dim hall, she felt the powerful impact of the man again. As if in subtle challenge, he leaned one hand on the wall near her head; unblinking, she stood her ground. At least his height and size no longer surprised her anew each time, nor made her feel at a disadvantage. Still, little flames of fire sizzled through her lower belly and ran like lightning down her limbs.

For the past few days, she had made a concerted effort to be somewhat kinder to him. She did not avoid him, spoke to him and even smiled at him, though she did not seek him out. It yet galled her when he lorded it over them as if he could have the entire country at his beck and call for a snap of his fingers, just as he commanded his own men. He seemed ever to want things done perfectly and immediately. She resented his invasion of her life and the bitter desire for vengeance he fed. His very presence spurred her to defiance. Yet her friends had judged shrewdly in deciding that they should not provoke him unduly. Perhaps she could discover where he might be at certain times or even what plans he had to find the smugglers. Now she forced a little smile to her lips and saw his dark eyes light in response.

"I was just keeping some of my accounts, my lord. It has helped my family and town financially to have all these visitors here, including you, of course."

"Do I detect a breach in the high walls of Mistress Rosalind's thorny independence, then?" he asked, his voice low. "In truth," he went on before she could answer, "it is concerning your guests here at the inn I wished to speak."

"Say on, my lord. Most of them are more in your control than mine these days, if you have complaints."

"But when the laborers are off what they consider my premises—the castle and barrack grounds—they feel they are at liberty to overindulge in ale and carouse here among the townsfolk. Though I have a royal warrant to command the entire region, I would rather not put that to the test until a military crisis comes. Too much control too early can work against ultimate control, you see."

At that, his eyes swept over her and she had the distinct, shivery feeling they were no longer discussing only military might in the region. Her stomach cartwheeled, but she did not look away from his penetrating stare.

"So," he went on, "I would like us to work together to control the workers circumspectly, as I have noted well how folks admire and respond to you."

She knew full well he had been watching her. She stiffened her backbone at his request they "work together." *Never, never,* her inner voice screamed, but she inclined her head as if to appear receptive.

"First, the carousing goes on entirely too late and is too noisy here in the Rose and Anchor," he informed her. "Once my workers get a bit of ale in them—"

"And you expect me, just a petite, delicate woman from little Deal, to control king's workers bestowed on us from big London?" she countered, instantly regretful she had taken that sharp-tongued tack with him again. "Besides," she said, "they quiet down whenever they see you."

His dark eyebrows crashed down over his eyes. She hated to admit it, but she still loved to goad him. She knew it annoyed him that his presence in the common room or taproom threw an immediate pall over the laborers' laughter and cavortings—and yet was that not what the man wanted! All he had to do was sit in with his precious castle workers here if he wanted them quiet! He ruled this region, she seethed, the way the king ruled the realm, with cold command and regal orders that were intended to further his own ends. She could tell she had shattered his steely calm now. She regretted that if she was letting the Rosies down, but she could not help but feel a thrill when she bested him.

"Just do not expect the king's largess to repay you if they get out of hand and break up the place some night," he warned her ominously, pointing a stiff index finger at her. "And on the morrow, I intend to assemble a military procession to take formal control of the castle, and I want a peaceful, sober crowd assembled along the route of march."

"You will be moving out of here then?" she inquired a bit too eagerly.

"My quarters are not yet completed, but it will be soon. Since you hold some sway here, I would appreciate it if you request that the townsfolk turn out in appropriate fashion along the way from the inn to the castle. Now that we have had horses sent and the supplies we lost replaced from London, the townsfolk should honor their king by showing their respect as we officially move the garrison to the castle."

She managed to bridle her temper and her tongue. How dared he demand the citizens of Deal honor the king who had tried to ruin them! How dared he order her like some lackey to pass on his orders! She detested being trapped between her desire for honesty and protest and her need for subterfuge and submission. She was tempted to tell everyone to bring mud clods or rotten eggs to his military parade, but she remembered her Rosies and calmed herself.

"I shall see they all hear of it," she said demurely.

"I am heading for the castle now. I believe, then, you and I have agreed you will help me with my two requests."

Their eyes met and held. His clever choice of words such as *agreed* and *requests* did not fool her after this exchange. He was still dishing out orders he dared her to defy.

"I shall do what I can," she managed, "though I am not some omnipotent commander to order folks to do that they would not, Lord Spencer."

"And if that means by implication that I am, I would command you to call me Nick as my friends do—since we have begun this past week to understand each other better. And I shall call you Rosalind."

She did not know whether the prickles at the back of her eyes and throat meant she would laugh or cry. And she had thought Franklin Stanway was slickly menacing and manipulative! By the saints, she meant to manipulate and menace this man, too, and hoped he would not know it until it was too late for him!

"Again, I can say only that I shall try, my lord. Good day."

She yanked at her door latch, stepped inside her chamber and closed the door quickly. She leaned against it; her legs felt as if she had the sea wobbles. Did he think her some sort of simpleton he could order about, then win over with begging favors and granting familiarities? She heard him— the king's foster son Nick—close his own door across the hall as she sank to a seat at her table to try to think things out.

"Did she agree to help, my lord?" Stephen Delancey asked Nick as he returned to his room.

"As much as I could hope for."

"The frost is starting to melt, eh?"

"But there is still a damned cold wind blowing, Delancey," Nick admitted grimly as he gathered up the drawings Franklin Stanway had done of the castle, dungeon to parapets. "She is very secretive, but that just corroborates the obvious. I warrant whoever runs the smuggling band in these parts probably congregates with his men here at this common meeting place. They've all learned to keep mum. Neighborhood loyalty and all that. This inn has had so many patrons lately, who would notice smugglers in and out? But the inn's owner might know something of it."

As he spoke, Nick continued to pack things he would need at the castle today. Delancey stood as if at attention, listening. "The thing is, I have got to get a bit closer to Mistress Rosalind before I can ask her about it, even indirectly. She'd clam up if I simply ordered her to tell me what she knows about suspicious goings-on. I need to know if she had noticed men with foreign accents or strange shipments of goods, especially at night. We shall get Franklin to ask her sister, too. His majesty told me to hunt out the most ruthless, brawny lout in the village and start there with suspicions and surveillance, but the town is full of brawny bruisers."

He ticked off possibilities on his fingers. "Rosalind's cousins. The brewer, Wat, whom I've seen her whispering with. Half the fishermen in town. So far, any man for miles around but Percy Putnam and his lackey, Roger Shanks, is a suspect, as far as I can see. Our bad beginning has set me back, Delancey, but I shall flush him out fast now."

"Putnam's a strange one for a revenue agent, my lord. Usually they're the most detested souls around."

"Mmm," Nick agreed as he tied his cloak around his shoulders. "I cannot say why, Delancey, but the man rubs me the wrong way. Just too ingratiating, I guess, like half the hangers-on at court. I would rather have someone tell things to me straight at any time. Bring his majesty's letter now, as I intend to read some of it to the men from the castle walls and save some of it to read tomorrow after the procession. Let's ride.''

But Nick had only just reached the hall of the inn when he heard a commotion outside. Shouts, a hubbub. The tap-room was emptying of its early patrons. Rosalind ran ahead of him out the door, and he tore after her with Delancey in his wake. As if Nick's speaking of Putnam had summoned him, the revenue agent rode back and forth in the cobbled court, waving a sword and screaming. His dart-eyed assistant, Roger Shanks, sat on another horse off to the side with his sword drawn, too.

"Attack! To arms!" Percy shouted. "A fleet of war-ships sighted off Sandwich! A goodly number! All able men down to the castle to make a stand!"

Putnam started when he saw Nick elbow past Rosalind. He had obviously not expected to find him here yet this morning. Delancey ran for their horses as Percy addressed Nick.

"Ah, there you are, my lord. Your men will have to make a stand on the unfinished walls! Seven ships! To horse! To arms!"

"Seven ships, Putnam?" Nick bellowed back over the noise of the crowd. "But headed south, not north, aren't they?"

"You have seen them from here? Coming from just north of Calais, I'd judge. I shall ride with you, then return to protect the townsfolk with a stand at the inn! I shall—"

Rather than argue with Putnam from the disadvantage of standing while the man pranced back and forth on his fine stallion, Nick ran over to mount his big black steed that Delancey had brought around from the stables in back. Nick rose stiff-legged in his stirrups and shouted, "Quiet here! No need for panic!"

The growing, murmuring crowd hushed. "Those are English ships sent south from Gravesend to Andalusia in Spain!" he went on. "I have a recent letter from the king telling me that they would be passing through today! My men at the castle are preparing to sound a volley to wish them well as they pass by. Delancey, the letter," Nick concluded and held out his hand.

Delancey, now mounted also, fumbled in his side pack and produced a piece of vellum much like the one Rosalind had seen on Nick's bed. Nick opened it and read a section of the king's letter, while Putnam turned red as an apple and his sword arm wilted. Rosalind itched to get her hands on and read the rest of that missive Nick flaunted. It could contain something about stamping out the smugglers! For the first time, she even considered risking searching his chamber. If caught, she could claim she was tidying the room— No, anyone who knew her would never believe that. And Nick sometimes sent riders back for things he needed. Perhaps there was a safer way than venturing into his room. If she were careful and clever, mayhap she could simply get him to tell her his plans for snaring smugglers himself!

She watched Percy ride over to the doorway and slowly dismount. On the ground, he was not the daring, dashing form he always tried to appear when mounted. Nick rode over to him and glared down.

"Next time, Master Putnam, come direct to me and do not create public chaos. I do not need boys calling 'wolf, wolf!' before the enemy is really at the door. And remember, *I* hold ultimate command of the castle and region if there's to be a call to arms." Nick wheeled his horse away and, with Delancey in his wake, rode toward the castle. The crowd melted back into the tavern or straggled down the street toward town.

Once again, Rosalind seethed at the arrogance that was the true core of Nick's character. Though she admired how he had kept control of the volatile situation, she still felt sorry for poor Percy. She sought him out inside.

"I suppose the closer to the king they work," she said, trying to soothe the obviously shattered man, "the more

they know and the more they flaunt it. It was an honest
mistake on your part, and we are all grateful you were so
watchful.''

Percy turned away from her without a word. He limped
through the inn and perched on a wooden bench outside,
overlooking the autumn gardens that still ran rampant, for
they had not had a killing frost yet. He could not bear to
face any of them right now, especially her. Was the little
bitch trying to make it worse by hashing it all over again? he
fumed. How dared the king's lord lieutenant dismiss and
scold *him?* How dared the whoreson bastard imply he was
like a boy here crying wolf! It made him recall the nightmare of that terrible day of his boyhood all over again! In
chilling waves, the memories rushed back.

Percy's father had been the revenue agent at Sandwich
before him. He had adored his father, a vibrant personality
and marvelous horseman, though the man had had little
time for him. But one day when Percy was ten, his father
had brought him on his horse with him to Deal. It had begun as one of the happiest days of the boy's life. Deal was
even smaller then; his father put in only the occasional appearance, hoping that would keep the lid on any possible
meagre smuggling here.

The boy had waited right outside this very inn in the cobbled courtyard while his father met with folks and took his
ease inside. Percy had watered his father's fine horse, curried it, fed it. And when after a long time his father still did
not return, the boy decided he would take the restive horse
for a little ride just down the dusty road to exercise it.

But he did not really know how to control the beast. It
cantered through the shallow valley and down to the shingled beach. It began to gallop, to fly. Percy held to the reins
and mane for dear life, but the horse stumbled on one of the
lines that tied the Deal luggers to the shore. The big beast
tripped, rolled and crushed the boy's leg beneath it.

Fishermen who had seen the accident put an alarm out. As the Deal folks were so adept at doing, the beach quickly swarmed with rescuers—and his furious, ranting father. His father, screaming at him that he had broken the horse's leg, had to have his valuable steed destroyed. Someone put the big animal out of its misery, but little Percy's misery had just begun.

Percy saw his father cry over the loss of the horse. But even as he was carried back up to the inn where the Delands dosed him with brandy and tried to repair his leg, his father said it was all the boy's fault. Percy lay screaming in agony on a table while they set and strapped the mass of broken bone as best they could. But to this day he bore a deeper agony than body pain: everyone in the inn and all of Deal knew that the horse meant more to his father than his son did. The little five-year-old blond girl Rosalind had stared at him that day in such pity that he had hated her! Her father loved her, that was obvious! It did not matter to Percy that she evidently remembered not a thing about that day, for he hated her for being so beloved.

He detested Deal—especially Rosalind—for its pity and its knowledge that Percy Putnam was worth less than a horse. He had felt a bit better when he contrived to have their damned luggers, which could trip a horse on the beach, ruined. When Lord Chamberlain Cromwell visited Sandwich, Percy found in him the perfect, powerful master, the man to deserve the love his father had betrayed. And all the while, he fed his hatred and waited for his chance to crush Deal and then control it all.

He shook his head as he was jolted back from his horrid memories. Today he'd been shamed once again before the folks of Deal and Rosalind as if he were a worthless, stupid boy. Now he had one more person to hate. Though Percy would strive to appear to be his friend, he would see the king's fine lord lieutenant, that self-satisfied bastard Nicholas Spencer, ruined, too!

* * *

Rosalind forced herself to join her fellow townsfolk to watch Lord Lieutenant Spencer's procession to the castle the next morning. Considering the pitiful, initial entry he and his men had made to Deal, they carried this off with aplomb. Yet it infuriated her to see Tudor green-and-white pennants paraded through town and vale to the castle. A single drummer led the procession with twenty mounted men in shiny silver breastplates following on sturdy steeds.

Ceremonial sword at his side, Nick Spencer was at his glittering best. His shoulders so broad, his back erect, his ebony hair glinting bluish in the sun, the plumes on his cap dancing, he sat astride his big black horse. His eyes went over her as he rode by, as if he owned her as well as the entire town, curse the man! His chin jutted with pride. His nose—she felt he held it haughtily in the air—had greatly healed now. At times, she wondered why she had set it. Her cleverness at the task had only made him both more handsome and more rugged looking.

This military display—the last array of soldiers here had ruined their boats and almost their town—impressed upon her the royal might that Nick and his men represented. Yes, perhaps even Meg had given her wise counsel. No doubt, one could catch more spiders, even rugged, handsome ones, with honey than vinegar. Perhaps it was actually time she seek out Nick Spencer, strictly for her own ends.

There were few cheers in town, but excited children and barking dogs chased the parade all the way down to the rising walls of the castle. From there, Rosalind heard tell later, Nick had made a rousing speech and read something else from the king's letter. Then the parade had disbanded amid clangs and shouts as the castle laborers returned to work.

All that day, Rosalind bided her time and laid her plans. Near dusk, when Aunt Bess and Meg went visiting Hal's family, she bathed in lilac-scented water. She took great care to sweep her wayward tresses back in a trim knot, but then on a whim, loosed some cascades of curls along her fore-

ead and temples. She donned her second-best, tawny-hued
elvet gown. It had ruffles along the square-cut neckline that
opped the taut brocade bodice, and tight slashed sleeves
ith puffs of chemise peeking through. She adorned her-
lf with the topaz necklace and drop earrings that had been
er mother's.

She was intentionally going to "bump into" Nick Spen-
er when he returned this evening and make him promise her
tour of the castle tomorrow. Now was definitely the night
 strike; tomorrow smugglers would be bringing in a haul,
nd someone needed to have Nick occupied at that time. She
as going to congratulate him on the parade and the way he
ad handled Putnam's panic, as the townsfolk were calling
. She was going to smile and be sweet. Either tonight or
on, she was going to find out from Nick what the king's
rders might say about smugglers. And most daring of all,
e would request that he take her on a tour of the castle
ter dark tomorrow, at the very moment her Rosies helped
eir French cohorts unload the big haul on the farthest
retch of beach and hid it in the vale. With a swish of skirts
nd trail of lilac scent, she went upstairs into Meg's room to
atch from a darkened window for Nick's return.

Chapter Four

It was after dusk when Nick rode back to the Rose and Anchor. All in all, he felt pleased with the day, for he had finally taken command of part of his purpose here. He had hastened progress on the castle, and he had officially established his presence and power in the area. Now, and it would be best if he could manage it before he moved into his quarters next week, he needed to obtain some information on the other charge from his majesty—the smuggling.

So far he had seen no sign of it, though the king's revenue man, Percy Putnam, when questioned, had admitted he and Cromwell—damn, but the man admired crafty Cromwell—suspected smuggling here. But then again, Nick mused, how could he himself have seen a sign of smuggling? He had begun his stay in Deal unconscious, then had been confined to a sickbed where he could hardly expect the leader of the smugglers just to come calling! But now that he had control of other things, surely it would not take much to flush out and snare the rustic ruffians of Deal who dared trade illegally with the French foe!

Unfortunately, Putnam had no proof or definite leads to offer him, even after several years of seeming to get on well with the citizens of Deal. So, Nick thought, if it had not worked for Putnam, perhaps his plan for a friendly demeanor, careful questioning and secret surveillance was loomed. Still, he was not Putnam. And he was not ready yet to turn to threats, or to toss someone in the new dungeon until he had a solid lead as to which Deal bully might be the brains and brawn behind the smugglers.

But he had reasoned out some things. Since Putnam had no clues, the smugglers were more clever than he had imagined. Bordeaux was the nearest well-known smuggling port in France, yet apparently no one in this area was absent for enough days to sail there and back! The fishing and rescue luggers were the craft no doubt used, but even with their skilled crews they could not reach Bordeaux and return in the time of an overnight fishing trip. Calais was English, and so off limits. But there was one town with a fine harbor where goods could be collected and brought back almost overnight—Boulogne-sur-Mer. And the first time he got the chance, he was going to look into that possibility.

He left his stallion, Raven, with the boy in the inn's small stable and headed across the dark lawn to the back entrance of the taproom. From here, he could already hear the rumble of conversation and laughter inside. Despite his rush to complete the massive castle, he had no choice but to release nearly half the workers at night. There were not enough torches or lanterns to go around, and some of the masonry suffered from being handled in dim conditions. But, Nick complained to himself, did most of the laborers have to come here before they stumbled back down to their pallets in the barracks? Surely the first good snow would keep them from walking the new path they had worn through the vale to get up here!

He set his jaw hard at the thought that workers and townsfolk alike would quiet the moment they noted he had entered the inn. Not that he wanted to share in their raucous pastime, nor that he saw himself as part of them. But it still annoyed him they could not simply greet him and go on with their fellowship while he was in their midst. If he was given such cold-shoulder treatment, how could he ask a few clever questions? There was hardly a chance he could even overhear something. It was only after he took his nightly pitcher of ale and went to his room that their frolic resumed to such a pitch he could hardly sleep.

It painfully reminded him of how people at court had never been at ease with him after King Henry made him his ward. Not the men at least. The ladies apparently found his majesty's friendship enhanced his attraction. Sometimes the way men hushed when he approached and closed him out of their circles recalled the devastating loneliness he had felt when his mother re-wed and moved to distant York. She had claimed she left him at court for his own good, so he could make his way in the world, but he had missed her terribly. The loyalty of the men in his command was a far different thing from friendship; he still suffered from that frightening aloneness. Sometimes, but for the king, he felt his fierce dedication to duty was his only friend.

He was nearly across the gardens when Rosalind opened the door. He halted with a jolt. She stood a moment, silhouetted in its light, beautifully gowned and alluringly coiffed as if she were stepping out to meet a lover. He wondered if she would see him when her eyes adjusted to the darkness. How he wished, foolish as it was, that she had come out to greet him. She knew everyone in town; most of them were her friends. But to his amazement, she waved to him and stepped out to close the door behind her.

"Mistress Rosalind!"

"You said you would call me Rosalind now, Nick." He heard her voice quaver, but she went on, "I was just stepping out for a breath of air. Meg and I decided to have a formal family dinner tonight, you see. I love the October nights, so crisp and clear with the smell of leaves and smoke."

He almost pinched himself to see if he were dreaming. Could this be the same prickly woman he had dealt with heretofore? He had not favored her shrewish tongue nor the way she dared to defy him, but it had made him more determined to bring her to heel. As willowy and fragile as she looked, he had been surprised by her backbone and vitality. He had even hoped her tartness was a different way of rustic female flirting. He favored his women sweet, but not cloyingly so, and Rosalind was a smacking antidote to that!

"You will catch a chill out here in that gown," he said as his eyes went over her at closer range. "Is that French silk and lace?"

"French? I really would not know, though I suppose many things we English wear are imported from the Low Countries, Spain—from somewhere."

Even in the dimness of the wan light reflected through the bull's-eye panes of the mullioned windows, he could see the soft stretch of her shoulders and the upper swell of her breasts over the taut bodice of the golden gown. Her neck was graceful and framed now with tumbled ringlets of honey-blond hair that shone like a gilded halo behind her. And she smelled enticingly of lilac-scented gardens.

"Indeed, my lord, I am not cold and much more hardy than you seem to think. By the way, the parade looked regal today, and I was glad to see you put Percy Putnam's panic—that's what they're calling it in town—in its place, though he was most annoyed by your rebuke."

She strode a few steps past him to stand at the edge of the gardens. He was pleasantly surprised she had offered him that bit of news about what people were saying and thinking. And her compliments made him go all hot deep in his belly. He wondered, if he played his cards right, might she not offer him more information about all kinds of things? Perhaps he should inquire directly if any Frenchmen—perhaps from Boulogne—had been through here. But he did not wish to break the mood. He could not have been more amazed at her warmth and her willingness to be alone with him in the dark than if she had sprouted wings and flown.

His sword belt creaked and his spurs clanked as he moved to stand even closer behind her.

The realization of how much he desired her hit him with stunning impact. He longed to lift his hands to cup her nearly naked shoulders, to slide the soft velvet down her white arms, and lean over her to touch and taste the skin of her throat with his lips and tongue. Her sweet scent intoxicated his senses. He tingled all over, and felt a distinct tightening in his loins. She had always had such an effect on him, even when they argued, but this sudden welcoming warmth made her more luscious and alluring than ever. He had to say something. He was gawking like a moonstruck dolt.

"I am glad the procession impressed you," he managed. "Since you deliver compliments *and* complaints, I value your honest opinion." He saw her stiffen a bit. "I yet believe you are cold. Pray take my cape," he offered, though he hated to have her cover herself.

He swirled it around her before she could protest, and she pulled its edges closer, almost as if she hugged herself. He longed to do that himself with such intensity he could hardly stop from doing so. He had to keep control here, for she was finally coming around. She must have realized after the parade and the panic today that he was the one in command, the one to whom she owed proper respect and submission. And perhaps, like other women he had known, albeit those were sophisticated court ladies, she had decided he was desirable, too.

"I was wondering," she said, her voice uncharacteristically soft and shaky, "since I was busy here and could not go all the way down to the castle today, if you would show it to me sometime. The thing is, I am always so busy during the day, and it is this time of night I am at liberty. But I suppose a torchlight tour would be too much trouble for a busy man such as yourself...."

Aha! He reveled in his first glimpse of victory. He had her now! A private tour of massive Deal Castle, the ultimate demonstration of his might and right. A few kisses and she would tell him anything he wanted to know. A bit of love play, and she could be his to enjoy during the months he was here. He almost suggested they get his horse and ride to the castle straightaway, but he did not want to reveal his hunger for her, since that might make her bolt. Damn, but his privy chambers there were not furnished yet! He would get something in there tomorrow, especially a comfortable cot or bed. If she went there at her own request and gave just one little sign that she meant all that her willingness implied, nothing would stop him from enjoying her and then having all he wanted: mistress, informant, perhaps even his accomplice later to catch the smugglers!

"Any night you are free," he said, "I am certain I could arrange it."

"Tomorrow, then?"

"Tomorrow. The sound of the sea on the pebbles under the parapets can almost lull one to sleep. It's a far cry from the bustle and noise here."

"Despite how fickle and unforgiving it can be, I love the sea," she said. Her teeth flashed pale in the dark, and her eyes gleamed.

He felt so strangely weak-kneed near her that he was utterly relieved to know she would be his soon. Once he possessed her, he would not yearn for her so intensely; he never had with another woman. Yet however hard he drove himself overseeing things at the castle or when he wrote to his majesty or even to Penelope, this stubborn woman tramped through his thoughts.

But now he saw her for what she was. Poor Rosalind, he mused, forced to don a hard shell of armor when so much man's work had fallen on her slender shoulders at her husband's and father's deaths. Now he was being allowed a glimpse of the soft, sweet, submissive woman beneath. He had slowly won her over these past weeks by not rushing her, but not giving her much slack, either. He congratulated himself on how masterfully he had handled her! She was probably so in awe of a man close to the king that she had been frightened at first.

He could not keep himself from touching her. He lifted one hand to cup her cheek. He felt her shudder with emotion, but she did not move otherwise. A huge jolt of lightning crackled up his arm and coiled in his chest and loins, waiting to strike.

"It has been difficult for you to be without a man," he dared to say.

"I have my family, my friends."

"You are trembling again."

"We had best go in."

"So I can quiet the crowd?"

"We could sit with them and have some ale. Then they would see you are not such a threat."

"I want you to know that I am no threat. When you are helping me—and thereby the king—and when we are on your tour of the castle, I shall not be a threat."

She nodded, but he felt her shudder again. He wondered if she would simply sway into his arms, since her longing for him was so obvious. He reached for her, but she deftly sidestepped and walked to the door.

"I shall go in first," she said, "so that no one talks. And when I come to the castle, I shall meet you there. My reputation, you understand," she added breathlessly and slipped inside.

He threw back his head and sucked in a deep breath of night air, wondering if he could have dreamed the past few moments with her. He felt triumphant. She was so changed, just as he had wished. As he strode inside, he chuckled to recall she still had his cape around her. Did she think people would not talk when they noted that?

It was warm inside the paneled, oak-beamed taproom. Silence swooped around him; he scanned the crowded area for her. Men, many of whom he recognized, clustered over drinks, card games or talk. He saw her then. She wore no cape now and, holding two mugs of ale, had made a place for him next to her on a bench by the far wall.

Feeling all eyes on him—did she not think everyone would note this, too?—he ambled over and slid in beside her. Then he realized a woman of her status would want to show off that she was friends with him. His position with the king must be even more of an amorous stimulant with her than it was with highbred ladies!

When she subtly elbowed him and nodded, smiling to the room, he nodded and smiled, too. The laughter and talk built again like the sibilant sound of a wave hissing on the shore. He took a good gulp of ale. For the first time here, he felt almost happy. How easy this victory had been! The woman he wanted to tame had as good as capitulated, and he, more or less, was sharing a drink with his workers and the men of Deal.

Rosalind's hands shook as she tied the cords of her russet cloak over her deep blue linen gown. Now that Nick had agreed to let her visit the castle, it would do no good to garb herself as finely as she had last night. Alf gave her a boost up on her mare and whispered, "No one, even him, is a match for you, Ros. When you hear my imitation of a dog's baying outside the castle, the coast is clear, so don't you worry."

"Not I!" she lied to Alf as she had to Wat earlier today. "I have simply requested to look around the castle. Who knows but it might not help us to know that fortress inside out sometime, too!"

"Sure, and mayhap we'll hide our next French shipment in the king's own dungeons!" Alf teased. They both laughed nervously.

"I shall be just fine, Alf. Tell the others that!"

He nodded and reached up to squeeze her hand over the reins. "Godspeed, cousin."

"And to the Rosies, too! I shall miss being with you."

She walked the horse from the stables and watched Alf disappear into the thick trees of the vale before she rode away. Though the Rosies knew where she would be, she had not told Aunt Bess or Meg, who were visiting Hal's family again. Aunt Bess would have worried, and Meg would have used the fact as ammunition to argue that she should be allowed off alone with Franklin Stanway.

Rosalind let her dark brown horse, Chestnut, pick her way slowly through the vale, then gave the mare her head on the beach. She recalled Nick had a black horse, so perhaps he would not note all the horses in town were dark-hued, so they might be used to haul goods when night fell. She knew to keep Chestnut's hooves away from the low, stretched tethering lines of the luggers. Surf sprayed skyward. Since she was going calling, Rosalind pulled up her squirrel-lined hood to guard her face and hair. It was wonderful to have this entire stretch of beach to herself. Few townsfolk stirred at night but the ones in the trade. Tonight those folks were behind her on the beach, awaiting the delivery of wine, brandy and luxurious yard goods from several small, swift French cutters. She reveled in the feel of freedom, as if she were sailing over the sea at night. Her control of the racing horse built her courage for facing Nick Spencer.

She finally slowed Chestnut as she passed the last lugger in the line. Now that the lord lieutenant would be living here, the Rosies must decide on a rotation of boats. Boats for fishing for fish, of course, but also for fishing for free-trade goods from the busy docks of Boulogne. The lord lieutenant and his men must note naught amiss when luggers were out at night. And Deal needed as many loads of goods as possible before the coming winter weather kept them off the seas.

Past the ribbon of surf, the massive castle loomed ahead just off the beach. The pale gray masonry of the walls looked ghostly tonight; the stone had been partly pillaged from a nearby priory. Their terrible king, she thought with a shudder, had ruined so much in the Reformation. What was one pretty Kentish priory when he had banned the Catholic church in England in order to divorce his queen and marry Anne Boleyn, thereby alienating the Catholic kings of Europe?

She pulled Chestnut to a halt and squinted at the brooding hulk ahead of her. Deal Castle had two rings of rounded parapets set inside two deep, dry moats and outer earthworks. Its thick walls formed a double, six-sided rose with storerooms, a well and quarters for the commander and garrison within the center of the castle. This much she knew from observation and from hearing the workmen talk at the inn. What other surprises lay inside, she would perhaps learn tonight. And she would definitely put her knowledge to good use for the Rosies.

She gave a wide berth to the sprawling wooden barracks town and reined in on the stone ramp leading to the single castle entrance. As he had promised, Nick Spencer emerged from the narrow entryway to greet her.

"You came," he said as if he had doubted she would, but he sounded pleased.

"I hope no one thinks it amiss I came at night, but I thought it would be hard to see with so many workers as are about in the daytime, besides the fact we are both busy then, I mean."

She had not meant to blurt out all that, but he seemed not to heed how nervous she sounded. She scrambled down from Chestnut before he could reach up to help her. He took the reins from her and, cupping her elbow, led her and the horse in. Rosalind feared he would hear her heart thud as hollowly as did their feet across the long wooden drawbridge that spanned both moats. They passed beneath the drawn-up portcullis that looked as if it could come crashing down at any time.

"This single guarded entrance keeps everything secure," he told her. "It is nigh impossible for anyone to get in or out without permission." He pointed out the murder holes above the gate-house door where boiling oil could be poured on hapless invaders who made it between cross fire from the parapets.

After he tethered Chestnut, he showed her the trapdoor in the gate house that led to the newly completed dungeons below. Just a glance down the narrow steps to that black pit made her feel as if the thick walls were closing in. She felt again the power of the king and this man she so detested.

As they walked farther in, tall, wavering torches in wall sconces lit their way, though Nick carried one now, too. With each step, she came to realize it was indeed an impenetrable fortress that one could never hope to capture and from which one could never escape.

"But where are the men who work at night?" she asked him. She had not seen a soul except some guards near the entry.

"They are between shifts now. The next group will get busy in an hour or so."

Probably sensing she was hesitating now, he shared with her some humorous tales of how things had gone wrong in the rush to complete the castle. Still, she dragged her steps even when he touched the small of her back to urge her around a turn or up some steps. By the saints, she scolded herself and silently cursed her Rosies, why had anyone thought this was a clever way for her to keep Nick Spencer occupied!

Before they reached the parapets, he put his flaring torch in a pronged wall holder. "The sea air smells sweet tonight," he observed as they climbed a final narrow turn of stairs carved in the inner walls. His voice seemed so rich and warm; it wrapped itself around her in its intimacy even with this vast edifice. "Let's stroll the parapets before I show you the living quarters below. Captain Delancey is setting out wine and a little repast for us."

"Oh. But I am certain I shall like the view from up here best."

Her mind ran riot. What if something went wrong with the smuggling tonight, and the men were discovered? What if he threw the Rosies in that wretched dungeon and someone admitted her part in everything? Would he imprison a woman here? What if he touched more than her elbow and the small of her back? And if she tried to flee, what if she could not find her way back out of this maze? She felt each step took her deeper into the weblike passages of the castle and into her confusing emotions with this man.

When they emerged on the upper, windswept parapet walk, she breathed a sigh of relief. She felt safer up here, not all closed in with him. Her hood blew back; the stiff breeze ruffled her hair, though when she darted a look at him, each hair on his head looked perfectly in place as if it dared not stray. Still, he took his flat cap off so as not to lose it as they walked the outer perimeter. They leaned almost together, elbows on the outer bastion in a three-foot-wide indentation for shooting guns or arrows.

"The castle reminds me of a big stone battleship heading out to sea," she said as they stared over silver-etched waves.

"So it does," he agreed and moved so close to her that his right arm seemed melded to her left one.

She shuffled slowly away to the next crenellation while he explained where the different ordnance of cannon would go to blast the French from the sea. Butterflies began to beat their wings in her belly when his voice became so stern, determined, even passionate like that. This was indeed a man to be reckoned with. And when she squinted far down the beach in the direction of where her Rosies would be awaiting their haul, she made two terrible discoveries.

First, from this height one could see much farther than she had imagined. Unfortunately, the sky had cleared even more since she had set out. Though free traders always worked on moonless nights like this one, from this vantage the pewtery cast of cold starlight was amazingly bright and provided visibility for quite a distance. A boat might appear as a dark shadow in the regular march of white breakers to the shore.

Second, Nick Spencer had stepped close behind her. With his long arms resting on either side of her, she was as good as blocked in. And he was facing the same direction as she was. He might see something amiss—even if it were only one little glint of sail or steel!

Her legs went weak. She would have to do something to distract him further, perhaps get him to take her somewhere other than this side of the elevated parapets.

"Shall we stroll down below now?" she asked without daring to face him.

"I thought you liked it here." His hands touched her shoulders. He stepped closer, pressing her skirt and petticoats into the backs of her legs. His body heat radiated through her. Prickles of sensation shivered along her skin.

"I cannot tell you how pleased I am that we trust each other now," he continued, his lips so close to her ear.

She stood almost in his embrace. This closeness both fascinated and frightened her. At least with his lips in her hair, he could not be peering down the beach!

"Rosalind, Master Stanway told me earlier today about the accident at sea where you lost your husband and father. And I heard it was in rescue of a royal galley. Now I understand your unwillingness to be with me at first, thinking the whole incident of my arrival would renew sad memories for you."

She held her breath. How much more had he learned through Master Stanway—therefore, no doubt, through Meg? She hoped she could trust Meg not to let word slip

about the smuggling, but her sister was sore smitten by
Nick's master mason. How much could Nick guess? That
she had vowed vengeance against the king and his men?
That she had fostered a group of free traders not only to
salvage poor Deal but to make his precious king pay? But no
such accusations followed, only his next amazing, unset-
tling words.

"Rosalind, I am no doubt here for the duration of this
conflict. Let's work together to make Deal a stronger place.
Let's pledge we will be honest with each other. And I shall
show you how we can seal our bargain," he murmured and
turned her to face him.

I would make a bargain with the devil first! she wanted to
shout in his face. He extolled honesty and trust to her when
she intended just the opposite for him. But he did not—
could not—mean it. He was here to stamp out smugglers, to
punish or imprison them! When he tipped her back gently
in his arms, she almost yanked away. But in his embrace, her
tumbled feelings of both pleasure and peril kept her from
fighting him.

"The choice is yours," he whispered, his mouth so close
in her ear that his breath scalded her. Her mind raced. What
choice? To work with him? To be honest? To seal the bargain? She could not think when his lips drifted down her
temple, then slid across her earlobe and her cheek to poise
inches from her parted lips.

"Oh, but—" was all she had time to say before his mouth
descended.

After seeing all his power, pomp and pride, it was not the
crushing kiss she had expected. Though he held her tightly,
his lips teased and beseeched. They softened and slanted.
Her legs went weak as water. But the moment she surrendered the slightest bit, he invaded.

He tipped his head while his slick tongue made a skilled
foray between her lips. He challenged her there. She opened
slightly to him and they dueled with tongue tips. He

breached her defenses further to ravage her mouth. Her
senses reeled; she sagged against his stiff leather doublet.
His muscled legs encased in black hose and high leather
boots propped her up.

Suddenly, she was really kissing him back. She tried to tell
herself it was simply to distract him from the beach, just to
throw him off the track until she found a way to destroy
him. But none of that made sense now as she felt herself
capitulate. Mutually, they deepened the desperation of the
kiss. Thoughts of resistance and refusal scattered like sand
before crashing breakers.

The kiss went on and on. She wanted it never to end.

"I knew it, knew it," he muttered. He breathed as if he
had run miles. His lips left hers only momentarily, to take
better aim. He fluttered kisses on her nose, her eyelids, her
cheeks, again her mouth, again. "So delicate and yet so
passionate, my Rosalind!"

His hands marauded, too, down her shoulder blades and
back to grasp her small waist just above the fullness of her
skirts. One hand crept up her ribs to where the swell of her
breasts pressed against her tight-bound bodice. She wished
she were free of it, she wished—

He tilted her back and showered kisses down her throat.
Who she was, why she had come—all that seemed as distant now as the sea roar in her ear. She grasped the powerfully molded muscles of his back under his doublet. The
solid fortress beneath her feet seemed to sway and spin as
their mouths met hungrily again. In her rapture and her
need, she felt exploding within her emotions that she had
hidden deep inside all these years, just as surely as her men
must be hiding smuggled goods right now.

Her men! Smuggled goods! "Oh!" she cried and pulled
away from him.

"What?" he said and caught her back.

Reality flooded her. She could not stand up here, keeping him distracted *this* way! She had lost control, her very

mind! This was not why she had come. She had to stop kissing him and then stop *him* from standing here and touching her. He had said Captain Delancey was below with a meal. Yes, however much she detested being inside this place, that would have to do.

"I think we should go below for that little repast you promised," she told him breathlessly. She lifted three fingers to waylay his next kiss. She put her hands on his and gently disengaged them from her waist.

Nick was surprised when she suggested they go below, for she must know that meant even heavier love play. He had planned to suggest it soon, but she had beaten him to it! Though he only dealt with a rural lass here, he had to remember she had been wed, no doubt to a strapping, lusty man, like most of that ilk around here. She clearly knew full well what she wanted from him in his privy chamber, just as he knew what he wanted from her. It was only that he had thought to woo her a bit more first.

Still, he did not want the next guards up here; he had told the two usually here now on watch that he did not need them. Perhaps she was worried for her reputation, too, if someone saw them here. It suited him fine if this seductive little bout had made her as ready and willing for a tumble as it had him. He wanted the beauteous, petite Rosalind so much right now that he could have bedded her here on the stones! In this moment, he desired her over any other woman in the world—including Penelope, whose visage he could barely recall when he stared so hotly at this lovely, blushing face. After all, things between him and Penelope had been mostly business. The white-hot need he felt for Rosalind now was a far cry from that.

"Yes, I am ready, too," he told her. "Let me take you there."

He escorted her down and around the spiral staircase, into the central catacomb of the living quarters. He planned to move the entire garrison in next week, but only a few guards

were in these narrow halls and rooms now. He was grateful
he had had a cot put in here today, though he had thought
it would take much more to get her to it. He hoped he was
her first man in her years of widowhood. Surely she was not
emotionally attached to the ones who frequented the inn,
especially not that burly Wat Milford. He had been thinking of Milford as his first smuggling suspect to investigate,
and he did not like how close the man seemed to Rosalind.
Hell, perhaps after he tumbled her she would tell him anything he wanted to know about wayward goings-on she had
observed in town or at her inn. Though he talked little after
enjoying a woman, women always seemed warm, trusting
and chatty then.

He put his hand on the door latch to his small suite of
rooms. Suddenly it amused him that he would dare to love
her in this fortress meant for war. He would dedicate this
place not by conquering a formidable foe or seizing the head
of the smugglers, but by bedding this desirable, delicate
woman. He opened the door for her and she entered.

He saw her look around. The room was shaped like a slice
of pie with its ceiling just high enough to miss his head. It
was sparsely furnished as of today with the cot, desk, four
chairs and a table where Delancey had left food and drink.
The narrow hearth vented just outside through a shaft instead of a chimney. There was one deeply set window overlooking the outer battlements and sea. The other door led
to a small storage room and garderobe.

"I thought you said Captain Delancey was here awaiting
us," she said and jerked back against him when he closed
and latched the door.

His hand tightened on her upper arm. "I said only he was
below setting things up for us, my sweet. Do not pretend you
did not know we would be alone here."

He turned her to him, his hands under her cloak again.
Panic pierced her. She wanted to hit out at him and flee, but
that would give her away after asking to come down here.

He was a pompous, prideful blackguard to think she longed for his touch—and yet, she did. And she had showed him so. She was no green girl, so how had she managed to get herself into an even bigger kettle of fish than she had been in up on the parapets?

His hands were so skilled on her again, his kisses so sweet they swept her away. She had foolishly let all this happen, she scolded herself. By the saints, she would just allow a moment more of this, then insist they go out. But with only one window in this room and it facing the other way, it was the perfect place to keep him while her Rosies worked. However, next time the friendly French came calling, someone else could keep him occupied!

Not breaking their kiss, he untied her cloak and dropped it over a chair. He moved them smoothly toward the narrow cot across the room, never halting his skilled barrage of sweet caresses. She hoped the French had come early; she prayed she would soon hear Alf's warning call that would signify the coast was clear. But what if she could hear none such down here through that one small window? What if when she said she must start home Nick insisted he ride with her down the beach? She was desperate for some ploy to stay that did not include clinging to him on his cot!

Her hands splayed flat against his leather doublet, she pushed him away. "Wine," she gasped. "Some wine?"

He looked so dazed she might have spoken in a foreign tongue. Slowly his hands on her stilled.

"Now?"

"If—if you would not mind, my lord."

"I hardly feel the need, but, of course."

He half stood—not too steadily, she noted—and leaned over the table on one arm to snatch the bottle. In the same big hand, he seized two heavy goblets by their stems and plopped back beside her on the bed before she could rise. He handed her the goblets. Their hands shook, but he poured the goblets half-full and set the bottle on the floor.

"To us—and to the king!" he muttered and clinked the rim of her goblet with his. He downed the contents of his in one good gulp.

She had no choice now but to drink the wine. As fine as it was—and obviously French!—it tasted like bitter gall after his dedication of it. She tried to rouse herself to flee. She was demented to be here! Her body had played her false when it had responded so irrationally to this man. She could not fathom how he could affect her so deeply that way when no other man had, including, God bless him, dear Murray. She tried to stare Nick down, but his eyes seethed with dark desire. His nostrils flared. His square chin thrust out determinedly. She stared at him as if mesmerized. He took her goblet and set it with his on the floor.

"G-good wine," she stuttered.

"Is it? I taste only you."

"I—have I seen all the castle you wanted to show me?"

"I thought you might enjoy lying on your back here and looking at the ceiling overhead."

"No, I—really, I am not—ready."

"A pity. I was so certain you were. I could get you ready."

"Really, my Lord Spencer, I—"

"You promised to call me Nick," he said and took her hands in his big, warm ones. He bent his head to kiss her knuckles, then turned her palms up to tend to those with lips and darting, deliberate tongue. A traitorous ache for him feathered up her arms and leaped to her breasts before swirling sweetly down into the pit of her stomach. She clamped her thighs tighter together under her skirts. Even so, she felt hot and ready for him there. He shifted closer as if he knew. She tried to rise, but he tugged her back and was suddenly sprawled beside her on the cot.

Their heads shared the single pillow. It was so narrow her bottom bumped against the wall behind. As it had when they had lain together on a bed the first day they talked, his bent leg rode easily over hers to hold her down. But this time *she* felt dizzy as if she were the one who had been banged on the head and lain unconscious for days—as if she had tried to rise too fast. The wine, the feel of this man, his kisses, the fact she wanted him with all her being absolutely terrified her. Yet she opened her lips as if in willing surrender when he kissed her again.

Things spun further out of her control. She met his kisses and embraced him, too. She helped him when he unlaced the ties on her back to loosen her bodice. She felt so deliciously disheveled with his big hand ruffling up her skirts to clasp her stockinged ankle, knee and bare thigh above her highest ribboned garter. She gasped when he stroked flesh there, bared now to the lick of cool air and his burning gaze. But then he returned his avid attentions to her fluted collarbones. A pulse beat wildly in her throat as he bathed her with wet kisses there. While his hand on her leg rode higher, his lips marauded lower to the damp valley between her breasts that was now freed from her bodice.

"So slender, yet so full here," he muttered against her breasts while he scalded them with kisses. "Your skirts and chemise—let's take them off."

She nodded. She tried to remember her hatred of him, but it had slipped away like the sleeves from her shoulders. She only held to his big shoulders as he reached behind her to unlace her gown farther. Like a madwoman, she nibbled at the hard sinew on the side of his neck, then flicked her tongue in his ear. He froze for a moment; she heard him gasp raggedly. Suddenly, she sat in his arms, bared to her waist with her bodice and chemise peeled down and his eyes and hands everywhere. He cupped and molded each firm, high breast. She arched her back for him; her arms were caught at her side by her sleeves until he freed her. He licked a callused thumb across the pink tip of one breast and bent to pleasure the other with his lips and tenderly tormenting tongue.

"Let me love you," he gasped, "love you."

Love!

He did not mean it that way, of course. But she clutched the huge shoulders of his doublet with her fingernails as he laid her back on the bed and stood to tug her rumpled gown off her hips. Love! But she had come here for hate, hadn't she? For vengeance, not for all this that she now wanted so desperately. Not for love, nor those other things he had said, like trust and honesty! Never! But now that she had come this far with him, would he let her go? Worse, did she want him to let her go?

"Nick," she said, "I cannot—"

"I know. We will not tell anyone. I hate dissimulation and lies, but for both our sakes, we will keep this quiet, the times we meet. I swear to you I will guard your safety and your secret if you will just be ruled by me willingly instead of—"

He had bent to kiss her again when there was a sudden banging on the door. Rosalind squealed and sat up so fast her head slammed Nick in the chin. He bit his tongue and cursed under his breath.

"My Lord Spencer!" came Captain Delancey's voice through the door. "Something has come up!"

Nick jumped off the bed. It was only then she saw he had removed the velvet codpiece between his thighs and that, through the stretch of dark hose, something had indeed come up. She grabbed up her gown so as to cover her bare breasts and shoved her skirts down over her legs.

"What then?" Nick yelled as he wiped away blood from his mouth on his hand. He glared at it, then her. He lurched to retrieve and to replace the codpiece from the floor to cover himself.

"Some of the guards down the beach are in a scuffle with men they've caught! You'd best come, my lord!"

"Go and I'll be with you!"

Nick straightened his hose and shirt. He slammed the lid of a trunk open against the wall beside the bed, grabbed his belt, sword and pistols, then slammed the lid down again.

Rosalind's heart slammed, slammed even louder. Men caught on the beach! Her men! Everything had gone awry, everything!

She scrambled to arrange her gown, but she would never manage to lace it all the way up herself. Curse the vile seducer! And he had glared at her as if this chaos were her fault. She only prayed it wasn't, but right now she had to get out of here to see if her Rosies needed help. They could not be caught on the first haul since this wretch had come to Deal!

"Wait, here, Rosalind. I shall return after this business on the beach," he vowed, his gaze intense, his face still flushed with passion. "I swear I will make it worth the wait."

She gaped at him. It shocked her speechless that, considering the way she had responded to him, the brazen words he spoke were no doubt true. As furious with herself as him, she smacked her fist on her knee when he ran out and banged the door closed behind him.

Chapter Five

Left alone in Nick's rooms, Rosalind jammed her arms into her sleeves and yanked up her gown. In her haste, she laced it as tight as she could, then pulled her cloak over it. She was tempted to take time to search Nick's chest and desk for correspondence from the king, but she had to see what men had been taken on the beach. Her legs were shaking, but if Nick Spencer thought he could order her to await his return here, he was sadly mistaken! What a fool she had been to think she could challenge him on his own territory. From now on she would fight him in town, at her own inn where she could keep her head.

She opened the door and peered into the deserted hall, relieved to see he had left no guards to hold her here. She started down the narrow corridor they had come in by, then realized it went up to the parapets. She turned, went back and turned again, going downstairs instead of up, then through a maze of dimly lit halls. She was grateful she met no one. At last, she smelled chill air and saw stars overhead. Holding her skirts and cloak high, she ran across a small court, cluttered with workmen's benches, where she had left her horse.

"Come, girl, good Chestnut!" she whispered and led the mare through the gate house. Grim, armed guards still stood stolidly here, but both doffed their caps and let her pass. She mounted Chestnut on the drawbridge, rode down the stone ramp and turned toward the beach. Once past the noise of the barracks, she heard the ruckus that must have summoned Nick and his men.

Fearing she would see her Rosies surrounded, she raced toward the noise. At first, torches blinded her. Nick and Delancey stood in the center of a crowd; Nick was shouting. She strained to scan the men hemmed in by soldiers with pikes and poles. No, thank God! None of her Rosies, not even citizens of Deal, although the faces of those caught looked familiar!

"Guess we kin 'ave a bit of frolic on our own time, commander!" one fellow shouted at Nick from the cluster of ten or so men surrounded by at least twenty guards. Nick backhanded the speaker to the ground. His next words were not to the man he stood over, but to the others gathered around.

"Not if you cannot hold your ale. You disturb your fellows who need sleep for first shift on the morrow!" Nick's voice carried crisply on the beach breeze. Rosalind dismounted and walked her horse close to the group.

"And how can I trust the likes of you up at the inn or in town, either?" Nick demanded. "Captain Delancey, these men are confined to barracks until further notice. And the next knaves who act thus will have their pay docked! Let the word be passed among all from lowest fetching boy to Master Mason Stanway himself! I am putting a quota of four drinks per day apiece at the Rose and Anchor! The owner will keep a list for me of anyone who demands more than his due! Get the names of everyone here, then toss these sodden, sorry louts in the surf to sober them up. The king has trusted them to build his castle to defend the realm, and they are not fit to speak his name!"

Rosalind seethed anew at Nick and his king. But she stood agape at his speech, especially his brazen pronouncement of counting drinks at the inn. How dared he declare himself

arbiter of what was served there! Or command that she and
the inn's staff keep lists for him of his own rogues' names!
Now that he had seen his sensual power over her, he evidently thought he could make her do anything! But he'd
find otherwise! He was a low, vile wretch who could not
abide what a fine time folks had at the Rose and Anchor,
where he was most certainly not welcome!

Yet, as she hurried away, she was so grateful his men had
not discovered her Rosies' work this night that relief began
to mute her fury. That was until Nick saw her and jerked to
a halt. He strode over so fast his feet spit sand. His men
dispersed behind him. Torchlight faded to leave the two
alone in the windy night.

"I thought I told you to await me in my chambers," he
began without ado.

"You did, but I am not some low fetching boy nor even
Master Mason Stanway to have to take your orders. And I
resent enforcing *your* rules for *your* men's errant behavior
at *my* inn. I shall have no part of it."

"I told you before it might get out of hand there, and so
it has. You will do as you are bidden."

"I assume you mean in bed as well as out, seducer!" she
threw at him and spun away. He yanked her back to face
him. She wished desperately she had remained mounted so
she could flee now. She was so angry with him and her own
behavior this night she could have smashed his nose back in.

"We will return to the castle and see about that challenge!" he insisted. "You asked for and wanted all you received this night!"

"I did not! But, I repeat, I will not be commanded by
you, my lord."

"Hell's gates, you shall!" he insisted and seized her arm
that held her horse. "I will not be gainsaid, misled, led
on..."

She shrilled a laugh. "*You* have been led on?"

"By a mere wench who needs to be taught her place here in this damned, defiant town."

"Indeed, if you cannot even control *your* own men—"

By her upper arms, he lifted her from her footing in the sand. She dangled, the toes of her shoes bumping against his booted shins. This close, she knew she dared not kick him.

"I cannot fathom how such a shrewish, stubborn woman can make me forget myself the way you do!" he gritted out. "I could confine you, too, for disobeying. How do I know you have not arranged this escapade tonight, told your tapman to get my workers drunk to plague me while you kept me busy? Dare I wonder if all those smiling, chatting men in the taproom last night were not in on some plan of yours to make me have to move down here sooner so they can have their raucous fun up there?"

Her eyes went wide as saucers at that accusation. It was wrong and she would deny it, yet it touched near the truth of her intended trickery. At least he evidently thought she was merely trying to harass him because of his earlier complaints about noise at the inn and his men drinking too much. With great difficulty, she seized control of her rage.

"Please, my lord, you are hurting me."

He set her down, still holding her firmly, but she went on, "I swear I had naught to do with such a plan. Your accusations are most unjust. It is only that we strive hard to earn what we can at the inn in a friendly atmosphere. That will be ruined by list keeping and doling out numbered drinks to grown men who only want a little respite from their labors!"

He nodded, though his jaw stiffened. "We have both been disappointed that things did not end tonight as we would have wished. There will be another time for us. Others may have seen you now, so best ride back to the inn. I shall send a guard along as I have things to see to before I return tonight."

"I assure you, I can ride back alone."

"Not tonight, with men abroad who might harm you."

He helped her mount. *Men abroad who might harm you.* The words echoed in her head. She, who was usually so careful, had almost let herself be harmed this night and by the very man who stared up at her now. Except for the king, he was, quite simply, the only man she had ever hated. But she feared him, too. Imagine his having the gall to assume there would be other times when they would take up where they left off! Now that she knew Nick's amorous powers over her, she would be much more on her guard.

Yet, despite the odds, she could not keep herself from still wanting to bedevil him. She could have bitten her own tongue as she blurted, "At least your tongue is not bit clear through, my lord. A pity if it had harmed your fine speech-making or other pursuits."

His eyes narrowed and moved thoroughly over her. He licked his lips slowly, deliberately. "Some things are worth a great amount of pain," he muttered low and turned away to call for a guard to ride back with her.

Rocked by emotional turmoil, Rosalind lay behind her locked door that night, huddled up in bed. She agonized over how her plans to outfox Nick tonight had gone so terribly awry. Their passion had exploded to anger, then they had both bridled it before they parted. But there would be so much more to come between them if he had his way!

She agonized, too, wondering if all had gone well with her friends. She dared not leave the inn to find out. Nick might be back at any time; she had not heard him return yet. With his rooms completed at the castle, he could surely bed there now, but would he? She was surprised he had taken his time moving down there, unless he had just meant to keep an eye on the town—and perhaps on her. She did not doubt for one moment he had his own plans for ferreting out smugglers and delivering them trussed up for torture to the king.

She flopped over and pulled her blanket topsy-turvy. She jolted at the familiar rap-rap-pause-rap-rap on her window. Wat? Hal or Alf? She yanked the blanket around her and deftly wended her way through the piles on the floor to the window. Shoving the velvet drapery aside, she unlatched the casement and swung it open.

"Ring-a-ring of rosies," Alf whispered.

"Pocket full of posies," she answered, completing their password. "How did it go?"

"Got stuff stowed safe, and they cast off. Pierre bids a special hello to you. But now the stuff's hid, I think some of what was promised is missing. You got the list?"

"Go home and don't fret. I can check it on the morrow. Have Wat meet me near the cave midmorn. Spencer's still out somewhere, so watch yourself. Fine job!"

"For you, too? You all right, then?"

"Yes, of course. Good night."

"And, Ros, I hear tell Putnam rode into town after dark, but his horse is not in the stable. Doubt if there's trouble coming from the likes of him, but thought you'd best know."

She tried to reason that out, but she felt so tired, so spent. It was not Putnam's regular day to visit Deal, and he seemed such a creature of habit. Surely Nick could not have sent for him. And if he was in town and his horse was not in the stable here, where was he?

"Yes, I'll be sure neither Putnam nor his lordship see me meet Wat tomorrow. Don't bother Wat now if he's gone home."

"Aye, he has. A good night's rest for us all, then, and I'll tell him in the morning," Alf said and disappeared into the darkness.

She closed the casement, tugged the drapery closed and sagged against it. Whether the entire cache promised was there or not, they had survived this first haul under the lord lieutenant's very nose! Elation filled her, yet fears nipped at her, too. There was no way they could do this each time a shipment came in either via the French or their own boats; she would never risk "amusing" Nick Spencer again! Besides—

She heard boot steps in the hall and darted back to bed. Her door was locked and she had even tipped and jammed a chair against it. Yet she could feel Nick staring at her door, seeing no rim of light, wanting to knock. She cursed him for making her feel unsafe in her own home. She cursed herself for melting like butter in his hands tonight! She had to keep him at bay in such a way that he did not wonder why she had changed her mind when she never let him near her like that again! Would he accept that his edict limiting her profits in the taproom would make her avoid him? But she still knew better than to alienate him. Oh, *sacre bleu*, as Pierre would say, what a mess a man could make of one's life!

A floorboard creaked in the hall. She strained to hear, holding her breath. A chill of foreboding racked her. But Nick's steps went into his room, and his door closed quietly.

Wat Milford jerked to a halt in the doorway of his house adjoining the brewery when he saw Percy Putnam sitting at his table. The visit itself was not unusual, only the day and time of it. Percy often made friendly visits around town. Wat usually enjoyed hearing his news and gossip, at least in the light of day while he worked. Now, the single, fat tallow candle on the table magnified the man's darting shadow on the wall, like a lurking black bat Wat wished would take flight.

"Good evening, friend Wat!" Percy said, and lifted a flagon to him with a smile that bunched his cheeks up cherublike. "Your apprentice said you'd stepped out, but he let me in. Never tasted better brew. Been out for a walk, then, or just catting about town?" he inquired and chuckled at his own jest.

Wat hardly felt like laughing. It had been a long day. "Walked to town to see someone, not catting round, not me," he said as he ambled in. Percy poured him a drink that he gulped straight down.

Not many smugglers had the local revenue agent making jests and smiling when they came home from a haul, Wat thought. Besides, his muscles ached and he was sick with worry thinking about Rosalind going to the castle tonight to distract that handsome, well-bred lord lieutenant. No matter what the others said, he was going to insist she was quits with that. He gulped more ale and nodded to thank Percy, who kindly refilled his mug.

"Of course, you would never be unfaithful to your lady. Courtly love, et cetera," Percy pursued with a grin.

"What?"

"I mean, you would never go catting, not a man who admires a certain woman we all know and love. Speaking of whom, I need your advice on how to help our dear Rosalind." Percy leaned intimately toward Wat, who slumped across the table.

"What about her? You mean she's in trouble?"

Wat forced himself to calm down then, reminding himself that Percy must be held at arm's length, despite his bumbling nature. But Wat, like others in town, had no real fear that Percy was not a friend, whatever occupation the poor man had inherited.

"Alas, I am sore afraid she's *going* to be in trouble," Percy said and poured Wat more of his own brew. "Lord Spencer has his eye on her, you know, and I hardly think, bright as a penny as she is, she'd be a match for him if he demands she become his mistress while he's here in boring little Deal—that's the way he no doubt sees the place after years in London, I mean."

Frowning, Wat drank deeply, but made certain he kept his head. Percy's observation fed his own fears. Who could not adore Rosalind? But this talk of London scared Wat stiff.

Percy had met people from court like the king's minister Cromwell. He probably knew a lot about Spencer's citified tricks. If Wat just shared a drink with Percy, maybe he could find out a few things and warn Rosalind. He hoped she was safe after tonight, but at least he had the reassurance of having seen her horse was back in the stable on his way up from the beach.

He finished his ale and poured himself a bit more from a second pitcher. "Spencer's a slipp'ry London-bred tomcat and Rosalind sure knows that," he said. "He's the one pro'bly goes cattin' 'round!"

"Indeed, and I don't want to see her ravished and ruined any more than you do, my friend." At least, Percy told himself, not ravished and ruined by Spencer. He inclined his head toward the slope-shouldered man across the table. "Since you are obviously her closest confidant outside her family, Wat, I thought you would be the one to keep a protective watch on her. I suppose if there's such a thing as guarding a widow's virtue, we must do it."

"Aye, and shall!" Wat declared and drank to his own vow.

Percy had never seen Wat Milford drunk, but he had gambled—and won, of course—that the man could get pickled over his pitiful love for Rosalind. He had seen Wat's longing glances at her for years, even before Murray Barlow drowned. Oh, yes, Percy recognized such torment, but never in himself. He'd have Rosalind Barlow begging at his feet yet, and not because he loved and spurned her! No, it would be because Percival Putnam destroyed her!

He was careful not to play too completely on Wat's emotions for Rosalind until he had poured a few more drinks in him. After all, this night was turning out to be quite fortuitous. He had ridden to town with his man, Roger Shanks, who was now waiting with the horses out back, to see if Spencer had moved into the castle yet. For some reason, Cromwell wanted to know about that and soon. But, lo and behold, they had seen Rosalind ride up to the castle and dare to go inside alone with Spencer! Since Percy did not want either Spencer or Rosalind to know he'd seen them, he'd not spring that information on Wat unless absolutely necessary.

Indeed, it was not primarily to turn Wat more against Spencer that he had come. Rather, he had surmised something from the lord lieutenant's questions in their first interview, one Percy had not wanted to have, but that Spencer had insisted on. Spencer evidently suspected Wat had some knowledge of the smugglers Percy had wanted to unearth for years. And, as a first step in his own newly inspired inquiry, Percy had decided that a great deal of ale poured into the lovesick man might turn up some tidbit on smuggling before Spencer questioned Wat on his own. Who knew but he might not be able to use Rosalind to make Wat talk somehow? Percy had to discover the smugglers before Spencer; it was only one of the ways he vowed to get back at him for humiliating him before folks the day of the parade.

Percy saw the tall, dark-haired Spencer as his opposite, the threat to his dreams, the foe and bane of his desires. Whatever it took, Percival Putnam had dedicated himself not only to his original plan of climbing to the pinnacle of power over the ruins of smuggling in Deal, but also of doing it over Lord Lieutenant Nicholas Spencer's degradation and utter demise, too!

But as the night wore on, Percy was amazed at the amount of ale Wat could hold without becoming talkative. He tried again to jolt him from his drunken stupor.

"You know, friend Wat, everyone's problems here could have been solved if Spencer had just drowned at sea."

"I know, don' I know," Wat agreed and drowned his sorrows in another gulp of brew from their third pitcher. "An' she's the one said let's save him and then saw he was alive in my lugger."

"Surely the town smugglers would have applauded his demise," Percy dared to say. He watched Wat closely.

Wat's shaggy head jerked up. "Wha' smugglers?"

Once again, another carefully baited hook went for naught, Percy fumed. At least, he doubted by morning the oaf would remember he'd even inquired.

"Why, it's a jest, my friend. I mean one like yourself who has smuggled a tender heart for Rosalind around for years! A man who has withstood all life's storms but the one of attaining the fair hand of the woman he adores! We were only speaking of what was best for her, of helping her, weren't we? Indeed, I've always admired her as a friend, the spokesman of the town, as it were, but I warrant she's more than that to some, eh?"

Wat nodded as he drank, sloshing ale down his chin and neck. He collapsed at last, his big head on his crossed arms on the table.

"Always loved her," Percy heard him mutter. "If only Murray ha'n't been my bes' friend, I would of fought him for her, but I'd kill Spencer to protec' her honor, sure I would...." He was instantly racked with heavy, sodden snores.

"You swilling Deal swine!" Percy hissed. He banged his cup on the table and slopped out the bitter ale he'd been nursing for hours. His precious time spent for almost naught, he fumed. But there was something in that last, longest speech the drunk had made. He knew now he could prey on Wat's passion for Rosalind and his deep need to protect her—at any price—from Lord Spencer. Meanwhile, if Spencer's apparent suspicions about Wat being in with local smugglers were correct, he would have to prove that another way. He'd get Roger Shanks on it first thing in the morning.

Percy lurched to his feet. He wobbled out the door, but only because of his short leg. He was stone-cold sober and stone-cold full of hate.

"Shanks, to me!" he shouted into the crisp night air. He heard his man instantly bring their horses around. As they rode to the inn, he explained exactly what he wanted Shanks to do.

The next day Rosalind kept to her room until she knew Nick and Delancey had left for the castle. She worked on her accounts, going over the lists of last night's purported shipment until she knew the items and quantities by heart. It was not worth the risk to carry that paper, even secreted on her person, when she went out to meet Wat in the vale to compare the order with their haul. She would not even use the secret tunnel to the vale, for it was too valuable an escape to risk unless it was absolutely essential. Instead, she took a big basket as if she were going after walnuts and strolled out the obvious way to meet Wat.

The day was gray with a threat of rain. Just down the path into the shallow valley—she intentionally avoided the busy lane that cut through it—she stopped to look back. Folks went about their tasks up and down the road by the inn; few customers headed for it yet, though by noon the place would be busy. She did not see Wat, so perhaps he had gone on before her. Enjoying the crunch of early leaves under her feet, she headed down toward the hidden cave where the Rosies had stashed last night's haul. Just to be convincing, she did stop to gather enough black walnuts to fill her basket partway full. On cold winter eves before a fire, she, Aunt Bess and Meg would chat while they picked the nutmeats out, and their fingers would be stained for days.

"Ring-a-ring of rosies!" Wat's whisper floated to her before she saw him. He peeked from behind a tree; they grinned at each other.

"Pocket full of posies, and what a surprise to meet you here," she teased as she strolled over. Before they spoke again, they went on a ways, deeper into the vale. She saw Wat had not managed much sleep last night; his eyes were bloodshot, and his face looked as wrinkled as his shirt. By the saints, she had not gotten much sleep either with Nick Spencer just a narrow corridor away!

When Wat started to speak, she held a finger to her lips and cocked her head. She was ever cautious when they neared a drop spot, but lately it would pay to be even more careful. She and Wat stood behind a clump of trees, listening. Bird sounds, hoofbeats on the distant road, the rustle of a squirrel through the leaves. Then, just when they turned away, something more.

They peered around, both straining to see in the direction of the sound. Footsteps of something big. But no deer or bear had been seen here since their childhood. Rosalind grabbed Wat's wrist. A man—oh, no, Nick Spencer's Captain Delancey!—bearing drawn sword came down the hill the same way they had, then stopped to look around.

"He must be following me and may have seen us," Rosalind mouthed to Wat, her back pressed to a tree trunk, her eyes directed heavenward. Wat's face crumpled in a fierce frown. Her heart pounded. Damn Nick for siccing his man on her like a watchdog! Was it only because she had defied him last night or because of something more?

"We cannot just disappear, or he'll look farther. We must give him some reason we're here besides these," she whispered and pointed at her paltry collection of walnuts.

Wat nodded, his eyes intent on her. Then she knew what she would do. It might make Nick Spencer angry again, but it would give her a motive for being here—and get him to leave her alone! How dared he imply last night that she desired him! Curse the blackguard, even if she did desire him, she didn't *want* him! Maybe when he heard about this, he would realize it!

"What?" Wat asked, when she could hardly recall what she had said.

Time and again these stalwart men had looked to her for ideas and leadership. She hoped Wat would be willing to trust her this time, too. She placed her basket on the ground.

"Over here," she mouthed and motioned to him. They moved behind the trees, then partway into the open. "We'll have to make him think we met for this," she said and stretched to her tiptoes to hug Wat.

She was surprised that he seemed not to grasp her meaning at first; at least, he went stiff as a board against her. "You know, a lovers' tryst," she murmured close in Wat's ear, hoping it looked at though she were kissing him. "Delancey won't dare tell anyone in town what he's seen," she said encouragingly.

That must have done it! Wat's ham-hock hands clamped her tight to him. He did not merely pretend to kiss her but planted his mouth right over hers, hot and heavy. Now she went still a moment, then hugged him back, her arms around his thick neck. Wat was cleverly putting everything into this ruse. How secure and comfortable this felt, she thought, not at all like that vile royal lackey's hot-blooded touch last night. She let Wat tip her back in his crushing embrace; she'd like to embellish things even more for Deal's lord lieutenant himself, but she only hoped Delancey was taking it all in.

"Mmm, Wat, can't breathe," she murmured and managed to pry herself away from her friend's barrel chest. She fluffed out her skirt. She only hoped that had been enough to convince Nick's spy as to why they had come down here. They dared not go near the cave now, though it was barely twenty paces from here.

Without turning her head, she scanned the vale and saw that Delancey had disappeared.

"Whew!" she said.

"Whew is right!" Wat agreed. "Wouldn't mind a bit more convincing like that."

She poked his arm playfully without looking at him while she scanned the hillside again to be sure. No one was anywhere near where Delancey had been.

"We'll have to get someone else to check our imports when we know where both Spencer and his captain are," she said. "Oh, Wat, you're beet red. You couldn't breathe either!" she commiserated when she noted how hard he was breathing.

He turned away. "Anything for the Rosies," he said gruffly. "Rosalind, I don't like the look of things right now. Percy Putnam was at my place last night for a chat when I came back from the beach, and now Delancey is hanging round. What if Spencer and Putnam are going after smugglers together?"

"Not after the way they argued at Putnam's panic!"

"I s'pose. But till we go to Boulogne next time, maybe I should just stick to fishing and sitting tight at the brewery. And maybe you should go see your other sister in Sandwich like you do sometimes. Both of us should—you know—stay away from Spencer for good reason, till he, well, cools off."

"Perhaps you're right," she admitted. Every time she thought of facing Nick after last night, she went all wobbly-kneed and weak-stomached. She almost wondered if it was not her hatred of him that made her feel that way; with Wat she had hardly felt a thing but regret it had come to this.

"Meanwhile, all of you could get the luggers going out each night for fish," she suggested. "And Nan's second child *is* almost due in Sandwich. It is just that, until that king's man at least leaves the inn for the castle, I do not feel I can leave things there unguarded."

"But we're on to him and he don't know that. We'll be on our guard!" Wat vowed. "Go on, then, and I'll go back down by way of the lane. I'll watch you go till you're safe."

He had said all that facing away from her. She patted his shoulder and started to climb the hill. But even with dear Wat, she no longer felt safe from Nick.

But if she had seen how deeply their mock kiss had disturbed her friend Wat, she would have felt surprised and saddened. And if she had known she and Wat had been watched by a second man, she would have been worried indeed. From his spot flat on the ground behind an outcrop of rock, Roger Shanks had also seen everything, including their intentional dissembling of a lovers' embrace for Delancey. Shanks had been following Wat and not Rosalind as Delancey was, and so he had been in place when she appeared, saw the lord lieutenant's man and put on an obvious show for him. Percival Putnam would be very interested to hear, Shanks thought, that, whether or not Wat was actually a smuggler, the clever Mistress Rosalind was pretending she was his lover. And no doubt she was doing so just to inflame the jealousy of the man she met last night on a real lovers' tryst, the lord lieutenant of Deal Castle!

"She did *what?*" Nick roared and slammed his chair back from the table so hard it barely missed Stephen Delancey. It toppled over with a bang onto the stone floor of his room in the castle. "With Wat Milford? Hell's gates, just as I feared." He grabbed his sword, spurs, cape and hat. Soon after, he was thundering across the castle drawbridge on Raven's back.

Surely, he thought, a country girl like Rosalind could not just be stringing him, *him*—the king of England's lord lieutenant—along for her own amusement! Of course, she was mere amusement to him, but that was different. Watching the king's convoluted love affairs over the years had taught him enough about women to read their thoughts and handle them. Perhaps Rosalind was just playing a rustic version of what court ladies called "the jealousy lure." Yet he could not believe she was that devious or skilled in pursuing men. And it was, of course, ridiculous to even contemplate that a woman would have simply desired a tour of a military edifice and was not angling for his affections. Her ready response to him negated that wild thought.

By the time he was ready to turn up through the vale, he slowed the big stallion to a walk. Rosalind seemed such a solitary soul at times despite her array of family and friends. She stayed in her room a great deal and went out for walks alone. He could not quite accept that she was hungry for one man by night and another one so different the next morn. Nor could he believe a woman of her quick wit could be mad for a man like Milford. Perhaps if Wat were involved with smugglers, he had some hold over her. He supposed rural folk either admired smugglers or were afraid of them. Maybe she needed them to help supply brandy or wine at the inn.

It still ate at him that she could—probably did—know who the smugglers were. Her inn could be their meeting place from time to time; at the least, she could have overheard something. Yes, he had a few questions to put to Mistress Rosalind, but not one would concern why she was kissing Wat Milford in the woods. Best he not tip his hand by letting her know she had been followed. But he would never let himself be outwitted by an innkeeper, and a petite, delicate wench at that! Since he had not managed to seduce information from her last night, he would have to be a bit more direct. Soon he was once again spurring his horse up the lane through the vale.

He tied Raven's reins to the old anchor before the inn and hurried inside, spurs rattling, sword clanking. As usual, the common room silenced as he strode through. He spotted Rosalind in the hall with the door to her room open behind her, huddled with her sister in earnest conversation. Both women looked up, and Rosalind blanched white as his shirt.

"Excuse me, Mistress Meg," he said and shoved Rosalind's door open wider. "I have some unfinished business to discuss with the proprietor of the Rose and Anchor."

"No, my lord, I have not invited you in my room—" Rosalind began.

"I am inviting myself." He pulled her in, closed the door behind them and leaned against it.

Panicked that he stood at the very heart of her private world, Rosalind spun away to calm herself. Her table was awash in papers, but the dangerous ones were stowed in the hidden cupboard above her bed. Wine crates weighted down the rug over the trapdoor. She turned back to face the furious man with her hands on her hips.

"Well, have your say then and get out. If you were a true gentleman you would not shove your way in here and would promptly apologize for last night."

"But apology takes regret. I regret nothing last night but the fact we were interrupted." He surveyed the room as he spoke. His eyes narrowed; his mouth tightened to a thin line. "This place," he declared, "is a mess!"

Her temper flared hotter. Her very life had been a mess since he arrived!

"Not everyone can be as perfect as you, my lord! I do my work here. And I dislike my chamber being invaded as much as you would your chamber at the castle!"

"I liked it a great deal when you invaded it last night."

"I cannot abide your jesting. And I do not appreciate your asking my own sister about my past! Didn't you? Just what do you think you are doing, inquiring about my past?"

"The past molds the present. And *I* will ask the questions here, Rosalind!" he insisted and pointed to himself as if she would not understand. He must have realized he looked foolish, for he slapped his hand down onto his sword hilt.

She almost accused him of having Delancey watch her, too, but she did not want to tip her hand by telling Nick that

she had seen his man. Her knees were so weak she leaned her
hips against her table. It was all she could do to muster a
fierce glare at him as he strode closer, frowning at the disarray, glancing at the wine crates on the carpet. He lifted the
lid of one box and examined a bottle. Her heartbeats thudded clear up in her throat. Surely, he could not suspect her
or have stumbled on someone who told him about the Rosies. Not someone in this town. They were loyal to the last
man and woman. She would stake her life on it, and perhaps she was doing just that.

"Ah, fine French wine, just like the bottles I have bought
from your tap man, even what you so eagerly wanted a taste
of last night at the castle," he observed, his voice smooth.

"We had that supply of wine before the French embargo
began."

"What good fortune! The king loves this Alsatian
malmsey."

She bit her lip, restraining herself from rising to that. By
the saints, that was probably why there had always been a
sky-high duty on it! Horrid Harry guzzled it while folks in
this area could never afford to enjoy it before her Rosies had
started bringing it in. She met Nick's eyes and prayed her
thoughts did not show on her face.

"Of course, lately," she said hastily when he looked from
her to the crates to her again, "unless someone as well-to-do
as yourself pays for the few bottles left, I just store these,
and we mostly rely on local ale."

"And the local ale brewer," he muttered ominously as he
came closer.

"Of course, ale is one of the few things to eat or drink
that we are not forced to cart in from Sandwich, since his
majesty will not give us a market license here. If you want
to make Deal stronger, as you said last night, mayhap you
could get that for us."

"When it was legal to import French wine, did you send
for it or have someone sail over to fetch it?" he asked, ig-

noring her hint. "In good weather, I warrant a town such as, oh, Boulogne is but a few hours off."

She fought to keep her voice and gaze steady. "There are many suppliers of wine, you know. I guess most of our stock comes through Dover where the customs men get their due."

"Rosalind, you must understand that I am just trying to ascertain how much certain Frenchmen—they are all our foe now—have been through these parts. If they have been here before, know the area, have contacts, they will be a risk to security should the French decide to lead an invasion army back in."

So much, she thought, for the honesty and trust he had prated to her last night. The man was obviously fishing for information about English smugglers and where they got their booty. But at least the fact he was asking her meant he did not suspect her, didn't it?

"I—well, to tell the truth, my lord, of course, there were Frenchmen through here. Some spoke only French. Some spoke English with an accent. And if you ever plan an invasion of French shores and need a guide or translator, I suppose you could find men up and down the Kentish coast who used to visit France, too."

"You do not speak French, do you?"

Her insides lurched. What if he knew she had actually been to Boulogne several times in the past three years and spoke quite fluent French?

"Poorly, a few words here and there. I speak a bit of several languages learned from folks who have passed through. A few phrases of Spanish, too, even High Dutch from a woman we rescued once. We saved her life, just as we did yours."

At that reminder, the tensions between them uncoiled to leave only the one that always made them so aware of the potential for passion between them. After all, she assured herself, he could never suspect her as leader of a band of smugglers.

After all, he told himself, even if she did know anyone among the smugglers or their French contacts, he would probably have to find another way to learn it than by seduction or direct questioning. Perhaps she had even been threatened to keep her silence. He would win her over to trust him to protect her or, if that did not work, would as a last resort, make her even more afraid of him so that she would confess all.

"You see—" he stepped even closer, so that he was almost pinning her to her position against her table "—in your capacity, you know a great deal of what is going on in Deal. I rely on you to help me keep an eye on things in these perilous times."

"Then I hope you will be making no more accusations, such as the one that I asked my tap man to get your workers drunk."

"It is just that I expect to be obeyed and abetted. I am here to protect everyone in Deal and all of England."

"Then I shall have my tap man count your men's mugs of ale. And I shall let you know next time I see Frenchmen passing through the inn. I hope, in return, you will grant me permission to visit my elder sister, Nan, in Sandwich. She is heavy with child. Interrogate Meg again, if you need someone to vouch for the fact that I visit Nan at times, and am not just running away from—anything."

"I see. Then perhaps I shall leave Captain Delancey here at the inn in his old room upstairs to keep a lid on things until your return. I am moving to the castle tomorrow. But I shall have time to see you arrive in Sandwich safely, as I should like to survey the layout of the town."

"How kind, but there is no need to escort me. Percy Putnam is riding back, and I said I would go along with him."

"Putnam's here? And will you be taking anyone else along for the ride?"

Their eyes locked again. Sometimes he said things in such a way that she wondered if he meant to insult her or whether he knew a great deal more than he was saying. But she reveled in treading the very edge of the abyss to insult him, too. Both cooperating with and fighting Lord Nicholas Spencer were the most terrifying and exciting things she had ever done, bar none.

"When would you leave, then, Rosalind?"

"I thought tomorrow."

"So soon. But that will give us time to have supper here tonight and chat about how we intend to work together. Here, I think, at this table, if you can find the top of it."

He leaned closer to her, and in doing so knocked his fist on the table through a pile of papers. She arched herself back, just inches away from him. His stern look challenged her, dared her to gainsay that order couched so carefully in the form of a request. It was almost as if she could read his thoughts. He would let her go to Sandwich *if* she entertained him here tonight and answered more of his leading questions.

"Supper, how pleasant," she choked out.

"Until tonight, then."

She was convinced that he would touch her, that he would kiss her. She could tell how much he wanted to. Her arms and legs went limp; her lips trembled and tingled. She became utterly aware of her body. She knew he wanted to push her back under him on this table and take what she would not give. She forgot to breathe when he studied her so intently, so close. His gaze widened. She could see herself in the dark tidal pools of his eyes. She watched his taut face in fascination as his nostrils flared and his lower lip slowly protruded so she could see its slick interior. Already, in the depths of her stomach, she felt a kiss that did not exist. She gripped the edge of her table as hard as she could to steady herself for what was coming.

"You have the look of a woman who has recently been thoroughly kissed and skillfully handled," he said. "Damn, I must have done an excellent job of that last night!"

Her mouth fell open as he spun away and banged the door as he left. Was he, indeed, that vain, or had he heard of her and Wat already and was teasing? And why had he had her followed? Cursing under her breath in French, Rosalind scooped up fistfuls of papers. Wishing they were lances, she heaved them at the door, but they only sifted to the floor like snow.

Chapter Six

Rosalind was terribly nervous that night as she awaited Nick's promised—or was it threatened?—visit. She had to keep him both amused and busy while he was here dining with her, and yet not let herself lose her head with him again. She rushed to straighten the room and set the table. She ordered a saddle of mutton, fowl pies and apple tarts from the kitchen, and opened a bottle of the French wine he had examined earlier. And though she was expecting him, she jumped when a knock resounded on the door.

He looked ridiculously handsome with his hair mussed and curled by sea spray. His black leather boots and jerkin creaked when he entered. Yet when she saw him looking so smug at the fact she had put the room in order and worn a good gown, she could not bite back a challenge, however indirect.

"I feel I must really count your glasses of drink tonight, my lord, since we at the inn have been so commanded."

"If I thought you would obey my every whim, you would have an immediate and quite revealing list of them," he countered, and got the best of her by dropping a quick kiss on her mouth before she could step back.

"The food smells delicious," he commented and rubbed his palms together in obvious anticipation. "I've always favored your inn's partridge pie."

She was surprised at his good nose, and hoped his talent for smelling things out went only as far as food. Right now, his big, booted feet rested directly over the hatch to her tunnel under the rug.

"Won't you sit down so we can begin?" she inquired as sweetly as she could. She pulled a chair out for him before scooting around the table out of his reach. But to her dismay, he followed her and held her chair for her. She blushed, not only because of the courtly gesture, but because he stood so close to her. Fortunately, he retreated to sit across from her, his eyes devouring her as if there were no food in sight to eat. She cleared her throat.

"Shall I offer grace?" she asked.

"Please."

"Dear Lord, we are grateful for the food we are about to share, especially since such is so dear in this town, which does not have a market or good arable fields of its own. We ask you to protect us from all foreign invasion and assault. Amen."

Now he cleared his throat as she poured the wine. "Why do I have the notion," he inquired with one thick eyebrow cocked, "that that prayer was aimed at me as much as at the Lord? And, as for me being a foreign invader or assaulter—"

"Hardly. I meant the French, of course, so—"

"I am moving out of the bosom, so to speak, of your family to the castle tomorrow. I guess I should give thanks that you did not give thanks for that."

"You really read far too much into my words, my lord."

His big hand closed over her wrist and she slopped the wine. He took the bottle and set it down with a thump. "Then be honest and deal straightly with me, so I don't have to read things in or search for them where they might not be, Rosalind."

Their eyes held as did their hands. Her mind raced. Was that a warning or a threat, or did he mean nothing dire by it? By the saints, what was this man really thinking? she agonized.

Damn this wily, little spitfire, he thought. He desperately wanted her in his arms, even though he felt he should hold her at arm's length. What was she really thinking?

"We'd best eat while it's hot," she said breathlessly.

"Yes. Yes, I'm starved."

They ate quickly at first, then slowed as she spoke of the trials and pleasures of living in a small town. They discussed the dangers of fishing in swiftly changing seas and the worries of tenuous political times—almost anything but the way they made each other feel.

"I hope that while I am away my sister and your master mason will be kept busy at their own appointed tasks," she said, at last daring to speak of something more personal. It was a warning she had long wished to express to Nick, since he obviously controlled Franklin Stanway's whereabouts.

"They adore each other," he declared and tossed down his napkin. "I have nothing but sympathy—and a bit of envy—for them."

This, once again, was not the way she had meant the conversation to go. She decided not to ask more directly that Nick keep Franklin busy when she was away. He'd no doubt have some double-edged retort if she did.

"I regret I must be getting back to oversee the men. Night work is not yet going to my satisfaction," he told her and rose to come around the table to her. She jumped up quickly as he slid her chair out. Once again, she had the most disturbing—delightfully so, damn him—feeling that he said one thing and meant another. She had no intention of fencing further with him in this way.

"Then allow me to wish you the best of luck with your workers while I am in Sandwich," she said as she walked to the door and reached for the latch. But as she pulled the door open, he moved behind her to close it firmly and quietly.

"And may I wish you a calm rest away from all your endeavors here," he countered.

"Thank you."

"The meal was delicious, and the company, too."

"Thank you."

"I wanted to kiss you earlier today, Rosalind, even when we fought."

"Did you?"

"It was written all over your beautiful face that you knew I did, and I assume it was the same for me. Don't play coy or foolish or try to deceive me, Rosalind."

He turned her to him, though she had refused to meet his eyes as he spoke. He tipped up her chin and pulled her closer so her body settled against his from their hips down. Their gazes linked; their breaths entwined; his mouth descended.

The kiss, at first, was as gentle as a skimming breeze. He smelled of ocean wind yet, and leather, and something indescribably wonderful, like—freedom. Her fists opened against his chest, then crept up to grasp his powerful shoulders and encircle his neck. She returned the kiss fervently, and felt so dizzy she could have spiraled out of herself.

When he felt her respond, he deepened the embrace. His big hands moved down her back to her waist and her bottom. He pressed her closer, cupping her to him. She stood on tiptoe and slanted her mouth across his. Their tongues invaded, dueled and danced. She felt the tensions in her unwind, disappear and then become another taut, driving force. How desperately she desired this man, this danger, this possible destruction. His strength—if only she had this wonderful power that poured from him to make her stronger and surer! His touch made her want to lean on him in every way, to share with him her deepest needs and knowledge—

She returned with a jolt to reality and pulled back. That was no doubt what he wanted, for her to surrender her body and all she knew. How foolish of her to forget the man in her arms was the enemy of all she must hold dear.

"You'd best go," she tried to say with conviction, but the words came out a breathy moan.

He kissed her again, once, twice, quickly, then set her carefully back. "Godspeed on your trip, and we will continue this—in depth—when you return."

Willing to agree to anything if he would just leave before she grabbed him and kissed him again, she nodded. At least they would part calmly now, and she had not nettled him into demanding answers to more questions, nor into searching the room as she had feared earlier today. She stepped back and pressed her elbows over her belly, grasping her upper arms with her hands as if to don chest armor against him.

But again, he managed to get the best of her with a surprise move. He reached behind her to pat her bottom and plant yet a final, possessive kiss on her pouted lips before he opened the door and departed.

During the week Rosalind was in Sandwich, it amazed and annoyed Nick to find that he missed her. He had never given much thought to any woman once she was out of his sight. Now he found himself glancing up hopefully each time a woman entered the inn or walked beneath the castle walls. He found himself going back over their conversations—even if they'd often been arguments. At the oddest times, he recalled her lilac scent, the softness of her honey-blond hair, the feel of her slender, strong body pressed against his, the taste of her lips opening under his. He had but to close his eyes to envision her vibrant face, her determined walk, that taunting tilt to her chin when she defied him.

Then, too, the realization that he had pried absolutely nothing useful out of her about smuggling in the area had made him do a great deal of thinking while she was away.

There was no one else to question, since he was not willing to risk what trust he had earned in Deal by tossing someone like Wat Milford in prison for interrogation—not yet. With the building of the castle going full tilt, he made a decision to discover the smugglers' identity another way, even to learn who masterminded the band.

Surely, the smugglers' imports must originate in Bordeaux, the most infamous French smuggling port. But he was still convinced their deliveries must be fetched at or delivered from someplace closer, like Boulogne. It was the nearest French trading port and one, he heard, where it was possible to sneak in and out along a fine sand beach. It was a place well known for its fishing trade, just as Deal was. Boats away for long spells would not be missed and foreign fellowships could be easily made.

He decided to gamble that he could learn who the Deal smugglers were at Boulogne instead of Deal. His plan was indeed a bit risky, but he was getting impatient. Risky, because he might get caught there in a hostile foreign country, risky because some here might misconstrue his trip to be treasonous. But the king had given him wide powers to do what he thought he must and Henry trusted him. Both he and his majesty had believed exposure and punishment of these criminals would be swift and certain, so he had to move soon. Yes, this ploy would surely work, for who would expect some of King Henry's men would dare set foot in France during these tense times—especially, the king's lord lieutenant of Deal Castle!

"Even after your tour of duty in Calais," Stephen Delancey interrupted Nick's thoughts as he helped him pack his leather pouch, "your French is not smooth enough to question the froggies in Boulogne, my lord."

"I shall do as little speaking for myself as possible. Since I want the word to get out that I am heading up a new band of English smugglers, they will not expect me to speak their tongue. I shall have Sergeant White along for translation, and Perkin Rich speaks a bit of French, too. Anyhow, as I suspect we shall be dealing with waterfront ruffians, I'll get by. I want a good look at whether they are building coastal fortifications, too. Now, about your keeping a close watch on things here the few days I am away..."

They reviewed again Nick's plans. Stephen was to stay in Nick's quarters at the castle while Nick took six men with him in a small sailing boat to Boulogne-sur-Mer. Four Kentish men who knew the area had been relieved of duties at the castle to sail the boat, and two translators were going along as well. The boat would be launched from a deserted beach between Deal and Sandwich after dark tonight, so that no one here would know of the plan. The people of Deal would be told that during this time Nick was visiting Sandwich.

"I am going to ride into Sandwich before I meet the boat tonight," he told Stephen as he strapped on his sword. "I thought I would look in on our absent Mistress Rosalind Barlow, just to get a notion of when she will be returning. As best you can, should she return before I do, assign someone circumspect to keep an eye on her," he added and shouldered his two attached leather packs.

"Of course, I could not care less if the little chit actually lies with Wat Milford in the woods," he continued, his voice hardening ominously, "but she may lead us to someone else interesting who could be part of the smugglers' band."

"Of course, my lord. Fear for naught here while you are on king's business among his enemies."

Though Nick could have turned Raven directly toward Sandwich, he first rode the horse up toward the Rose and Anchor. No telling if that stubborn woman had ridden back today or not, so he might as well have a quick look before setting out. He was convinced Rosalind had seen Frenchmen here, for the contradictions in her manner showed she was hiding something. She was not telling him because she was protecting the Deal smugglers!

A wild thought had occurred to him that perhaps he should simply take the frustrating wench with him to Boulogne. It would keep her out of trouble here, and he could dangle her there as bait in the hopes she would hook some French smuggler who knew her from these parts. Surely, such a man would be curious why the English innkeeper had come over. Or perhaps the French wretch would believe Nick's ruse more readily if he had her in tow.

He had to admit that such a thought was foolhardy. She would be even more trouble than usual if he took her to France with him. He did not need a woman underfoot, especially Rosalind Barlow. What quicker way for all Deal to learn he had been spying out smugglers among England's enemies than to take that little shrew along? She would chatter of what she knew to Wat Milford or to the other oafs in the area. And he did not need Percy Putnam hearing of his voyage and misinterpreting his motives for visiting France. The bungler might inform his idol, Cromwell, of it, too, and that could cause trouble. The king trusted Nick, but Cromwell had never liked Nick, and might misrepresent the true situation to the monarch.

While he had no time for it today, even if Rosalind had returned to Deal, he was planning to demand she give him a complete tour of the inn—attic, cellars, every corner of every blasted room. He could, of course, just ransack the place himself without her on the premises. But he wanted to see if she would give aught away when he tore into things. And he wanted to impress upon her that she could be pulled down with the smugglers if she didn't tell him all she might have seen or overheard. Still, he hated the idea of turning her against him after the fairly civilized conversation they had exchanged at dinner last week. At least most of the inn's chambers were not buried beneath debris like those piles of things in her bedchamber! Damn, but he could not abide an untidy woman!

Yet, he mused, she was not slovenly in her appearance nor demeanor. Whether she was gowned in a blue linen work dress and apron or in her ruffled, tawny velvet, she lured and seduced. Those green-gray eyes flashed fire and her pouting lips that could say such bitter words could taste so sweet in a kiss.

As he rode away from the beach into the vale, he recalled the last night he and Rosalind had been together. Over supper in her chamber—which someone had greatly straightened since his previous glimpse of it several hours earlier—they had spoken of many things. Yet in all his leading conversations, she had never given him one hint that she knew who could be "simply free trading" with France, as she had once called it in defiance of his insisting it was "smuggling, theft and treason, pure and simple!" The freezing glance she had given him then before she cloaked it added to his nagging suspicions that she knew something. Still, when he had held her and kissed her good-night, the mere touch and scent of her had made every suspicion of her fly from his mind. He shook his head to clear it. He realized he had been woolgathering over her again while a silly little smile played on his lips.

He tied Raven's reins to the big anchor in the yard, but decided to walk around in back. He entered through the kitchen garden door where he would be least suspected. One never knew when something might be discovered this way. Or, if Rosalind were here, she might not be warned in time to distance herself from someone "foreign" passing through. He walked as stealthily as he could in his heavy riding boots.

He could hear the distant chatter of cooks' voices in the kitchen as he passed the pantry and flour bolting room. A fine dust of sifted flour floated in the air just inside. Nick sneezed twice, the explosive noise as loud as crashing cymbals.

"Oh!" a woman cried, and two dim figures leaped apart on the other side of the half-open pantry door. Nick stepped back and glanced into the small room. He wanted it to be Rosalind, as if his suspicions and desires could conjure her up. But it was a taller, darker-haired woman who had been half entwined with a man. Not a kitchen maid and her paramour from the stables, but—

"Mistress Meg and my own master mason! My apologies for the intrusion," Nick said as Meg smoothed her skirts and Franklin's hands returned reluctantly to his own hips.

"Just came up for a bite of breakfast before work, you see, my lord," Franklin ventured.

"I do see. A tasty bite, was it? Well, while the cat's away, the mice do play, eh, Mistress Meg?"

"My sister said we could be together here on these grounds!" she blurted defensively. Even in the dimness here, Nick could see she blushed, and he regretted teasing them.

"I shan't breathe a word to the mistress of the inn," Nick promised. He reached in to clap Franklin on the shoulder. "As long, that is, as the castle walls rise apace with other things, my man. And you had best both brush off the floury prints on your back before you venture out. We never know when the queen of the inn might return, do we?"

Nick doffed his cap to the astounded cooks as he walked through the kitchens into the common room. What had possessed him to be so jovial with Franklin when the man should be down at the castle? A bite of breakfast! Hell's gates, it was early afternoon! Did being so enamored mean one lost track of time?

Strangely, though, the minute he left their presence, a pall descended on his temporary good humor. They were obviously so in love, so desperate to be together that risks meant nothing. It made him fear for himself. Yes, he ached for such, but not from his own promised fiancée, Penelope. At least the couple's actions had answered his question as to whether Rosalind had returned. They would not be so bold then, even to meet covertly in the pantry.

His anger at Rosalind's obstinacy flared up again. She ordered her sister about. She rejected the king's lord lieutenant's support of the king's master mason as a suitor. She went off to Sandwich for days on end. And that was the worst of it, blast the minx!

He strode through the suddenly subdued common room and banged out the front door. He had mounted before he spotted Rosalind's Aunt Bess gathering newly dried and freshened sheets and bolster covers off the bushes at the side of the inn. Slowly, he walked his horse toward her.

"Good day, madam. You have not heard when the inn's mistress is to return, have you?"

He saw she jumped, not at the sudden voice of a man behind her, but when she realized who it was.

"Oh, my lord, good day. Nary a word have we had from Rosalind after the news she sent with Percy Putnam that her dear sister Nan was delivered of her second child Tuesday last."

"Rosalind has other friends in Sandwich to keep her there besides her sister's people, I warrant."

"A few, I suppose," Aunt Bess said as she gazed up at him. He knew it was her nature to be chatty, yet she said no more. She only crinkled her face as she looked up at him against the afternoon sun and awaited what else he would say.

"I am going to stay in Sandwich for a few days, and thought I might call on her. Her sister's husband is a cobbler there near the waterfront, I believe."

"Oh, yes, and makes the finest gloves, too. You ought to buy yourself a pair. Fine Spanish imported leather and—"

"Difficult to get in these times, no doubt."

Aunt Bess turned back to gathering armloads of sheets. "I suppose, my lord. Forgive me, but I must be off now. You know the old saw, 'Men may work from sun to sun, but women's work is never done.' Tell Rosalind I miss her here if you see her. Good day, my lord," she called over her shoulder as, laden with linens, she scurried toward the house.

"As slippery as her niece," he muttered under his breath as he turned Raven toward Sandwich. The old lady missed Rosalind, he mused. Hell's gates, he would die before he admitted aloud he missed the little spitfire, too. And about women's work never being done, he guessed that was true of Rosalind if not of many of the other women he had known. He admired that, for he valued his own dedication to duty. He knew Rosalind drove herself hard, doing her accounts, spending time with townsfolk, burning the candle at both ends far into the night. He had seen lights in her windows and under her door several nights. Was it just the burden of running the inn, or could she be meeting with men who did their dirty work at night? Before he had forced her to house him at the inn, had she allowed smugglers to meet there after dark?

"Come on, boy," he said to Raven and spurred him a bit faster. "We are going calling on a wench, and we shall see what we'll catch her doing. I doubt if it will be laundry, but it had best not be embracing someone in secret. On, boy!"

Rosalind longed to return to Deal, but she feared to do so. It was not just that she worried Nicholas Spencer's questions would find their mark. And it wasn't because she hated him. No, unfortunately, quite the contrary. During the night, during the day, however busy she was helping Nan with the new babe or suffering through Percy Putnam's unwelcome visits, she missed that arrogant, aggressive king's man. And admitting to him she cared for him even one whit was what she feared!

She sat now in a window seat, holding her five-day-old nephew in her arms. The window overlooked the harbor from the rooms her kinfolk owned above the shop of Morris Dalton, cobbler and glover. Why, poor Morris would have lost his trade and shop with this unjust king's blasted embargo if the Rosies hadn't brought in Spanish leather when they could! She was expecting some fine cordovan hides in the next several loads, both those the Rosies would fetch from Boulogne and those Pierre Lyon and his men would deliver to Deal. Feeling sleepy in the shaft of sunlight, she rocked the baby and sang to him a little song she knew in French, called "Frère Jacques."

"What does that mean, Ros, 'Frère Jacques, dormez-vous?' " her elder sister asked as she laid out pewter plates for dinner. Nan was brown-haired and brown-eyed and very happily wed, even if she sometimes missed her family in Deal. Her love for her husband and two children made Rosalind happy for Nan but sad for herself at times. She cuddled the new child and wished for a fleeting moment that Murray had left her with a child to hold like this.

"The words mean, 'Brother John, are you sleeping?' " Rosalind explained.

"Mmm. Watching you just now, I'd say, Sister Ros, are you dreaming?"

"Was I nodding off?"

"Just that faraway look in your eyes again. Something's changed in your life since I saw you last, and I would surmise it is *that* man." The two of them had shared several discussions about *that* man, especially after Percy Putnam had blathered about Nicholas Spencer to Nan as if it were the rarest gossip.

"It is not him the way you mean," Rosalind insisted so vehemently the baby stirred before she lowered her voice.

"I know well 'tis not Wat after all this time, nor Percy Putnam!" Nan insisted. Whereas Rosalind had ever been able to cow the younger Meg with a grace or a scolding—at least before Franklin Stanway crashed into their lives—Nan had always spoken her mind right back.

"Certainly not! Wat and I are just friends, and however many gifts for my new little nephew Percy showers on us all, never him!''

"Then I must be right!" Nan announced pertly and went to kiss her gangly, red-haired husband as he scuffed up the stairs from the shop. It was a good thing Morris arrived when he did, Rosalind told herself, for Nan's temper had turned a bit sour in her lying-in with this child! Still, as she usually did this time of day, she left Nan and Morris with their new son and took the four-year-old Andrew down into the small yard at the rear of the row of attached shops and houses. They tossed a leather ball back and forth for a while and chatted, but once again Rosalind's thoughts were not on what she was doing.

It was time for her to return to Deal. She should go this afternoon. She could be back before dark, before Percy Putnam made himself an unwelcome guest again. Despite the largess of his gifts, the man had driven her to distraction lately. He had tried his best to worm out of her what she thought of Nick Spencer, when she wanted nothing more than to forget him. Yet she could not forget him, nor stop worrying that he was trouble. Trouble for the Rosies, trouble for her. It had actually been a relief when Percy moved on to gossiping about King Horrid Harry!

She imagined she could hear Percy's high-pitched voice now. It often became shriller when he had some tantalizing tidbit he wished to pass on.

"The king will wed the German Anne of Cleves at Yuletide. I have it on the best authority," he had boasted, his thumbs stuck importantly in his doublet.

"I suppose that piece of wisdom came from your master Cromwell," she had said.

"My *friend* Cromwell, dear Rosalind. More like a friend as these years go by, and he and I both make our way in the world. You see, Cromwell has arranged the royal marriage as both a matter of state and a matter of hearts. The king's favorite artist, Hans Holbein, painted a miniature of Anne that his majesty much favored. His grace's friends have highly praised her beauty. To him as to all us men, a favorable countenance on the female we bed is of utmost importance! The king's not one to favor a political match unless there's passion, too. I hear the lady will arrive sometime in December. Mayhap I shall go to greet her with my Lord Cromwell, if he is not too busy, that is. And as reward for all Lord Thomas Cromwell's service to the king, he's to be made an earl, you know, and many will rise with him!''

"Meaning you, I take it," Rosalind had said. "But *I* have it on good authority that many nobles think Cromwell is overstepping his bounds. Like Cardinal Wolsey who fell before him, he takes too much power on himself. Many detest him, I hear, and resent an arrogant son of a blacksmith running roughshod over them."

"Who told you thus?" She could hear Percy's outraged demand ringing yet in her ears. "Tell me who preached such poison and I shall warn my Lord Cromwell!" But since she could hardly tell him that it was her French friends in Boulogne who had said that, she had been hard-pressed to shift the topic.

Yes, she decided, before Percy came calling later, she was going home to face Nick Spencer. Her mind still on the French song, she sang others to little Andrew as he ran about the garden. She smiled as he scrambled for the ball, then had to turn to chase it herself. She and the child laughed, and she called to him in English he could clearly understand this time, "Aunt Rosalind has to go home today, my sweet, and I will miss you so!"

Nick still sat his horse on the other side of the garden wall. He recognized the voice singing the songs—and, damn it, he recognized that they were in French. She had told him she spoke but a little of that language and yet these lilting songs—

He shook his head. So what if she knew a child's song or two? She had said Frenchmen passed through the inn, but would men like that have taught her children's songs? He felt so confused he almost dismounted and marched into the yard to demand to know everything, but thought better of it. Then he heard her say she was heading home today. As he was riding back that way to catch his ship, he would wait for her to leave town and be sure she got started safely. Since he really did not want her to know his whereabouts, best he not do more than be certain she was safe. His questions, unfortunately, would have to wait until he returned from France.

Hoping she would leave by this back way, since she had a horse, he moved Raven farther down the small street under a tree and waited for her to leave. But he had barely situated himself when a cloaked man let himself in the back gate with nary a knock. It was not Putnam or Shanks, and he wondered if it were just some friend of the family—or perhaps someone come to court her while she was hiding out from him in Sandwich. Now another feeling mingled with his anger at her and festered inside him. He seethed, waiting out in the street while who knew what went on inside.

It was almost dusk when Rosalind and the man emerged from the back door, both riding her horse as if they were the best of friends, to say the least! Nick mounted quickly, angry that the man was cloaked and hooded, so he could not glimpse his face. They headed out of town and toward Deal along the seaside road. They would pass right by where Nick's men awaited him with a boat below the cliffs to sail at dark.

He kept a ways back. But when, up ahead as darkness fell, Rosalind's guest dismounted, Nick did, too, and in the shadows of the rocks he crept closer. Damn, but the two of them were having a lengthy farewell as she bent down to speak with him. At least they had not melded their profiles in a kiss, not yet at least! Then, on the swift sea breeze, Nick heard they were speaking French, and not some little children's songs.

"*Adieu,* Pierre," came clearly to his ears.

"*Adieu, ma chère* Rosalind" followed as the man melted away into the growing shadows between the rocks as if they had swallowed him whole.

Hell's gates, Nick fumed, a French lover! And one who was heading down where he might find Nick's men! Or did he have some secreted boat of his own waiting below? Damn, but she would answer all his questions now. What other falsehoods besides that of not speaking French had she fed him? Had he gobbled them up because he desired her? He knew now there was much she had not admitted.

If he could just question her somewhere alone, where she could not run to her family, he would learn what he needed to know. Perhaps the Frenchman was over here in England because he was a contact for the smugglers. Perhaps he told Rosalind things she passed on to the brigand band. Back in Deal, no longer hindered by his presence, she would construct some elaborate battle plan against him by the time he returned. She might clear away the evidence that smugglers had met there before he could force her to show him around in a thorough search!

Perhaps he *should* take her with him to France. There he could keep an eye on her and question her privily! If they needed someone who spoke better French than either of his translators, she could not deny him help or he would have her dead to rights. She would obviously not be missed at home. She had bidden her family in Sandwich farewell, and her folks in Deal did not know when she would return. And, he thought, and reached back to touch his saddle satchel, besides the king's declaration he could go where he must to find the smugglers, he carried signed papers stating that he could question anyone, detain anyone he desired. Anyone he desired!

But now there was no time to stew. Rosalind had turned her horse toward home, and soon both she and the sneaky Frenchman would be out of his reach.

He ran back toward Raven, startling one other single rider coming down the road. The man, evidently scared by Nick's sudden appearance, wheeled his horse around and headed back toward Sandwich. Nick scrambled up on Raven's back and spurred him after Rosalind.

The October shadows grew as Rosalind cantered down the familiar road high above the sea toward Deal. She had been shocked to see Pierre today, although he had assured her the presence of King Henry's lord lieutenant did not mean they were not still in business. But when Pierre had asked her for a farewell kiss, she had refused. No reason to complicate her life more than it was with Nick Spencer. He's the one she should refuse kisses to, if she were in her right mind! Dear Murray seemed to drift farther from her memory these days while that blackguard Spencer stomped through her dreams and hopes and ravished her once-chaste heart.

She tried to calm herself by enjoying the beauty of the scene. Tall cliffs rose from slices of sand beach along the sea here. Booming breakers echoed on the wind, while seabirds soared in eddies and drafts above her head. After sunset, pink puffs of clouds wandered the darkening meadow of sky like lost sheep. Sometimes here in the light, she fancied she could see the distant thread that was France on the blue-gray horizon. Now, of course, the road was not busy, though an occasional late dray or cart loaded with food for Deal creaked along.

Someday, she vowed, Deal would get a market license from this dreadful king who would devour the likes of Anne of Cleves as he had his previous wives. No doubt the woman had no notion what she was getting into. Poor thing, to come across that sea from her homeland to wed a monster like the Tudor king!

She heard hard, swift hoofbeats behind her and twisted around in her saddle. A lone horseman, riding quickly enough to be a messenger, galloped toward her from behind. As he approached, Chestnut shied and she had to cling to the mare's neck. When the horse settled, Rosalind reached for the dagger she kept up her big-cuffed riding gloves. There had been no highwaymen on this road for ages, but—

"We meet again," the horseman said and seized her reins as he halted by her side.

She recognized the voice and sat stock-still, though she longed to flee. "Whatever are you doing here?" she demanded.

"Chaperoning you and your French lover, it seems."

She gasped. "What? You—you've been following me?"

"Put the dagger away, Rosalind, or I shall take it from you."

She defied him by grasping its hilt to hold it upright. "Did you come to accompany me back, then?"

"I came," he said, and drew closer, his horse's head to Chestnut's tail, "to take this—" he wrenched her dagger away, daring to grasp its blade with his gloved hand "—and, yes, to accompany you. But not back to Deal. We are going on a little ride, and you're going to tell me the truth about so many things, beginning with that Frenchman."

"A customer of my brother's I dropped off where he asked," she insisted. She had begun to quake. She feared the determined look in his piercing brown eyes. She could tell he was angry. A pulse beat at the base of his throat, and his jaw looked hewed from stone. When he reached for her reins, she hit his arm with her fist, but he did not budge. "Nick, going on a ride *where?*"

He pulled Chestnut behind his horse off the road between jaws of rock and down a sloping path to a spot where he quickly dismounted. He reached up to haul her down. On the next turn of the path she saw a waiting man, who now strode up to take both their horses.

Nick yanked her saddle pack from Chestnut's flanks and threw it over his shoulder with his own. It was only when he lifted her down that she noted he was not garbed as usual. He looked much more the ruffian now with a worn leather jerkin over a rough-woven shirt and seaman's cap.

He took her arm in a strong grip and walked her down the twisting path toward the sea. "We are going on a little jaunt to France," he said. "After all, you are a woman who likes sailing, and evidently mysterious Frenchmen, too, so do not bother to protest. If you would like to see the royal warrant allowing me such rights of detainment, I shall be delighted to share it with you—as we shall share other things truthfully and completely these next few days."

"Detainment?" she sputtered. "Share what things?"

She gaped at him in stunned surprise. This could not be happening! She must be dreaming this. She had had nightmares since he crashed into her life in that tempest at sea, but this was far worse than any imagining. He was abducting her—with the king's permission, no less! Both of them in collusion again, the two beings she detested the most in God's great universe! She had no illusions. He was not doing this because he wanted an amorous interlude. He had caught her speaking French with Pierre, and clearly suspected her of more. As yet he evidently knew nothing else of her involvement with smuggling, but it was clear he planned to question her closely about her links to France.

She tried to stiffen herself and pull back, but the path was part pebbles, part sand. She slid and bumped against his hard hip and shoulder as he alternately supported and pulled her along. He pointed with his gloved hand. The sea wind flapped his black cloak like great birds' wings around them both, so she had to bend forward to see. A two-masted boat, not a Deal lugger, awaited them below, guarded by four men who looked as small as a child's stick figures from here. For one moment she feared he had discovered Pierre's crew, but then she realized the men were his.

"I will not go with you," she dared to say, though her voice wavered like the wind through clefts in the rocks.

"If you wish me to carry you down and tie you in the boat, I am ready," he replied with infuriating calm that verified she was indeed trapped.

"I must tell you the truth. I have always detested your arrogant nature, my lord. I shall hate you more now!"

To her amazement, a hint of a smile twisted the corners of his taut mouth. "That is what I want from you, for starters, sweet. The truth. But as for hate between us, I have observed quite something else."

He pulled her along again. She knew she had no choice now but to face her fate as bravely, even as brazenly, as possible. Behind him, she went down step by steady step, like a prideful cat, trying to hold herself erect and aloof, her chin up, determined he would not make her cower nor get the best of her. Yet what beat in her breast was not hatred, but a stunned realization that he had indeed become her beloved enemy.

Roger Shanks had to scramble on hands and knees and crawl on his belly to find a good spot on the rocks where he could see below. He had only intended to keep Mistress Rosalind in distant view after she left her sister's house. Master Putnam's bad leg pained him sorely today, and he had sent Roger to deliver gifts for both the new Morris babe and Mistress Rosalind. Ah, he had had no idea when he followed her that Nicholas Spencer rode behind her, too. At least Spencer had evidently not recognized him when he bolted past earlier.

Wait until his master heard this! Though Percival Putnam mostly kept his own counsel, Roger was sure his master fancied the woman. He had escorted her to Sandwich last week. And his temper had been most aroused that night they had seen her visit Lord Lieutenant Spencer at Deal Castle. Nor had Master Putnam taken well to the news that Rosalind had been playacting, kissing Wat Milford in the woods in order to inflame Spencer with jealousy. Now, apparently Spencer was jealous again of the man she had given a ride to, for he was pulling her down toward a waiting boat. What did the wench expect when she made a hot-blooded man jealous? And now at dusk, they were preparing to set off somewhere in a small boat with a crew of men he could not identify from here.

Ah, his master would be pleased to hear of the clever surveillance job Roger had done, though undoubtedly he would first lose his temper because the woman was eloping with a man he detested—a man who had publicly humiliated him and imposed his own control on the realm of Master Putnam's jurisdiction.

Roger squinted into the stiff wind as he edged out to see better. A man below and to his left held the lovers' horses. Spencer and the woman had reached the half-moon beach below, but they were evidently waiting for darkness before casting off. Blast, but he'd have to risk getting closer so he could tell Master Putnam the direction they sailed.

Carefully, he started down another path, taking care to keep away from the man holding the mounts. Ah, but he would have to guard getting too close to the master when he told him all this. When he heard his lady love was whoring for Lord Spencer, who knew what curses or missiles he would throw?

But Percival Putnam's abuse was worth it all. Worth it for the coin the master paid. And worth it to work for the man who had promised he would be powerful Lord Cromwell's strong arm in all of Kent as soon as the local smugglers were arrested and foul treason with the French foe could be proved.

* * *

The boat set out from the beach as darkness fell. The crew, wherever Nick had found them, Rosalind thought, seemed to know what they were doing. Several of them spoke with a Kentish drawl, but they were all strangers to her. She sat straight as a board in the seat beside Nick, even as the men hoisted sail and the little vessel rocked and pitched its way toward France. She did not look at him; she tried desperately not to so much as bump him.

"Where exactly is this brigand crew taking me?" she asked at last as curiosity devoured her. Whatever he answered, she had vowed not to demand the why of it in front of others, but she had to know where.

"A little coastal town named Boulogne-sur-Mer for a day or two."

She felt the color drain from her face and throat. Boulogne! She could be recognized there! Or worse, some of the Rosies' contacts could come to speak with her. Pierre Lyon himself might accidentally give everything away, for he would be shocked to see her there when she had seen him that very night and not said she was coming for a visit. Had someone told Nick that the Deal smugglers used Boulogne as a storage place for their smuggling, or had he guessed? She had no illusions he would not continue to question her. He would probably be even more forceful than he had been before, now that he had her off alone.

But the worst of it was, no matter how hard she tried to fight him, even when she tried to tell herself he was touching her against her will, she simply melted in his arms. In truth, he had never touched her against her will. She had responded wildly to him, as if, like that piece of driftwood looming closer on the inky sea, she were pulled to him by great powers over which she had no control.

"Rosalind, you are trembling. Are you cold?"

She must not let him know her fear of him and of herself. She must not let him know that in choosing Boulogne he had greatly endangered all she must protect. She did not look at him as she answered. Mayhap the humble attitude of a damsel in distress would suit her best.

"I am a bit chilled, I guess."

He covered her, legs and shoulders, with his cape as if it were a blanket.

"Thank you. Such kindness for a prisoner."

"You are my guest unless you decide otherwise."

She snorted with laughter and shook her head. So much for the helpless damsel facade, she thought. This man infuriated her so much she would never carry it off.

"I'll not fence with you, words or weapons, my lord. I take it I am at the mercy of your goodwill."

"What has been between us has never been mercy nor goodwill. But I would advise you to put your head on my shoulder and try to sleep. It will be late before we put in, however late you are used to staying up for your own amusements."

There was nothing she could put her finger on in his apparently kindly suggestion, but she still sensed the challenge in his words. She'd stay awake clear to Spain, she vowed silently, rather than put her head on his shoulder!

But later, she did doze sitting up. Soon it seemed the ghostly stretch of beach lying beside the familiar harbor loomed straight ahead. Their prow crunched on the sand, and two men jumped out to drag them farther up.

"I will walk!" she told Nick when she saw he meant to carry her from the boat. He indicated his permission with a sweep of hand in the direction the men piled out. And he managed to keep his face sober when she found the sand so sloppy wet she sank in to her ankles.

The crew dragged the anchor from the boat and buried its claws in the sand. Nick took her arm; she thought to shake him off, but decided not to goad him further. Even in silvery predawn, she knew the way, but she pretended not to. There was no telling what he suspected her of, but she would not confirm his suspicions.

The scene was unchanged from her earlier visits. The medieval wall still encircled the hillside that held the old town called *la haute ville,* with its cobbled streets and its gabled houses of gray stone. Most windows looked shuttered against the chill sea winds of October.

The dimness made the scene even more familiar to her, for the Rosies often came and went at night. There were, after all, French informers who answered to king François in these parts, and some of those could not be bribed. She half hoped Nick and his men would be discovered, but it would mean disaster for them all. The calves of her legs hurt at the pace Nick set up the hill and ramparts and through one of the four great gateways, where one of his men spoke French to the guard and slipped him some coins.

Just as when she had toured Deal Castle with Nick, she felt trapped by the enclosing walls. But it was her relationship with him and not the walls of stone that made her feel so. This place was familiar, and yet she still felt she was sailing with Nick into the uncharted future of her tumbled feelings for him.

Finally they halted on the narrow street under an inn sign, Le Canard. It was, to her relief, not one she was familiar with, though unfortunately Pierre did not live too far away.

"Go inside and rouse someone to see if we can have two chambers for two nights," Nick told his man who spoke French and handed him a pouch of coins.

Rosalind breathed a silent sigh of relief as they waited. He was going to give her her own chamber, even if he did put a guard at her door! Mayhap, if she had her privacy, no matter what else happened, she would survive this clash of wills. At all cost she must keep from capitulating to him both as her enemy and as the man she admitted to herself that she desired.

"Thank you for that, at least," she whispered. "I will not try to escape."

"For the two chambers, you mean?" he said so close in her ear his breath scalded her. "One is for my men, and we shall share the other. You will not escape this time, and we will settle everything between us."

She bit her lower lip and leaned back against the cold stone of the inn. She pressed her back, bottom and calves there for support. She, who had never been ill a day of her life and could take the wildest storms at sea without blanching, felt her stomach cartwheel and her legs wobble. This man was the only tempest in her life she had ever feared she could not conquer. But, she vowed to herself, neither would he conquer her!

Chapter Seven

The chamber the elderly, bleary-eyed innkeeper, Simon, gave Nick and Rosalind was up under the eaves on the third story. It had a slanted ceiling and creaky, crooked floors that attested to its age. He lit a fire for them and promised food and hot water before he hurried out. Nick's men were housed in a room one floor below.

Rosalind felt both bodily exhausted and mentally invigorated. She prayed Nick could not discern how hard her heart beat at his mere presence in the intimacy of their surroundings. She strolled the perimeter of the room as if she were interested in every dim, dusty nook and cranny. Both windows were shuttered against the cold. She sensed she had to go on the offensive, especially as she surveyed the meager furnishings of table, two chairs—and the biggest canopied bed she had ever seen. She spun to face him with hands on hips.

"So exactly why am I here, my lord?"

He nodded toward the bed. "I would like to say it is because we both want to finish what we began before—what we both want. It's obvious we're gunpowder and fire together."

"Your arrogance continues to astound me. Our last night together in Deal, when we shared a civil dinner, I had glimpses of a gentle man."

"I can be that, if you will let me. But you seem unwilling to cooperate. You see, you are also here to answer directly—without interruptions—the questions I have put to you before. I asked you whether you knew any Frenchmen who passed through Deal for covert purposes and you denied it. And yet now I have caught you red-handed, chatting in French to one of them!"

"Appearances are not always what they seem. Will you bring out the instruments of torture now to force confessions from me? I swear you will need such before I'll confess to what is not true!" she said boldly.

He dropped their packs on the table and strode over by the hearth to prop one booted foot on the andiron. "I wish you would talk straightly with me, Rosalind. I would take whatever confessions you offer and give you a few in return. I admire you greatly, Rosalind. Needless to say, I desire you, too. Despite past problems and possible future complications, I want you. And I should like to hear such truth from your lips, too."

She stood her ground by the table. She knew, of dire necessity, that she could lie to him about the Rosies, but she could not deny her desire for him. And though she hated to admit it even to herself, she had come to admire him, too. Though she had oft accused him of being arrogant, she knew that it was his powers of strength and leadership that made him seem so. She had seen he was brave and self-sacrificing when he risked his life to rescue his men instead of saving himself during the storm. He had thanked her and the folks of Deal for their care and rewarded them handsomely. He had touched her with gentleness as well as driven her to distraction with his demands and accusations. Though they believed in different causes, she knew how hard he worked, just as she did. She had seen him in his weakest, most intimate moments as well as in his public, powerful ones. And she sensed that sometimes, like her, he was deeply lonely, no matter how many people depended on him and looked up to him, including her sister Meg, whose love for Franklin Stanway he had championed more than once.

So, despite all the conflict that had passed between them, she longed to surrender to him. Yet could she surrender to him as a woman and not surrender as a smuggler? Would her desire for him risk the Rosies or help keep them safe? Mayhap when she denied all knowledge of any Deal smugglers—for that confession must be what he was ultimately angling for—he would want to believe her more if they had loved each other. All their struggles aside, yes, curse the man, she wanted and desired him, too. She almost told him so, but the innkeeper bustled back in carrying a tray, with two heavily laden, sleepy-looking boys in tow.

"Baked crabmeat and wine sauce in pastry warmed from supper," the innkeeper told Nick in French as he set the tray on the table. Rosalind decided not to translate for Nick. Besides, the man pointed to each thing as he named it, so the meaning was obvious enough. The innkeeper might not know he was addressing a lord, Rosalind thought, but the way he bowed and scraped showed that he liked the look of Nick's English coins.

"And some beer, bread and cheese," the man continued. "Ah, yes, and the boys have four big buckets of hot water in which your *chère amie* can bathe, eh?"

She certainly would not translate that, she fumed, as they were left alone again. Nick strode over to shoot the bolt on the door, a bit ruthlessly, she thought. Unfortunately, he ignored the food on the table.

"Who was he, Rosalind?"

Her chin jerked up. She had been waiting for him to begin that line of questioning again. She knew she'd been skating on thin ice ever since he'd seen and heard her speaking to Pierre.

"I could be flippant and tell you that man was the innkeeper, but I'll not fence with you."

"Fine," he said and walked slowly back across the room to her. "Let's hear it."

"I told you he was a friend—a customer of my brother-in-law's."

"Do the two of you have many French friends? Perhaps, I shall have to haul your brother-in-law in for questioning, too."

"No! I mean, I don't have many French friends, I'm sure, but a man must make a living. Anyway, I was leaving so I dropped the man where he asked."

"I suppose he lives under one of the rocks there," Nick said, his voice dripping sarcasm now.

"I suppose he took a boat down on the shore, just as you did."

"I'll wager he did. Straight back here to France, I'm sure. I repeat, who and what is the man to you, Rosalind?"

"All right," she said and sat down in a chair at the table, where the smell of the food teased her nose despite the knots in her stomach. "His name is René Gaspar and he's an admirer of mine."

"Aha! And here you told me there had been no one for you since your husband died!"

"No one but you," she said accusingly, hitting her fist on her knee. "I must be demented! And as for René, he admires me and not the other way round, if you catch my drift, though none of this is any business of yours."

"I've made you and what you know my business," he insisted, but his voice was not so strident now. She was amazed to see how her half-truth admissions seemed to calm him. Surely the man was not jealous! No, it must be that he believed her story now. Or, mayhap it was her somewhat backhanded admission that she, too, desired him. That, she thought, was obvious each time he touched her. They were fated somehow. And that big bed over there just beckoning—

"If you don't mind, I'm starved," she told him.

He nodded and his eyes refocused on her. He had obviously been far away right then, calculating something. "I like a woman with a hearty appetite," he said and sat across from her. "Besides, we've a busy time ahead and should eat while we can."

A hundred questions came to her, but she held her tongue. If they weren't arguing, it was best that way. No use to give him an excuse to get back on his topic of Frenchmen or worse. She was famished and needed her strength, needed to postpone what must be the inevitable between them.

"Even though they put those buckets of water on the hearth, we should use them before they chill," Nick said after devouring an amazing amount of food in a short time. "I shall wash after you."

"I see no screen nor opportunity for privacy here."

He wiped his mouth and hands with a square of linen, then rose and came around the table. He took her hands and drew her to her feet. "Will there be need for such?"

"But—"

He silenced her with a hot kiss that shook her to her toe tips. This time, she did not fight him or herself. It seemed right that she should be here with this man, away from home, away from the path she once thought her life would take. Away from everything but the strength of his arms, the inflaming press of his lips, the very leather and sea-wind scent of him.

She wrapped her arms around his neck and leaned willingly into him as they deepened the kiss. All her fears and previously tortured reasoning flowed from her. He molded her more completely to him. Feeling strangely safe and secure, she leaned back in his iron embrace and ravaged the warm, slick depths of his mouth as he did hers. Then he lifted her in his arms.

"Mayhap," he whispered, his eyes so intense, his voice so raspy it shot shivers down her spine, "we can save time by just sharing the water."

Like one mesmerized, she nodded. He carried her to the hearth. After all, she told herself, she was no green girl, no counterfeit maiden to play coy. And she had never in her life wanted to be with—wanted both to possess and belong to— a man as she did this one.

Dreamily, smiling, they began to disrobe each other. "What is this little key on the chain around your neck?" he asked her.

She was jolted from her trance. She had forgotten that. She had not worn it the night she had gone to the castle, but had taken it to Sandwich. It was the key to the secret cupboard over her bed where she kept her Rosies' records in code.

"Just the key to my trinket box of jewelry at home, meager as it is," she told him. "But tonight, I think it is the key to my heart." She removed it herself and carefully dropped it down her boot before turning back to him with a smile. Then she unknotted her already windblown coif and shook her hair free. It tumbled in heavy waves halfway down her back to tickle her shoulder blades. She slanted a look up at him through her lashes. Despite his meal, he still looked ravenous; his eyes devoured her.

The hearth fire licked golden shadows on their skin as their final garments, his hose and her lawn chemise, puddled at their feet. She caressed his molded chest muscles, reveling in the crisp resiliency of his curly, ebony hair there. She ran her hands down his lean ribs while he clasped her waist and cupped her bottom. She was suddenly too shy to look lower, but she pressed her soft belly against his loins and felt his desire.

She recalled those first days at the inn when he had been in her control. In a way, though it was mutual now, she sensed her power over him again in quite a different way. What possessed her to become the coquette when she had never felt the urge before she did not know.

"You still owe me for fixing your nose for you," she said as she kissed the tip of it.

"Name any price!"

"Mmm." She rolled her eyes and pretended to consider. She knew she should insist that he not use her as a pawn to discover more about Deal smuggling, but all that seemed so distant now. "Well, then, I want you to wash my back for me," she teased.

"That and more!"

"Our water is getting cold."

"But we are not. We could boil the very sea if we swam in it!"

They ignored the waiting water longer. His hands cradled each breast while his big head bent and he tasted there. Sparks skittered through her, tingling every nerve. She ruffled his thick hair, which the wind never dared to muss. Each place he kissed her burned like red-hot coals aching to burst into flame upon the hearth. Although she could see perfectly well that he was champing at the bit he imposed upon himself, he caressed her from shoulders to hips as if they had all eternity for this. Her legs went weak; she held to him and nipped at the sturdy sinew on his neck. She stood on tiptoe, rubbing against him to flick her tongue in his ear. They each found new stretches of skin and curves and angles to explore with fingertips and tongues. They clung together, lost in eternal kisses. She touched him everywhere while he leaned his head back and breathed deeply with his eyes shut tight. She felt so dizzy that she stepped back to steady herself.

She bumped a bucket. Water sloshed under their feet to spread and hiss on the hearth.

He opened dazed eyes. "Damn. Well, let's use it quickly then. I need it to cool me off instead of warm me now."

He dumped the water into the wooden tub and climbed in, holding to her hand. It came just over his hips in little, lapping waves when he lowered himself in slowly. "Here, sit on

my lap," he said and helped her in. His hard, hairy legs
cradled her softer, smoother ones. Her ivory knees looked
so small and shapely next to his. He lifted her heavy, loos-
ened hair over his shoulder so it trailed down his back not
to get wet. She leaned back in his embrace. All this seemed
the most natural, important thing in the world to her.

"It's gone cold," she protested.

"It does not matter." He splashed water over her, but
soon the press of her back and bottom against him made
them hurry more. Dripping wet, they stood and stepped out.
He seized a linen towel and took a swipe or two at her and
himself. She laughed throatily to see the discarded towel
clinging to him across his hips like a white pennant of surrender. And then, indeed, she did surrender to this man she
desired, wanted—and more than that.

He carried her to the big canopied bed and yanked down
the bedclothes. Still damp-skinned, they tumbled between
the cold linen. They did not notice. They felt heat like the
July sun in a closed courtyard. Nothing mattered but their
being together now, the sharing of themselves, their bod-
ies, their lives, their love.

Love! she thought. Yes, that was it for her. Sobering and
frightening as it was, she loved this man. She regretted it,
but she could not help it. She loved him desperately despite
all that stood between them.

"Yes," she whispered in his ear as he rolled them over and
his weight took them down into the deep woolsack mattress. "I desire you, too, I need you, I lo—"

"I love what you do to me! I swear I have never felt so
with another, Rosalind, never!"

It was the last time either spoke except for murmurs and
muted groans. She could hardly catch her breath, let alone
shape thoughts or find words. She kneaded the hard muscles of his lower back and clung to his broad shoulders as he
moved up and down the length of her, kissing, touching,
demanding, giving. She thought she seemed so small next to

him; the length of him went on and on. She welcomed the gentle scrape of his beard stubble even in her tenderest places. She lured him with explorations of her own. And then he knelt over her and nudged her thighs wider with one big knee, then two, between.

Their dazed gazes met and held as he leaned closer. Slowly, deliberately he pushed his strength into her waiting warmth. She gasped. They were one. He hesitated only to ravish her mouth again. Then he cradled her to him and began to move.

"No one else?" he asked. "There has been no one else since your husband?"

"No one," she cried. She could tell he believed her. She was both fiercely glad she had saved herself for the glory of this moment, and yet regretful it was with a man who must yet be her enemy.

This was like nothing she had ever experienced before. Five years of marriage, twenty-seven years of life, nothing had prepared her for this sweep of stunning sensation. Riding Chestnut along the cliffs, pitching and yawing through the storm-swept sea—nothing. It was so wild and wonderful that despite her shock, she began to respond, to match his pace and then enhance it and challenge and drive it.

"Rosalind! Ros—"

They swept the world away until the entire universe exploded.

She realized they must have slept. She stirred and stretched her languid limbs luxuriously within the cocooned warmth of his embrace. Her hair was caught under him somehow so she could not lift her head. First in their passion and then their exhaustion the previous night, they had not pulled the crewelwork bed curtains closed. She could see dawn pearling around the shutters.

Reality struck. In the light of coming day, how could she face him? What could she say? What would he say and do?

She had no illusions; there would still be many battles between them. And yet how she cherished the precious moments when their only struggles had been to pleasure and treasure each other.

"Awake?" he muttered, his voice thick with sleep.

"Yes."

"We have a lot to do, and not only more loving."

There was that word again, she thought. If only he meant it as she did! He only spoke of loving how she made him feel. She had tried to tell him the truth of it for her last night, but had not quite managed to get it out. Of course, there was no future for them. No future beyond a liaison, at least. And mayhap not even that, she supposed, once he began to question her and she defied him. And, for certain, there could be no possibility of a real future for them, not for the king's lord lieutenant and an innkeeper from little Deal. Damn, the blackguard, but she wished she did not love him! But still she wanted every precious moment with him now. She could feel herself getting prickly hot, and those treacherous little butterflies beat in her belly again. She wanted to turn over to kiss him.

"Nick, my hair is caught."

"Mmm, the beautiful rest of you, too," he murmured. He slowly moved the palm of his hand in sweet circles over one breast and then the other as her nipples sprang to tingling nubs.

"What do you mean 'we have a lot to do' today?" She tried to keep her sanity at each new sweet assault he made.

"You're quite as adept at shifting topics as you are at other skills. I am going to take you for a walk through the town while my men are busy."

Oh, no, she thought. He meant to dangle her here like bait on a hook. And close to dawn or dusk was the most likely time some of the Rosies' contacts might notice her on the streets and get caught. But for all her concerns, she could not help the shivers of sensation that were shooting through her. Well, she thought, two could play at this game!

Intentionally, for more reasons than one, she shifted her bottom back against Nick while pretending to wriggle in his arms just to free her hair. It had the immediate effect she had intended and the long-term result she desired. It was nearly midmorn before they climbed from bed.

Finally, he forced her to stop dawdling over breakfast and fussing with the braiding and piling of her hair. He took her out—supposedly, for her first time—to see the little town on Boulogne-sur-Mer. Again she realized, though she could not help longing to lie *with* him, she would have to lie *to* him about so much to save the Rosies and herself.

"So, you have never been to France before?" he inquired as they strolled the bustling dockside.

"I see it is not so very different from home but for the language and some of the food," she countered. "That sauce in the crab pie and the one over the breakfast shrimp were delicious. And the cheeses—"

"We are not here to take back new ideas for the kitchen of the Rose and Anchor, woman," he insisted. "I said, *have* you been to France before?"

She saw his eyes darken and his jaw set harder. It was clear he was on to her ploy to keep him distracted, so she would have to find another battle plan.

More than once, the men he had sent out on some mission had appeared to report stealthily to him, then disappeared again. They went in groups of three, led by either Perkin Rich or Charles White, the two who spoke French. Fortunately, this was one such time his men returned, interrupting his line of interrogation. While he whispered with them, she kept her head turned seaward and hoped no one walking by would recognize her. She stared out at the forest of masts, the stretch of drying sprat nets and the long, wooden lobster traps that had always looked like ham hocks to her.

Nick was soon back with her, taking her arm to urge her along the busy dock. As they circled the wharf again, he also circled back to the questions she had earlier tried to side-step.

"As late as you stay up, Rosalind, surely you have seen or heard unlawful pack trains passing through Deal at night. Ponies of dark hue with muffled hooves, cartwheels may-hap wrapped with hemp, you can imagine the rest."

She could indeed, but she held her tongue. From a wooden tray strapped to a farm girl's neck, he bought her an apple and took a huge, noisy bite from his own. It both amused and comforted her to find he evidently intended to keep calm with her. But that was it! She would take her cue from his mood. If he seemed calm, she would match him. If he became amorous, or lost his temper, she could meet him halfway, too. That way, mayhap she would seem to play by his rules, seem to cooperate and agree, at least in tem-perament. To make him think she had not a worry in the world, she took the chance to fill her own mouth.

"As a lone woman wi' the inn, I though' I bes' no' ge' involved," she said thickly and almost choked. He had to pound her on the back. She spit some out and swallowed the rest. Her eyes watered; she had to fight to get her voice and poise back.

"I suppose," she began again, carefully clearing her throat, "there are coastal smugglers everywhere, but why should I make trouble for myself? If there are French smugglers passing through Deal, Sandwich or wherever, the less I know about it the safer I will be. Since I do not doubt whatever smugglers ply their terrible trade in our parts would be dangerous if discovered or crossed, I want no part of such."

"Good!" he agreed, but she knew nothing between them was one whit settled. He held her wrist as she lifted her arm for another bite of her apple. "But you *do* know something, Rosalind. Do not be afraid to tell me. Besides the illegality of smuggling, his majesty cannot have Englishmen trafficking with the French foe when security around the new castle is essential."

It struck her then that she was indeed playing with fire. In these hard times, the king could view smuggling with the French, especially near his precious castle, as something far worse than an evasion of—to her—unfair taxes. He might see it as spying—as treason! Mayhap they were not just talking broken boats and fines and possible imprisonment here. It might be broken lives, even torture and death to discover treason!

Now it was more important than ever that she win this struggle between her and Nick. She loved and desired him, but she had to defeat him. Yes, matching whatever tack he took might be her best defense. His earlier, kindly attitude seemed gone now and he had turned deadly serious, so she must, too. He indirectly threatened her, so she would subtly threaten him in return.

"You say his majesty cannot have anyone trafficking with the French foe, but that is what you are trying to do here!" she insisted. She had heard enough to know his men were going here and there trying to make smuggling contacts from whom Nick could pry information about contacts in Deal. "I cannot imagine why you have dragged me out on these streets, except to try to make it look as if I have something to do with French contacts when it is you who desires such!"

"Silence!" he hissed. "You may not have direct contact with smugglers in Deal, but I warrant you know who does! I want names, incidents, even if they may be improbable leads! And I still want to know more about that damned Frenchman you were whispering with—the one who called you his love!"

"A mere turn of phrase. I told you he favored me. Too bad you really don't."

"Never mind trying to turn the tables!"

"You're the one who has done that. It's obvious now the king sent you to Deal to chase smugglers as well as build and defend the castle."

"Hell's gates," he cursed and pulled her away, "will you keep your voice down?"

"Not if you insist on arguing in the streets."

He steered her up a narrow, cobbled close with overhanging top stories of gabled houses. "I weary of your gainsaying me, Rosalind! It will be better for you and Deal if you tell me all you know. I will do what I must to accomplish my ends, so best you help me!"

"I do not respond well to threats, my lord!"

"Then call it a promise!"

Damn, but this woman enraged him as no one ever had! He was on the edge of losing his temper, of shouting at her that he was going to search the Rose and Anchor, cellar to shingles, the moment they returned. Last night in his weakened state, he had considered offering her some bargain—of protection, of immunity, of reward—*if* she confided to him what she knew. Any sane man would think that after their shared intimacy last night she would tell him all. But tonight, he would just see! There would be no bargain, only her ultimate admissions and the smugglers' total defeat and destruction!

He heaved his apple core into the gutter in the center of the street and hurried her back toward the inn. He had ordered his men to put out the word they were staying at Le Canard and he was interested in arranging "free trading," to use Rosalind's term for it, between here and Sandwich, and he still longed to smoke the smugglers out. But Rosalind was so defiant, so adamant about her innocence that it confused him. She might be infuriating, but she was also the most fascinating woman he had ever known. And despite his temper, she still dared to chomp on her apple as if she were Eve leading him into the Garden of Eden!

That night, somehow, it was not the confession he wanted that slipped from her luscious lips, but the words "I love you!"

He wondered if she meant it, or whether it had tumbled out as wildly as he had tumbled her. She lay beside him now, disheveled, delicate and delicious looking. Although their breathing had slowed, their limbs were still intertwined.

He was loath to begin his questioning again. She had seduced his senses and his mind, and he reveled in it. As alluring as she looked, how could he suspect her? Might she not be completely innocent in the smuggling mess? Could she be telling the truth about that Frenchman? He knew it would do no good to ask her brother-in-law. No doubt, whatever the man told him would have been worked out before. Perhaps Rosalind was not even an observer.

He had tried both direct and indirect approaches with her. No one had appeared who knew her, though his men had met several dockside ruffians who admitted they could ferry French and Spanish smuggled goods to the coast of Kent without "King Harry's revenue men knowing aught."

But those men had refused to give any names from Deal as references. And so it proved nothing about Rosalind, nothing about Deal. Could any woman who looked this way, who trusted him so intimately with her body and her very heart, have become enmeshed with a hoard of dirty, ruffian smugglers?

"Nick?"

"What, sweetheart?" He traced her profile and then her lips with his index finger as she spoke.

"It does not mean a thing—not that I expect anything from you in the future—what I said to you just now—that I love you."

"Those words mean a great deal to me. Since you love me, you will trust me. That's the way it is for people who are intimate like this—they share everything." He had made love to her because of his desire for her, because he had not been able to restrain himself, but if, as a result of their emotional and physical closeness she trusted him, all the better for both their sakes.

"I believe we have shared everything," she told him. But this was, Rosalind thought, most definitely *not* the way she wanted this conversation to go. Nor was she so foolish as to share everything with Nick. He had said, *I love what you do to me* and mentioned he liked *loving her,* but no more. By the saints, he was probably so used to having women in love with him that it didn't mean a fig to him! At least he had not grilled her further about knowing smugglers since their argument yesterday. But she knew he was still capable of playing on her emotions, for he kept them stretched so taut he could have any tune he wished from them.

When he started to caress her, every nerve of her body leaped alive. He murmured in her ear, "You *can* trust me, you know."

"Nick, I cannot think when you do that."

"This?" he asked, his hands working wicked magic between her thighs. "Do not think, then, just trust me. Trust me and tell me what I can do to help you. If there is any pressure put on you to keep silent about suspicious things you have seen at the inn, I can protect you. If you have ever been forced to store things at the inn you didn't want, I can see it never happens again. Any information you can share would help me in return. I will protect you, the inn, the town, and you will help me root out any dangers— Damn, Ros!"

She had clamped her thighs closed on his hand and sat up so fast her head smacked his jaw, just as it had that night at the castle. She saw he was furious, but she was, too. Did he think she was so far gone at his touch, she would tell him everything? So much for matching this madman's moods!

"Oh, sorry!" she said, hoping he believed her. "You were making me so wild I could not hold still."

He touched his jaw tenderly. "I like my lovemaking wild, but not like that, curse it!"

She lay back and smiled up sweetly at him. She had overheard they were going back to England on the morrow. She regretted that in some ways, but was relieved in others. Both her dearest dreams and worst nightmares had come true with Nick here in this little town. But if he thought he could manipulate her even as he seduced her again, he was much mistaken. Once again, two could play at whatever tricks he wanted to try. She was up for the challenge of seduction or this latest game of his called "trust me."

"If your jaw hurts, I could kiss it and make it better," she crooned through pouted lips.

"I would like that. I am afraid, though, I hurt all over."

That time, in the blur of passion that followed, she did not repeat that she loved him.

Wrapped in each other's arms, they lay drowsily abed in the dusky early-morning hours. A fat tallow candle still burned low on the table to barely illuminate the room as a knocking on their door awakened them.

Nick rose on one elbow and muttered to her, "Probably Simon with food. I told him we must be away before dawn."

"Mmm. Or your men," she murmured and sighed as Nick got up and pulled on his shirt. But he unsheathed and held his sword aloft as he padded to the door. As he did, the knocking that had awakened them sounded again.

Rap, rap, pause, rap, rap.

Rosalind sat bolt upright in bed as Nick fumbled with the door bolt. The Rosies' secret sign! Just when she'd thought she was safe! The last voice in the world she wanted to hear—Pierre Lyon's—gave the Rosies' password in heavily accented English through the door.

"Ring-a-ring of rosies!"

Rosalind jammed a fistful of sheet against her mouth. He must have seen her or heard she was here! He thought it safe to reveal himself and things about the Rosies. If Nick opened the door, he would recognize him, catch him, and then the Rosies were doomed. She had to warn Pierre before Nick got his hands on him! Dragging the sheet around her, she jumped from bed and ran for the candle at the table.

Nick swung open the door, hiding his raised sword. The cloaked form of the unsuspecting Pierre stood in the doorway.

Quickly, Rosalind lifted the candle so that it lighted up her face, then gestured Pierre away with her other hand. He fled headlong, noisily down the stairs.

"Wait! You! Stop, *monsieur!*" Nick shouted in the first French she had heard from him. He tore after Pierre. She heard him call for his men below, and then a door banged.

Trembling, Rosalind put down the candle and scurried back to bed, trying desperately to settle the sheets. She sat up, straining to hear as, below, Nick's men must have leaped from bed. More footsteps. Shouts in both languages. She should have known Nick spoke some French, since he had been stationed in Calais.

She could tell that other guests had been awakened below. Murmurings floated up the staircase, a curse or two at all the noise. If they caught Pierre, she was doomed. As it was, he had given away their knock and part of the password, supplying Nick with more ammunition. She thought he had been starting to believe she knew nothing. Now he would have far more reason to suspect her.

She pressed her clasped hands between her breasts, feeling the thud, thud of her heart echoing the sound of doors being slammed below as folks went back to bed. She thought she might be sick. She hardly dared to breathe.

Soon she heard men's voices again, and Nick's deep voice carrying clearly above the rest. She was about to get out of bed in an effort to overhear what they said when Nick came back in. Banging the door behind him, he threw the bolt, then dropped his sword on the table with a clatter.

"Who was that?" she asked, her voice almost a squeak. "Did you catch him?"

"Bare-assed and barefooted on those cobbles? Across foul, slippery gutters when the bastard knew every turn of every alley?"

His voice was hard, his face furious. He walked gingerly over to their tub of water and swished first one, then the other foot in it. If she had not been so frightened she would have laughed, for his shirt only just covered his bare buttocks, and the thought of the king's lord lieutenant tearing through the streets that way was ludicrous.

"Our bait got a bite but the bastard fish got away," he muttered more to himself than her. "And here I am again, singing my old refrain, 'Who the hell was that, Rosalind?'"

She breathed a silent sight of relief, then realized she was premature. He seemed to stalk her where she sat in the bed, the sheet pulled up to her chin. He yanked it away, then the pillow when she tried to cover herself with it.

"The man came here with a secret knock or code, didn't he?" he demanded. "It is time you came uncovered with me, my little innocent!"

"I am cold, Nick. Give me that!" she dared to say, though she trembled at his anger. She drew up her knees and hugged them for warmth and modesty. His dark, angry eyes seemed to burn her bare flesh and bore beneath her carefully erected facade.

He leaned down and pushed her flat against the mattress, then vaulted onto the bed, pinning her beneath him.

The single candle threw his shadow big on her. His breath came ragged; his hands holding her down were harsh.

"Who was the man, Rosalind?"

"How should I know? Someone your lackeys running about the docks these past two days lured in with your counterfeit plan to smuggle, I suppose."

"Could he be that so-called René friend of yours?"

"How should I know! I didn't even see his face!"

"But you rose from bed behind me to warn him away, didn't you? He took one look at you with that candle and fled!"

"I simply rose to hold the candle for you so you could see him better."

"Really? Then explain to me why he said that old nursery rhyme, with your name in it as if he knew you."

"What? My name in it? You are imagining things."

Her blood coursed through her; she could feel it, hear it ringing in her ears. It was actually Aunt Bess with her love of the old childhood rhymes who had suggested the Rosies' password several years ago.

"Best inquire of your men," Rosalind said boldly, "why some ruffian they contacted would spout an English rhyme." Her voice quaked as much as she did, but she could always claim cold and fear at his anger. "Maybe he wasn't even French," she went on, stalling for time to think. "Since you are so convinced that I use my knowledge of French for illegal purposes, wouldn't some Frenchman who came calling speak in French? Now get off me, you big oaf! You are hurting me!"

He sat up and hauled her to him by shackling her wrists. He held her forearms pinned against his chest where he had not even had time to lace his shirt.

"You may be a delicate, petite wench, but you are far more clever than most men, sweet. It makes me wonder. Does that password refer perhaps not only to your name but also to the Rose and Anchor!"

"You're demented and obsessed! You're seeing things where there is nothing!"

"I tell you where I shall see things," he told her and hauled her off the bed. He steadied her until she got her balance. "We are heading back to Deal right now, and you are going to take me on an intimate, extensive tour of the Rose and Anchor. And if I find so much as one thing that casts suspicion on you, you will not escape me, Rosalind. And we will go on from there to get to the bottom of this. Now garb yourself. I do not need your French friend returning with his fellow bullies and, as usual, your beautiful and very willing body tempts me to waste more time. Now, before the sky turns light!"

She wanted to slap him, shriek at him and scratch his eyes. He enraged her further by patting her bottom as he loosed her. He was the bully, damn him, and so insulting! Those moments she had treasured he called a waste of time. And tried to put the blame for it on *her* being willing, the blasted blackguard! She would love to break the very nose she had so foolishly fixed for him. Why had she not let the wretch drown that first day! She hurried to dress but she still seethed inside; she had a hundred curses and names and excuses to hurl at him.

But she was scared too. If he really searched the inn, he could find her coded book with the embossed rose on the cover in her hidden cupboard, the trapdoor in the floor, and the set of false cellars! She hated him for using her like this the past few days, and detested herself for reveling in his every touch. But she must return home safely before she took him on again. She must somehow warn everyone never to use the Rosie knock or password again. She must get back with her friends where she was not this man's prisoner and hostage before she told him what she really thought of him.

She refused herring, bread and beer before they set out.

"Is your stomach unsettled with guilt?" he goaded. "A pity it will be a bit rough out on the sea."

"It is your touch that makes me sick," she told him through gritted teeth. She pulled her arm from his hand when he tried to escort her downstairs to join his waiting men.

"Then, one way or the other, you are going to be very sick," he countered as he hurried her and his men down and out through the graying streets toward the sea.

Chapter Eight

⌒⌒⌒⌒⌒

They beached the boat in the same spot from which they had departed England three days before. Nick's man appeared on the cliffs above with the horses. They made the long climb up without speaking. Rosalind caught Nick glaring at her from time to time, but she tried to avoid his gaze. When he helped her mount Chestnut, his grip was hard.

At Deal the two of them rode directly to the inn while the others clattered off for the castle. Rosalind's stomach rumbled from hunger; since last night, she had accepted nothing from Nick Spencer but several swigs of water. But worse than the hunger, fear gripped her belly in a tightening knot. She had rehearsed a hundred things to say if he uncovered her secrets at the inn, but if he found the codebook, she did not know how to explain it away. She hoped desperately she would have a moment alone with someone she trusted before Nick tried that knock or password on Wat or Alf or Hal. If they saw it was Nick, they would not respond, but in the dark of night who knew what sort of secret meeting that knock could get Nick into before her men realized he was privy to it.

Despite her quaking legs, she dismounted at the stable door before Nick could touch her again. She started toward the rear garden entrance, but he pulled her back. "No one, not even Meg or Aunt Bess is to know what we're about," he warned, his voice crisp and cold. "If you so much breathe a word to a soul before I have ransacked this place, they will be detained with you."

Nick stood at her side while she greeted her female kin, but he saw nothing amiss. He even watched to see that she did not slip either woman a note. The little vixen had evidently decided to behave. She told them several things about Nan and the new baby, then said the rest would have to wait. He explained he had stopped by in Sandwich to escort her back, for they had privy business in Rosalind's chamber. Both women raised their eyebrows at that. Nick wondered what they would say if they knew the sort of bedchamber business he and their precious Rosalind had shared the past two days. But, ignoring Percy Putnam's man, Shanks, who was leaning over the banister above them, he finally escorted Rosalind into her chamber.

She threw her cape on a chair and stood her ground with her arms crossed over her breasts. "If you tear this place apart," she began, "I'll not be responsible for what others say of you and your brutal ways."

"But you are responsible for driving me to such lengths," he clipped out. He surveyed the room. It was still cluttered, though not as badly as the first time he had seen it. "Pour me a glass of that fine 'imported' French wine while I begin."

Every word he spoke, each order he gave goaded her. But she obeyed, taking a bottle from a case on the rug, steadying her hands to keep herself from smashing the bottle over his head. "Shall I also empty each case so you can look for a note smuggled in a bottle?" she dared.

It was a mistake. He pulled her to him, though that move slopped wine down his chest and onto her skirt. "You will just do as I say and guard that tart tongue of yours!" He gave her an ominous shake, then turned away to survey the room.

Despite her dire straits, she could not resist sticking her tart tongue out at him behind his back.

"I shall start with the walls, I think," he declared.

Her heart thudded. "What?"

"Hidden panels or doors. I can wade through this litter of other things later. A crafty little female like yourself would not leave important things just sitting about while she is away, now would she? And I hope in my search," he said as he lifted the draperies away from her windows and peered behind each, "that I won't stumble on a hidden love note from the likes of Percy Putnam or Wat Milford or 'René.'"

"How dare you say that after—after your forced seduction of me. I may have been foolishly mistaken to trust you, but I guard my affection and my favors closely!"

"So you said in the depths of our bed in Boulogne. But if you have lied to me about some things, why should I believe I have been your first lover since Murray?"

Her temper flared. She clenched her fists so hard her nails bit half-moons into her palms as she fought to stem her desire to attack him physically. She almost told him that both Wat and Percy were to be trusted more than he, but she knew now how poor an idea it was to rouse his ire further. No, she would have to get through this nightmare somehow and bide her time. She would outwit and outlast this pompous, prideful lord lieutenant yet!

Evidently satisfied with the windows, the damned man peeked under the portrait of her mother that an itinerant artist on a pilgrimage had painted to pay a debt. Then he started for the arras over her bed.

Oh, saints, she thought, I am doomed.

"Aha!" he said when he spied the small, square door in the wall behind the arras. He pulled the tapestry down and flung it on the bed. "Come over here and open this for me." When she stood still, he shot her a piercing look over his shoulder.

"I keep my inn records there, and also some other things that are dear to me," she said. She had been terrified all along about the damning evidence of her codebook, but his mention of love notes and Murray had given her an idea.

"Where is the blasted key, Rosalind? Open this now!"

She knew he would break into it if she did not open it. Slowly she fished up the key by its chain around her neck. His gaze seemed to nail her to the floor as she handed it to him.

"The key to your heart, I believe you called this the other night when we loved. You little liar. Now we shall see what other things you have hidden," he threatened.

"You are the liar, my lord. Trust me, you said, and I did so with my body and my heart. I told you of my love and you gave me naught but deceit."

"Here is the deceit, sweetheart!" he crowed as he lifted out her things and dropped them on the bed amid the other piles there. He sat down, cross-legged, in his boots, curse him, and became immediately engrossed. But when she tried to edge away, he ordered, "Climb up here with me."

"Never again will I go near a bed with you on it or in it!"

He frowned at her. If she had not stood back from the reach of his long arm she was not certain what he would have done.

"We shall see," he said. Gathering up a pile of her belongings, he strode across the room and tossed them on the table. "Come here, then."

She sat across from him, her hands folded demurely on the table. He peered into her box of coins, though she had most of her savings buried beneath various rosebushes out in back. She hoped he could not see she was shaking as he pawed roughly through the pile, which held mostly inn records, peering down at them. Then he came to the black leather book with the gold-embossed rose.

"Ring-a-ring of rosies," he declared, pointing to the cover. He flopped the book open and leaned close to her carefully coded script. "What is the next line of that rhyme?"

"I think it is something like 'ashes, ashes, you will fall down,'" she said, trying to bluff her way through this. "That book, as you can probably tell, is where I keep my private diary in code, just so prying eyes like yours will never know my deepest woman's thoughts, should it be found. I liked the rose, as if it were a picture of my name. I hope you will be gentleman enough not to make me read it to you, as it contains some of the only treasures I have left from my marriage."

"A diary of your marriage? So these headings here and there are dates?" he asked, pointing out symbols with his finger.

She nodded, fighting to keep her eyes steady on his. She hated to lie to him, though she knew she was fighting for freedom and for the very existence of the Rosies, this town and herself. For all she believed in the rightness of what she was doing, she still felt great remorse not only in using the memory of Murray this way—but also in manipulating Nick's emotions.

"Dates on which Murray and I . . . did special, sentimental things together," she faltered. His gaze was intense as she spoke. "Dates we—tried to make a child on that very bed you have walked all over to ravage my precious, private memories."

Praise God, she thought, the man actually looked embarrassed. In the depths of their bed in Boulogne the second night they had exchanged memories of their marriages. His had been a matter of politics and no love match—all arranged by Horrid Harry, of course. His wife had died in childbirth with a stillborn babe. Rosalind's marriage, she had explained, had been a natural blooming of a friendship that grew and flourished like a flower until Murray's life had been cut short.

She had thought as she shared that with Nick, though it was too dark to see his face, he not only had been touched, but also had yearned for something like that. She had even shared her greatest regret that Murray had not left her a child. Nick had held her tight as if to comfort her. Now, mayhap all of that might make him soften toward her. She prayed he would not demand a symbol-by-symbol translation of these detailed records of what French shipments had come in and when and where they had been stored and sold. For then she would have to quickly create many more lies than she already had.

"Clever of you to use your own code," he observed, "but then you are a clever wench."

"But obviously no match for you, my lord. Please do not give that book to others to scoff at. As you can see, I never meant for even Murray or Meg to read it. Even after I died, no one would know my heart's secrets. It—I, well, some of the things you and I did I would hate for others to know, but these things were in the sanctity of the marriage bed."

She saw him shoot a look over at the canopied bed and the open, emptied compartment above it. "I grant you," he said, "I have a safe in my bedchamber in my house at Greenwich. Many do. Then, for now, I shall search further."

She wrung her hands while he knocked on walls and went through the three coffers that held her clothes. He rattled through her baskets of shells and other treasures, then lifted the wine cases off the rug and scuffed it to the side.

"So," he said, his voice triumphant again, "what have we here?"

She launched into the defense she had planned on the boat trip back from France. "Why, I just never fathomed such things as family safe spots and escapes would come under suspicion from you," she said, feigning surprise. She rose from the table to join him as he lifted the door by its recessed metal ring and peered into the dark, dusty depths.

"It's a secret escape tunnel. It goes under the gardens and comes out on the edge of the vale," she told him. "In a coastal area like this, where we have lived with the threat of invasion over the centuries, from the time of the Romans and Normans on, many houses have escape routes. It's tradition and just plain good sense. And, now that this king has persecuted the church he once defended, there are many such tunnels and hiding places in new-built houses, too, where folks live who once espoused the old faith before our king replaced the pope as head of his own church. Why, who knows when the times may turn again, especially with the French threat? Here, let me escort you down the tunnel, though we'll have to fetch a candle. Then I'll show you the double cellars we could use for storage or hiding in case of a French invasion. Before we knew the castle was to be built to stop the French, it seemed a good idea."

She hoped her willingness to help and her abundance of freely offered admissions would set him back. Obviously, they did. His eyes widened, his lower lip dropped before he set it hard again.

She only dared to offer all this because she knew another delivery had not come while she was gone. The Rosies knew better than to hide contraband anywhere about here these days. The inn's drop spots were all temporarily empty. She had sent all the goods on from the tunnel here when she first heard the king was sending a lord lieutenant to this area. Even if Nick found the cave in the woods or discovered the empty tombs at St. Leonard's loaded with the most recent hauls, he could not directly tie them to anyone specific in Deal and would have to suspect the entire town!

"Shall I fetch a candle, my lord?" she asked helpfully, as he continued to study her without speaking. "There is one right out in the hall."

"No, but I shall send a few of my men through the tunnel when they arrive. Let me see the double cellars then and what other wonders this perfectly normal place has to offer.''

He marched her through every room, sometimes routing out late sleepers. He hoped they did not uncover Franklin Stanway in or under Mistress Meg's bed, but they did not. He searched the attic, and spent an hour traipsing through the cellars, with her as an apparently willing guide, while his men searched the tunnel.

It angered Rosalind when she discovered that Percy Putnam's man, Roger Shanks, was hanging about, though she was relieved not to see Percy. But she guessed he'd know soon enough now that the lord lieutenant of Deal Castle suspected her and the Rose and Anchor of something. By the saints! All she needed was petty Percy on his guard about smuggling, too!

They were back in her bedchamber with Nick poring over her other papers when three of his men climbed back up from the depths of the tunnel. They looked dirty and squinteyed. She watched the tall one blow out his candle and walk to Nick. The man put some scraps of lace and satin in Nick's hands. Another calamity, just when she thought she was convincing him! Those must have been snagged from bolts of smuggled yard goods when they were toted in or out!

"Pretty dainties," Nick said, when the men left the room. He let the scraps of cloth flutter down before her on the table. "I have not seen you wear a gown made of such fancy stuff."

"Far too fine for me," she retorted, trying to match his mood and tone. "It looks like something that one of your court women would wear."

"Exactly, and there are none such around here."

She shrugged. She was so hungry, so tired, so on edge.

"Will you tell me next, sweet, that the Romans or the Norman invaders left these behind? If Catholic priests ever used your tunnel when his grace closed the monasteries, they were strange holy fathers to dress thus. Or mayhap some court ladies just happened to be down there gambling at cards the other night, and you forgot to tell me. No, it is you who have been gambling here, my bold beauty! Contraband must have been hidden down there, and I surmise you knew it and knew it was empty now. What sort of a fool do you take me for?''

"One who seduces a woman who cares for him and then turns on her," she said. Her voice was low at first, but it rose in volume as she went on. "Evidently, one who plays with hearts for his own selfish ends."

"What passed between us at the castle and Boulogne is separate from this. You are the deceiver here! And so, until you decide you can share with me the names of those you have surely seen—if not directly abetted—who have smuggled goods through here, you may consider yourself under arrest."

"You dare not!"

"It is that or the new dungeon in the castle, and I had rather reserve that for others I shall question."

"My reputation—the inn."

He rose and took her codebook, then evidently changed his mind. He dropped it back down on the table between them. "I have the strangest feeling that when Deal citizens learn that I suspect you of collusion, it will only serve to enhance your reputation, my sweet. The lovers' book is yours to cherish. Pity, that you will not be able to write of us cuddled in the night, that there will be no memories of your vowing your love for me. You see, I know now *you* were the user for your own ends, too. Just used your beautiful body to blind me to your cause, didn't you, you little liar? And you dared to say you loved me!"

"Oh, no doubt, I lied on that. I must have been demented, you bast—"

"Now the house rules for you!" he interrupted, raising both his voice and finger like a tutor to scold her. "I do not deceive myself that keeping you where I know your loca-

tion will stop what communications you have with folk in
Deal, but it will serve as a stout warning to everyone. I intend to assign a guard here, though, to keep you from cozy
chats with the likes of Wat Milford and your cousins. You
may have the privacy of this chamber, but you are only to
leave the inn by public entrances—'' he strode over and
slammed the tunnel hatch closed ''—and only then when
you specifically receive permission from me, which you
must write to request!''

''You cannot mean this! By what right—'' she began before she recalled the writs with the king's seal she had seen
in Boulogne. Those had given him the right to detain, imprison, question under duress and other dire things. Damn
his vile king and this man who was but the loyal royal arm
here!

''And if you break my orders for your arrest, I shall have
to see you are kept, shall we say, closer to my person at the
castle where I can see to you privily.''

Her head jerked up. ''I would rather die than be close to
you ever again!'' For the first time, tears stung her eyes. As
much as she had lied to him to save her town, her Rosies,
even herself, she could not dissemble about how she felt for
him. Beneath the fear and pain, she still longed for his smile,
his care, his damned deceiving arms around her. She still
loved him even as she silently cursed him to the devil.

''Then we understand each other,'' he said.

''Indeed.''

He nodded and strode to the door. He looked back at her.
''Do not think things are finished between us,'' he concluded and closed the door behind him.

She crumpled in the chair, her fists on the table. She collapsed over them, racked with sobs. It was only when Meg
and Aunt Bess hurried in she realized she was crying all over
the Rosies' codebook.

* * *

To the attention of the Lord Lieutenant of Deal Castle, Nicholas Spencer:
This nineteenth day of November, the year of our Lord 1539, Mistress Rosalind Deland Barlow humbly beseeches that your lordship bestow upon her written permission that she might step out the back entrance of the inn called the Rose and Anchor to assist her sister, Mistress Margaret (Meg) Deland, in the yearly winter cutting back of the apothecary and kitchen roses in the gardens. No other living soul will be addressed at said time without your revered, written permission. Your prompt response to this meek entreaty will be greatly appreciated.
Postscriptum. This courier has imbibed only the amount of ale set forth in the lord lieutenant's regulations.

"Hell's gates," Nick shouted at the poor man who had handed him the note, "not another of these niggling requests! Will the woman never cease!"

He dismissed the laborer with a wave of his hand, and the man gladly scurried back to his job. Nick glared at Rosalind's now familiar script, then stuffed it in his leather pouch already full of them. In the two weeks Rosalind had been under arrest, she had deluged him with these petty, provoking epistles. She humbly begged to step outside to bid farewell to guests, to help her aunt gather eggs, to shake a tablecloth, to see her horse was curried. Damn the woman! In following his orders to the letter, she was intentionally driving him to distraction with a deluge of piddling requests that his own laborers delivered from the inn—and only too often with a snide postscript attached verifying that the courier had only imbibed the allowed amount of ale!

How he had kept away from her these long days he did not know. At first he had vowed to himself that he would let her stew for a week before he visited her again; meanwhile, he had ordered Percy Putnam to visit about the town to see what he could overhear. The man should report back today. But Nick still could not bear to face her. They would surely argue, and it would rip at his insides to hear her admit again she did not care for him after the way they had loved—that is, seemed to enjoy—each other in Boulogne. Worse, he was terrified she was guilty of deeds he would have to pursue and punish her for. He had to break her, though he could not bear to.

Then, too, he had thought his obsession with finishing the castle walls would help keep his thoughts from her. They had to get further before bad weather, and certainly before spring, when a French fleet could well appear on the horizon. But not even his duty to the king's castle had kept his mind off Rosalind. Nothing, *nothing* had worked to rid him of his desire for her! And these blasted notes were a daily—an hourly—reminder of all that had gone wrong between them.

He knew he had to cool his temper before he gave another order to his soldiers or his laborers. He strode the nearly completed battlements and glared in Rosalind's distant direction, though he could see no more of the inn from here than two crooked fingers of chimney smoke drifting in the air above the vale.

Nick could only hope the town's favorite daughter's detainment would force someone to act or talk out of turn. Since the little vixen was fighting back in her own way, he was strongly tempted to haul some of her closest friends in for individual questioning without waiting for someone to make a wrong move. Nick had no doubt that the moment he left the inn, she had somehow warned others he had heard a secret knock and password. But his only alternative was to confine her here, and he was not ready to do that to her. Besides, if she were that close to him, his desire for her would lead inevitably and fatally to ignoring his duty.

He heaved a huge sigh as he leaned against the wall below which masons were completing the final sturdy portholes for cannon. He had taken pity on Franklin Stanway's moping today and allowed him go up to the inn for a dinner break. While Nick was away in France, Franklin had been forced to stay here day and night when he had wanted time alone with his lady love without Rosalind about, and on his return Nick had driven everyone so hard there had been no time for dalliance. Nick had finally taken pity on the lovelorn mason, but he had also thought Franklin might pick up more information from Meg about Rosalind.

The inn seemed very quiet to Rosalind as she came in from plucking linens from the bushes. Aunt Bess was out, and she had been glad to take over this duty—though of course she had written a note to Nick requesting his kind permission. Nick's guard, Tom Shallcross—one of the six he rotated on assignments watching her when she was not in her chamber—came right behind her, his arms full of sheets and bolster covers. She rather liked all of Nick's men. She'd never let him or them know, though she did slip them extra ales when she could. She had been pondering her next "nice and sweet" note to Nick—mayhap one thanking him for allowing her to curry her horse, which she had finished just before she started on the linens. She had already left a note with the tapman for Franklin Stanway to take back if he came today, one begging she might take a walk outside.

In the hall outside her chamber, she took the linens from Tom, left him at his post there and carried them into her room. It was quiet in the inn today. Usually at this time of day Aunt Bess was downstairs sweeping the taproom floor, making all the men move their chairs and feet in the process. The good-natured, two-way ruckus was discernible all over the inn. It was as if Aunt Bess had become both townsmen's and castle workers' mother away from home, and they all reveled in teasing her, then noisily, grudgingly obeying. They loved to be ordered about.

"Too bad, *he*'s just the opposite," she muttered under her breath. "*He* does nothing but dish out orders and would probably never move so much as his feet for his mother—if such a monster ever had a mother."

She could not stem the growing antagonism she felt for Nick Spencer. How dared he curtail her freedom! How dared he bed her, say he admired her, then treat her this way! But worse, she detested the fact she still cared for him, even missed him, the wretch! Damn the king's man! These notes she bombarded him with were probably so much water off his back and did not nettle him one whit. She could just picture him wadding them up and tossing them off the parapets onto the wet sand! She'd have loved to tell him how she felt in person, but coward that he was, he'd been staying away.

Then, as she paced in her room, she realized that silence no longer suited her. She used to love solitude or just the rustle of waves on the sand. But lately she had been such a jumble of anger and noise inside, she longed for a good argument—or at least some raucous singing from the taproom. And where was Meg right now? Why wasn't she coming in to ask if Rosalind wanted a drink or to share a moment's chat?

Well, she'd just go find Meg after she put these sheets in the linen press in Aunt Bess's chamber. Each time she entered that room lately, it bothered her, since she could still picture Nick lying there in bed, looking innocent and helpless as she fixed his nose and nursed him. Whenever she was in the room, she'd gaze at the bed his big frame had seemed to dwarf and recall that time they'd both toppled there together and he had held her down—

She gathered up the sheets and nodded to Tom when he jumped to attention. "Changed my mind, just going across the hall," she said, "if you'd be so kind as to get the door."

He nodded and hastened to oblige. Her mind drifted again. How dared she treasure moments like that with the king's man! She'd seen the true Nick Spencer now, and she would not fantasize this time about her lying with Nick on Aunt Bess's bed!

"Handle's stuck, mistress, but I'll just—" Tom said and put his shoulder to it.

The door banged open, shoving a chair that had been wedged against it inward. And there on the bed where Rosalind had too often thought of herself lying with Nick—

Meg squealed. Franklin tried to cover her, but only succeeded in making their current involvement more blatant.

"Meg!" Rosalind shrilled.

Both embarrassed and enraged, Rosalind could not at first decide what to do. Then, with her bottom, she banged the door closed in Tom's face. She ran toward the bed and dumped the clean sheets on top of Meg and Franklin. It had been overly obviously that both were buck naked on top of the counterpane.

"Get—get at least a sheet around you, Meg, and get this man out!"

What she had seen was causing Rosalind's knees to buckle. She crumpled in the chair next to the bed, head in hands. She could not believe it had come to this. Yes, she'd seen Franklin's love poetry. Yes, she'd known the two were in love, and she'd given them permission to be together on the grounds, but not like this! She found her strength again as Franklin, a sheet over himself like a tent, evidently scrambled into his clothes on the other side of the bed. Meg sat, a sheet clamped across her breasts and under both armpits, glaring at Rosalind.

"How dare you intrude thus!" Meg cried.

"It's my inn! Aunt Bess's room! Get out, Master Mason and stay away from ruining my sister's virtue! I'll not rear some babe from a king's man!" Rosalind shouted and pointed to the door as Franklin emerged from his tent, sloppily half-garbed.

"I love him, Ros! I will wed him!"

"You'll not. He only wants one thing and—"

Meg, her once-shy sister Meg, vaulted from the bed, almost tripping on her sheet. "You'll not scold me, Ros, and not forbid us either! I'm full-grown, and besides—"

"Sweetheart, maybe we should let it go for now—" said Franklin.

"No, she has no right, especially when she's mayhap done exactly what we have. As for loving a king's man or bearing his child, she—"

"Now, you listen to me, Margaret Deland!" Rosalind cried, hands on hips. "You've known for years that the king's men are treacherous and not to be trusted one whit!"

"Speak for yourself and your lord lieutenant!" Meg blazed back. "I love Franklin and will wed with him, even if you toss me out with him!"

Rosalind turned away and yanked open the door. She wanted to throw Franklin out and confine Meg to her room, but she knew she was beaten. Beaten not only by the strength of Meg's love but by the agonizing fact that she herself loved Nick, just as Meg had said. She would never have her lover again in bed—let alone in wedlock. The gulf between them was too deep, too far. Could she sentence her sister to the same fate?

"I would suggest you report back to work—king's work," she said to Franklin in a just barely civil tone. She could not bear to meet Meg's eyes again. Leaving the door to Aunt Bess's room open, she fled across the hall and slammed her own door. Its bang shattered the quiet of the inn.

* * *

Nick was pacing the parapet walls, kicking himself for not having brought Rosalind's coded diary to the castle so that someone could have taken a better look at it. But he cared for her and wanted to believe her so badly. According to word from the guard he had posted outside her room at night—and also from the one who was stationed at the other end of the escape tunnel on the edge of the vale—she was cooperating by not leaving the inn without written permission. Cooperating, that is, except for this hell-bent barrage of bothersome notes she knew would puncture his pride and control as only she could do!

He banged his fist on the stone wall behind him and silently cursed Rosalind Barlow. Then he saw Franklin striding across the walkway, his short cape flying behind him in the breeze. Before Nick could even ascertain why the mason had such a dour look on his face, the man thrust a note at him.

"I need not ask whom this is from," Nick said.

"A request to take a constitutional walk about her own lawn, so I hear," Franklin replied.

"The usual tripe," Nick muttered to himself. "But I believe I shall actually respond to this one with leave denied!" he announced grandly.

Franklin nodded, hat in hand, standing on one foot and then the other. Nick nodded his permission for the man to speak further.

"My lord," Franklin went on, apparently choosing his words carefully, "your feuding with Mistress Rosalind on paper has not taken the edge off her tongue in the flesh."

"She took out her anger at her arrest on you?" Nick asked, storing this note away with the others.

"Not exactly, my lord, but she is angry as a slapped hornet and gave me the tongue-lashing of my life. That one can outshout the royal Tudor, can't she, now? You see, my lord, here's the way of it. She took the guard you put on her door out to the stable when she obtained your permission to curry her horse. Actually, I gather, she had him doing the work for her.''

Nick smacked the wall again. ''He is there to keep her in sight unless she's in her chamber, not to take her orders! She is not to lead her guard about by a ring in his nose! They answer only to me. Mayhap leg irons—and losing her ink and paper should be next,'' Nick growled and ran a hand through his usually kempt hair.

''But the thing is, my lord, I thought she was clear of the inn for a spell, and Meg and I took advantage of the time to—ah, borrow her aunt's room. Well, Meg said the old lady had gone visiting, but I guess we lost track of time. Mistress Rosalind returned, this time with her arms full of new-washed linens. Came into her aunt's room, she did, and then, there we were—rather intimate, you see.''

The man looked away, then threw back his shoulders to face Nick squarely. ''I love and would wed Meg, my lord, but Mistress Rosalind carried on about the treachery of king's men. Said a lass could not trust such men one whit, and ordered me out. But Meg stood up to her and told her we would wed with her blessing or not. Mistress Rosalind wrote that note I gave you 'fore she found us, my lord, or I don't reckon it would have been as civil as it is. And I guess it won't be telling tales out of school to repeat one thing Meg said to Mistress Rosalind—that she had no right to deny our being together when she was obviously sweet on a king's man, too.''

Nick set his jaw hard and clapped Franklin on the shoulder. He wanted to believe that Rosalind had told Meg she loved him and meant it; but he could not afford to think that even this was not some sort of trap for him. *He* was the one who should be laying traps and snares here!

''The little shrew needs settling down again,'' he told his master mason, and silently hoped at least she would be angry enough to make a misstep. ''As to your wedding Mistress Meg, Franklin, the lass is of age and you have my blessing. I shall be happy to stand as your supporter, no matter what Mistress Rosalind says.''

"She's a shy thing, Meg, my lord. And torn because she doesn't want to hurt Mistress Rosalind, whom she loves dear. But aye, we are willing, and if you will stand with us, I think we'll risk it soon as we can. My heartfelt thanks, my lord. I'd best head back to work.''

Franklin's words reverberated in Nick's head amid the buzz of files on stone and the clatter of hammers on chisels. *Torn because she doesn't want to hurt Mistress Rosalind, whom she loves dear,* he had said. Yes, damn it, he, too, was torn by his feelings for Rosalind, but he hardly loved her. Did he? Impossible! Still, she haunted his very dreams. Intentionally avoiding her only stoked his passion for her. Meanwhile, he was going to put a covert watch on Wat Milford and her cousins. His next step might just have to be to have anyone Rosalind knew well hauled in here for very stringent, lengthy questioning!

"Hello, friend Wat!'' Percy Putnam chirped as he interrupted Wat's noon repast of ale and cheese in the small storage yard behind the brewery.

"Master Putnam, 'tis not your day to come to town!''

"I am only here because I knew you'd have need of my aid,'' Percy said smoothly—much more smoothly than the way he rocked his way over to Wat and leaned against a stack of barrels. "You know, to get you inside the castle and know which room is Spencer's and all. Matter of fact, I even did a sketch for you.''

Wat's jaw dropped, a hunk of cheese halfway to it. "What in creation you talking 'bout?''

Percy leaned closer. "That night we talked,'' he whispered, "you vowed you'd kill the lord lieutenant if he tried to sully Rosalind's honor. I tell you, he intends to make Rosalind his mistress. The time is ripe, my friend. And I am willing to be your accomplice when you strike him down!''

"Naw, everybody knows he's only got her under arrest, 'cause he thinks the inn might have been some smugglers' drop place once," Wat protested. "Which of course he's dead wrong about! And he hasn't been near the inn once, not since she came back from seeing Nan in Sandwich."

"I'm pleased to hear you've been keeping a good, if distant, watch on her. But you see, friend Wat, I have, too, when she was in Sandwich. I bear her great respect and affection for her kindness to me over the years, and that was one way to repay it. And to tell you true," Percy added and glanced around as if the barrels had ears, "Rosalind disappeared from her sister's almost three days before she came back here. My guess is she and the lord lieutenant, who put out the word he was in Sandwich when he was not, went off together, eh? And now he's evidently told her to avoid all her old friends, and I for one miss her sore."

Wat nodded slowly. His eyes were misted with obvious agony at those revelations.

"You see, Wat, I am afeared that Rosalind's become enamored of him, sly seductive courtier that he is. I don't just mean she's had him join her for a solitary supper at the inn! I'd wager he has plans to move her to his quarters at the castle, and that's why he has such a push on to complete the walls before the cold winter months, so they can be all cozy there!"

Wat stood up so fast his cheese flew and his ale spilled. Percy stepped back. Wat looked the part of some gargoyle carved from stone, hawk-faced, clamp-jawed, tormented, just as Percy had hoped. Wat seized and studied the sketch Percy had brought of the still uncompleted castle.

"Of course, you'd have to get a cap or hood to cover your head and face when you march in with the workers from their camp and then lie low inside...." Wat heard Percy say before his roiling anger blocked out the man's voice.

Wat gripped the edges of the sketch so hard his hands shook. Through Aunt Bess, Rosalind had gotten the word out to the Rosies that Spencer was suspicious of her and, by implication, of them all. She had begged them to steer clear of her and smuggling until further notice. And she had warned them never to use the Rosies' knock or password again because the man was on to it. He had taken her to Boulogne, she claimed, and managed to lure Pierre Lyon to his door before Pierre fled, though she hoped he would not recognize the Frenchman again. And she had assured her comrades that despite her abduction she had not been harmed, and they were not to commit any rash deeds.

But what if she had been seduced there as Percy implied and now was pining for that handsome blackguard! Even if the lord lieutenant had no amorous designs on her, what if Spencer was planning to imprison her for suspected smuggling at that impenetrable castle? Wat would not let the Tudor ax fall on Rosalind, however brave she was! He had seen Spencer's strength and cunning, yet he would protect Rosalind with his very life. He could not bear to see her and all they had fought for here in Deal destroyed by this king's man.

"What say you, Wat?" Percy Putnam's voice broke through the blur of his fear and rage.

"What's in it for you?" Wat challenged.

"Only Rosalind's safety, as I said." Percy tried to meet Wat's stare without blinking. He knew Wat was deceptive; his big burly looks and abrupt speech cloaked a wily man beneath, like several others in this sinkhole of dirty Deal. Why, he'd never have dared this with Wat if he hadn't discerned the man's weakness for Rosalind. He decided to risk a bit of truth with the lies to reel Wat in.

"Besides," Percy admitted and hung his head, "Spencer's shamed me in public before all of you—my friends. I was quite pleased with being the king's top man here before he barged in with his commands and orders—and his lust for Rosalind he will slake until he casts her off, besmirched and broken, mark my words!"

Wat nodded, frowning. "I shall think on all this, Master Putnam, but keep your sketch of Deal Castle. A man would have to be demented to sneak in there. No, if an accident befell the lord lieutenant, it would stand a better chance in the vale some night as he rides through. And justice would then be served, for he would probably be riding to see Rosalind again. And," he added with emphasis on each word, "she is innocent of all he claims about knowing smugglers, as pure and innocent as new-fallen snow."

Percy nodded and took back the map of the castle. He tore it to shreds as he said, "You're right, of course, about it all. A clever man would probably just run a fishing line or net across his horse's path and when Spencer's all wound up in it, slit his throat, quick as one-two-three."

Percy Putnam fought to keep from smiling at the picture of Nick Spencer with his leg crushed beneath his big mount before he lost his life. "Good day to you, then, friend Wat. You know, I've already forgotten why I came here," he said as the shreds of the sketch drifted to cover the spilled ale and cheese in the dirt under his departing feet.

That afternoon, Nick stared down at the most recent of Rosalind's mockingly deferential notes spread out before him on the table in his room at the castle:

To the attention of the Lord Lieutenant of Deal Castle, Nicholas Spencer:
This nineteenth day of November, the year of our Lord 1539, Mistress Rosalind Deland Barlow humbly beseeches that your lordship bestow upon her written permission that she might at least put her head out the front door of the inn called the Rose and Anchor to wave to her cousins' children as they pass by. Though their sweet faces and pleasant company are sorely missed, mere children must not be the next innocent citizens of Deal to come under your suspicion nor be

reported by your guard as trying to smuggle greetings
to their beleaguered kin, Rosalind.

Your prompt response to this meek entreaty will be
greatly appreciated.

Nick swore a string of sailors' curses he had not used since
he had last set to sea on a royal galley. That was the last
straw! He had to go to see her and stop this siege she was
waging against his position and sanity. Besides, his hands
tingled to touch her, even if it was to shake some sense into
her. His ears rang already with her voice as she would
adroitly argue, shrewishly scold or cleverly cajole. He was
going absolutely mad denying himself her presence!

But as he yanked open the door in order to shout for
someone to saddle his horse, Captain Delancey came down
the hall with Percy Putnam in tow.

"Finally news from town, Master Putnam?" Nick asked.

"We've hit the bull's-eye, you and I, with both our arrows!" Putnam boasted before Nick escorted him in and
faced him alone.

"Well?" Nick prompted, annoyed at the simpering smile.

"I told you I thought Wat Milford might be one of the
smuggling band," Putnam began, clasping his hands as if
in great expectation.

"Say on."

"I believe you have become such a detriment to that band
that he must surely be part of, that they are ready to strike,
and then we will have them!"

"You have learned of French contraband coming in?"

"No, my lord, even more damning than that, I'd say. The
smugglers of Deal are going to risk violence against your
person. In short, they plan to assassinate you. And I know
how you can set a trap to catch at least one of them and then
torture him to tell all he knows. And then hang him as a
warning to the rest you don't pull in, while we send word to
the king and Cromwell that—"

"Who?" Nick interrupted. "Wat Milford?" Even as he spoke he took Rosalind's latest note and rolled it smaller and smaller between his fingers.

"Just so, my lord. Wat Milford!"

"I knew it!"

"Well, I must tell you, when I was first king's revenue man in Kent, I used to believe the band was headed by the former innkeeper, Rosalind Barlow's father. But as he's long left us, mayhap Wat has filled his shoes since. Lord Spencer, did you hear me?"

Nick stood transfixed, staring at the note crushed in his fingers no smaller than a pill. Wat Milford, assassination—that was one thing, but this new information that the band might once have been headed by Rosalind's innkeeper father racked him. Then, might not the mantle of leadership—like the ownership of the inn—have fallen to her? Even though she was a petite and as yet a young, widowed woman. It was obvious everyone looked up to her, and he had long thought the inn the perfect place for covert meetings to go undetected and for goods to be hidden, though he had found but a few scraps of material there.

"I can even tell you," Percy's shrill voice went on, "how I believe the attempt on your life will come and how you can snag the perpetrator, my lord."

Nick tried to thrust the impossible but nagging suspicions about clever Rosalind from his mind. It could not be—besides, he had her contained now and she was obviously smarting. But he could not fathom she would have any part of urging an attempt on his life!

"Yes, fine," he managed. "Sit, Master Putnam, and let me hear all you know so I can plan. And, if this threat proves true, I cannot thank you enough."

"I do all for love of the king, even as you, my Lord Spencer. No need to thank me. No need at all."

Chapter Nine

The next day, Nick had Percy Putnam carry word to Wat Milford that Nick was riding to the inn alone that night. Percy himself embellished the story to include the detail that Nick was intending to seduce Rosalind.

Percy was pleased with himself. Although he had every intention of ruining and disposing of Nick, he did not want that honor to go to Wat. He would not allow Nick to become a martyr for the king's causes, or for the king to send more forces here to rout out insurrection and get in his way. His scheme was to pull Nick down at the same time that he ruined Rosalind and Deal. But he saw that for now he must worm his way into Nick's trust, just as he had done with the people of Deal.

Once again he was acting with Thomas Cromwell's knowledge and approval. His master had never liked the way his majesty favored Spencer and was most annoyed to hear from Percy that Nick intended to try to get Deal a market license the next time he saw the king. That would have a wretched impact on Cromwell's covert control of the market at Sandwich, which was feathering his nest for the future.

So Nick rode into Wat's trap, but only after Stephen Delancey and sixteen handpicked men had secreted themselves in the woods of the vale at dusk. They snagged Wat easily before the fishing lines he strung across the path could harm Nick. The fish-gutting knife in Wat's belt was evidence enough for Nick to believe all Percy Putnam had told him.

By midnight Nick and Captain Delancey had begun to interrogate Wat none too gently. But they made little headway and, exhausted themselves, tossed him in the dungeon for the night.

"You sorry bastard! You have usurped the honor of being our first guest," Nick accused, as he glared at the stunned but defiant Wat through the small grate in his cell. "I had expected to see the French foe here first, but being English, you are a viler enemy. A fellow countryman's rebellion against the rightful powers of his king is treason. Even if you will not admit it, I now know who is the leader of this villainous band of smugglers. I can only hope you have not been passing information to the French as well."

"Lord Spencer!" Wat roared as Nick turned away. "What you asked about Mistress Rosalind, whether she had knowledge of anything, I deny it again!"

Nick peered back into the cell so new it had not gone dank yet. But it breathed out a chill that would soon cool this man's passion and his courage. "But of course you would deny she has knowledge of your smuggling band, you poor wretch. You admitted you love the little deceiver. And no doubt you would do anything she said, included dispense with the king's lord lieutenant who is here to crush your smuggling."

"No!" Wat shouted as Nick walked away. "The only one who had a hint of my plot to snare you was Master Putnam, not Rosalind!"

Nick grabbed the rungs of the iron ladder and started out of the dungeon. The poor wretch protested just a bit too much about Rosalind, he fumed. Wat had claimed that his attempt to waylay Nick had everything to do with protecting her honor and nothing to do with protecting any smuggling. More than anything Wat had said or not said, the man's admission that he had loved Rosalind for years angered Nick the most. That, too, Wat claimed she did not know and never should. Nick pitied the man so for his unrequited love that he felt no need to tell her Wat's tormented secret. Nick had no doubt a man far gone on Rosalind would take terrible risks: his own passions had been strung to the breaking point these past weeks, just from the necessity of dealing with her.

Then, too, Wat's claims that Master Putnam had urged him on as well as just set the trap fed Nick's growing unease about Putnam. Nick knew Putnam would claim Wat was lying. But the more he observed the king's revenue man, the less he liked him. And yet he obviously owed the man his life. If Putnam were not on Nick's side, he would have surely let Wat kill him.

All that aside, Nick felt he had to hear from Rosalind's lips that she had no part in this plot against his life. But then, whether he judged she lied or told the truth, he did not know what he would do next with her.

He emerged from the dungeon and strode toward the small stable inside the castle walls. He ordered Raven saddled and rode out again, heading for Rosalind and the confrontation he had been both dreading and desiring for weeks.

Rosalind was dreaming of Nick again. They were at sea in a great storm, swept around and around in crashing circles. Then she and Nick were pulled this way and that by black, cresting waves, apart, then together. They held to each other, then were ripped from each other's arms again. Her cork belt did not save her—nothing did.

Meg went by, calling out for Franklin. "I will wed him no matter what, matter what.... You love a king's man, too." Her voice resounded in Rosalind's ears through the shriek of wind.

Wat and Percy Putnam flowed past, then the king himself, tugging at Nick before Rosalind managed to grab him again.

"I hate you, hate you!" she tried to tell the king, to tell Nick, but water filled her mouth, choking back those last words. She was terrified she would drown; she was drowning in her desire for Nick. He clamped her to him, his strong legs separating hers until she wrapped them around his waist for dear life. And then they moved together in the ebb and flow of eternal tides and tempest—

She sat bolt upright in bed. She had thrashed the bedclothes to wild waves around her. The nightmare had awakened her. No, something else. She heard a horse's hoofbeats so close, so fast. Outside her window? She cowered in bed as the knock sounded on her windowsill.

Rap, rap, pause, rap, rap.

She had told her men never to use that signal again. Still, what other did they have if there was a crisis? She leaped from bed and ran to the window to pull aside the curtain. A big form stood silhouetted in moon glow. Wat, Hal or Alf? Nick? It could not be Nick!

"Open this damned window, or I will break it in!"

Nick and none other!

She stood like a sleepwalker, her heart thudding. She opened the casement just a crack. "You! Go away! It's the middle of the night. I shall still be here in the morning, rotting and cursing you yet under your blasted arrest!"

"No better time for a smuggler. I am surprised you were not sitting up until you heard from your accomplice, though we have detained him late."

"What? Nick, go around to the front door if you must. I shall dress and let you in."

"I do not want everyone aroused and underfoot if I have to haul you off! Now open this farther," he insisted, and like a night thief put his gloved hands on the casement to pull it wide.

As he clambered in, she ran back to pull another garment over her night rail. She had barely donned her robe when he thudded down to the floor. He strode over to seize her, his hands hard on her shoulders. He dragged her back to the window where moonlight poured in on them both. His big hand seized her chin and tipped her head back.

"Did you know of Wat's plan to kill me!"

She gulped night air. She grabbed his arms for support. "Wat? Kill you? No—I—"

He nodded, and his tense body seemed to slump. "I shall hope that for once you are not lying. I did not think you were quite so stupid."

"About Wat—you must be wrong. There is some misunderstanding. Wat would never—"

"Have you seen him privily since we returned from France?"

"Cannot the guards you have set to breathing down my neck answer that?"

"I want not more questions, but answers! I want to hear it from your lips."

"No, I haven't seen him privily, though he delivered barrels of ale here off and on. We chatted with your guard hanging between us, as you no doubt know!"

"Have you sent secret word to him?"

"I sent word to all my friends through my family that I was fine, despite your unjust keeping of me here like some dog in a kennel. He tried to kill you? How?"

"He set a trap in the vale to trip my horse and then planned to cut my throat."

She shook her head to clear it. Trip his horse... Some memory she could not quite place from her childhood, of a tripped horse and a screaming injured boy here at the inn, darted through her thoughts and then was gone. She shook her head again. He loosed his grip on her chin at last.

"But why?" she asked. "I cannot believe it. Where is he now?"

"Cooling his heels in the castle dungeon until his interrogation begins anew on the morrow, and then who knows what we shall discover."

"You have not tortured him!"

"That is the crown's concern. Of course, you would believe it of me! *I* at least want to believe your innocence in this latest plot, but *you* believe I would torture a man first thing to wring from him the truth—or lies like yours."

"I am not lying!"

"You lied about loving me. A woman who loves a man trusts him and shares what she can to help him."

"And a man who cares enough for a woman to bed her joyfully does not try to hurt and destroy her and those she cares for in turn. Please let me go."

"I am afraid not, Rosalind."

She tried to back away from him, but he only propelled her faster. His grip tightened. Her thighs hit the side of her mattress, and he tumbled them back on it. His sword hilt pressed against her hip. She froze, so afraid of what he might do and she might do in response. This close, with his hands hard on her, she admitted to herself that, despite everything, she had missed him. Missed him and longed for him, however much she detested him.

"You and I know all about torture and lies, don't we, sweetheart?" he goaded, his breath scalding her throat.

"Never call me that again. I don't know what you mean. May I visit Wat? He has no family. May I take him a hot meal at least?"

"You indeed know all about torture and lies," he repeated as he tried to seize control of his temper. He fought to ignore her concern for Wat. He almost told her then that Wat claimed he had adored her for years. But again he sympathized with the lout for that, and held his tongue.

With one big hand, Nick pinned her free hand over her head. With the other, he opened her robe. She held her breath and went absolutely still. She longed to kiss him, to throw her arms around him, but she would not give him that satisfaction. He placed his hand on her flat belly and slid it slowly up, over her rib cage, up the swell and crest of her breasts where her nipples leaped erect at his touch. Through the thin linen of the single garment, he flicked his thumb across one peak gone hard as an acorn as he spoke again.

"No, you may not visit Wat in his cell, and I warn you not to disobey. I do not wish to be forced to put you in a cell of your own. As for the hot meal for my prisoner, no, but you may deliver one to me at sunset on the morrow, for we have much to discuss. Will you do as I command without a fuss, or shall I take you with me now?"

He could feel her heartbeat under his hand. He cupped the fullness of her breast, molding it, longing to bury his face against it. He held himself rigid, fearing one movement from her in either rage or tenderness and he would be lost. Then he would show her how desperately he had missed her and still desired her. He longed for her under him, opened to him, telling him she loved him and wanted him again.

"I have no choice but to agree," she whispered when he had almost forgotten his command. Bitter jealousy bit at him at the thought that she cared deeply for Wat, that she admired him. Though whether as friend, neighbor, lover, fellow smuggler... Damn, he did not know. But *he* wanted her admiration. He wanted her so badly in so many ways that it scared him spineless. Quickly, before he revealed his feelings, he got off the bed and turned away.

"The guard will bring you to me at sunset," he said crisply, though his breathing still seemed labored. "And you are yet under arrest here until that time."

She turned only her eyes to watch him climb out the window. His sword caught and he had to come back in and start out again. He cursed. Ordinarily, she would have laughed, but she feared if she so much as moved, he would come back and she would cling to him and cry and mayhap even tell him all about the Rosies and beg for his mercy. His mercy and his kisses and his touch. How had this happened to her, this growing web of danger and deceit? And worse, to love the very spider who lured her deeper and deeper in.

She listened to him ride away. Cool air was swirling in through the open window casement and drying her feverish warmth. He had dared to use the Rosies' knock. With poor Wat his prisoner, she feared it was the beginning of the end for them. She had seen the king's concept of justice once when their boats were destroyed; she shuddered to think of what could be the price this time. But she saw no alternative but to fight Nick and the king. She had no fear, no matter what they did to Wat in the dark depths of that dungeon, that he would give one thing away. So it was still her burden to find a path out of this predicament. She must get all those in Deal who depended on her through the coming winter and beyond.

Unsteady on her feet, she went to close and latch the window. She leaned her forehead on the cool glass. She still tingled in every place Nick had touched her and throbbed in one place that he had not, curse her weak woman's body. She sobbed once before she regained control, but tears tracked down her cheeks. Wrapped in her robe, her legs trembling, she stared out long into the moonlit back gardens, trying to harden her heart against the enemy she knew she loved.

In his bustling suite of rooms at Hampton Court Palace, one floor above his majesty's rooms, Thomas Cromwell worked steadily through stacks of documents and met briefly with various visitors and informants. Yet all the while he listened, read, conferred and spit out orders, his thoughts were on something else—the latest epistle he had received from his eyes and ears in Kent, Percival Putnam. He had no doubt the man was loyal, slavishly so. And his latest message warmed Cromwell's heart.

Putnam claimed Nicholas Spencer was not true to the task with which his monarch had entrusted him. Spencer had secretly taken a paramour, Putnam claimed, a woman quite unsuitable and suspicious in her dealings. Though she might know a great deal about the smuggling there, Spencer had not interrogated her, but had instead closeted her away from other men for his own devices. And he had left the castle the king had sent him to oversee for a three-day tryst with her somewhere in France.

In France, Cromwell mused, as a hint of what some might call a smile crimped the corners of his mouth. Judas Priest, in Catholic, enemy France where who knew what machinations might be going on. Men sneaking off to France on privy business these days took great risks, so Putnam need not have underlined the words *in France.* Did the crippled little revenue man think he was dealing with some rural dolt here? That handsome, arrogant dog Spencer would never have been disloyal to the king's causes, but that wasn't the point. All Cromwell needed—and Putnam knew this well—was the mere appearance of deceit.

Putnam had also stated that Spencer was being soft on a smuggler he held—held, thanks to Putnam's maneuverings—because the prisoner had been the woman's former lover! This woman of Spencer's must be exceptional then, Cromwell thought, if she could protect her past lover thus when most men would be all too willing to rid themselves of a former lover. Before this, Spencer had ever been content to take wenches and then leave them, but this one must have her claws deep in his stubborn hide.

In France. Cromwell kept coming back to that. He had worked hard to keep his majesty hostile to France so this coming Protestant marriage would enhance Cromwell's growing power. The German bride was due to land in England somewhere in Kent near Christmastide. And Crom-

well would be furious if it were the king's ward Spencer who
was there at his new castle to greet the woman soon to be
come queen! A queen for whom, damn it all, Cromwell had
manipulated his grace's affections so he would take Anne of
Cleves to his bed and his heart. After the prolonged Boleyn
catastrophe and the loss of meek Queen Jane, his majesty
was as skittish as a colt around his first filly!

"My lord, the next report," his secretary, Lawrence, in
toned and slid yet another piece of parchment before him.

Cromwell skimmed it, yet he could not help but relish
again the implications of Putnam's epistle. Yes, Cromwell
would like nothing more than to rid the king of one more
royal adviser, just the way he had rid him of Cardinal Wol
sey and that rapacious clan of Boleyns and Norfolks. Surely
with Putnam's help, he could devise a way to make his grace
believe that his man Spencer was dealing with the French
foe! Many jealous courtiers would rejoice at Spencer's fall,
though not as many as would cheer if great Cromwell him
self went down, he mused smugly.

"But we shall see, we shall see," Cromwell muttered.
Though Putnam's fawning had both amused and annoyed
him in the past, perhaps if he used the man well, he could
ruin Spencer and yet earn credit with the king for wiping out
that band of smugglers. After all, anything an Englishman
did privily in France in these times could be construed as
treason!

"Lawrence, sit and take a letter," he commanded. And
he used to think it such a pity, Cromwell mused, that his
sending men the king knew nothing about to stave in Deal
boats at Putnam's request had not stopped the smuggling.
Now he knew it was fated that when the Deal smugglers
were smashed, Nicholas Spencer would be, too!

He shoved the other documents aside and fished out
Putnam's letter again. He began to dictate to his secretary.

To the king's revenue and excise agent, Percival Putnam, in Sandwich, Kent:
The contents of this missive are to be kept covert knowledge until the time is ripe just after Christmastide. Then the new queen will have safely arrived on our shores and will have been royally wedded and bedded. Meanwhile, your instructions are as follows....

Nick had written to the king at Hampton Court Palace to inform him that he would be honored and pleased to fulfill a royal request tendered as a personal favor. As lord lieutenant of Deal castle, he would greet the future queen here and escort her to his majesty at Greenwich Palace when she arrived next month near Yule. Reading between the lines of Henry Tudor's letter, Nick had discerned his majesty was a nervous bridegroom, albeit that it was for the fourth time. What a woman could do to a man's resolve, even if he was the king, he fumed. However, he had assured the king that most of the castle would be complete when Anne of Cleves arrived. Even better, though he would wait to give a full report until he saw the king at Greenwich, he vowed to him that the band of slippery smugglers would be under his control by then.

"They must be!" Nick muttered as he paced back and forth in his small chill chamber waiting for Rosalind to arrive with the meal he had commanded. "They must be!"

The fire in the small hearth did little to warm these stone-walled rooms when the wind whipped off the sea from the northeast this way. Nick only hoped it was seeping into the dungeon to cool Wat, too. Grudgingly, he admired the strength, stamina and loyalty of the man. For hours today the big brute had stood, trussed like a pig for the spit, and refused to talk. Nick's and Delancey's questions about smuggling and trafficking with Frenchmen all went for naught. In a rage, Nick had thrown him back in his cell and sent Delancey and some men to break open every barrel at the brewery. They might turn up some hidden booty, and he'd have Master Milford then! But the threat of that had not made Wat blink an eye, so Nick had ordered Delancey to fetch Rosalind to him in a loud enough voice for Wat to hear. *That* had had the bastard pounding on his door and howling as they left him in the dark.

Delancey knocked on the door and escorted Rosalind in. She wore a moss-hued cloak that made her eyes look more green than gray, Nick thought. But her gaze was still storm-tossed as she glared at him. She carried a basket covered by a cloth; the smell of bread and meat made his nostrils flare. He felt a wave of pure pleasure sweep through him. For once she had apparently obeyed him to the letter. If only that luck would hold! He tried not to show that he was thrilled to see her, but he was so happy to find she had come without a fuss that he felt like a simpleton with a sweet.

"Find anything in your search?" he asked Delancey, forcing himself to frown.

"Nothing in the empty barrels but bugs and dirt, and nothing in the heavy ones but ale, my lord."

Nick saw Rosalind could hold her tongue and temper no longer.

"You are just like your king, Lord Spencer!" she exploded. "Not only unjustly accusing folks of smuggling, but breaking everything you can to ruin their honest livelihood. Three years ago it was our fishing and rescue boats, and now an innocent laborer's ale barrels!"

"Innocent of smuggling goods in his barrels, mayhap, but I could hang him yet for his plot to murder me. And I know about the boats being staved in years ago, but surely that was some mistake."

"Indeed it was!" she flared, intentionally misunderstanding him.

"That will be all, Captain," Nick said, fighting to keep calm. It was obvious her obedience to his orders had not been bred of a contrite heart or sweet temper. And it most annoyed him that she had once again defended Wat. Meanwhile, Delancey nodded and closed the door to leave them alone.

Nick went instantly on the offensive. Leaning against the table with his arms crossed on his chest, he leveled a hard look at her. "What would you say if I told you Wat had confessed to being part of a smuggling ring your father headed once and you head now?" he said, drawing his bow at a venture.

He watched her eyes widen. Her high color, set aflame by sea wind and anger, drained from her face. She set her basket on the table.

"Why, I would say either you lie or he did," she said. "And I must tell you, all that unkegged ale will go to waste if you do not rescind your earlier order that patrons of the Rose and Anchor be kept to four mugs daily."

"Ever adept at shifting topics, aren't you? I shall send my men back on the morrow to put the lids back on. So, what have you brought me there? Shall we sup together before our further business?"

Rosalind trembled at his accusations, his implications—and his mere presence in this place. But she had to keep her wits about her. Still, that did not mean she must abandon the use of her temper against him, nor her attempt to match his quicksilver moods. But her heart pounded in her breast at the thought that Wat must have told Nick something that made him come ever closer to the truth about her father's band of smugglers that was now her own.

Slowly, to steady herself for what came next, she set the food before him: two half-moon-shaped chicken and turnip pastries, a half loaf of fresh bread, cheese, butter, honey. He sat across from her—smugly, she thought. This time, she vowed, he would be the fly caught in her web!

"Of course," she dared, "you'll have me taste each thing to be certain I mean not to poison you."

She bit her lower lip so as not to reveal she enjoyed the worried look that sprang to his face. Had the blackguard not considered that?

"Here," she said and took back from him the pie she had put on his pewter plate, "now, let me see." She plunged her spoon in it and took a bite. A succulent odor escaped with a puff of steam and gravy.

"Mmm," she muttered, "not poison, mayhap, but hardly worthy of you. This is the sort of thing we stupid, rustic folk of Deal would eat, not the king's lord lieutenant. Oh, dear, and the same is true with this town-baked bread and foul country cheese, nothing like what you favor at court, of course. And who knows, since some of the townsfolk are ever close to starving with no king's market here, some of this might have gone bad on its way from the Sandwich market or somehow been imported from enemy France. Food of rural louts like Wat and me is worth naught for the likes of a king's man!"

"Ro—sa—lind!" he began, his voice first wary, then threatening.

"And so," she went on, "I shall just dispose of it before it taints you, as having to live among all of us has no doubt done!"

She managed to grab most of the food before he could react. Running to the single window, she shoved the casement wide and heaved the food out, plates and all. Somewhere below, pewter clattered against stone and someone yelped. Oh, saints, she cursed silently, she had not meant to toss the plates, too, but this man forever enraged her. She must have hit the castle laborer she had bribed to salvage what he could under the window. Even to best Nick Spencer, she had not been able to bear the thought of wasting food with such hard times coming for Deal this winter.

She had expected Nick to yank her back, to shout or yell. Instead, he stood gaping at her, his face crimson with fury, his fists clenched stiffly at his sides.

"There," she said, wiping her hands on the linen napkin she had brought. "Deal food might have done for the likes of poor Wat, but not the lofty lord lieutenant."

"Are you quite finished with that protest?" he demanded through gritted teeth. "I swear it shall be your last. Come over here."

She walked slowly toward him, but on the far side of the table. "I said *here!*" he repeated.

She circled the table and strolled closer, anxious now as he took a scroll from the small desk behind him. Her heart, still thudding from her show of defiance, began to thunder even harder. An arrest warrant for her? Orders for Wat's execution? Percy Putnam had been whispering in town that this was imminent, although he had also vowed he would write the king himself to plead for his life.

"What is that?" she managed, but her voice squeaked.

"A list of the men in town who will also be under arrest in their homes until someone admits to the truth," he informed her.

He handed her the scroll. She unrolled it. It rustled loudly in the room, silent but for the crackle of the small hearth fire. She gasped when she saw the long list of names—most of the men in the town! Granted, many of them had helped somehow with the smuggling, but they were hardly all Rosies. Yet, as far as she could tell at first glance, Nick had gone overboard. He had included every man strong enough to pull an oar or lift a box.

She did not dare meet his eyes. "It's absurd and unjust. Townsfolk will starve without men to work. Am I supposed to believe that, under duress, Wat named nearly the entire male population of Deal?"

"I am saying that *I*, under duress, have named them as perpetual patrons of your inn, that suspected hotbed of sedition and smuggling. They may ply their legal trades by day, but the streets will be guarded by night, and they will stay home. Any man caught abroad after sundown will join Wat permanently in the dungeon.''

''But the names of men who saved your life and the lives of your soldiers are here! You ingrate!''

He seized her wrists, and the scroll rattled closed between them. ''Then help me, Rosalind. Help me get to the bottom of this before the odds and punishments escalate!''

She gaped at him. She felt torn in two. True, he had not ripped these men from their families or arrested them for smuggling without proof, as the king's warrant certainly allowed him to do. But his action would stop the free trading, for without these men she could never manage alone to handle a haul, even one delivered to their doorstep by the French. And it would also mean worse times than usual for Deal this winter. Already fishing weather had turned risky. Bitter days with food supplies miles away down rutted, wintry roads in Sandwich always meant hard cold weeks of gaunt-faced children. Each winter, Rosalind doled out coins she had hoarded during the year, but without even a sporadic smuggling trade to keep them going through the cold months, extra food supplies would be unavailable.

''Well?'' Nick's stern voice slashed through her agonizing. His eyes were slitted and cold as steel. She felt she faced a barrage of weapons, as if she were trying to take this very castle. A chill of foreboding raced up her backbone, but it stiffened her resolve. Surely, there was no way to help him without consigning herself, the Rosies and the town to certain destruction.

''What is there for me to say, my lord? You once vowed to me you wanted to strengthen little Deal, but now you ruin her. I would like to leave now. I think there is nothing left between us.''

That parting declaration angered and hurt him more than anything she had ever said or done. Another outburst of her temper would have been better than this demeanor of resigned defeat. She dropped the scroll on the table and took her empty basket with her to the door. He moved quickly to hold it closed when she lifted the latch.

"Nothing left?" he challenged. "What about our feelings for each other? The way you respond when I touch you?"

He wanted to sweep her into his fierce embrace and kiss her so hard he would leave his imprint on her very flesh. He wanted to delve into her clever brain and demand of her stubborn heart that she trust him. He wanted to force her to admit she loved him and to mean it, too, but he knew better than to risk all that.

And so he slowly placed his open hands on the door on either side of her head. Gently he pushed back her hood. He felt drunk with her very presence. Her eyes widened; he could see his image in their gray-green depths. Neither of them breathed. Her lower lip trembled. He stepped carefully closer, not to press her to the door, though she pressed there herself. He barely touched her. But he prayed desperately she would find a way to help him. He did not want to be forced to destroy all she loved.

Rosalind felt suspended in time and space. She should push him back, flee from him. She should step on his foot or knee him, or— But she could not. She realized, with the sudden stunning impact of a blow, how alike they were, despite their oft-declared enmity. Granted, he was orderly and disciplined; she more—well, casual and carefree. But they both were fiercely loyal to what they believed in and to the folk who trusted them. Worlds apart as their pasts might be, could not their futures somehow blend in peace? But she knew the answer. Even as she yearned for that, it could not be.

Still, she savored the scent of him as he stood so close; she drowned in the leather aroma and smell of sweet cloves he often chewed. She could only relish his nearness, his strength, this fierce power that leaped and arched between them like summer lightning on the sea. And she would cherish this tenderness that he sometimes showed.

He moved so slowly closer that the tips of their noses touched, then brushed. He slanted his head to caress her slightly parted lips with his. So soft, so sleek, she thought. His breath burned her cheek. His tongue teased and tantalized. She breathed out in a great sigh as she responded by opening her mouth to his skilled ministrations. But the kiss lasted only a moment. As his lips withdrew she stood frozen like a statue against the door, mourning the end of all they had shared.

"*That* will always be between us," he whispered, "whatever I must do to you or to this town to stop the smugglers and ensure the safety of the castle here."

Dazed, she nodded. She understood his plight, but it only made things doubly worse that he, too, was torn and would yet fight on. Somehow, this felt like farewell. She stepped aside as he opened the door for her, his wrist just grazing her hip.

"Captain!" he called. "Escort Mistress Barlow back to the Rose and Anchor, where she will remain under arrest from dark to dawn. During the day, with an escort, she may go about the town to visit friends."

Rosalind's mouth dropped open in surprise before she thought to close it. He was putting her on the same terms as the men. She was grateful for the new freedom, but she realized he might just be giving her more rope to hang herself. Hang herself, as Percy had implied Nick might do with Wat. Oh, damn this man!

Her basket on her arm, she turned away to follow Captain Delancey out of the maze of halls into the cold night outside.

At the last moment, on a blustery morning in mid-December, Rosalind agreed to stand up with her sister at her wedding. She had apologized days ago for trying to come between her and the man she loved. She had found the strength to give the wedding her blessing, no matter how she herself hurt inside—and still mistrusted any king's man. But for Meg's sake, she would make an exception and be kind to Franklin. After all, a master mason was more like an artist, someone free-spirited who could break away from the king, whereas a soldier did naught but take Horrid Harry's orders. Yes, Franklin could be family, but never Nick.

"Meg, please do not cry on your special day!" Rosalind pleaded as she and Aunt Bess helped her dress.

"But, oh, Ros, I'm so happy now that you'll not only be there, but stand up to support me! And to Aunt Bess for giving us her chamber until we can find a place in town. I cannot thank you both enough!"

"You'll be a better supporter for her, Rosalind," Aunt Bess chimed in. "My old legs could not take all that standing on that cold stone floor!"

Aunt Bess blotted the bride's face again as Rosalind laced the embroidered pale blue brocade gown up her back. At first Rosalind had refused to attend because she'd made such a firm stand against the family ever so much as... as mingling with a king's man. Then she had said she'd go, but could not stand up with Meg. But now, as hopelessly in love as she was with Nick, who was much closer to the king than Franklin Stanway was, she recognized her own hypocrisy.

The fact that Nick would be in attendance had held her back at first. She could not bear the thought of standing up with Meg while his eyes bored into her back from the congregation. Although he should have been hated in town since the house arrests, it was clear the Deal citizens had come to feel a grudging respect. These past few weeks had been a battle of wills, a stalemate, as he waited for someone in Deal to crack or misstep. Still, nobody, not Wat, not any of the other townspeople and especially not Rosalind Barlow, was giving in to the king's lord lieutenant!

By the saints, Rosalind vowed to herself, she would not allow her painful love for him to affect her manner. She would just be civil to him at the church and at the wedding breakfast here at the inn, but not allow one moment when they could talk privily! Just as she had done these past few weeks, she would keep herself busy. It was best for everyone if she never had a moment alone with him again!

Bundled up in cloaks and blankets, the little party was driven into town in the inn's wagon. As they passed Milford's brewery, Rosalind hardened her heart against Nick again. Poor Wat was rotting in a cold dungeon while his friends attended a wedding! But life must go on, she told herself. Even if the French attacked, even when Nick left the area someday, even if he never so much as touched her with desire again—that was obviously all it had been with him, desire—life would go on.

At the little gray Norman church of St. Leonard, Franklin came out to greet them and help them all down. The love for his bride that shone in his face made Rosalind blink back tears. Inside, she shook the faint dusting of snow from her cape and stamped her booted feet to keep warm.

The moment she took Meg's hand to wait in the vestibule with her, she came face-to-face with Nick Spencer, where he leaned an elbow on a carved stone tomb that served as a Rosies' drop. It was still stuffed with bottles of French brandy and Spanish cutlery, if he would but shove aside the heavy lid of the sarcophagus to look. Surely the reason she blushed hot was at the memory of Alf dropping an entire case of brandy here on these flagstones. Rather than lose it all, they had taken off their shoes and scooped up what they could to drink it quickly. How their giggles had echoed off the vaulted ceilings in that week before Nick came and all their new troubles began!

The memory heated her blood, but his fine appearance did even more to her. He was elegantly garbed all in black, with silver slashings in his velvet doublet. His cape lay neatly over one arm. A jaunty black velvet cap flaunting a large topaz perched on his sleek ebony hair. He looked a bit on edge, too, as he tugged up his big-cuffed leather gloves, then whacked the other hand between each finger as if the custom-sewn leather would dare gape away from his skin.

"Good day, Mistress Barlow."

She barely inclined her head. "My Lord Spencer. I am sure your master mason is grateful you could take time to attend."

"He had better," Meg put in with a nervous little laugh. "Lord Spencer is Franklin's supporter, just as you are mine. Oh, Ros, there is the sign we should go in!"

Rosalind had no time to react to that new bombshell. Aunt Bess thrust in her nieces' hands small ribboned bunches of holly mingled with red-orange bittersweet. With a little push from Meg, Rosalind preceded her sister up the aisle. Franklin and Nick had hurried around the perimeter of the small sanctuary and awaited the two women before the draped altar; the minister stood ready. How could Meg have been so muddle-headed as to have forgotten to warn her that she and Nick would both be supporters? Rosalind seethed.

As she turned to face Nick at the altar, everything else blurred for her: the radiant bride and groom, the holy words, Aunt Bess's sniffles, the shaft of sun that slanted through the blue-and-red stained-glass windows to drench the wedding party in royal purple.

For Rosalind, as if in a dream, there was only Nick. Nick, staring at her. Nick, so tall and handsome, yet stern. Nick, the man she longed so to hate but could only love.

"With this ring as a token of unbroken love..." The minister's words broke into her thoughts.

Strangely, then, the words that came next to mind were from Franklin's poem that Meg had shared with her but two months ago: "Yet when I breathe the air you do, my hands and heart doth tremble too. But when your smile says I belong, then my weakness makes me strong."

Rosalind was jolted back to reality. She found herself staring at Nick's firmly chiseled lips; no smile there. But his eyes, directed wickedly sideways, slowly perused her, toes to knees to waist to breasts. Next, to her blushing face, to her hair, swept up in coils and ringlets. From the corner of her eye, she forced herself to meet his dark brown stare unblinking. Then, his eyes meandered again.

"My hands and heart doth tremble too," she seemed to whisper her own vows in her heart. Well, she thought, when had she ever backed down from a game the blackguard played? She would see if her weakness would not yet make her strong against him!

So, brazenly, apparently disdainfully, she let her eyes study him, polished boots to winking topaz jewel on his cap. His square, arrogant chin, his wide shoulders and strong chest, tapering to hard ribs and flat waist and narrow hips that flared to powerful thighs. The slanting steel of his silver ceremonial sword glittering amethyst in the window lights. The black velvet codpiece mounted at the juncture of his long legs. Her mind skipped to their passionate bouts in Boulogne. She remembered where she was and flushed hotter yet.

"And so, by God's great might and the king's good grace, I do solemnly pronounce that Franklin Stanway and Margaret Deland are man and wife together," the minister intoned. "My good man, you may kiss your bride."

Franklin beamed, and Meg cried again. They kissed long and lustily. Radiant, linking arms, they turned and exited down the aisle before Rosalind realized she and Nick were to follow suit in the progression. He extended his arm to her. With so many of the townsfolk's eyes on them, she almost refused. But for the sake of Meg—and her husband, Franklin—she placed her gloved fingers lightly on Nick's arm and, head held high, accompanied him out.

Suddenly, all the way down the aisle, as witless as the idea was, she wanted this for herself—with Nick. She and Murray had wed here once, but had she ever really chosen Murray, or had Murray chosen her? No, they had wed because it seemed the natural thing to do; they had had no barriers to surmount. What would it take, her thoughts tormented her, for her and Nick to wed? They would have to fight for their love, to choose it, to prove it. Unthinkable! She would never wed again. Her only vows now must be to do anything she could to help Deal survive this coming brutal winter. She must be strong until Nick would leave and there would be better times. Still, she could not help crying when she saw Meg's joyous face.

To Rosalind's relief Nick and Captain Delancey stopped only briefly at the wedding breakfast at the inn—barely long enough for Nick's bridal toast and his gift of a pouch of coins to the beaming couple. He bade Franklin and Meg farewell and kissed the bride briefly on the cheek. His gaze caught Rosalind's from the door; when she stiffly stood her ground across the room, he touched his hat and departed. But where she should have felt relieved, she only felt even emptier.

After folks had drifted off to get home before sundown, she helped Aunt Bess and her cousins' wives straighten the inn. With a final farewell, Meg and Franklin went off giggling to Aunt Bess's chamber. Nick was giving Franklin only one day away from the castle, Meg had said. There was an even harder push on to complete as much as possible before someone special came near Yuletide. If it were King Horrid Harry himself, Rosalind vowed, she would seek him out to say exactly what she thought of him and his lord lieutenant!

The Christmas season was but a week away, she realized with surprise as she glanced at Meg and Franklin's closed door, sighed and went into her own chamber across the hall.

And a bitter holiday it would be, too. Nick's presence here and now his containment of the Rosies would force her to dig to the very bottom of her dwindling reserves.

She recalled Nick's threat, "Any man caught abroad after sundown will join Wat permanently in the dungeon." Several men had volunteered to risk defying his edict, especially since Rosalind had received word from their contact in the market in Sandwich that Pierre was coming next week with a big shipment from Boulogne. How she would love to find a way to receive and sell those goods! That would surely earn them enough to scrape through until good fishing weather. Then, mayhap Nick would be called away or be more lenient when he had turned up nothing after so long. She'd like to find a way to pull off one more free-trading delivery right under his damned nose!

A rap, rap sounded somewhere. She jumped to her feet. Someone at the window? Her heart raced as she hurried over, but no one was there. Light snow sifted on the sill outside. Thud, thud, it came again. At her door! She peered out into the hall, but no one was there. And then she knew—thud, thud—what the sound was. She wilted back inside and quietly closed her door.

Thud, thud. The rhythmic sound reverberated through the floor under her stocking feet. It echoed in her brain in her memories. Meg and Franklin were thumping their bed across the hall as they loved. Meg and her king's man. Loving wildly the way she and Nick had done, but would never do again.

Like the young girl she had been once, the one without a care in the world, Rosalind ran to her bed and threw herself upon it. She held her pillow to her ears to block out the thud, thud. But she yearned so for Nick here to hold her that her heart soon outdid the noise the lovers were making, thudding far, far into the winter night.

Chapter Ten

Rosalind was desperate. So desperate, she was going to take the chance of her life. It was the only way she could see to get the many folks dependent on the Rosies' free trading through the winter. It would keep Pierre from getting caught. And that was important, for not only did she like the Frenchman, but with him a prisoner, Nick would have one more card in his hand toward proving smuggling—her smuggling. If she went down to the beach to meet Pierre when he arrived from Boulogne, she could warn him to lie low after this haul. And, outfoxing Nick Spencer would be reward in itself!

Surely her plan was brazen enough that Nick would never catch her and her cohorts. But if he did, he could not throw women in the dungeon. His warrant posted on the town commons declared that any *man*, not woman, caught abroad after sunset would be imprisoned. Not a group of wives, widows and mothers. If discovered waiting on the beach, they could claim to be rescuers. Rosalind would explain she and the seven others whose help she had enlisted were there for good reason. After all, one woman had seen a boat that might be in need of valiant rescue. What else could they do but go to the shore secretly to help salvage lives and goods? Thanks to the king's lord lieutenant's detaining them in their homes at night, the men of Deal who had saved his own life were no longer allowed to save others!

Rosalind knew by now that Nick had a man posted at the other end of the escape tunnel, so her band of women dared not leave the inn that way. She had supposedly invited the selected women to her chamber for a private Yule celebration on this night of December twenty-third, because their men were homebound. They would change their attire here, then go right out the front door of the inn as if they were departing patrons before they melted into the vale to reassemble on the beach. Several additional women were staying behind for a diversion, but the others had brought, secreted in a basket, man's garb, which they would wear for protection against the winter winds. Now, the only thing left was for Aunt Bess to lure Nick's guard away from her door in the hall.

It was not long before Rosalind, trying to encourage sounds of a happy gathering with her ear pressed to the door, heard her aunt's voice just outside.

"Oh, my good man, I've hurt my ankle. Please, could you help me into my niece Meg's chamber here—I don't want to disturb Mistress Rosalind with her guests.... It's so tender, I can hardly put weight on it, but if you'll just help me to sit down over there... Oh, I can't thank you enough...."

"Shh!" Rosalind hissed to the women.

"You know, Mistress Bess, my mother's about your age," she heard the guard say as his voice faded.

Our first little victory of many this night! Rosalind rejoiced. Aunt Bess's successful ploy was a good sign. Nick might have forbidden her guards to help her at household tasks—even the decking of the inn for Christmas—but he had not said they could not help Aunt Bess!

Rosalind peeked out into the temporarily deserted hall. "Now!" she whispered and beckoned with her hand. She nodded farewell to the four women who would stay behind to make some noise. Quick as lightning, the others fell into the rank and file they had arranged. They were out into the hall and through the common room before the guard managed to help Aunt Bess to the farthest chair in Meg and Franklin's room.

Outside, ice pellets smacked Rosalind; cold air bit deep into her lungs. Grass crunched underfoot as she strode away from the inn behind the others. She would have loved to take Chestnut from the stables but dared not. It was enough of a gamble that Aunt Bess's plea to the guard that he not bother Rosalind to tell of her aunt's "turned" ankle would be heeded. As for returning when all was done, there would be a new guard on her door by then. She was hoping he would not know there were far fewer women inside to leave than those who had first gone in. She would climb in her own window and be visibly there to bid them farewell. But for now, she and her companions must meet the French, then unload and hide the goods. The root cellar of the abandoned fisherman's cottage on the heights would have to do as a temporary drop, and the climb would tax women's muscles sorely this night!

Down on the sleet-swept beach, things went perfectly. Pierre Lyon and his men came early. His embrace and praise urged Rosalind on as she explained their precarious plight.

"Ah, you were magnificent to dare to come to warn me now, as you did that night in Boulogne, magnificent!" he told her in French. "That frowning ogre was the king's lord lieutenant, you say! *Sacre bleu!*"

Sacre bleu, indeed, Rosalind thought, recalling full well why she had given up Pierre's French curses these past few months. She was grateful when the sleet stopped and the Frenchmen helped carry the boxes and packs of things to the edge of the beach. Then she insisted they shove off. Pierre's rough beard scraped both her cheeks as he kissed her quickly before they put out to sea.

She was relieved when the French boat was out of sight, and she hurried everyone on to the next step of their plan. She used a long piece of driftwood for a scuffler to hide tracks across the stretch of sand. The women hoisted their loads and started up the winding path to the heights. Some carried packs on previously hidden poles slung across their shoulders; others carted boxes on their backs or hanging in fishing nets between them. Rosalind hefted a heavy, hemp-covered roll of brocade. The thrill of victory coursed through her veins, making her burden seem light. She had never been prouder of the people of Deal, but dire necessity had driven them to this.

Then the sky fell.

"Halt, all of you!"

Nick! Nick here. Rosalind dropped the roll at her feet and spun to face him and the four soldiers at his back. He seemed to have sprung from the very rocks she would have liked to disappear under. A big, black cloak blew back from his shoulders like the wings of a huge owl. It was so dark she wasn't certain he recognized her yet. Her heart crashed, crashed to echo the breakers on the shore.

"Drop that booty, lads, and back down to the beach, all of you!" came Stephen Delancey's voice from up above. The women, fear on their faces, hurried back down toward Rosalind. More men's heads popped up from behind boulders, perhaps twenty of them.

Two men huddled together against the wind struck a flint and lit first one lantern, then another. Still, Rosalind stood like a statue, her feet in the sand, the roll of material leaning heavily against her legs as if to hold her there.

She knew they were caught with the goods, doomed. Too late to claim a rescue of a ship. In her desperation, she had ensnared all these dear, trusting women with her. How they must hate her now. She could think of absolutely no way out of this. There was naught to do but confess all and throw herself on Nick's mercy, hoping he might let her bear all the blame and forgive and free these others.

"I told you this continued beach watch would pay off someday, Delancey!" she heard Nick exult. He stood a bit away yet, but the sea wind carried his voice to her. "The guards may have summoned us too late to catch the French suppliers, but we made it in time to net the ones from Deal. Still, they are not the big, burly louts I was expecting," he went on as he snatched hoods and hats off the women. "These lads are lasses, men, and I have no doubt we'll find their leader here. Mistress Barlow, step forward!"

Nick's sharp eyes found the form and face he sought. He strode up the path to yank her down to the beach with him, while his men herded the others behind. Holding her arm in an iron grip, he spoke close to her face.

"Enjoying your little gathering? How did your note requesting permission read?—so you could 'share humble Yuletide gifts with poor women of the town'? But you forgot to inform me the gifts were smuggled ones from France, Mistress Barlow!

"Gather everyone around," Nick ordered, raising his voice so all could hear. "I shall only ask my questions once, and arrests will be made at the slightest hint of hesitation or defiance. I want the names of the Deal smuggling band now, or I shall assume the worst. Then your men as well as you will be in the castle dungeon within the hour!

"Mistress Barlow, I will take the first name from you, and not a man's name, is it?" Nick challenged. His voice was so smug and sure she could not stomach it. He thrust his face close to hers again; lantern light threw demonic shadows on his strong features. "Well, shall I take them all in, then?" he goaded when she just glared at him.

"Though I can name no others, I am one of the smuggling band. We merely hired these women to unload some goods this night," she admitted.

"At last," he said.

For one moment she thought she glimpsed tears shimmer in his eyes, but it must have been the wind and wet. Her limbs felt like lead; she could not have fled if her very life depended on it, as indeed mayhap it did. He would have to understand how it was for her, for the folks at Deal. But she knew she could never explain her need for revenge against the king, for Nick saw him as the very zenith of justice in the realm—and as his foster father. He had admitted to her there must have been some confusion in the king's ordering the destruction of Deal's boats once, but she could tell he would never think ill of his precious king.

"You, woman," Nick went on, pointing at Hal's wife, Hester, behind Rosalind. "The next name of a smuggler!"

"Hester Deland. Though I can name no others, I am one of the smuggling band," she said, echoing Rosalind's admission of guilt.

Nick started. He turned to Charles Seabrook's sister, Alice. She stood holding hands with Charles's wife, Clare. "You, woman, a name! A man's name!"

"I, Alice Marlow, am one of the smuggling band!" she declared, her voice trembling on the wind.

"And I, Clare Seabrook, am another!"

A chill shuddered through Rosalind. These women were standing with her! But they had so much more to lose! They had children to care for. They were tied more closely than she to endangered men. Yet they did not blame her after all, but boldly cast their lot with her! Could this desperate ruse be worth a try? She feared most of the Rosies would turn themselves in at the castle the moment they heard. But mayhap Nick's fury would be easier to quell if he could be made to believe that women were the smugglers! His warrant had said he would imprison men! But before she could decide her next move, Nick's hands clapped hard on her upper arms.

"And the leader of the criminal band?" he demanded, tipping her back so she almost lost her footing in the sand and her boots slid against his for support.

"I am leader of the Rosies, named for our favorite flower," she dared. "I alone am fully responsible, and—"

"No, I am leader of the Rosies!" Ned Stone's wife declared. "I am responsible!"

"No, I am!" Hetty Deland chimed in.

"No, I am! I am!" came the cacophony of voices behind her.

Bless these friends, her fellow townswomen, Rosalind thought, and tears stung her eyes in joy and pride. But Nick's hands tightened until her arms started to go numb.

"Finally, we shall see!" he muttered. He shouted to his men, "Get these women's names and take the lot of them to their homes with their offspring and helpmeets where they belong. They are not to leave those homes. And tell everyone, women, that Mistress Rosalind will bear all Deal's debts until each smuggler signs his own confession."

"No!" Rosalind dared to say. "No one signs confessions just to save me! Tell the town that—"

He dragged her away down the beach. His cape flapped as if to swallow her. Women cried out her name. Rosalind tried to turn back to shout more to them, but the guards held them back with pikes.

"But why would they need to save you unless you are guilty?" Nick demanded, spitting the words from the side of his mouth. "You are the only one among them in a position—and with the heritage—to lead the smuggling band. Hell's gates, do all you women think I am a dolt to believe otherwise?"

Nick pulled her on. Tears stung her eyes like sleet and she didn't even try to break his grip. She only fought to keep her feet, to keep up with the pace he set, to keep whatever shreds of sanity and courage she could salvage in her fear.

In the first cove before the town, she heard horses. Four of his men appeared, one leading Nick's big black horse.

"Go help the others with the women and the booty," he ordered the men brusquely. He lifted Rosalind sidesaddle upon his horse's broad back, then vaulted up behind her. She could see, even feel the fury in him mingled with both desperation and exultation that he had her dead to rights now.

"Give me the slightest struggle, and I'll tie you behind me like a piece of goods," Nick threatened. "A *smuggled* piece of goods."

But she was too crushed and stunned to struggle. She gripped the edge of the big saddle to hold herself away from him as his arms reached around her for the reins. Futilely, she tried to keep her hip from bouncing back into his lap as he urged the horse to a fast clip down the beach toward the looming castle. His cape clapped like thunder around them in the cold, hard wind.

"Then instead of *who,* I will ask *why,* and you will tell me at least that!" Nick roared at Rosalind amid his barrage of intimidating questions and brusque demands.

She sat on the table in his chamber at the castle where he had roughly deposited her after he carried her in over his shoulder with one hand hard on her bottom and one pinning her legs to his chest. He had been obvious about avoiding the bed, she recalled. He had paced around the table like a chained bear, leaning his fists on it either to wheedle or shout at her. She dared to sit cross-legged now in her boy's garb, hands grasping her knees. She fought to keep her back erect, her chin up, but she was wilting. All she really wanted was to collapse and cry over all the good things that had been irrevocably lost this night: freedom for the dear folk of Deal, the town's income in hard times, her quest for justice and revenge and her desire for some sort of future in Nick Spencer's arms.

She struggled to keep her temper in check through his badgering, for she feared what she would admit to him if she lost control. She wanted to plead for mercy, but she would not give the blackguard the satisfaction or the opportunity to trick her. And he would certainly mock her or use it against her if she blurted out that she loved him, as she had before. Yet that had been true, and still was, blast the man! She was proud she had told him little so far, but yes, she thought, she would indeed tell him *why*.

"Just open your eyes if you need the *why* of free trading here in Deal!" she insisted. "Tudor revenues were ever sky-high! Both royal Henrys ignored pleas to license a market for Deal. You already know this king ordered our boats staved in as 'a reward' when Deal citizens rescued his sailors with loss of their own lives. The king has taken over Deal with this fine castle of yours! Yet except for the inn, the king lets profits from maintaining this unwelcome force on our doorstep go to Sandwich!"

Nick glared at her. "Yes, there have been problems, but I weary of hearing 'the Tudors, the king'! No king made you a smuggler, Rosalind! It is against the law of the land! And you have lied to me from the first about everything, haven't you? You even told me you loved me and let me have a taste of that luscious body to deceive me—"

"I deceive you?" she interrupted. She felt the pain from *his* deceit roar out of control. She could not stem the words she said, even though she did not truly believe some of them. "Best admit your deceits here, too, my lord! You are the one who abducted me to France! You are the one who forced me to share a chamber with you there. And you are the one who bedded me cold-bloodedly to seduce from me admissions I distrusted you too much to give! In our personal dealings, you are as much to blame as I! And if you dare drag me before your precious king, I shall tell him such! At least, I would rather you torment me than seduce me. Go to the devil and your king, for however misguided I was, I detest you now!''

Nick was gasping like a fish. His face flushed hot. His fists at his side clenched, unclenched, clenched. For the first time in more than an hour he sat down hard on the chair nearest him.

He could not believe it had come to this. Nothing had ever been cold-blooded between them, at least on his part. No woman, no person, had ever made him feel more alive than Rosalind did. But this woman—*a woman,* any woman, had duped him! Him, Nick Spencer, the king's lord lieutenant! This assignment was the chance of his lifetime to advance himself and earn the king's favor so readily bestowed in his youth. But a petite, fetching, delicate-looking country wench had made—an absolute ass of him!

For weeks he had told himself no woman was clever or strong enough to be a part of a smuggling band, let alone to command one. But the clues had been legion: her inn, her contacts, her codebook, her escape tunnel, her French, the Frenchman he had seen her with on the road from Sandwich, that man who knew her in Boulogne. Still he had been so smitten by her, yet so desperate to believe he was in control of his feelings for her, that he had looked askance at what was staring him in the face. Now, he feared he must face the fact he could control neither her nor his feelings for her.

He was still smitten by her, more than ever now that he saw for the first time the true depth of her cleverness and the strength of her character and commitment. Even in a man's world, she had made her own decisions and stood by them. She had been more loyal to what she saw as her duty than he had to his. Doomed though they were, enemy that she had made herself, he had never met a woman like Rosalind Barlow.

Even now—tonight when he told Delancey he would question her here alone rather than with him in the guardroom as was proper procedure—he had protected her and risked himself. Yes, damn her, risked himself by letting her go relatively unpunished this long when he had had suspicions. He should feel triumphant at unmasking her and her blasted Rosies at last, but the choices facing him now terrified him.

If he helped her, he would be going against the king's orders; if he punished her, he punished himself. Worse, he thought prosecuting her and Deal would be somehow unjust. Indeed, as he had seen before but ignored, the king's might did not make right. Somehow, he had to face the king about the apparent wrongdoings of the crown toward the people of Deal. For if he just abandoned Rosalind and Deal to the king's justice, he would never forgive himself.

He knew he should disavow anything to do with her. He should toss her in the dungeon cell next to Wat's. She had been so dedicated to her duty she had not even noted Wat adored her. He should hang Wat for trying to kill him, and send the other men of Deal with Rosalind to prison in Sandwich or Dover. He should summon that simpering Percy Putnam and tell him that his hint about Rosalind's father had put him on to Rosalind being the very heart of the illegal trading. He should write the king that the smuggling ring was smashed and bask in the royal rewards. And then he should inform his fiancée, Penelope, that he wished to wed her at Yule when he escorted Anne of Cleves to the king at Greenwich.

But he could do none of those things. He had come to care for Rosalind and this damned, defiant town of Deal. It mattered to him that they survived and prospered, and not only because they would service the castle on which his and mayhap England's future depended. He needed time to think and plan. He also needed Rosalind's goodwill, but he knew full well he would have to do without her help unless he could find some way to convince her that he had the good of both her and the town of Deal in mind.

"Come with me," he ordered her and stood to seize her arm.

"Am I off to the dungeon?"

"I will not have you whispering further sedition to Wat through the grates there, and I need you close for further interrogations. If you detest me as heartily as you have claimed, perhaps proximity to me alone will be a fate worse than death for you."

"I will not stay here with you!" she began when he marched her toward his narrow bed.

His tautly leashed temper snapped; he grabbed her by her upper arms and picked her off her feet. "You shall stay anywhere I bid and do anything I bid," he gritted out. "I cannot trust you, Rosalind. I want to, but I cannot!"

Her eyes were wide pools he could have drowned in. He let her slide slowly, heavily down his body before he realized she thought he was going to force her to his bed. That and his powerful physical reaction to her deflated his fury. Just now, he had felt her soft curves intimately through her boy's garb without her usual heavy skirts and stiff bodice.

"I swear," he clipped out, "I only came over here to fetch you some blankets." He held her with one hand and opened the chest at the foot of his bed with the other. He hauled out two thick wool blankets, shoving them into her arms. "The floor is no doubt hard and cold," he said, still fighting the temptation to keep her here with him.

He yanked his mattress and pillow off his bed, leaving only the rope webbing underneath. He walked her to the narrow door that linked his chamber with the tiny storage room and tossed the mattress and pillow inside. It was pitch-black and so damned cold when he opened it. But he had to at least lock her up, didn't he?

"I shall send for your clothes in the morning," he said, "but there will be no outside visitors. And since tomorrow eve begins the Twelve Days of Christmas, you may expect a special gift on every one of them—a visit from me!"

He moved her backward into the room with his hand
gently grasping her throat like a big, warm collar, then
slammed the door shut before he could reach for her again.
The thud of the door reverberated in the room and in his
mind. He turned the key in the lock but left it there. He tried
to think if there was aught stored in the room she could use
to escape or ruin or even throw down the garderobe shaft as
he could picture her doing. But no, battlement flags and
large pieces of his extra armor yet uncrated were the only
goods in storage there—that and the person he feared was
most precious in the world to him.

He slumped on the chair before the low-burning hearth,
his head in his hands. He could not bear to have her cold in
there, but she was tough enough. Tougher than he; she had
proved that. Until now. Now he would turn the tables on
her. He had to persuade her to tell him what she knew. Word
of her arrest would soon be all over town, and Percy Putnam knew everything that happened in Deal. And mayhap
the king's raven, Cromwell, knew everything Percy knew.
But there had to be a way out of this, a way to save himself
and still save Rosalind, too.

Rosalind stood still in the blackness of the room she had
barely glimpsed before he slammed the door. She decided
her life as she had known it was over. Her life as she wanted
it to be was doomed. She had to find the courage now to
save her friends, whatever it cost her. Curse the man—for
starters it was going to cost her any hope of him. At that, she
crumpled to the floor on his mattress, and soon began to
tremble so hard from nerves that she wrapped herself in the
blankets.

She heard no sounds in the outer chamber, but her mind
made much noise here. All this disaster and she still loved
Nick! How could that be? How unfair! She had become her
own worst enemy. It was a more cruel injustice than losing
Murray and Father. She actually understood Nick's need for

loyalty, for duty, and his abject pain at thinking she had lied
to him and used him. Oh, yes, she understood that well
enough, for he had done the same to her! How could they
be so different and yet so akin? If only there were some way
out of this. If only she had someone to trust, to really trust,
though Nick had said more than once in Boulogne that she
should trust him. Hopeless, her life, her future, her love.
Hopeless, even in this season of holiday hope, with Christmas and the beginning of the new year.

She cuddled deep in the pile of blankets, like a cocoon.
She was afraid to sleep, for then she might dream. Not
nightmares of prison, ruin or even death, but happy dreams
of her in Nick's arms, dreams now as barren and cold as the
room in which she slept.

The next morning, Nick sent Stephen Delancey into Rosalind's cell with her breakfast, water for washing and the
clothes her sister had sent. Stephen reported he found the
prisoner subdued and tousled from sleep. Even that innocent description made Nick more desperate for her, but he
still needed time to plan.

At dawn, Nick had ridden to the Rose and Anchor to
speak with Meg. She, like most in town, had heard the news;
he found her nearly hysterical. With Franklin's help, he settled her down as best he could. He ordered her to remain
there with her aunt, and promised to send Franklin for Meg
later. But by the time Nick was back at the castle, a child
from Deal had delivered to his care a confession of smuggling followed with columns and columns of townsmen's
signatures, or an X after a printed name if they could not
write.

Nick just shook his head. What an information web these
people had! All these names in but a few hours when so
many doors were barred and guarded. ''More than sixty
names! Hell's gates, that is near the entire male population

of the place!'' Nick muttered as he placed the paper in his pouch. "Everyone is standing up for her again!''

But despite himself, he wanted to stand up for her, too. He respected and longed for such loyalty and friendship for himself. She had earned it and deserved it. Rosalind's life here in rural Deal had been a far cry from his among his supposed friends at the king's glittering court, and he was starting to believe she had the better of the bargain.

Nick sent Delancey in again with Rosalind's dinner tray at noon, for he knew the first time he looked into her eyes today, the first time she defied him again, either tenderness or temper might consume him. And that could ruin what he had in mind for tonight.

His plan was a rash gamble, but he saw no other way; his feelings for her would allow no other alternative. If she did not cooperate, he would have to remove the last of his protection from her and let her be handled strictly by the law. He told himself he could do that to her if he must, for the sake of his duty to his king. And yet, could he? He agonized over that question again and again.

"My lord, Percy Putnam's here to see you." Captain Delancey's voice cut through his thoughts. Nick started to attention; he had been sitting at his desk, staring at the door to Rosalind's cell. He wondered if she might be able to hear through the door. And he did not want Putnam, whom he had been expecting, to know he kept her here so close.

"Tell him I shall walk with him along the battlements," he ordered Delancey and grabbed his cap and cape as he made for the door.

Percival Putnam's rage boiled even more when he heard he was being further insulted. Why else would Nick Spencer insist he go up to meet him on the battlements than to point out their obvious differences? Buffeted by wind, the king's lord lieutenant would stand and stride straight while Cromwell's revenue man would wobble like a ship in a gale!

This was just one more thing to bring the bastard down for, Percy seethed as he slowly climbed the stairs. Far worse was the fact that Spencer had now shattered his dearest fantasy—to have Rosalind his prisoner at his mercy when he commanded Deal. But it would not be long now before he had Rosalind and Spencer in prison, downcast and defeated, even executed, he hoped, gloating at the thought.

"Sorry to bring you clear up here!" Spencer greeted him.

Percy nodded and smiled, silently cursing the man anew as he limped toward him.

"My Lord Spencer, I hear you now have two of the smugglers to be forced to talk, even though one's in skirts—or should be," Percy began, quite out of breath. The sea wind he hated swept hard against him, yanking at his blond locks. "Mistress Rosalind—who would have thought it? But I was always suspicious, always. Too bright and bold as brass, was she not, my lord? And no doubt, luring Wat and who knows what other willing dupes into everything. Surely now you can tie her to every family in the village for your swift justice on them all, eh!"

"The investigation is under way and under my command, Master Putnam."

"So it is, but I mean, the powers that be in London would agree that with the French threat, we cannot have this foul nest of smugglers and spies rooted out any too soon!"

Percy noted well that Spencer's eyes narrowed and his jaw set hard. His and Cromwell's snare had to be sprung on Spencer soon, Percy vowed.

"Spies? There is no real question of spies, Master Putnam, at least not yet."

"But, alas, how can they avoid the taint of treason, my lord? Anyone who has darted over to France lately and sought contacts there—as indeed they must have done, no doubt when we were all unawares—must be suspect. And anyone who appears to coddle such criminals might be construed, wrongly perhaps, my lord, to be in league with them. Well, then, keep me informed, if you please," Percy concluded.

He started carefully away with one hand on the stone wall, for he wished to leave before he inadvertently gave aught away in his fury at Spencer. He had done what Cromwell counseled in his last letter, expressed an opinion of action that Spencer would not heed. And he had warned him of consequences with the king. Not directly, of course, but if it came to a trial for treason when Spencer fell, at least Percy Putnam could claim he had done all he could to urge the lord lieutenant toward what was right before informing on him.

Nick leaned his shoulder against the big, cold, thirty-two-pounder brass cannon and glared at Putnam as he departed without a by-your-leave or fare-thee-well. It was obvious to him that Putnam was feeling his oats. The man must have in mind claiming part of the glory for ferreting out the smugglers. His implication that he knew Nick had gone to France— No, Nick could not believe Rosalind or anyone else had told Percy such. The man must have been referring strictly to the smugglers' need to get goods from France.

Nick went back down another way to his rooms. He had more than Percival Putnam to worry about right now. He had Rosalind Barlow on his hands. Tonight would be a dice roll the results of which he could not predict.

Rosalind donned her forest-green velvet gown for warmth under her hooded cloak and wore her hair down to keep her neck warmer. She had been given winter garb and two hearty meals so far today, so at least her jailer did not intend to freeze her or starve her to make her talk, she mused, as she paced four jerky steps back and forth in her tiny cell. And she had the garderobe here, so the lofty lord lieutenant must be using a mere chamber pot, she mused, though that thought was cold comfort, even as the stone seat of the jakes had been.

It was getting dark through the small slit high up on the wall. This was Christmas Eve, the first of the Twelve Days of Christmas called Yuletide, and Nick had promised she would see him each day. So far, she had seen only Captain Delancey with the food trays and her clothing from Meg.

Daring girl, the once-shy Meg! Rosalind thought proudly. Her sister had included a note hidden in the sleeve of this gown that claimed children of the town had spread the word that the Rosies must sign a confession or the burden of guilt would fall on Rosalind. Every man who could write his name or make an X had signed, "for, even forcefully closeted in their homes, safe for now, Ros, they are all willing to stand by you, the dearest Rosie," Meg had written. On the beach last night Rosalind had asked that no one confess, but they were obviously not willing to let her face punishment alone. She wondered if Nick was out making widespread arrests this minute. Of the whole town? What a dreadful Christmas Eve, when her memories of such times were happy and warm! Now she would spend this one alone, besieged and afraid. So physically close to the person on earth she cared for most and had lost. Well, anyway, Meg's little note and further words of love had helped her.

For one moment, she thought she heard Meg's voice, but of course, it was her imagination. How much trouble the heart's longing could cause, she fretted as she paced. She had actually fancied once that she and Nick had a right to be together. She had thought her love for him might make a difference, should he ever discover the truth. She sighed. She, who had valued and longed for the truth so oft in her life, had turned into the worst of deceivers and liars. Deceiving Percy Putnam those years before—that had hardly seemed to matter. But with Nick, it all became so momentous, so difficult, so—

She heard a knock on her door, then the key grated in the lock. She whirled around to face the door as it opened. Nick stood there, looking ludicrously elegant in a forest-green velvet doublet with cloth-of-gold slashings, matching velvet cap, black hose and square-toed shoes. Her heart fell. He must be stepping out with his men or even up to the inn for Christmas Eve.

Warmth emanated from the bright chamber behind him. A golden glow of dancing firelight threw his long shadow to her feet and on her skirts. She thought she smelled pungent pine boughs and sweet beeswax candles. But she was certain she did smell food, roast beef with horseradish mayhap and spiced mincemeat. She felt tears prickle behind her eyes at the thought of all she was missing, all she would never have—a chance to enjoy the holiday peacefully with the man she loved. She heard the clang of glasses and the clink of pewter. Was all this to torment her on Christmas Eve? Defiantly, she swept off her cloak to show him she was neither cold nor to be outdone.

"I see you have dressed for the occasion," he told her and leaned his shoulder on the doorway to study her. His eyes seemed to illumine the room and heat her blood. Then he backed into his chamber and indicated she should step out. Slowly, wondering what she would see, she edged closer to the door.

"Please join us," he added, and his smile flashed white in bright fire glow. She sensed there were people behind him, but her eyes saw only him. "For Christmas Eve, all of us together," Nick prompted. "I trust you will not toss the food out the window."

She blinked and squinted behind Nick. A big Yule log crackled on the hearth. Pine boughs were looped across the mantel and draped over the window and door. A damask cloth and dishes of steaming food covered the table. And Franklin and Meg stood uneasily near the door, holding hands, leaning forward expectantly, as if wondering what she would do and say.

Rosalind wanted to pinch herself. She must be dreaming. She had expected another rough interrogation session from

Nick. She had dreaded but planned for more demands and threats and the knowledge she must struggle against the man she wanted only to surrender to. But this made her want to cry and laugh and—and trust him. This gave her a tiny glimmer of hope.

"Then you will join us?" Nick asked. "It would mean a great deal to me if you would."

Mean a great deal to me. His words echoed in her head. Still astounded, she nodded stiffly. She wanted to speak. She wanted to throw herself in Nick's arms, fool that she was. But Meg hurried across the room and hugged her.

"We have this one special night—a truce he's promised!" Meg whispered in Rosalind's ear. "Ros, oh, Ros, mayhap this can be a new beginning for the two of you—"

"Too late," Rosalind mouthed before she kissed Meg's cheek.

"No whispering, you two, unless it is over first-night presents, aye, my Lord Spencer?" Franklin said and came to bow over Rosalind's trembling hand. "All we need now is the king himself, dressed as the Lord of Misrule, to dole out gifts. My lord, were you at court that time they say his majesty bumped into the punch bowl and doused Queen Catherine and her ladies?"

"My first Christmas at court, Franklin," Nick admitted, his eyes still on Rosalind. Nick fretted that such hearty mention of the king would throw a pall on things, but Rosalind stared back at him unblinking and unprotesting. She looked like a Christmas angel, he thought, her beautiful hair loosed golden over her velvet-clad shoulders and the Yule log fire gilding her head in a rich halo. And that indescribable, other-worldly look on her lovely face.

"I am afraid I am here without gifts for anyone," she said, still holding Meg's hand. "But I am grateful for—all this," she added and swept the little room with a graceful arc of hand.

She would set any court woman he had ever known to shame, Nick thought, and took a step closer to her. No one could hold a candle to her wit, and fire, and beauty.

"Thank you, my lord," she said to him. "Whatever your plan here, I thank you for loveliness in the midst of fear, discord and pain."

"Come sit, then, and let's trust one another, even if for a while."

She let him take her arm and seat her next to him, across from Meg and Franklin. Trust, she thought. Surely, he did not believe he could mesmerize her by all this into suddenly trusting him. Nor that he would get her drunk, she thought as Nick poured her goblet full of red wine. Yet it seemed a night for trust, a night to be drunk with love. Christmas love and the love of this man she would surely not have into the new year. So she would treasure each moment of this now, she vowed, whatever befell her when Meg and Franklin would leave and the Yule log would burn low and Nick would turn to her again with eyes gone hard instead of soft and glowing.

"To Deal's future," Nick proposed a toast.

They all drank solemnly, as if testing one another yet.

"And to the king," Nick said and clinked her goblet. When she hesitated, he told her quietly, "It's one and the same, Rosalind. Things can and will change with our help and, I hope, that of his majesty, too. To the king."

It was then Rosalind gave Nick what she considered to be his First Day of Christmas gift. She nodded. For the love she would ever hide in her heart for Nick Spencer, she took a sip of wine in honor of his king.

Chapter Eleven

The Yule log still burned bright, but Rosalind feared their evening of peace and goodwill was ended. Stoically, she kissed Meg farewell at the door, and Franklin hurried his wife out into the hall. Nick closed the door behind them and bolted it. Surely he could not mean to question her tonight, she thought, not after all this sweet sharing.

"Let me pull two chairs to the hearth, Rosalind. We have much to say to each other."

Every nerve in her body snapped taut. He placed the chairs close, facing each other. She sat where he indicated, her knees almost touching his. This evening she had felt protected; now she felt stripped bare again. She gripped her hands in her lap and waited for him to begin. He cleared his throat.

"It is not just some Christmas fantasy, Rosalind, that we could be reconciled. You and I and the town of Deal, reconciled with the king you have all defied for years. I grant you there may be wrongs and misunderstandings on both sides. But if you and I cannot settle things between us to work together, everything will go up in smoke—" he kicked the Yule log so hard she jumped as its whole facade shuddered to silver embers "—and be nothing but ash."

She leaned toward him, her gaze intense, her attention riveted on him. "You mean it is not too late?"

"Almost," he said, his eyes narrowed. "Mayhap. But I believe in fighting defeat until the very end, and these past few months I have seen you believe in that, too."

"Yes. Oh, Nick, I want to believe you! I want to trust you, but I have been so afraid and still am!"

He leaned closer, elbows on knees, and took her hands in his big warm ones. "I, too," he said quietly. "Afraid and furious."

"At me."

"At the whole situation. Even at myself for holding back when I knew I should attack. Do you think I want to destroy or even punish the people who saved my life? Saved me when they knew who I was, since I announced myself so clearly from the deck of the sinking ship. Saved me when, evidently, all of you suspected I had come to ruin your free-trading livelihood. And it pains me even to think of hurting the woman I have grown so to . . . cherish and admire."

Tears blurred her gaze until she saw two taut-faced Nick Spencers. She blinked and sniffled. He handed her a hand-kerchief from his doublet. She took much too long to blow her nose in order to give herself time to think.

He did care for the folks of Deal! He cared for them at least as much as he did for his blasted royal duty! He had called their smuggling "free trading" and a "livelihood" instead of a crime or treason as he had last night. And he had said he cherished and admired her, though that came nowhere near the soul-shaking love she bore him.

"What must I—we—do to seize this chance to save Deal from defeat?" she asked.

"You have to trust me enough to tell me all that has happened with the smuggling here. Yes, damn it, Rosalind, names, places, times! You have to admit to me you hate the king—and then—" he held up a hand as if to ward off the protest he saw coming "—you have to put that aside. You have to be brave enough to forgive and forget the past. You must be willing to go with me to the royal court and face the king, so we can settle things with him directly. With Putnam's interference and his implications of possible treason with the French threat, things can no longer be solved locally. Throwing yourself on my mercy is not what is needed here, though I admit I covet such. Besides, his majesty has always had a soft spot for bright, beautiful women—if they can keep a civil tongue and temper.''

Breaking their touch, she slumped back in her chair, her hands again clasped in her lap. Forgive and forget? Nick would take her to court to face the king and be civil to him? Impossible, even if it were the only way. But then again, Nick, whom she had tried to hate with all her might, had won her over. And even if her back were not to the wall, she wanted so to be on the same side as he and not to fight him anymore. She wanted to help him and trust him, those things he had once claimed meant love.

''Well? Are you bold enough for all that, my little Rosie?''

''I am thinking. What do you mean about Percival Putnam's interference? He may be the king's revenue and exciseman, but he was on Deal's side when the boats were broken. His majesty never even deigned to answer Percy's epistle of protest, but Percy still vowed he would write a protest to the king again if Wat were to be hanged.''

Nick frowned. ''You trust Putnam, then?''

''No, and I never have. But I pity him, and it does no harm to be kind to him.'' A fragmented memory darted through her mind, a memory of pitying Percy. Pitying him when he screamed and her father held him down on the table at the inn. But when could that have been? The memory seemed some disjointed dream she barely recalled.

''As you have been kind to me from time to time?'' Nick was asking. He reached forward to cup his hands over her knees, then obviously thought better of it and sat back in his chair again.

"Being kind to you was far different. I have never felt one whit sorry for you, my lord! But when I was kind to you, I have not always lied to you and have been heartily sorry afterward."

He gazed raptly at her, a hint of smile lifting his lips. They both held their breath. The understanding that she did love him hovered between them in golden fire glow. He looked as if he would make a momentous announcement, but he said only, "Then tell me all now, sweetheart, the truth. I do not command, but beseech. Together, let us find a way out of this predicament without the entire town following you to prison."

She sat straight as a lance in her chair. "Could we find another way Deal folks can earn some money for food to last the winter? I tell you, Nick, if I could see the king I would ask he grant us a market license, especially with the castle here."

"You may not believe me, sweetheart, but I intend to do just that."

"Oh! Really? Good! Then, too, mayhap our men could be licensed as pilots to board becalmed vessels, for they know the treacherous Downs and the sea clear to France and beyond! Or the skill of Deal men could be put to use to patrol the shores against the French!"

It all tumbled from her then. The hard beginnings of her Rosies, the struggle to rebuild town spirit after Murray's and her father's deaths. The Rosies' methods of operation, their drop sites—the one in the tomb at St. Leonard's did not amuse him. Her desire for revenge against King Horrid Harry that made him gape at her audacity. Her friend Pierre, the Rosies' names, her pride in the women and folks of Deal who had stood up for her. She vowed to him there had never been intent to pass information to the French about England's defenses, nor had they ever done so.

"I swear, it was only simple free trading!" she said and saw that he believed her. Each time she divulged something to him, she shuddered, yet her woman's instincts told her she could trust him now. The burden she had borne so long felt lighter, even when she admitted she thought Percy had once favored her, and that was why he had trodden softly on the free trading. "But I did not favor him that way, and nothing ever came of it," she concluded.

"I think something may have come of it now," he said. "I do not trust the man, and I have never quite put my finger on the reason. I cannot help but wonder if he has not played both sides for his own aims."

Rosalind's earlier defense of Putnam as a friend to Deal had unsettled him. Putnam had let slip to Nick that he had ingratiated himself with the townsfolk he actually despised only to keep a better eye on them. The man had told him his epistles three years ago to the king were not protest but praise for staving in the smugglers' luggers on the beach. Who, then, Nick mused, had first told the king of smugglers here and urged such punitive action?

And there was more evidence of deceit from the man. Tonight Rosalind had claimed Putnam would write the king to protest Wat's possible hanging. But Putnam had told Nick he wanted the man hanged. And Nick suspected Putnam had goaded Wat for his own ends, though that meant Nick must take his would-be assassin's word over that of the king's revenue agent, who had apparently saved his life. Nick admitted to himself he admired Wat more than he did Putnam, and instinct counted for something. Could Putnam have simply arranged to save Nick's life only to try to ruin it in his own way later? And for what ends? This was starting to reek of Cromwell's familiar stench, for Putnam idolized the king's crafty lord chamberlain. Yes, Nick decided, first thing in the morning he would have Delancey ride to Sandwich and bring Putnam here for questioning.

"But when could we go to court?" Rosalind interrupted his agonizing. "You are kept here to finish the castle and watch the seas, are you not?"

"Another order has superseded that, one I cannot share with you yet," he said.

"Then I am alone in my trust and confession!" she countered.

His eyes met hers. "All right, then," he acquiesced with a firm nod. "The king's betrothed, Anne of Cleves, will land here from Calais as soon as weather permits. I shall be escorting her to his majesty at Greenwich outside London. You looked the part of a boy last night. No one in town or the royal retinue would know you were off with me to see the king if you were but another lad riding far back in the crowd."

Her heart galloped as if her horse already did. She had never been farther by land than Dover. To Greenwich and London? And with Nick to see Horrid Har—his majesty? But what if this were a ruse to spirit her away to coerce Deal to good behavior? What if Nick were to isolate her and then hand her over to others for brutal questioning or—

No! She would not believe that. He had seemed to trust her. She must trust him. This would work. It must. "All right," she told him. "I agree."

"Then, before we—take to our beds, I have something for you, a gift for the First Day of Christmas."

He stood and walked toward her prison cell. She got to her feet, one of which had gone prickly numb since she had been sitting so long.

"But you have already given me this night with Meg and Franklin," she protested gently. "And the opportunity, however much a risk, for a new life for myself and Deal. I do realize, my lord, that taking me with you to London is a great risk for you, in case someone should misread your reasons to aid me."

He came back, holding the key to her prison cell in his open palm. "Ah, but who is to say my reasons for aiding you, my sweet, are all so honorable? Who is to say there is not indeed something for people to misread in my motives?

I am but a man, Rosalind Barlow, and one entirely smitten with an amazing woman.''

She held her breath. She stared down at the bright key in his hand. "You mean," she faltered, "now that we agree on certain things, you will not lock me in?" She took the key from his hand before he changed his mind.

"Yes, but I am also hoping you will not lock me out. Remember the key you wore around your neck, Rosalind, the one you once called the key to your heart? Indeed, this is mine. I am trusting you to cooperate, and I am hoping against hope you will consider not locking that door between us. I am beseeching that you share my bed, narrow though it be for two. I've put another mattress on it, you see."

She pressed the key between her breasts and stared into his intense brown eyes fringed by thick ebony lashes. Whatever would assail her on the morrow, she soared with joy and longing now. She felt herself blossom from pure desire for him. She yearned to feel his strong arms around her, to hear his voice close to her ear whisper words she could ever treasure.

"Nick, oh, Nick, my love!"

He gathered her in his arms and they stood, pressed together for how long she did not know. The molded muscles of his back felt so good against her hands through the thick velvet; his chest was warm and sturdy against her cheek. She clung to the key as he began to disrobe her. Her thoughts darted to that other time, that other hearth in France where they had undressed and then loved. It seemed forever ago and yet the closest moment in her memory.

The big key got in her way when she unlaced his doublet and then his shirt and tugged both over his head. She smiled at the way his hair, ever so perfectly in place, stood endearingly on end. She put the key down her bodice, only to have that fall away under the skill of his hands. When she stood in but her linen chemise and he in his hose, they came together in a crushing kiss.

Deep and sweet, the caress went on and on. She seemed to spiral outside herself, she was so dizzy. She clung to him, rubbing her hips in luring invitation against the proof of his powerful desire for her. She stroked his ribs, grasped his lean hips. He held her bottom, lifting and molding her harder against him. Her peaked nipples grazed his curly chest hair as their tongues danced and dueled, attacked and surrendered. He stepped back only to skim her chemise to her ankles, kneeling as he peeled it away, then capturing her to him to rain slick kisses on her stomach and her hips. His tongue darted into her navel and flicked lower. Her legs buckled and she knelt, too, facing him. She felt perfectly at one with him in heart and mind before they even joined.

He sprawled them back on their velvet garments close to the hearth. Then his hands and lips wandered everywhere; she could hardly breathe. He whispered erotic commands she was eager to obey. She was so light-headed, but when had she not matched him move for move? Her hands ran rampant on him, then clasped the thrust at his loins with strokes that sent them both into realms of wilder desire.

"Now I will give you an order, Lord Lieutenant of Deal!"

"Anything!"

"Kiss me again while I hold you here and then— Mmm, Nick, you are supposed to give me time to—"

"Much more of that from you, and this celebration will be over before it has begun!"

She shot him a smile, and saw his face was stretched taut with passion. His eyes seemed to glow with love. Well, perhaps not love, she thought, for he had never declared such. But he held her so tight to him, then settled even closer. She responded; she helped him. He gasped aloud and met her languorous gaze.

"I have never met a woman so giving—so strong—and innovative as you, my love," he said, breathless.

She gasped, too, as he thrust deep to set a steady pace. She held to him, stunned at the wonder of it all, then began to match his rhythm. Everything spun farther out of her control, her breathing, her restraint, her thoughts. But she clung to one thing as she did to him—he had called her *my love!*

She was not certain when Nick had finally carried her to bed. They lay together on their sides spoon-fashion, with their arms and legs entwined. Sometime near dawn, they loved again. Each time, he swept her to the point of wanton abandon. She took—well, a certain matter into her own hands to demand he end the sweet torment. If such skills as his had been learned at court, it must be quite a place, she thought as she slid into slumber again.

When next she woke, it was broad daylight and Nick was gone. Ale, bread and fruit sat on the table, evidently awaiting her. Drowsy, she sat up and wrapped the wool blanket around her for a robe. She was still sitting there when the door opened and Nick ducked in.

"I cannot believe I slept that long," she murmured through a yawn.

"Neither of us had much sleep nor are we likely to until we get all this resolved." He came over to sit beside her and pulled her into his arms, nestling her tousled head under his chin. The scent of sea air in his clothes told her he had been out on the battlements somewhere. "A slight complication, sweetheart," he said.

She raised her head to stare at him. "Anne of Cleves is here already?"

"No. I sent Captain Delancey to Sandwich to bring Percy Putnam here for a chat with me. But he is gone—with that man of his, Roger Shanks."

"Gone where? Mayhap just to Deal."

"No. I had the town scoured for him. His servants claim they did not know his destination. I have the strangest premonition it might be the same place we are going when our guest arrives. Meanwhile, I have closed up the castle, tight as is possible with one part of the wall not yet done. And I have a guard in the hall outside this door should Putnam just materialize. You may have the use of these rooms. I have much to do and will see you when I am able."

"Tonight?" she blurted shamelessly when he stood.

"Oh, yes, tonight," he vowed with a taut-lipped smile. "And I have sent for more clothes for you, including that tawny velvet gown in which you once seduced me out of my senses in the garden at the inn. You may go to court looking like a lad, but it won't do to appear before the king that way. Until later, sweet." He dashed a hard, possessive kiss on her pouted lips and was out the door.

So, none of that was a dream last night! she thought. She knew the wild lovemaking was not; she felt deliciously tumbled and slightly sensitive in several key places. Key— the key. She rose and walked to the hearth and found the key under her discarded garments. She might still have no future with this man, but she would never give up the token of this key to his heart. It might bring good fortune to help them unlock a mutual future of better days.

No, she thought, as she gathered her clothing in her arms, none of what she faced was a figment of her fancies. When she and Nick had compared what they knew of Percy Putnam, he hardly seemed the hail-fellow-well-met she had thought, and now he had disappeared. And, with Nick's help, she was going to try to deal in flesh and blood with the king, Henry Tudor, the tyrant of her life. Nick had promised his majesty would be in a soaring mood, looking forward to wedding and bedding his betrothed.

Mayhap, depending on what calling a woman "my love" meant to a courtier like Nicholas Spencer, he just might love her, too! But no matter what, now they had a chance to right things here in Deal. She would give her life for that, but with her and Nick now sharing everything, her fears were not so fierce. They had a fine plan. Surely nothing could go awry to stop them now!

At dusk on St. John's Day, December 27, ten ships emerged from a sleet storm on the horizon and anchored just off Deal. The castle guards pounded on Nick's door, but spyglasses assured him that the ships were English and not French.

"I just hope a nearly finished castle will do to house the next queen of England and her retinue for one night," Nick muttered to Rosalind as he donned his best garments and she scrambled into her boy's garb as they had agreed. The largest room of the castle, the guardroom, had been scrubbed, and its floor covered with sweet rushes in preparation for the future queen's brief lodging here. A large canopied and curtained bed had been hauled from Sandwich, as well as great quantities of food.

Nick dropped a quick kiss on Rosalind's cheek. "I am trusting you," he told her, "that all will go well on your end. Stay well back even if you want a glimpse of the princess. She is reputed to be fair and comely, and you would put her to shame if anyone noted you were not a mere lad named Richard Rose." He patted her bottom through her tights and trunk hose and, striding out, banged the door.

Richard Rose. It was a good enough name for a Rosie, Rosalind decided. She felt knots of nerves tighten in the pit of her belly at what they dared. But as long as she had Nick to believe in, she would not question his methods nor his motives.

By the time Anne of Cleves and her ladies were rowed ashore, messengers had been sent to Dover, Canterbury and Greenwich with news that she had arrived. Before her procession set out on the morrow, foul weather or fair, to deliver her to her anxious royal bridegroom, the king's courtiers would flock to accompany her. Though some of her companions were staying aboard their ships tonight to avoid overwhelming Deal, Rosalind heard voices loud as the sea when she tiptoed down the hall to catch a glimpse of the welcoming ceremony.

Many folks had still come ashore with the bride-to-be, mostly English nobles who had gone over to Calais to greet her. Rosalind peered down a curve of stone staircase just as Nick bowed to a group of cloaked women and finely garbed men in the covered entryway to the central living chambers.

"Welcome to Deal and to England, my Lady Anne of Cleves!" Nick's voice rang out to send shivers up Rosalind's spine.

"*Ja, ja!*" a strident voice rang out from one of the women, followed by a guttural stream of High Dutch, which Rosalind caught some of. It was years since she had spoken that Germanic language of the Rhine with the woman called Frieda they had rescued.

"A bit of a problem with conversing, Lord Spencer," an elderly man with a ceremonial sword said to Nick, loud enough for all to hear. Rosalind started down the steps to get closer. "Not a word of English from her lips, it seems, and nary a one of us speaks her tongue. 'S blood, his majesty will not be pleased at that."

The crowd of courtiers muttered, and Rosalind overheard two Englishmen at the back of the crowd.

"The Tudor stallion will go straight through the roof, if you ask me," one said.

"I'd wager my hunt park on it," the other agreed as Rosalind edged behind them. "And not just for the woman's doleful lack of a civilized language. Cromwell's lied in his attempt to snare his grace in a Protestant marriage. If the Lady Anne of Cleves is fetching, I'd rather kiss a cow."

"And now with all the fuss and frippery awaiting us at Greenwich, his majesty's stuck with her."

"Is he? That remains to be seen! Everyone said he was stuck with Anne Boleyn, too, Jenkins."

Night was falling. Soldiers lit the torches in the little courtyard, but the crowd edged into the common room near the guardroom where the Lady Anne would spend the night. Rosalind slid in, too, but stayed at the back of the room nearest the door. She felt safe enough in rough lad's garb with her hair up under her cap; no one gave her a second glance. Besides, but for pitying the poor Lady Anne, she was enjoying this. It served the king right if he had to wed and bed a wife he could not abide!

How sad, though, she thought, that the English—Nick, too—were ludicrously trying to speak to their next queen with broad gestures, bobbing heads and silly smiles when a few well-chosen words would do. And they were making fools of themselves speaking in ever louder voices as if that would break through the language barrier. How could two great nations have been so careless as to not have someone here who could translate? Why, if Rosalind's pantomime as this boy weren't of utmost necessity, she would step forward to help this confused and exhausted woman, even if she was to wed Henry Tudor!

As cloaks were removed, Rosalind saw the assemblage glittered. Many of the English wore gold-embroidered velvet and satin awash with winking jewels. The Englishwomen looked beautiful with their gabled hoods setting off their pale faces. Even in her best attire, Rosalind would have felt plain and poor next to them. She noted, too, that even without the Englishwomen's rouged cheeks and reddened lips, the princess's face had unfashionably high color. For a moment Rosalind doubted Nick's brazen plan to take her to plead with the king, if this was what his majesty was used to in women. But the remarks of Jenkins and his friends, as well as her own observations, made her quite certain that Anne of Cleves was not what the king would want at all.

The woman was gangly and bony. Nick had told Rosalind that Anne was twenty-four, but she looked a good deal older. She had a pockmarked face and a high forehead that set off large, dark eyes, mayhap her best feature. But her nose and mouth were so wide as to give her a bovine look. And her garments—even with her lack of court experience, Rosalind could tell by comparing them with the elegant and graceful apparel of several lovely Englishwomen nearby that they were a disaster.

Anne of Cleves wore a heavily woven gown with a stiff, high collar reminiscent of a man's coat. it had tight sleeves instead of lined or turned or double ones. Her bodice opened slightly to display a chemisette drawn up to her throat with a narrow ribbon as if it were a winter night rail. Worse, she wore a large hat with its brim turned up in from where blond hair peeked out. Once again, Rosalind was struck by the great gap between the king's fiancée and his female courtiers.

But then, as she edged her way out to go up to pack her own gowns for the journey on the morrow, her ears picked up the chatter of the two pretty women ahead of her. She halted at once.

"I, for one, am going to bedevil Nick Spencer about deserting all of us at court for this wretched, damp cold place," the redhead said behind a kid-gloved hand. "He's done it all for his own gain, of course."

"Ever a clever dog, schooled by the king as he was," the other responded. "For not only did that rogue Nicholas leave us behind, but he left his fiancée Penelope Wentworth, too, though I warrant he'll wed her on the heels of his grace's nuptials."

"Hmm, by the looks of the royal bride, Nick's getting the far better bargain. Penelope always was a beauty. Nick is as fortunate as the lovely Lady Penelope Wentworth that the king got them together, for I hear she has a fine dowry, too. I just wonder how a hot-blooded man like that has been amusing himself without her these past months, hmm?"

Rosalind wanted to tear into the two women. She wanted to rail and scream at Nick. But she clamped her arms around her stomach and propped herself against the wall with stiff legs. She shook deep inside. Nick had never mentioned a fiancée; since he had said he was widowed, she had stupidly not asked. Penelope—he had muttered her name that first night in his delirium, but she had assumed it was his mother— Damn the blackguard, she had assumed too much! "Trust me," he had said, and she had bedded with him ecstatically and loved him deeply!

But how could she trust him now when he was no doubt going to betray her as soon as he got her out of Deal? He, a man "schooled by the king," was hardly going to take his rural mistress before this king who arranged his betrothal with the lovely, well-dowered Lady Penelope Wentworth! Nick had no intention, then, of letting her ask the king's help for Deal! No, more likely after he had amused himself with her at this distant assignment, he would toss her in some London dungeon, wed Penelope and then return here to smash all the other Rosies whom she had so naively identified for him! He had asked her to admit she sought revenge against the king the other night, no doubt in order to bring additional charges against her. And she could just hear his voice saying to her on Christmas Eve, "Ah, but who is to say my reasons for aiding you, my sweet, are all so honorable?"

She bit her lower lip so hard she tasted blood. She turned and ran from the room. Still trembling, she hurried back to Nick's chamber. She could try to flee the castle, but it was well guarded. And what good would that do? Yes, Lord Nicholas Spencer had given her good advice on one thing at least. She did have to face the king, explain and ask for help. But since Nick obviously had no plans to permit her to get that far, she would just have to find another protector, one who also could get her near his majesty and act as her intercessor. And that person was downstairs now, afraid and as desperate as she was that no one would help or understand her!

Rosalind shed her boy's clothes and shook out her tawny velvet gown. Bejeweled cloth of gold and crimson satin it was not, but it would have to do. She stretched her arms behind her as far as she could to lace it up her back, then reached back over her shoulders to complete the task. If she could just keep Nick from spotting her until she stood close enough to Anne of Cleves to speak. No courtiers knew her, if the guards did not stop her....

Over her pinned-up hair, she jammed her best gabled hood with its linen pleated veil. She did not even change her shoes, but hurried out and down the steps toward the guardroom.

She passed folks in the hall who shot her curious glances. She entered the yet crowded chamber that was to be the future queen's this night; fortunately, Nick's back was turned.

In High Dutch—the best she remembered—she said in a tremulous but loud voice, "Your Grace of Cleves, my Lord Spencer, please forgive my delay." She pushed forward and curtsied to the startled woman, trying to ignore the fact Nick looked as if he could spout cannonballs. "The lord lieutenant of the castle asked me to accompany you to the king as your translator, your grace. My name is Rosalind Barlow."

A huge grin lit the woman's broad countenance, counterbalancing Nick's furious frown. Nick made a move to grab Rosalind, but Anne of Cleves was quicker.

"What a kind, sweet surprise!" she said in her language, and took both Rosalind's hands in her own while grinning and nodding at the shocked, seething Nick. "*Danke schon, Lort Spen-zer, ja!*" she told Nick as she drew Rosalind to her side and began to tell her about her sea voyage through hail and sleet.

It stormed the next day, hail and sleet again, as the encourage set out on the first leg of its journey. Nick's face, too, was a continual storm cloud. Rosalind managed to stay close to Lady Anne where he dared not accost her.

The second day, Nick dismounted fast enough to lift Rosalind from her mount while Lord Admiral Fitzwilliam and the Duke of Suffolk tended to Anne just one horse away.

"Hell's gates, are you demented, Rosalind?" Nick hissed, and gave her a good shake before he set her down. "So much for trust—"

"How dare you preach trust! Did you think I would not learn of your own fiancée?" she spit back at him.

"What? But I had not even thought—"

"By the saints, at least I uncovered your purposes—exposed your lies—your 'trust me' and 'here's the key to my heart'—before you kept me from even getting to the king. But the future queen will see I get my interview with him, you wait and see!"

Nick gaped at her. He tried to drag her away, but Lady Anne called for "her dear Dutch Rosalind," saving her once again from his clutches.

When the entourage mounted and started on next time, Nick rode ahead alone, thinking, brooding. He was angry, but more than that he was in agony. He should have told Rosalind about Penelope, explained it all. But right now, he was not sure he could have explained it even to himself.

Now his betrothal to that woman seemed a distant dream, and one he would like to awaken from. But he owed an explanation to Penelope, and to the king who had arranged the betrothal, too. What would he tell them? That he had found a woman—an innkeeper and smuggler—who had made him forget his duty, his fiancée, his own straight path in life? That he could not stomach a coldhearted arrangement where he and Penelope—he knew it was the same for her—wed each other to please the king and elevate each other's political, social and financial status in the realm? It seemed suddenly so bloodless! The fact that Penelope had evidently chosen not to accompany the courtiers who came to greet the Lady Anne, when she could have been reunited with him after months apart, spoke volumes: she was in no greater hurry to see him than he her.

He felt no real emotion toward his marital deal with Penelope; Rosalind evoked soaring passions in him. Passions did not add up to love, of course, but he felt a growing need both to protect and to possess Rosalind. For all their sakes, he had to do something about Penelope. He had no doubt her emotions were not at risk here, but her pride was. He must see her soon to explain, or write to her—or at least explain his stand to the king so word of his reluctance could be as officially passed on as this betrothal had been arranged. Though Penelope probably would not care if she ever saw him again, he owed it to her to explain how he felt. But hell's gates, Rosalind was the one he must see right now to explain how he felt before the little spitfire did who knew what to make things worse!

He smacked his horse's reins and spurred the big beast on around the next bend, as if he were just eager to secure the road ahead, instead of to still the twistings of his heart.

On the second day they rode from Dover to Canterbury, where a torchlight procession and salute of cannons awaited them. Once again, sticking close to her savior, Rosalind glimpsed Nick's furious glare. If he could have literally shot her amid the boom of guns, she was certain he would have done it. For one moment, assailed by precious memories of Christmas Eve, she wavered. He had been a tender lover, he had—

No! she railed silently at herself. He had never been a lover at all, for she was mere amusement to him until he could dispose of her and wed his dear Penelope. He would never gainsay his king, his foster father, on that or anything else! Rosalind did not believe in jealousy; these murderous feelings she newly harbored were surely not that.

They were for being betrayed along with her beloved Deal, which Nick Spencer had vowed to protect.

The entourage stayed the next night at Sittingbourne and reached its temporary destination of the bishop's palace in Rochester on New Year's Day, 1540. On the next day, the ever-growing retinue would push on to Greenwich to be greeted by king and court. Pageants, tournaments and other lavish festivities would herald the wedding.

She had been right to think she would never keep Nick Spencer into the New Year, Rosalind told herself. Now, with each step toward the king, she mourned the loss of what she had thought might grow to mutual love between her and Nick. She had wanted him so, cared for him deeply, longed for his touch. And curse the man to the devil, she did yet!

The women and their liege lady settled in a sumptuous suite in the palace. Lady Anne had chattered incessantly to Rosalind about her husband-to-be, wondering this and that, hoping for his approval and goodwill. Rosalind felt great fondness for the poor woman, and realized that the only way she had ever disappointed the nervous bride was that she had not seen the king. That Rosalind needed to see him as soon as possible she was saving for a last-moment plea to her grace just before they reached Greenwich.

Fortunately, the Lady Anne still kept her close, for she had seen Nick lurking just outside the women's suite. When someone entered or departed, he either glared in at her or desperately gestured for her to come out. But she had stepped into his traps more than once before and would not again.

"The king has gone *where?*" Thomas Cromwell roared. His messenger flinched as if he had been struck. Both Percival Putnam, seated across the wide table, and Roger Shanks, standing behind Putnam's chair, jumped.

"On a royal whim, my Lord Cromwell," the messenger tried to explain from a safe distance down the long, cluttered table, "with two boon companions to Rochester to see the next queen privily before the formal public ceremonies."

"Be gone!" Cromwell ordered and turned to Putnam before the door closed. "Judas Priest, this is dangerous! I had hoped to have Lord Spencer detained and charged before his majesty saw him. But if his majesty receives proof of perfidy in these times without Spencer there to deny it, perhaps he can yet be convinced. You said the woman is with Spencer in Lady Anne's entourage?"

"My source at Deal Castle says Lord Spencer assigned her to act as translator for the unsuspecting Lady Anne," Putnam elaborated. "If Lord Spencer and Mistress Barlow are working for the French, might they not try to harm the Protestant bride or even the king himself?"

"Exactly!" Cromwell clipped out. "Or so the king might be led to believe. If I play this right, it will make his majesty even more anti-French and protective of his bride, who owes me her position! Perhaps with the taking of Spencer and the woman, and the proper pressure applied to extract confessions to place before the king— Indeed, what you told me of your own clever dealings indicate you know well how to make a man in power believe the threat of looming assassination."

Putnam could not stem a proud smile, however awed he yet felt in the very presence of his idol. "Anything I can do to help, my Lord Cromwell, you have but to name it."

"Let me borrow your man Shanks here to take a message straightaway to the king. I shall inform him of a plot by one close to him who would betray him." Cromwell grabbed paper and a pen and began to write as he spoke. "Perhaps this will fetch his grace back to Greenwich before he sees the Lady Anne. If not, my men hard on your man's heels will arrest the traitors, but not in his majesty's presence. When his grace returns here, I shall keep him busy with the plans for the vast reception while we make the lovers talk. Using your man as a courier will keep the word from spreading to anyone who might want to help Spencer. Even I, I fear, have leaks and those who would play me false. It never does to be too careless trusting others, you know, friend Percy."

"Indeed, I do know, my Lord Cromwell. And I shall revel in telling Spencer that when he's on your rack. As for the woman, how I wish I had her for myself—I mean, to . . . chasten and correct."

Cromwell peered up as he sanded and sealed the letter. "Is that the way of it? The wench must be a rare one, then. But no, if he goes down, she must, too, his whore, a smuggler and a link to the French—a Jezebel, indeed. We'll have to make her talk, too, of course, to accuse him of—of whatever we ask of her."

Putnam nodded. He shifted excitedly in the hard chair. His long-tended dream to break Rosalind Barlow personally was gone. But it was worth it to have Cromwell's favor. And he could still be given Deal to crunch under his boot soles. Yes, that would have to do. Lord Spencer and the clever Rosalind had made their own bed, and now they must lie—and die—in it!

Chapter Twelve

That night, Nick stalked the torchlit hall outside the women's suite, waiting to give a passionately pleading letter for Rosalind to the next person who went in.

So a woman, and a country wench at that, had brought him to this, he marveled. She moved him so deeply he was actually more worried about her well-being than his own! Damn, the depths to which a woman could pull a man!

If this missive did not convince her, he was frustrated enough to don women's garb to go and haul her out. What vile fortune she had somehow learned of Penelope and jumped to all the wrong conclusions! He really should have settled things in his own mind and told both Penelope and Rosalind that the betrothal must be broken. But, God knew, he had barely thought of Penelope for weeks when he should have. After this emotional tempest he had been through with Rosalind, the thought of wedding sweet, cloying Penelope had been far from his mind—anathema, even. Hell's gates, Rosalind had probably ruined him for wanting all other women, anyway! As soon as possible he had to fairly, firmly end things with Penelope for both their sakes. And he had to find some way to convince Rosalind of his good faith before they met the king. On her own, who knew what Rosalind would say or do to the volatile Tudor? And the royal temper—which was not going to be good once his majesty beheld his betrothed—could blow them all to bits, especially if Putnam or Cromwell got to him first.

Nick started as a man he recognized from court strode down the hall toward him. His short, fur-lined cape blew back in his haste. Sir Anthony Browne, the king's old friend and master of the horse! Sir Anthony's arrival usually heralded the king's, though surely that could not be the case here. His majesty was at Greenwich, preparing a grand welcome for his bride.

Nick and the older man greeted each other with mutual bows.

"Lord Spencer."

"Sir Anthony, how fares the king at Greenwich?"

"A pox on his boyish, impatient heart," Sir Anthony complained, his voice low, his thick eyebrows high. "He's not at Greenwich but hard on my heels. You might know he could not pass the night without gazing on the exquisite face of his beloved. He's convinced Holbein's portrait did not do her justice. Is Lady Anne inside then? This is to be a suitor's surprise, you see."

"A surprise? Yes, she is inside, but—"

"Good," Sir Anthony grunted and turned back to gesture down the hall. Looking like two overage and overweight schoolboys sneaking out of studies, Lord John Russell and the king hurried down the hall, chortling and elbowing each other. If his majesty's ulcerous leg was bothering him tonight, no one would have known it. No other retinue, and no blasted warning, Nick fumed. And if they crashed in there and got a glance at the Lady Anne, and then Rosalind stepped forward with her plea or some shrewish scolding of his majesty—

Nick crumpled his letter into a small ball in his fist and swept the king a bow with a flourish of his cap.

"Nick, my man! My thanks for delivering my bride safely to me. The king is only a man in matters of the heart." King

Henry lowered his booming voice and leaned closer with a wink. "You've seen her. What think you?"

"The lady is difficult to describe—with her rough sea voyage and such a long ride in the storms we have had," Nick floundered. "Love, they say, your majesty, is in the eye of the beholder."

"Aye," Henry Tudor said, grinning and clapping Nick so hard on the shoulder he almost bounced him off his feet. "And I cannot wait one moment longer to eye her or to be her holder! Come with us, then, Nick. The door, Sir Anthony..."

Sir Anthony dared to guffaw at the king's jest as Nick just gaped. Nick knew this was no time to dare to bring up the fact he wanted to discuss not wedding his own fiancée. At least this was his way into Rosalind's sanctuary, and mayhap he could snatch her away in time before the king saw her or vice versa. Nick's heart thundered as the king nodded, and Sir Anthony swept wide the door to the room where Nick had glimpsed Rosalind earlier.

"Just a humble visitor, a humbly expectant visitor," the king told the first two women who recognized him and, surprise on their faces, swept a low curtsy.

Now, Nick thought, mayhap those who had told the king his fiancée was most fair would begin to get their just comeuppance! Nick jolted to a halt beside the king.

Rosalind had evidently been speaking with the Lady Anne after the bride was prepared for bed. Rosalind still wore her only good court gown, the tawny velvet one that made her glow golden. Her head was uncovered and her thick hair tumbled loose. Nick had never seen the little spitfire look more alluring, even if he would have liked to strangle her right then. The Lady Anne was sitting on a stool, gazing up while Rosalind spoke to her in that infernal, guttural chatter of theirs.

When the room suddenly hushed, Rosalind turned in midsentence and caught sight of Nick and the men. She gasped. Nick wondered what was going through that quick mind of hers on first facing the Tudor monarch. Or did she even know it was the king? The Lady Anne looked frozen where she sat, a brocade robe over her night rail, her large mouth hanging open. She was a brunette now, for her blond locks—a wig—dangled from the hands of a lady-in-waiting. All the other women curtsied low, but for Rosalind, who stood gaping from one man to the other.

"His majesty, the king!" Nick muttered with a downward jerk of his head. Did the rural wench not know to curtsy, too?

"No, Nick," Henry intoned. "This paragon of beauty shall not bow before her future king and husband! Indeed, I, as her lowly suitor, must bow to her and only pray the lovely language that came dripping like honey from her tongue will soon include the words 'I love you, husband!'"

Before Nick could move, Henry Tudor, King of England, thumped down on his good knee before the mute, wide-eyed Rosalind.

Nick knew things could only go from bad to worse: he scented disaster for them all here. He had to try to salvage things now. "How clever of you, your grace," he said, and laid a hand on the king's huge, padded shoulder. "You knew not to overwhelm your bride without giving her a moment to compose herself. This is, as you of course knew, the translator, your majesty. Your bride sits there and cannot speak a word of English, so I'm sure she appreciates this brilliant pantomime of yours. You were always skilled at theatrics, sire."

"What! Uh, yes," the king choked out and went ruby red to his very jowls. He lumbered back to his feet; his eyes narrowed as they went over his intended, who rose slowly, then wilted into a shaky curtsy, holding her robe tightly around her lanky form. As Rosalind shuffled away, Nick pulled her back against the wall.

"I do not love or intend to wed Penelope," he whispered, surprised at the firmness of his words, but this was a night for surprises. "Besides, you and I may be rotting in a dungeon on the morrow, considering the chaos you have made when I trusted you!"

"You trusted! Chaos I've made? I—"

"Silence! His grace will not be taken with the Lady Anne. She is doomed with him, but it will be you and I with her if you do not come with me. Now!"

He thought for a moment she would argue or fight him. He considered clapping his hand over her mouth and dragging her out. But the king's voice drowned Nick's final plea.

"Not a word of our language and looks like—like this, when I was led to believe . . . otherwise?" the king ranted, speaking to no one in particular. "'S blood, there will be someone who pays dear for this deception! Betrothed or not, I like her not!"

The king's words almost gave Nick hope, but not quite. He had seen the king in his rages before, striking out at even those closest to him. And right now Rosalind, by appearing to be a pretty Lady Anne at first, had no doubt contributed to riling the king. And Nick himself had delivered Anne to him, and then when asked in the hall, had not dared to say he knew his majesty would dislike his new bride. Dislike! That was not the word for the sputtering fury that was starting to erupt here!

Rosalind evidently grasped all this, too. After all, she had told him her father had a vile temper that she was sometimes afraid she had inherited. Whatever her thinking, Nick did not even have to escort Rosalind toward the door. Her feet were as swift as his as the two of them hurried out through the corridors into the crisp January night.

"Where are we going?" Rosalind asked, hurrying so fast she almost tripped over her skirts before she lifted them in both hands. Neither of them had taken time to retrieve so much as a cloak. "The king and Lady Anne will wonder—"

"I just hope his grace has a translator or two at Greenwich so he can at least speak to her, as I have been trying to speak to you for days!" Nick interrupted as he pulled her toward the stable block of the bishop's palace. "And as for their wondering, they're probably wondering at how they both got into this mess!"

Nick was wondering the same thing about himself and Rosalind, but he knew they must flee now and make a new plan. Their only hope was that the royal wrath over being misled about the beauty of his bride would not spill over onto them. Everything had become such a risk, and the odds against them kept escalating.

He touched his index finger to his lips to signal silence as they approached the stable. He would find both their horses and they would ride to his house at Greenwich and spend the night there; it was the safest place nearby he could think of. Then, as soon as possible, especially in case Putnam had Cromwell meddling in this, he was going to smuggle—yes, damn it, *smuggle*—himself and Rosalind in to see the king. They had to speak with his majesty before Cromwell did! And one thing he had to dare—he hoped the king's displeasure with his own betrothed would help—was to ask to be released from his promise to Penelope.

"I just want you to know," Rosalind said, as if she could read his thoughts, "I have not forgotten or forgiven your not telling me about your fiancée."

"You have mentioned it every time we have talked the past few days. Why should I think you'd forgotten? There's no time now, but I spoke the truth about not wedding her. I swear to you, Rosalind, when it comes to love, she means no more to me than you claimed your French friend, Pierre, does to you. I believed you on that."

"You did not. You were green with jealousy!"

"Would you be quiet! I was just furious that you were intimate with the French foe! And as for Penelope, she hardly has her heart set on me, either. The entire thing was an arranged marriage—"

"By the king, whom you dare not displease."

"Betrothals can be broken, Rosalind," he said far more loudly than he'd intended.

"So can promises," she clipped back, "but for the time being, I have to trust you."

He again held up his finger for silence, as they entered the stable. He was relieved to see the stable boys sprawled in the hay in sodden slumber. Nick located the horses; Rosalind helped him saddle them and tighten the cinches. Her cool head and willingness to help when she had been defying him for days amazed and moved him anew. She was not one to stand about wringing her hands as most women he knew would have done. Or perhaps Rosalind, of all the women he knew, did not grasp the danger of the royal wrath.

He gave her a boost up and put her foot in the sidesaddle stirrups under her voluminous skirts. He mounted and they moved their horses at a slow walk out the back way. They would have to ride by the palace to take the river road. He prayed they would not be seen. With everyone trying to cover his own culpability, mayhap courtiers would not think a thing of his suddenly departing his duty. He could always say that once the king arrived, he knew Lady Anne was in good hands—bless the poor woman.

"And bless us all," Nick muttered as they started slowly around the corner of the brick palace.

But they both reined in at the sound of a single horse's swift hoofbeats. The rider's face was lit by torchlight as he rode by hoodless and dismounted before the building.

"Nick, that's Putnam's man, Roger Shanks!"

But Nick had already dismounted. "Stay back!" he hissed and loped around the corner of the building. He ran the short distance in the grass and tackled Shanks before he had climbed two steps. They hit hard together on the stone stairs and rolled down. Shanks grunted. Quickly and effectively, Nick silenced him with a blow to the jaw that knocked him cold, then dragged him into the shadows and around the building where Rosalind waited. He ran back for Shanks's horse.

"Nick, what can it mean?"

"Nothing good for us. Hold his horse's reins while I tie his hands and boost him over his saddle. Master Shanks is going with us!"

Nick divested Shanks of his cape and handed it up to keep Rosalind warm. She settled it around herself with a slight shudder. More anxious now, they cut through the dark gardens. Soon, they were galloping down the river road.

In the two-stall stable behind Nick's small house on the Thames just north of Greenwich, he lit a lantern, dumped the now conscious Shanks, gagged and trussed, in the straw and searched his saddle packs. Then, none too gently, he went through the man's clothes.

"Aha!" Nick gloated and held up a folded missive. "Hell's gates, Cromwell's seal," he muttered as he carefully slit the wax from the parchment and leaned under the lantern to read it.

Rosalind watched as Nick's face, usually such a sun-struck brown, paled. "More bad news?" she asked, her hand on his arm.

"The worst, but we shall overcome it. Only I cannot offer you my hospitality here this night as I had wanted, sweet. I hope I may some other, better time. We shall have to move on now."

"Why? What does it say?" she demanded and reached for the letter. *Some other, better time.* His plaintive words echoed in her brain. Would there ever be such for them? Could she really trust him now? But she must! She not only must, but she would! But things seemed to be spinning so fast out of their control now. They must flee now, and more and more powerful people could seek their demise.

While Nick boosted Shanks upright in his saddle this time, she skimmed the letter. She, too, interpreted it the way Nick must have, reading the lines—and between them. The fact that Shanks was the carrier meant Putnam had gone to Cromwell with his poisonous lies. Unfortunately, it was easy to guess the identities of "the traitor close to the king's heart and the woman who has seduced him from his senses to smuggling and foul treason." She realized, as Nick must, that Cromwell could have sent someone to arrest them. Besides, it must be a crime to abduct a messenger with a letter sent between the lord chamberlain and the king. They were truly fugitives together now, no doubt fleeing for more than just their freedom. Whatever trials Nick had brought on himself, she felt a deep stab of remorse that she had brought Nick to this.

She refolded the letter and stuffed it down the front of her gown. Cromwell's seal felt cold against her flushed skin, as cold as the serpent that the man himself must be. She did not even question Nick about their destination this time as he helped her mount. She had cast her lot in life with him; if he took her to far-off Araby or the savage Americas, she would follow.

But he only took them to a small inn at a hamlet a few miles farther north. As he dismounted and helped her down, longing flooded her for the Rose and Anchor and that other inn they had once shared in France. And how she wished she could have seen the inside of his small house in Greenwich tonight so she could have imagined just once that she was entering it as his bride. But no, besides the immediate dangers, there was still the problem of Lady Penelope Wentworth. She of beauty and dowry and the king's favor, the king whose goodwill Rosalind and Nick needed now for their very survival. Nick might want to break his betrothal, but could he do it now and keep his coveted position? Could he do it now and still have enough power to help Deal and to save her? Could he himself survive? And if he must do as the king said, could she be strong enough to let him do it?

"Rosalind, are you all right?" Nick's voice pierced her agonizings. "Keep a stout heart. I know the innkeeper here. I shall be inside but one moment, and then we shall go in the back way."

True to his word, he was not gone long, though it seemed an eternity to her. He returned and led her and the horses around to the back of the half-timbered building. He untied Shanks's ankles and shoved the frightened man ahead of him up narrow wooden stairs, lit by the innkeeper's lantern. Rosalind followed as she saw a boy lead their horses away. The second-story chamber seemed quite lavish compared with the look of the exterior.

"Never mind building a fire. Food and water later when I call down," Nick told the wiry innkeeper, who nodded, left the lantern and disappeared.

While Rosalind lit candles from the lantern, Nick pushed Shanks into a chair. The man's eyes glowed as big as gold sovereigns; he tried to mutter through his gag.

"Best turn your back if you do not want to see this," Nick warned Rosalind. "The wretch is going to tell us all he knows of Master Putnam's dirty dealings, or he will wish he had never seen the light of day."

Shanks gasped so hard he almost swallowed his gag. "And when I am done with him, he is going before the king to tell all," Nick went on, his voice cold and calm as he shoved Shanks's head back against the chair with a tight hand on his jaw. "But first, let me just gauge the loyalty of this knave to his master—the master for whom he will hang after we are finished with him!" He pulled the gag from the man's mouth.

"Please—none of it my fault—taking orders, my lord . . . just earning some coins to live by," Shanks croaked out.

"Then you will tell us all," Rosalind cut in.

"Aye, mistress, if you be certain I'll have my life in fair trade. I only did what I was told, I only—"

"But why? Why does Percy hate us so?" she demanded.

"Mayhap 'cause you cared for his lordship here, who has usurped Master Putnam's place to command Deal," Shanks blurted, obviously eager to please. "Other than that, don't know, but there's much I do know!"

Rosalind frowned and shook her head. She felt she should know from whence Percy's deep-seated hatred sprang, but she could not quite fathom it. For someone to be so jovial and ingratiating on the surface and so festering with hatred inside—it had to be more than a crooked, short leg that warped a man so.

"All right, let's hear it from the first," Nick demanded.

"You mean the spying?" Shanks asked. He was sickeningly eager to please, Rosalind thought. But she, too, had feared when she had faced Nick's wrath—though it was more fear for her Rosies and Deal than for herself. Somehow, after the first time Nick touched and kissed her, she had known deep inside he would not brutalize her no matter what. Shanks had no such protection or hope.

"Yes, the spying," Nick demanded.

"Well, there was the night Master Putnam and I watched Mistress Rosalind get off her horse and go into the castle with you, then the time she was pretending to kiss the brewer, Wat, in the vale—"

"You were there, too?" Nick exploded.

"Sure. You had your man watching her, too, like a jealous lover."

Rosalind dared to roll her eyes as if to say, I told you so, when Nick glared her way.

"And you say she just *pretended* to kiss Wat?" Nick demanded.

"Oh, aye, I saw it all. No doubt to get your dander up, my lord. Then there was the night I saw you haul her off toward that boat along the Sandwich road—"

"That's where Putnam got onto the trafficking-with-the-traitorous-French idea," Nick said to her.

"Yes, but it was a risk!" Rosalind countered. She was shaking at Shanks's admissions of watching her. Nick looked so furious she was grateful Shanks had not given him a chance to pummel him.

"A calculated risk I was prepared to handle," Nick dismissed her protest. "Say on, Shanks!"

"Well, then 'ventually, we went to Cromwell with it all, 'cause he'd like to see you fall, just like Putnam would for shaming him 'fore the town the day of the parade and all..."

Rosalind listened as the interrogation went on and on. Her stomach twisted tight on the realization that someone as powerful as Thomas Cromwell wanted to see Nick fall, but her thoughts chiefly concerned the man she had once erroneously called Petty Percy. She knew there was something deeper there than Shanks's belief that Putnam wanted her for himself. He'd never made the slightest move that way. No, Percy Putnam hated her and Deal, and she felt she should know why. But it would not come to her. She grasped why the limping man who had once thought he commanded the town and would find the smugglers out himself could detest Nick. But where was the key to Putnam's evidently maniacal hatred of the kindly folk of Deal?

After their lengthy interrogation of Shanks was complete, both Nick and Rosalind stood stunned. She understood not only Percy, but Nick, better now, for she knew why Nick had questioned and threatened Wat and her. She shuddered to think to what lengths she would have stooped had Shanks not been such a mercenary and a moral coward. With scant prodding but Nick's threats, he had spilled all the details of his spying in Deal and Sandwich and all of Putnam's and Cromwell's plans.

Nick's stomach clenched tight as a fist. He could not believe he had come to this looming precipice in his life. His dear monarch mayhap turned against him. Crafty Cromwell so much more deadly than he had ever imagined, pulling tight his snare. The woman he was betrothed to in a mutual business arrangement a far cry from the flesh-and-blood woman he really wanted. The woman he should arrest or abandon for his own survival the most important person in his life.

"Nick, we still must go before the king, but he was so angry tonight," Rosalind said.

"In facing him, I shall have to rely on the strong relationship I have built with him over the years." He turned to face her. Despite Shanks staring up at them, Nick put an arm around her waist and tipped her chin up with his finger. "And you will have to rely on the relationship that has bloomed between us these past months—despite overwhelming odds."

"Trust."

"Yes."

"And love, Nick. That was never a lie, though I warrant it is one of the overwhelming odds."

He started to speak, then nodded. She saw his eyes glisten. He squeezed her waist, then went out into the hall to call his friend, who came quickly up the steps.

"Hold the food until about four in the morning, Lester," she heard Nick say. "But if you would watch our prisoner for us, I will see you are handsomely rewarded."

"You takin' on my boy Stephen as your man and raisin' his name with yours all these years, my lord, that is all the reward I'll e'er need," Lester said. He pulled Shanks to his feet and led him out. Lester must be Captain Delancey's father, Rosalind realized, but there was no time to ask. So Nick, too, had friends who were loyal to him and would risk all to help him. Yes, at the very core of their beings, they were alike and made to be together! she vowed.

Nick came back in and lifted her in his arms. Both fully clothed, they lay on the bed, facing each other in a fierce, mutual embrace.

"We must try to sleep till four or so, then set out for Greenwich Palace to see the king soon after he arises," Nick whispered. "Somehow I shall obtain an audience for us before Cromwell stops us."

"With all the coming celebration in the afternoon, it should be a busy place."

"I just hope Cromwell does not have guards there to arrest us. But even if they go to my house, they will not find us here, my sweetheart. Can you get a little rest? We need it sorely, I am afraid."

"But Nick, even if I could rest, I am not certain I want to. Not when we are together like this, and mayhap if things go awry—or if to save yourself you must wed Penelope—time like this will not be ours again. Oh, Nick, I know I've nothing to offer like the king's favor or prestige or dowry or—"

His lips silenced hers. He splayed his spread fingers through her hair to cradle her head. "I have always done what his majesty asked," he muttered in her ear when their lips parted at last. "But I wed once at his royal will, and in Deal I have seen the advantages of deciding some things for myself. I hope and pray that the king's disappointment in his own bride will not make him want company by having others wed those they would not have. Wedding Penelope now—it would be a last-ditch effort, only if all my other efforts to save you and Deal fail."

His voice and face were so intense. Rosalind thrilled with hope. But the king was the king, and indeed, Nick had ever sought to please him. Besides, even if he did not wed Lady Penelope, it did not mean he would wed Mistress Rosalind, innkeeper and smuggler.

Yet she threw her arms around him and held him close. If this were the last night of her life she could ever lie in his arms, these final memories would have to last a very, very long time.

"We shall not disrobe, my love, but that does not mean we cannot be one," he told her breathlessly. Yet soon her gown was gone, her petticoats strewn and her chemise up to her chin. They joined, holding hard, then became still and content before the storm came.

"I love you, Nick, and ever will!"

Propped up on his elbow, he lifted his head to gaze down at her. He realized then that he had never told a woman he loved her. But things were yet in so much chaos he feared he still could not say it, could not dare to mean it.

"I— Trust is all I can offer now, my Rosalind. That and my undying admiration of you, no matter what befalls us. I pray it is enough for now."

She nodded. It was not all she had hoped for, but it was the only rock she had to cling to now. And then the tempest swept them away together.

At last Rosalind lay quiet in Nick's arms, drugged with sleep. But fears assailed her, fears for her future without him, regret that her past had not been different. If she could but go back to when she was a child, a child before memories began. A child before there was danger and deceit and desperation—even before Percy came to town to take his father's place as the king's revenue man.

Rosalind's eyes flew open. She was wide awake. Her body stiffened in Nick's arms, but he slept on. It was not a dream she had, but the memory she had buried about Percy that came crashing back.

She must have been newly five years old that time Percy's father's horse tripped on the lugger lines on the beach. And the boy had been so horribly crushed beneath the big beast. Yes, she recalled it now, as horrendous as it had been.

She had been there, standing against the wall to see her father strap the boy's shattered leg together to save it. He had not let the carpenter cut it off or the blacksmith cauterize it, though both men stood ready. Yet Percy's cries had made her shake and cry.

After it was all over, she sidled closer to the sobbing lad. She pitied him that his father had seemed to mourn his lost horse but not his son. He had blamed his boy and stomped from the room to drown his sorrows in more fine wine. But little Rosalind had patted Percy's hand and said, "Poor lad. My father is the one set your leg. My father says—"

But he had shrieked at her and called her names. He had cursed all of Deal. Her father had run back in and, arm around her quaking shoulders, ushered her out.

"Best to leave him be, Ros. His pain has made him wild. Nothing to be done for him right now by a mere slip of a wench."

That's it! she thought, lying rigid in Nick's arms. Percy was older than she. Percy recalled that day and somehow hated her for it! Mayhap hated her father when he should have hated his own. It was not his leg that had crippled him, but his hateful, selfish father. And now they had to face Nick's foster father, Henry Tudor, in but a few hours. She shuddered and Nick's arms tightened as he woke.

"Are you all right?" he asked. "My friend said he would wake us when it was time."

"I just recalled something about Percy. Nick, it's not that he cares for me and is jealous of you. I think he hates me as much as he does you. He must have always hated me, and I just did not know!"

His lips moved in her tresses behind her ear. "Wat was just the opposite. He has loved you for years, and you did not know."

Her stomach cartwheeled. All those years while Wat was Murray's friend, and then hers? That day she had kissed Wat in the woods and made light of his blush and his heavy breathing? And mayhap he had tried to kill Nick to have her for himself. Poor, dear Wat! She had known Pierre cared for her, but Wat had suffered years in silence, just as she might have to do now, if she lost Nick.

"Oh, Nick, I have been so stupid, such a failure!"

He turned her to face him. "You, stupid? You outfoxed me! You, a failure? You kept Deal going for years and showed me what friendship can be! It's what I longed for and never really had, Rosalind. I had no real friends at court, only acquaintances and rivals, but for the king. The men under my command were loyal, but that is not like having friends. But your entire town would have died for you! It is just that you have tried to be too much to too many! Besides, I tell you, it was Wat's feelings for you that made me treat him as gently as I did. If we get back to Deal, I shall find a way to pardon him. It's obvious that a man in love with you can do crazy things!"

She hugged Nick hard in gratitude. "I'm not sure that was a compliment, my lord. You mean you pitied him because he cared for me?" she asked.

"I think I understood him, that is all. I used to feel I was in control of my life—even when indeed it was the king—but that went heels up when I met you. You are the most unique, precious person I have ever known, my Rosie. And if we manage to get out of this—"

"My Lord Spencer!" Lester Delancey called through the door. "Nearly four of the clock!"

"Time to go," Nick said and kissed her soundly before rolling off the other side of the bed.

Rosalind sat up and scooted off her side. Time to go, indeed, but to what? Nick's future, her safety, Deal's very existence, her love for him, which he had never admitted he returned—all was at hazard now. How she yearned to go down to their horses and flee to live anywhere with him! But they both had responsibilities, duties. And they were going to fight for their futures. She only hoped and prayed those futures could be together. The room was icy cold but she felt flushed with hope.

Within twenty minutes, they headed their mounts toward Greenwich Palace, with Roger Shanks, tied and seated on his horse, behind them.

On the way, they made multiple plans for what they would do and say if Cromwell's men tried to impede their access to the king. They hoped the lord chamberlain would think they had returned to Deal once his men did not find them at the bishop's palace or Nick's house, if they had gone there.

As they neared their destination, they saw early preparations for the royal welcoming festivities through the silvery morning river mist. Boats were being decked for a water pageant on the Thames, perfumed bonfires were being built and tents for courtiers and displays by city merchants were being erected. A broad way was cleared for two miles across Woolwich Common and Black Heath to the very gates of Greenwich Park, where a pavilion of cloth of gold awaited the formal meeting of the bride and bridegroom.

Deciding a brazen front would be their best chance, they left their horses with a stable boy and entered the front gate of the palace. With Rosalind on his arm and his pistol hidden by his sleeve but pointed at Shanks's back, Nick approached the first set of guards in the king's wing of the sprawling, red brick building.

"The Lord Lieutenant of Deal and the companion of Lady Anne of Cleves to see the king," Nick informed them with an impatient gesture toward the closed doors. Damn, he thought, but the regular guards who would just pass him through must be preparing for the ceremonies today.

"An' him, my lord?" the guard asked, pointing to Shanks. Both pikes still barred their way.

"My valet, of course, sirrah!"

At his fierce look, the guards let them pass, despite the fact a valet would never have walked slightly ahead of his master. They kept a good pace down the polished parquet floor toward the king's audience chamber. Nick felt Rosalind trembling, but she held her head high. Though petite and delicate, she seemed tall and strong. Despite all they had been through, she still looked stunning and defiant—regal, really. Yes, he had no doubt Mistress Rosalind Barlow could hold her own at court. And he admitted he would like to see her rapier wit duel with some of the forked-tongue courtiers here.

Luck was with him! The guards at the king's doors recognized him, though one protested, "My Lord Spencer, his grace has been up all night, and no one's to go in."

"But he told us to come at the crack of dawn, and on this day of days, who could disobey, eh?"

The guard leaned closer. "Last night his ire was up. Some say he won't go through with it." He shrugged, then opened the pair of oaken doors. Nick felt Rosalind stiffen as they stepped inside. So far, success, he thought as they entered the deserted audience chamber.

The draperies were still drawn, closing out the morning light. Mayhap his majesty's mood was foul enough that Cromwell dared not yet approach to spout his poison of smuggling and treason, Nick mused. Or the dark raven might think his message had been safely delivered by Shanks, and that his grace would take his own precautions against being approached by anyone close to him. Mayhap that was why the suite still looked deserted. According to the next step in their plan, Nick handed Rosalind his pistol and whipped out a length of cord to retie Shanks's hands behind his back. As an extra precaution, he gagged the man, too.

"If anyone enters and protests, remember, Rosalind, do not resist. Merely call for me, and I shall come running. It would be folly for you to hold a gun on any member of the king's court or his guards, though you may certainly shoot this one if he makes a move. I shall be out to fetch you and our singing bird here as soon as I can manage.''

Nick dropped a kiss on her lips. The thought hit him he must be mad to trust Rosalind with a loaded gun within the king's privy chambers—she who had once vowed revenge. But she was an intelligent woman, and she saw the best hope for their future. He trusted her.

But he feared, in the back of his mind that he might still have to fulfill his vow to Penelope in order to appease his majesty. If it were the only way to save Rosalind and Deal, he would do it. And if he were forced to wed his betrothed, he only hoped Rosalind would understand. If their parting were the only way he could save her and Deal, he hoped she would believe his great esteem for her.

But there was no time for other vows or orders or even farewells. He tried to smile at her, but his face felt as if it would crack. He strode away and knocked twice on the withdrawing room door. Of course it was still early, and the king could be in his bedchamber in the room beyond. No answer, no sound.

''My lord king, 'tis Nick Spencer. Important news that cannot wait, your grace!''

The door opened into the dim room and, praying Cromwell had not come before to do more damage, Nick stepped in. The gentleman usher who had opened it closed it quietly behind him and retreated far across the room.

Henry Tudor sat in a big carved chair, facing the eastern window and holding a large flagon. His dark blue velvet gown seemed a shroud around the huge man. As Nick approached, he saw the robe was draped over the same garb the king had worn last night. Keeping their distance, two gentlemen ushers, three valets and a secretary hovered on the far side of the room. Nick had imagined he would find a raging inferno, but the voice that greeted him was bitter and listless.

"You were wise to disappear when I saw her last night, my boy," his majesty said without turning his head. He lifted his injured leg down from the padded stool and shoved the stool toward Nick across the wooden floor. He drank deeply from his flagon as Nick came closer.

Nick bowed, then sat as silently bidden. So far, so good. But his head was much lower than the king's; he felt at a great disadvantage. Though that fact would have rankled with him a few months ago, he took heart from the fact the king had called him "my boy."

"What momentous news, then?" the king asked, his voice a monotone despite the fact he was obviously seething. "Unless it is that Lady Anne of Cleves was as affrighted by me as I by her and is taking a boat back to the Rhineland, I care not to hear it."

He took another big swig and wiped his wet mustache with the back of his hand. His face looked creased, his eyes bloodshot. It was obvious to Nick the king of England had not slept at all last night, and lack of rest always made him especially ill-humored.

"I grieved when I first saw her, your majesty, for I knew that she would not find favor in your eyes, though many had led you to believe she would."

"God's truth," the king gritted out through clenched teeth. He had not yet looked at Nick.

"But your orders said to deliver her safely to you and—"

"And you have ever been dedicated to my orders, Nick."

"Yes, your grace, as best I could. And your rewards and care have flowed most bounteously to me. Now, not to mislead you of my true intent, I would ask a few moments of your time, however important a day this is."

Henry Tudor snorted. "The day I place my head, unwilling, on the marital block! I, who should have the last say in all that affects the king's majesty! In an hour my courtiers and my people will line the way for a glimpse of my new queen, one I would not wed or bed!" He heaved the heavy silver flagon against the wall, where it spilled red wine like blood. No one else in the room moved. Silence reigned again.

Nick knew time was of the essence. Though Cromwell was no doubt running here and there in an effort to control the events of the day, it did not mean the crafty raven—even with Putnam in tow—might not be here soon. From his doublet Nick removed the letter he had taken from Shanks last night.

"Your grace," he said as he extended the letter to him with a shaky hand, "I tell you I have discovered the smugglers of Deal and also a way they might serve you well. If you would but read this letter, I shall explain more."

"A confession?" the king inquired as he snatched the letter.

"Of sorts, sire."

"But with Cromwell's hand and seal." The king frowned as he skimmed the letter, then read it carefully again. Nick watched the beady eyes move up and down the page. He prayed he could complete this interview without Cromwell's intrusion.

"'The traitor close to the king's heart and the woman who has seduced him from his senses to smuggling and foul treason'?" the king read aloud and turned to Nick at last. "What is this? *Who* is this?" he roared and jabbed his thick finger at the page.

Nick tried to sit straight and stay serene. This must be done deftly and quickly, then Rosalind and Shanks brought in. But he could see the vein in the king's bull neck throbbing; it ever heralded a fit of royal spleen. Nick feared he had been demented to try this after the Anne of Cleves debacle. He tried to sound calm, not craven.

"Cromwell is the one close to your heart who has failed you, and I would tell you why. To tell true, your grace, Cromwell accuses me and the woman I—I love. A woman from Deal."

He was astounded at what he had just said. He had not even admitted his love to Rosalind. If things went wrong here, he might only be able to tell her of his love in parting from her.

"'S Blood, Nick, you! And the woman you love! I take it you do not mean Lady Penelope! No one is bidden to love a woman when the king is tied to that—that horse-faced German!"

"Tied only by Cromwell, your grace. Alas, he has tried to maneuver you as he has others."

"You speak bold and dangerous words. Cromwell maneuvers others, *not* his king! But for this marital mishmash— 'S blood, do not stare like a dolt! Say on!"

"First, your majesty, if you would permit me, I would bring in the woman of whom I speak and a witness we have captured—the courier of that letter."

"I am sick to death of even the thought of wenches!" the king exploded, then lowered his voice. "So, what sort is she, this so-called seducer accused here of smuggling and foul treason?"

"A sweet but somewhat spirited woman, your grace, unjustly accused. This report of her is as cleverly misleading as that given you by Cromwell about Anne of Cleves. Your majesty, you voiced your approval of this woman from Deal last night in the presence of your courtiers and the Lady Anne. If I may but step out to fetch her in..."

The king's red-gray eyebrows had risen higher and higher at that last speech. He gestured brusquely and muttered, "Yes, yes, I'll hear the rest of it and see her. Fetch this sweet, somewhat spirited woman, then!"

Nick jumped up and hurried to the door. A spate of answers he could have given to the king's question, "what sort is she?" raced through his mind. Now, everything depended on Rosalind's proper, careful handling of the king.

He yanked the door open and gestured to Rosalind to come in. Across the room where he had left her holding the pistol on Roger Shanks, she now also held a second man at gunpoint. And that man, hands in the air, sputtering with fury, was the Lord Chamberlain of England, Thomas Cromwell!

Chapter Thirteen

❦

"Rosalind, that is Lord Cromwell!" Nick protested.

"I assure you," she said without turning her head, "he announced himself quite plainly. When he recognized Shanks and told me who he was, I had to stop him to give you time!"

"Foul sedition!" Cromwell shouted, bringing the king lumbering to the door. "A woman armed in the king's chambers!"

"'S blood, Nick," King Henry roared, "is that your 'sweet, somewhat spirited' woman? Have you brought Cromwell, too?" he demanded as the raised voices brought his two guards dashing in.

The king waved the guards away and motioned to the others. "In here, the lot of you! I never did favor women with any sort of power in their hands, Lord Lieutenant of Deal!"

Quickly, Rosalind handed Nick the gun. As if to rid herself of guilt, she hastily wiped her hands on her velvet skirt as she sank in a low curtsy before her king.

King Henry came closer, peering down at her in the dimness. "Indeed, I know you, do I not, young woman? Cromwell, open a drape," he ordered, as if he were addressing the lowest lackey. Cromwell sputtered in protest, but hastened to obey.

A shaft of sunlight leaped across the floor to bathe Rosalind in gold. Her blond hair and tawny velvet gown seemed to glitter. Still windblown from the ride, she straightened and stood her ground, staring up at the tall king through her thick, sun-gilded lashes. Nick and Cromwell glared at each other. Shanks, still gagged, hung his head and shuffled his feet. But the moment belonged to the colossus King Henry and the petite Rosie from Deal.

"Your grace, I regret our first meeting was so confusing," Rosalind began. "How long I have looked forward to telling you what is in my heart. And then, last night, to have such a misunderstanding and case of mistaken identity—my fault, of course."

"Ah, yes," King Henry said. "Would I had not been mistaken. But you were only doing a service for the Lady Anne. It seems my lord chamberlain, who agonized over most details—did you not, Cromwell?—forgot to find a translator for the Lady Anne."

That small accusation against Cromwell gave Rosalind hope. Mayhap this would not be so dreadful. But even if it were, she was here to fight for Deal—and for Nick.

"And you say you have wanted to tell what is in your heart?" the king prompted. He extended a bent arm to her. Daintily, she placed her hand on it. Inclining her head, she looked up at him as he escorted her slowly toward the door to his withdrawing chamber.

"I have longed to tell you," Rosalind said, "how my little town needs your help and goodwill, your majesty. To tell you how grieved I am that I mayhap have been victim of misunderstandings—just like your majesty—before you saw me with Lady Anne."

Nick stood amazed at the instinctive female weapons with which Rosalind waged her war with the king. Once he had feared she would be a ranter and a raver like the fated Queen Anne Boleyn. But now he saw the core of sweetness in Rosalind that had made the king love his departed Queen Jane

Seymour. Yet jealousy ripped through Nick as remembrance racked him. Rosalind had been hostile to him in the beginning. She had tried her honeyed words on him and he had fallen headlong for her. Indeed, she had to coddle the king to coerce him, but did she have to look and act so charming? And as ever, despite his temper and current predicament, his grace was responding as if a new beauty had been brought to court at his whim!

But Nick was not the only one struck by Rosalind's rapport with the king. Cape flying, Cromwell strode after the king and Rosalind while Nick dragged Shanks along in their wake.

"Your majesty," Cromwell clipped out, "this woman heads the ring of smugglers in Deal. I have a witness—your own revenue and exciseman from Sandwich. She trafficked with the French! And she's seduced your ward, Spencer, to vile complicity!"

"Where is your witness?" the king demanded as he rounded on Cromwell.

"He felt he must return to command Deal—I assigned him to do so—when he realized Shanks, this man, was missing," Cromwell floundered.

"Then we shall hearken to the witness we do have," the king insisted with a nod to Nick. Nick pulled out Shanks's gag, and with no prodding, the mercenary coward spilled what he knew.

"The knave lies!" Cromwell insisted at several points in Shanks's narration. "They have obviously threatened or bribed the rogue!"

"You, of all men, ought to recognize such," King Henry retorted.

Rosalind saw that set Cromwell back on his heels. He glared darts at her and Nick, but dared not gainsay the king.

They entered the withdrawing room. The king indicated that she should sit on a stool, positioned before the big carved chair in which he sat. Nick and Cromwell hovered at either arm of the king's chair.

"Who speaks true, mistress, this rogue or my lord chamberlain?" King Henry demanded.

"This rogue, your majesty," Rosalind replied and clasped her hands on her knees before her as if in supplication. "I do not understand lord chamberlains, but mayhap they have reasons to lie, even to their sovereign lords at times."

"Indeed, they must have their reasons," King Henry muttered.

"Then I beseech you to let me tell my story, your majesty," Rosalind pleaded. "I admit complicity with Lord Spencer, but not as Lord Cromwell claims. My complicity is only that I came here to tell you all the truth, which some close to you would withhold and distort. In Lord Cromwell's letter, which Lord Spencer showed you, the one close to the king who would betray him is not your loyal Lord Lieutenant of Deal Castle!"

"Your majesty, will you be preached to by a mere rural wench, and a criminal at that?" Cromwell demanded, though he kept his voice well under control. "Not only does she lie, but you have not the time to hear such excuses. You must be about your business now to greet your queen this day."

"*Your* business to greet *your* queen *you* have saddled me with!" King Henry roared. Cromwell held his ground but flushed scarlet. His pudgy jaw hardened to stone.

"And," Nick put in, "besides choosing a queen who was obviously more suited to his needs than your grace's, I daresay Lord Cromwell has had other business he chose not to tell you of until much too late."

"Such as?" King Henry demanded, silencing Cromwell's sputtering protest. "It is Cromwell who told me of smuggling in Deal."

"But he surely did not tell you the rest of it, your majesty," Rosalind said quickly at Nick's nod. "He didn't tell you the whole truth about Deal. More than three years ago, Deal seamen rescued your sailors from a ship wrecked on the Downs. Deal lost a boat of men that night, including my father and husband.''

''So you are a widow?''

''Yes, your majesty. And I inherited an inn from my father, the Rose and Anchor, which would be honored for your presence should you visit Lord Spencer and your castle at Deal. Your master mason, Franklin Stanway, has wed my sister.''

''She intends to take you 'round Robin's barn, your grace,'' Cromwell insisted. ''She also inherited a smuggling band and has sold information of the castle to the French—with Spencer's aid, I tell you. That trip to France this man Shanks discovered was obviously for such perfidy.''

''Nick?'' King Henry said. ''We have Cromwell's word against this witness of yours and Mistress Rosalind's, it would seem. You have ever been loyal to me. Who tells true?''

''Lord Cromwell lies, sire. I went to France with the unwilling Mistress Barlow in tow to try to ferret out who the French smugglers were. I thought, since she was a familiar face at the Rose and Anchor, someone would recognize her and might unwittingly step forward. I felt the writs and warrants you had given me allowed me to go wherever I must to fulfill your orders, though if there had been time, I would have asked for your permission first, your grace.''

The king only nodded in encouragement of Nick's recital of events. Everyone hung on his words.

''Afterward, your majesty, I found Mistress Rosalind was a part of the smuggling band, but found no evidence of spying. Ask Cromwell who it was who sent some of your soldiers to stave in the very boats of Deal that had rescued your sailors three years ago! Ask him who tarnished your majesty's good name in Deal! Your lord chamberlain, who should be striving to build the crown's popularity with your people, caused an unfortunate rift between your grace and Deal. Just as Cromwell lied to you about the appearance of your next queen, he—''

"'S blood, 'tis true!" King Henry declared. He smacked his fist on Cromwell's chest and the man recoiled several steps. "And if you lied to your king about a wife, what a small thing to lie about doings in Deal, for your own ends, eh, Cromwell? I do not doubt but you have some spy there for your own purposes and take bribes or such to profit yourself in your quest for power, when it should be *my* power you protect!"

"But I ever strive thus, your grace! If I failed to inform you of my righteous punishment of some stupid band of smugglers, it was only in my industrious quest to lighten some of your grievous burdens," Cromwell said brazenly, but he backed away from the king's reach. "A minor decision three years ago to punish thieves and smugglers in a pitiful town—"

Rosalind leaped to her feet. "Pitiful only because for years it has been denied a royal market license, a denial that forced good, loyal citizens to take to the sea to earn their keep beyond fishing and rescuing!" she exploded at Cromwell. "And I see now that was probably not our gracious king's doing, but yours indeed!"

How long she had envisioned herself screaming such at the king himself, but now Cromwell had to do. Besides, she realized now, mayhap most of the blame was Cromwell's, with Percy Putnam in collusion. Despite his grief and anger, the king had been quite kind to her when she had expected a foul monster. Why, he only had a temper like her father's and her own, so she felt quite at home fending off his quibbles and his questions! In a whoosh of skirts, she sank back on her stool.

"But *are* Deal people good and loyal?" King Henry demanded, with a glance at Nick, then back to her. "Smugglers cannot be good or loyal!"

"Your Majesty," she answered, "Deal folk are good and loyal enough to risk their lives to rescue your men on the sea. They did it twice, the second time even after they thought you had no care for their first rescue. And they would do it again. They are loyal enough to pledge their help to you now, should you need their boats to patrol the shores against a French incursion. Loyal enough to ask that you might grant them permission to pilot your vessels in the dangerous Downs where Lord Spencer almost lost his life when you sent him to Deal."

"She argues like a clever cleric, Nick."

"I know, your grace."

"And in a pretty package, too."

"I do not argue, your majesty," Rosalind said, blushing at the way the king's eyes studied her, head to toes. Yes, she thought, Nick Spencer was indeed this man's foster son in some ways.

"Your majesty," she went on, her voice becoming steadier all the time, "I beseech you to reach out your hand to Deal, which longs for reconciliation with you. Lord Spencer said you were merciful and just, and that has given me courage to plead the case of my people before you, even in the presence of Lord Cromwell."

"Whom, I believe, has much to do today, with the arrangements *he* has made for *his* new queen to arrive," King Henry intoned and glared at his livid lord chamberlain. For one moment, Cromwell gasped like a fish out of water. It was obvious to Rosalind that he knew he was clinging by a gossamer thread to the king's goodwill.

"Indeed, there is much to do, your majesty," Cromwell acquiesced. "Shall I take this man with me for safekeeping?" he inquired smoothly, pointing to Shanks.

"No, leave him. And leave me!" the king demanded, his voice rising. "We shall talk much on these things after we get through this farce you have fashioned for your king today! Out, get out!"

Fuming, Cromwell did just that.

"Now," King Henry said, "Mistress Rosalind, I will ask you a straight question. Have you smuggled in Deal?"

"Yes, your grace. I am here to make amends and cast myself on your mercy."

Nick thought Rosalind had never looked more alluring. Though bereft of jewels and clad in a wrinkled, windblown gown, she seemed to him as lovely as any lady of the court. She was adorable, and he adored her.

King Henry evidently agreed. He patted her hands, which she was gripping before her, and nodded in apparent understanding and forgiveness. Nick breathed a sigh of relief. If he could just end things now and spirit her away, mayhap they would have a chance to survive all this.

"And, your majesty, I must also admit I love Nick Spencer," Rosalind declared.

Nick's insides cartwheeled. Did the woman dare to plead for everything she wanted? On this subject, she had best tread more carefully today, considering the king's own lovelorn predicament. And what if the king announced that Nick had said he loved her, too? There was much yet to accomplish to settle things fairly with Penelope, to manage the citizens of Deal and to capture Percy. He could surely not think of telling Rosalind he loved her yet, nor of any sort of commitment beyond. He held his breath.

"I realize," she went on, while both men stared at her, "that Lord Spencer regards you with the utmost loyalty and affection. When I nursed him through a deadly fever after he almost drowned, even in his delirium he declared you were to him as a beloved, trusted mentor, almost a father—"

"Well," King Henry said and this time put his big hands over her small clenched ones, "perhaps not enough older to be a father, but a trusted and wise friend. True, my man?"

"It is, your grace," Nick said. He took a deep breath and came to a decision. For the first time in his life, he would defy the wishes of his king. The king seemed gracious enough now, but if the royal temper was roused again, Nick only prayed he could save Rosalind and yet break his betrothal to Penelope. The king must mean to go through with his unwanted wedding to Anne of Cleves. Nick had feared he might have to do the same to prove that very trust and obedience he had just proclaimed.

But he knew now that such vows of total obedience to the king or Penelope were impossible for him to make, even if his new-sought independence got in the way of his God-given—that is, king-given—duty. He wanted to free Penelope from a betrothal as cold on her part as it was his. He wished her well, that she might find love someday, and he would write such to her if the king allowed it.

"Your majesty, I would ask another favor from your generous nature today. For personal reasons, I would like your permission to break my betrothal to the Lady Penelope Wentworth. She and I, I fear, entered into the arrangement for the wrong reasons."

The king's beady eyes darted to Rosalind's face. She fought to keep it calm. "I believe I see the allure of your personal reasons," he said. "And I, on this of all days, can appreciate wedding for the wrong reasons. Let this request of yours be granted, then, Nick, and if she wishes, I shall find Penelope another fine match. You, I take it, are best left to your own devices."

Rosalind bit her lip to keep from exploding in tears of relief and gratitude. The king frowned down at his fists on the arm of his chair. Shanks just shook his head and leaned against the wall.

"Above all, kings should be the ones to choose their own wives, and they are not," King Henry muttered, though to no one in particular. He leaned back in his chair and closed his bloodshot eyes for one moment. "I should be and I am not. Trapped, trapped, but I will find a way out of this."

Nick sat on the edge of Rosalind's stool and they clasped hands. He was surprised to feel her trembling more than he. Despite the lift of her chin and set of her face, tears tracked silently down her cheeks.

It was quiet in the room for a moment, though Rosalind longed to touch the king's hand as he had hers. She had come to care for poor Anne of Cleves, but she felt this man's grief as well. He was indeed as trapped by his birth as anyone in Deal. She had felt trapped once, too, by her dedication to her duty and her thirst for revenge. And then, thanks to the king's sending Nick to Deal, she had found a way—found this man she loved—to save herself.

"I thought I was trapped before," she whispered, "but times and people can change, your majesty." She realized she mayhap meant the words for Nick as much as the king. Nick, who had done so much to change her life, and had changed himself. Nick put his arm around her. But it was Henry Tudor, King of England, who then changed both their lives even more.

"Master Secretary, to me!" King Henry bellowed. Everyone jumped. The secretary scurried across the room, pen and paper in hand, and plunked them on the table near the king.

"I shall need these documents at once," the king told his secretary without a glance his way. "A pardon for the citizenry of Deal—for various misdemeanors and misjudgments, et cetera. A market license for said town, especially to help supply the new castle. A note censuring Lord Cromwell for ignoring that need. A warrant for Deal fishermen to keep themselves occupied with lawful acts of piloting royal vessels through the Downs and patrolling the Kentish shores. And a promissory note that Nicholas Spencer, Lord Lieutenant of Deal Castle, may wed whom he chooses, of his own accord and free will."

"Your Majesty!" Nick and Rosalind cried together. Rosalind's heart pounded in her chest. But, she reminded herself, though she had begun to hope Nick really loved her, he had never quite said the like and, as for marriage with her, when his career was so important and he had always set his sights so high—

"And one more thing." The king interrupted her thoughts. "An order to my lord lieutenant that he is to return forthwith to Deal—not lagging here for any of this playacting on Greenwich Green today—and arrest this Percival Putnam for me."

He looked at Nick. "I shall keep this man Shanks for further evidence, but I want Putnam in my—as crafty Cromwell put it—safekeeping, until his testimony is needed, too. From what Shanks told us, I would wager you and your lady's return to Deal might just flush Putnam out."

"I warrant it would, your grace," Nick agreed.

Rosalind's head spun. Deal saved, Putnam doomed, mayhap Cromwell doomed, too. And whatever befell her and Nick in the future, the king of England had called her Nick's "lady."

The next day Nick took Rosalind back into Deal as his apparent prisoner. He put out the word that he had been reassigned to Calais across the Narrow Seas and would be taking Rosalind with him as a token of Deal's future good behavior. He extended further his house arrests for the menfolk of Deal. He and Rosalind could only hope that this subterfuge would pull Putnam into their trap for him. Surely, he would want revenge on Nick or Rosalind before they both got away.

Nick and Rosalind had disagreed about whether to tell her family the good news behind the apparent bad. But if they did and Putnam were in the area somewhere, he might find out the truth; obviously Shanks, and who knew who else, had been feeding him information for years. Rosalind had wanted to tell at least Meg the good news of Deal's salvation, but she felt so sick to her stomach on the ride back that she did not argue long with Nick's decision for complete secrecy. Evidently, she thought, the trials that had bothered her for weeks were now making her feel that she could not keep a bit of food down.

She stood now in the single window in Nick's castle chamber, breathing in fresh, cold sea air while Nick ate alone at the table. Even the smell of his food churned her insides.

"I have pulled the back guards from the final breach in the unfinished wall to give Putnam a way in so we can trap him here," he told her between mouthfuls. "My Rosie, you have ever had a hearty appetite. Are you sure you do not want some of this barley soup, at least?"

"No, I couldn't. I am just feeling sea wobbles until we get our hands on him. He's lived with such hatred, Nick. I see that now. He's got to be stopped and then admit everything to the king."

"Mmm. But even if Putnam has fled, I think you have convinced his majesty of everything."

He shot a blinding smile at her across the little room. "And, I'm beginning to think, my sweet," he told her, "you could convince me of anything and everything, too."

"I'd like that," she said, smiling back despite her physical unease. "Conquering the King of England was nothing in difficulty next to convincing you to trust and love me and this town."

He looked as if he would make some important revelation, but he said only, "The townsfolk will be pleased when we can share the pardon and permits with them."

"There will be dancing in the streets," she said, her chin propped on her arms. "And we'll have to allow as many drinks as anyone wants at the inn that night, my favorite lord lieutenant!"

"If so, I shall have to release Wat and put him on probation to brew as much ale as that little brewery can handle."

She turned to smile at him when their eyes met. She latched the window closed and sat down on the edge of Nick's narrow bed, which they had shared so joyously on Christmas Eve. It was after that night, she realized, she had started to feel this queasiness. Mayhap something she had eaten then had roiled her stomach, and it was not just apprehension at facing the king and now Percy.

Then they heard the quick knock on their door, the signal from Captain Delancey to prepare and beware. Nick leaped to his feet, brandishing his sword. Rosalind grabbed the small pistol she had hidden in the knot bag hanging from her waist. But then the knock came again and they both started as they recognized it.

Rap, rap, pause, rap, rap.

The Rosies' secret knock? Here and now? But Captain Delancey did not know of that, and, they hoped, neither did Putnam! Carefully, sword raised, Nick walked to the door and unlatched it. He had barely opened it a crack, when it slammed in and Delancey, gagged, was shoved in first, his arms held securely by Rosalind's cousins, Hal and Alf. Other townsfolk, men and women, spilled in behind, including Meg and Franklin. Some held fish-gutting knives, some staves. Nick stood, sword raised, aghast. He hesitated and was quickly seized by Rosalind's Rosies.

"All right, we got him now, folks!" Alf cried. "And look at our Rosalind, all frighted and peaked! No struggles, your lordship! We got a couple of your men trussed like pigs and we hold the final breach in the wall. You will be shipped out on a galley bound for far Cathay, Lord Spencer, but not till Rosalind's taken our meager life savings and is so far away you'll never see her again, even if you do come back."

Rosalind's heart overflowed with love and gratitude for these Rosies and their town. They risked all by this. She knew how loyal they had always been to her. But she knew, too, that she had to stop this rebellion before they were in so deep Nick and the king could never forgive them.

"Alf, list—" Rosalind got out, before Alf cut in with the longest speech she'd ever heard from him in her life.

"See, your lordship, if you make it back someday, the whole town would deny anything you said. Just got yourself knocked on the head and took by brigands or slavers, that's it. 'Sides, though all of us admired you for some things, no one hurts our Rosalind and gets away with it. Bring him, lads! Bring the lord lieutenant right out here so Master Putnam can see he gets to the boat."

"Wait, no!" Rosalind cried. "Is Putnam with you? I have to tell you all that's happened. But Putnam's the one we have to watch—"

"Silence her!" The familiar voice emerged from the crowd of faces as Percival Putnam stepped forward with a pistol pointed right at Nick's chest. "I told you this man has seduced her and she would plead for him, my friends. Hold her here, men, and bring Spencer along with me."

To Rosalind's shock and horror, Alf reached for her and clapped a hand over her mouth. Others pinioned Nick's arms behind his back and started to pass him through the press in the small room and crowded hallway. Percy disappeared, evidently planning to precede Nick out to wherever he was being taken. She knew Nick would never make it alive to some boat to Cathay. She had no questions where Alf had come up with money for her to supposedly escape. Percy's face, in that brief glimpse she had, looked demented with agony and fury. But a strange, fierce victory had gleamed in those once-cherubic blue eyes, too.

She clutched her pistol in the folds of her gown, but she could not shoot Alf or any of her friends who clustered close. Then cheers broke from many throats as Wat Milford, unkempt and unshaved, appeared in the doorway. If the Rosies had even taken over the dungeon of the king's impenetrable Deal Castle, Rosalind had no doubt that, under Percy's control, they would all eventually be imprisoned, even executed, there!

"Wait!" Wat cried. Slowly, folks quieted. "What my rescuers said Putnam told them—that Lord Spencer had tortured me. Not a word of it was true! I say Putnam's lied to us about many things over the years. It's Lord Spencer who is honorable, not Percy!"

Rosalind bit Alf's fingers so hard that he yelped as he released her. She lifted her hand and shot her pistol at the ceiling. Stone and plaster sifted down. The echo of the loud retort deepened the silence.

"Percy Putnam is the deceiver here, not Nick Spencer!" she shouted. "We have full pardons from the king for all the Rosies' smuggling! We have a market license and pilots' licenses, but someone grab Percy!"

People screamed. The men holding Nick released him, and the crowd surged, swayed, then stepped back as Nick, Delancey and Wat tried to shove their way out to chase Putnam. A distant shot cracked the air.

"Up, up the stairs he went!" a muted voice cried. "That way!"

Chaos ensued. Nick managed to push his way through the crowd with Rosalind close behind. Finally, people stood back to let them through. Rosalind could not fathom how Percy had gotten such a start on them nor how, crippled as he was, he could still be eluding them.

Despite the clinging queasiness in her belly, she climbed the steps behind Nick to the windswept battlements, where people pointed. Wat was just ahead of them. Rosalind realized that, everywhere she looked, she saw citizens she recognized from Deal. A major mutiny! Despite his earlier largess, what would King Henry say when he heard the citizens of Deal had stormed his castle?

Wind ripped her hair and clothes on the battlements where she and Nick had stood together the day she had come to decoy his attention from the Rosies down the beach. So much had happened.

She heard a scream from the crowd below. Percy, whom the king had ordered them to deliver safely for questioning against Cromwell, had somehow climbed the crenellations at the top of the wall and leveled his gun at her and Nick.

Nick shoved her down and threw himself low toward Putnam. Wat leaped, too, big arms outstretched. Rosalind waited for the shot, expecting to see Nick or Wat grab the screaming Percy.

"I will bring you all down, all of Deal!" Percy shouted. "Pity me, think I'm worth no more than my father's horse, will you? I—"

But as Wat reached for him, Percy's arms windmilled in the air. His shot went awry. For a moment he looked as if he would fly, as if that stunted leg would never weigh him down again. And then, where he had stood screaming at them, there was nothing but blue, blue sky.

Rosalind rushed to the wall and peered over with Nick. Below on the pebbly beach, Percy lay still in a distorted pile that told them he would never lie or deceive—or suffer—again.

Rosalind leaned back so she would not be ill over the wall. Nick steadied her. "Everything is out in the open now," he said, and lifted her in his arms. Meg and Aunt Bess rushed up for hugs and kisses all around. But Rosalind still felt so shaken, Nick carried her below, away from the hubbub of the crowd.

"I feel I've waited too long to say all this," he began, as he sat in his chair and cradled her in his lap. "But I had to be certain we had Percy—and the town—under control."

"The riot's over and Percy's gone for good, when the king wanted him imprisoned."

"Shanks can tell his grace all he needs to know about Cromwell. I tell you, sweet, that vile deceiver will not be long in power."

"But we've survived, you and I," she said and encircled his neck with her arms to press her head under his chin. "Survived and—"

"It's a bit late for speeches, but I think we've survived and conquered. You have conquered me, that I know, my sweet," he said and sat her up straight, lifting her chin so she looked right into his intense gaze. His eyes glazed with tears. "It took me a long while to realize and then accept it, but I feel much more than passion and admiration for you. I feel love, Rosalind, the first time in my life that I have felt such for a woman, I swear it. I fear I did not even know what it was when it came knocking."

"Oh, Nick, that's all I need. Really, it's enough to live on the rest of my days."

"Hell's gates, it's not enough for me, and I was hoping you would demand much more."

"I long for more, but I am no fool. There are gaps between our positions in life, between our pasts, Nick, I see that."

"I, too, see that, and our ambitions, fierce as they both are, have been for opposing issues. But what if we could combine them? What if I were as passionate for helping Deal and you for furthering the realm? What if we bridged our different pasts into one road for the future?"

"Yes, Nick. Oh, yes!"

"Then you would consider marriage to me? We could live here for now. Later, perhaps keep a house here, and if we must be at court, use my Greenwich town house."

"I never even got to see inside it, you know. I would like to," she said, and smiled through the wash of joyous tears streaming down her face.

"You shall, then, soon, as my wife. If Meg and Franklin would just stand up for us as we did for them—"

"Oh, yes!" she cried and threw her arms around him before he could say more. After all, what else in the whole, wide and lovely world could there be to say?

* * *

Later, they went back up on the battlements among the still-rejoicing townsfolk. The sun shone bold and bright.

"There's really a market license for Deal?" Aunt Bess asked as Rosalind's family clustered around them again.

Nick nodded and explained. But before he or Rosalind could announce their good news, Aunt Bess skipped off, clapping and singing, "To market, to market, to buy a fat pig. Home again, home again, jiggedy-jig!"

"And there's to be a general pardon?" Meg asked.

"Better yet," Nick told them. "There is to be another wedding, as soon as Rosalind gets over this sick stomach that has been plaguing her."

"A wedding!" Meg shouted so loud the Rosies and other townsfolk on the level below hushed and looked up. "Well, as for having a sick stomach," Meg continued while Franklin beamed, "I'll be company for you, then, Ros. Franklin and I are certain I am with child. I cannot keep a thing down, and the mere smell or sight of eating does me in."

"Oh!" Rosalind said as her eyes met Nick's. "But all the years Murray and I tried—nothing."

"I shall buy you a leather-bound book for our wedding to keep records of our children," Nick said, and threw back his head and laughed.

Despite herself, Rosalind laughed, too. She held Nick's hand tight, even when they stepped to the edge of the ramparts to shout down to the citizens of Deal who gathered below, looking up now as if waiting for the announcement they longed to make.

"My betrothed, Mistress Barlow, and I thank you for joining us to celebrate the near completion of Deal Castle on this day!" Nick called out to them. "And I have several documents from your king, which Captain Delancey will read to you. You are all invited to the wedding at St. Leonard's to he held, well—" he glanced down at Rosalind beaming in his arms "—as soon as we can possibly arrange for all the food and ale. Captain Delancey, read the town their greetings from their grateful king.''

Nick and Rosalind cuddled in the protection of the walls while Delancey read each document to cheers and shrieks of joy. Despite the cold winter wind whipping from the sea, their world was warm and wonderful. They embraced and kissed.

"A baby, it must be a baby," she breathed in his ear, and he held her to him. Her hands gently touched her flat belly in amazement.

"You told me once my merest touch made you sick," he teased.

"And you said I must plan on being very sick, then," she recalled with a smug smile.

"So be it, the future Lady Spencer, my Rosie."

"And no more tempests in our lives but the ones we face together, king's man."

"And the ones between us when we love."

They embraced and kissed again, only to have the hurrahs from below blast the air. Holding hands now, side by side, they waved and smiled at the people of Deal. The spirit and love of these folks swelled around them like the sea. Everyone cheered wildly again as Nick and Rosalind hugged and kissed, right on the edge of the castle walls and of their new life together.

Author's Note

Lord and Lady Spencer divided their lives between the big stone house Franklin Stanway built for them in Deal and their town house in Greenwich, which they resided in when they were at court. Though the French invasion did not come, the invasion of their hearts was complete. They shared a full life with their six children, the eldest of whom was named for the king. Franklin Stanway became a builder in Deal, and he and Meg ran the Rose and Anchor.

The king wed Anne of Cleves to avoid endangering the Protestant alliance she represented. But his majesty postponed his wedding two days. He bedded with her, but never consummated the marriage and soon divorced her. Anne, happy to escape with her life after the former Queen Anne's fate, declared herself the king's "loyal and dear sister" and lived happily in retirement in England until her death in 1557. King Henry, of course, went on to two more wives.

Thomas Cromwell's position was greatly weakened by his miscalculations in maneuvering the Cleves marriage and his continual misuse of royal power. His enemies rose up, and the king charged him with treason. He was executed in July 1540, a scant six months after this story ends.

Today Deal is still a lovely seaside town, with many houses connected to the beach by underground tunnels. A museum there also contains remnants of the town's smuggling, rescuing and seafaring past. Once completed, sturdy Deal Castle was not attacked until the English Civil War, although during World War II it took a direct hit from German bombs. It has been restored, and is now a popular tourist attraction.

Just as in this story, barriers are still coming down in England today. The "Chunnel" in Dover, not far from Deal, will provide a new link to France, and the European Community nations are making a stronger, united Europe. Thus it was with the once-opposing forces of Rosalind Barlow and Nicholas Spencer in the tempest of their times.

Caryn Cameron

* * * * *

Harlequin

HISTORICAL

CHRISTMAS

STORIES · 1991

Bring back heartwarming memories of Christmas past,
with Historical Christmas Stories 1991, a collection of
romantic stories by three popular authors:

Christmas Yet To Come
by Lynda Trent

A Season of Joy
by Caryn Cameron

Fortune's Gift
by DeLoras Scott

A perfect Christmas gift!

◆ *Harlequin Regency Romance*™

WHO SAYS ROMANCE IS A THING OF THE PAST?

We do! At Harlequin Regency Romance, we offer you romance the way it was always meant to be.

What could be more romantic than to follow the adventures of a duchess or duke through the glittering assembly rooms of Regency England? Or to eavesdrop on their witty conversations or romantic interludes? The music, the costumes, the ballrooms and the dance will sweep you away to a time when pleasure was a priority and privilege a prerequisite.

If you are longing for the good old days when falling in love still meant something very special, then come to Harlequin Regency Romance—romance with a touch of class.

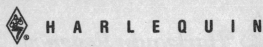

HARLEQUIN

A Calendar of Romance

Be a part of American Romance's year-long celebration of love and the holidays of 1992. Experience all the passion of falling in love during the excitement of each month's holiday. Some of your favorite authors will help you celebrate those special times of the year, like the revelry of New Year's Eve, the romance of Valentine's Day, the magic of St. Patrick's Day.

Start counting down to the new year with

#421 HAPPY NEW YEAR, DARLING
by Margaret St. George

Read all the books in *A Calendar of Romance*, coming to you one each month, all year, from Harlequin American Romance.

American Romance®   COR1